The RISE *and* FALL *of* MAGIC WOLF

The RISE and FALL of MAGIC WOLF

TIMOTHY TAYLOR

Publisher: Meghan Macdonald | Acquiring editor: Russell Smith
Cover designer: Laura Boyle
Cover image: Alamy/Zoonar GmbH

Library and Archives Canada Cataloguing in Publication

Title: The rise and fall of Magic Wolf / Timothy Taylor.
Names: Taylor, Timothy L., 1963- author.
Identifiers: Canadiana (print) 20230566995 | Canadiana (ebook) 20230567002 | ISBN 9781459753198 (softcover) | ISBN 9781459753204 (PDF) | ISBN 9781459753211 (EPUB)
Classification: LCC PS8589.A975 R57 2024 | DDC C813/.6—dc23

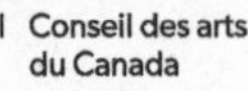

We acknowledge the support of the Canada Council for the Arts and the Ontario Arts Council for our publishing program. We also acknowledge the financial support of the Government of Ontario, through the Ontario Book Publishing Tax Credit and Ontario Creates, and the Government of Canada.

Printed and bound in Canada.

Rare Machines, an imprint of Dundurn Press
1382 Queen Street East
Toronto, Ontario, Canada M4L 1C9
dundurn.com, @dundurnpress

For Jane and Brendan
And for my parents, Richard and Ursula

1

PARIS

Père-Lachaise

It was the one-year anniversary of my mother's death when Magic Wolf first came into the world. I didn't see the coincidence at the time because I didn't really see something being born that moment. But something was. And my mother, Lilly, was there from the start.

I was twenty-four years old. It was a Sunday, my day off. I was lying there on my lumpy futon in my below-grade studio flat in Rue des Partants up behind Père Lachaise Cemetery, watching the ankles of passersby in the high window, watching the light ripple on the low ceiling. I was thinking about her on that day, of course, thinking of my mother in our family kitchen in West Vancouver making bread. One of my earliest memories: me sitting on the counter next to her, age three or four, riveted by all the action in that kitchen. She struck me as enormously powerful, my mother. And she was tough too, I know now. Holocaust-survivor tough. Flinty resilience, loyalty, compassion. These are the things I remember most about her. And that bustling kitchen was the stage on which I saw that first played out, making those endless loaves of bread. It was very physical: banging out the cups of flour, tossing in yeast and water measured by eye, mixing and gathering everything on the big board with her hands, punching down the dough. I remember how sometimes she'd wipe a stray hair from her forehead with the back of her wrist when she couldn't use her fingers because they were caked in sticky dough.

So I had these childhood images running through my head as I lay there in my apartment in Paris that day. The sharp pain of her death had receded by that point to the dull ache of absence as my own life took on its direction in the kitchens of Paris, my own callouses and burn scars forming. And that was the moment when my childhood friend Magnus chose to call.

No introduction. No hello. He started in as if he'd stepped right into my thoughts. He said, "Your mother. I only just heard. I'm sorry, Teo. Really am. I've been in England. Cancer was it?"

And I answered as if it hadn't actually been a decade since we'd spoken, since long ago West Vancouver in our teens, West *Van* as it was only ever known, just as Magnus Anders himself — in his burgundy corduroy jacket and yellow Adidas Kopenhagens, his inextinguishable slant-grinned confidence — had only ever been known as *Magic*.

"Cancer, yes," I said. "Colon. Then liver. Then everything else. It was brutal."

"I remember her really well," he said. "Lilly."

"That's right."

"The way she'd call you in for dinner. 'Teo-oh!' Like she was singing. I remember her voice."

People said my mother had an accent, a musical, European lilt. I wish I could have heard it so I might remember those melodies now.

I said, "How're you doing, Magnus?"

At which point I lay there listening to Magnus Anders talk about life in London for a while, about the wife and kids he apparently already had, all the while thinking myself of Magic rolling tires off that bridge above the railway tracks. Magic starting up that bulldozer that ended up crawling down onto the beach and out into Horseshoe Bay. Magic taking a rock to the head during a street game we simply called *War*. And I saw that last part in slow motion while we spoke, the blood spray, Magnus falling backward flat in the grass, blood pulsing out between his fingers.

After West Van we lost track of one another, which is the way things go. My family moved. Or more accurately: my father became restless one last time. My father, Arthur Wolf, with Japan, Hong Kong, Vietnam, and Spain behind him already. Met my mother, Lilly, in Ecuador, where her family had fled after the war she refused to speak about. All I knew was that she'd been a refugee and ended up in South America while Arthur had been a nomad wandering around somewhat aimlessly when their paths finally crossed. They were married in three weeks, the story went. And by the end of the decade, had three kids, all born in San Tomé, Venezuela: Simone, then Jonah, then me — Matthew as I was named, but who was only ever called "Teo" due to the nickname given me by local kids.

What I couldn't see then, and what is so plain now, is that no man who travels around for so many years and has his children in the middle of the Orinoco jungle is going to settle permanently in groovy 1970s West Van with the neighbour who grew pot under his back deck, the draft-dodger sculptor across the way, the transcendentalists and yogis, the eccentric architect who built the airplane in his basement.

"Remember the Thierrys?" I asked Magnus that day.

So we pulled it back together, that summer day the airplane came out of the house in pieces and went onto a flatbed truck. A stubby wing, a fuselage, a tail assembly. We sat on our bikes in the road, mustangs and banana seats. We imagined flight.

So did my dad. So did everyone. Permanence was not in the coding in old West Van. And so my father had voyaged onward and my long-suffering mother, who I imagine would have been happy to settle just about anywhere after surviving the Nazis, made not one sound of protest.

Of course, no one ever asks the kids. So me and my two older siblings, Simone and Jonah, we were just along for the ride, this time to the sky-domed prairie, Edmonton, Alberta, the land of rural routes and four-by-fours, megachurches and farm equipment in primary colours, the infamous oil sands, the fields of dirty snow and distant beige treelines, and where for all my father's big plans and the powder-blue vastness above, every door seemed to slam shut immediately and lock tight around me.

"So, England," I said. "Doing what?"

"Making money," Magnus said with a sigh, like that was just a thing people decided to do. Boring really, he said. Something about technology, private equity investment pools, European partners, computer trading systems, and the new ways that banks moved money around.

"And married?" I asked. "Who would marry you?"

Zaina was her name. Her family had come to England from Lebanon early in the civil war when she was a baby. Two boys already, three and four years old: Caleb and Zach. They had a place in Chelsea off Sloane Square, but Zaina and the boys were moving to a house on a bit of property in Essex. I didn't know enough to realize what any of this meant. *A bit of property.* Magnus barely twenty-five years old at the time. Meanwhile, I was dragging myself off a borrowed futon to listen to this part of the conversation, standing now and drifting into a kind of trance, my gaze through the black iron window bars to the fan-patterned paving stones in Rue des Partants. Something was shaping there in the swirls and crests. Something in Magnus's intent that I sensed but could not yet see.

"How's your father?" I heard Magnus ask. "How's Mr. Wolf holding up?"

Always the formal address when it came to my father, who was a legend to Magnus from the time we were boys. *Served on the sweeps in the Med. The minesweepers. That was some hairy shit there.* That was Magnus telling me, not my father who always gave incomplete answers on this topic. My father would say that the mines made a plume of water ten stories high when they exploded. Brought up a black slick of oil once, though the Germans did that from time to time, loaded up the tubes with garbage and used engine oil, shot it out to make it look like they were sunk. *Sardines in a can*, he said that time. *Poor bastards.* But then he'd change the subject as if he'd gone too far.

"He's good, thanks," I said. "Bought a farm before my mother died. So he's a farmer now. Or he's not, really. He rents the fields to a local guy who grows canola. But he has a tractor and he drives around. He built a big greenhouse. He's into orchids. He has dogs, these huge Anatolians."

"Mr. Wolf with his orchids and his dogs," Magnus said.

"He misses her. We talk every couple of weeks, much more than we used to."

"Always admired him," Magnus said.

Which I knew to be true. So I said, "It was his idea I move to Paris, in fact, to learn from the best."

Why tell this lie? It had been my mother who really encouraged me to go when I told her the idea. I'd been studying English at university and suddenly had to get out. She seemed to understand immediately. And it's doubly unfair, as I think back on it, because even though he never objected particularly, I'm not sure my father ever really paid much attention to my decision to leave. First he was consumed with caring for my ailing mother. Then he was grieving her. And after I'd gone, he didn't seem to think I'd made an impulsive mistake in going to Paris any more than he thought Simone was a paragon of wise choosing for becoming a cardiologist (which she was) or that Jonah was foolish running off to be a photographer in Japan (which he wasn't really; he was very successful, in fact). Leaning in over his orchids with shears and reading glasses, walking those dogs along the frozen berm down to the steel-cold lake, grieving my mother intensely every moment, his mind was cast out along the track of that long journey around the world to find her, again and again. And when I called him a few weeks after returning to Paris from my mother's funeral, lost in the blur of those first weeks in a Paris kitchen, I remember he asked me why I was calling so early in the day and I realized he'd forgotten I was in France.

Maybe I told Magnus what I thought he wanted to hear: a heroic lie about a father figure he admired. Maybe I told him that because I sensed that my mother's death couldn't possibly be the real reason Magnus was calling, that he had some other motive that day. And once again, Magnus seemed to tap directly into my thoughts with the next thing he said.

"But Paris!" I remember him saying. "Now that is really something. You cooking in Paris. Who picked you for the future celebrity?"

I laughed. *Celebrity.* Give me a break. But Magnus was insistent. And he was going to prove no different than a lot of other people here who thought cooking was some sort of glamourous vocation.

I tried to talk him down. I gave him the basics. My job was at a place called Le Dauphin, one of the big ones up there in Montparnasse where they produced celebrated Parisian bistro fare for hundreds of diners daily — tourists, regulars, visiting famous people. The place was never not slammed, without question the hardest work I'd ever done. Twelve-hour days, six days a week. And on the seventh day, you worked only eight hours because we didn't do Sunday dinner.

"As in," I said, "zero glamour."

"But wicked fun!" Magnus said.

"Wicked exhausting," I said.

"Working with such cool people."

"The chefs patrons are completely psychotic honestly, though the sous is great."

"What's a chef patron?"

"They own the place," I explained. "Chefs Denis and Marcel. The Pellerey Pricks as they are known."

Of course, Magnus immediately wanted to know *psychotic how?* So I told him there, in that very first conversation, neither of us really hearing it the way I hear it so clearly now.

"Psychotic like hitting people," I said. "Like throwing plates, grabbing you by the balls."

And I was saying this remembering the brandy-inflamed face coming in over my shoulder just the week before, the hand clamped over my testicles from behind. Screaming, "C'est quoi ce bordel?"

Magnus was howling. You'd think it was the funniest thing he'd ever heard. And I was laughing too, no point denying it. Because laughter was absolutely necessary to survive that shit. Not in the moment, certainly. You never laughed to their faces. But the Pellerey Pricks cussed out the servers daily, slapped the dishwashers for nothing at all. They'd brandish blades and weaponize butane torches at the apprentices and the junior cooks. They'd hurt you, those two. They'd call you *fiotte* or *sous merde*. And you'd bark *Oui, Chef!* And get back to it. You had to. That was the order of things.

But you'd laugh later. Up at the bar in Pigalle. You'd tell the story, you'd wear the burn mark proudly, you'd have the second drink, the third drink, the fourth. It's how you kept your sanity. Or so we thought.

"And the sous?" Magnus asked.

"François Coté," I said. "Frankie. He's a great guy. Came over from Montreal to Paris about ten years ago."

Friend of a friend, I explained. Which had been my angle, because no way was I getting a job at Le Dauphin otherwise.

"And look at you now," Magnus said. "Living the life in Paris."

"All day every day," I said. "Eighty hours a week."

"Life of Riley," Magnus said. "And partying like crazy after hours, I'll bet. So you single or what?"

I misheard the spirit of this question. I should have seen that Magnus was making a display of largely courteous envy about the lifestyle he imagined. Single and cooking in Paris. Bars and booze in Pigalle. Life of Riley, sure. Only, what I sensed in the moment instead was the chasm yawning between his situation and mine, the very different distances we'd managed to travel over precisely the same number of years. Even if I didn't understand what kind of dough a house on a property in Essex actually meant, or for that matter a wife and two children and another on the way — the alleged tedium of doctors, daycares, school applications, rushing home by car service from Heathrow after a last-minute trip to Moscow — I sensed immediately the enormous value of property and family to those in his sphere. So I nudged my own reality toward what I imagined was his, not really knowing what I was doing, much less planning it at the time.

No wife, I said. But yes, there was someone.

"Come on," Magnus said. "Who is she?"

She was a professional cook, a very good one, I said, both true. We had mutual friends though we weren't exactly dating, true and true. But lately, I told Magnus, something seemed to have clicked between us. And I thought we were really beginning to imagine a future together. And at that point, in a conversation between two old friends reconnecting, I veered into the wholly aspirational.

There would have been more. I would have told Magnus that her name was Stephanie, that she was originally from Seattle. I would have told him some short version of the story that Stephanie knew an old girlfriend of mine from high school, that Stephanie was the one who then put in a word for me with Frankie Coté. Graduated Culinary Institute of America, top of her class, came to France for the same reasons I had only five years before. I might have even told him that Paris hadn't been easy for her, that she'd struggled to advance in the all-male sanctuaries that were restaurant kitchens in the city still at that time. Maybe I told him that Stephanie seemed sane in our insane world of kitchens. That she mentored young cooks without hitting them. That she could laugh at herself, at all of us. At me. Maybe I mentioned that she was writing on the side, that she'd published stories in magazines about her time in France, that she was mulling over when might be the right time to return home. Maybe I told him all that and how beautiful she was too, her intensely observant green eyes, the golden hair that she shook in a certain way to clear her face.

I can't honestly remember all that I told Magnus that day, only that I would have been thinking about all these things, and that there was a dense quality to the silence that then followed, whenever I did finally stop speaking.

That silence seems notable to me now. I can hear it still. And I'm forced to wonder if it was in that very silence that the idea came to Magnus, that the design was revealed. Not Magnus's biggest idea ever. Just the one that would end up making the biggest difference to me.

He said, "So you cook in Paris. You rise through the ranks. You learn from the best."

"Sure," I said. "That was the plan."

He said, "You love this woman, Stephanie. Who sounds great, by the way."

Did I love her? I hadn't thought that far ahead, though as he said it, I was easily persuaded.

Magnus said, "So we do our work. Then in a year's time, maybe two ..."

I waited. The silence stretched. Finally, I said, "Then what, Magnus? In a year or two what?"

"You and me, back in Vancouver," Magnus said. "You and your family. Me and mine."

"Doing what —" I started. But here he cut me off.

"You and me," Magnus said. "And *Magic Wolf*."

Montparnasse

So that was the birth moment, the first time someone actually said the words. Not the name of a restaurant either. It was a restaurant *group*. That's what my old friend Magnus had decided we were going to do together.

"Magic for my old nickname," he explained. "Wolf for ..."

I thought I had the gist of it. And I was flattered, certainly. Only, no way was I ready. In one year in Paris — and I tried to explain this, only it communicates poorly to those outside the trade — I'd worked my way up from apprentice to the most junior of juniors, what was called a *commis* in French kitchens. In my case *commis* at the *poissonier* station. In twelve months I'd worked my way up to being the assistant to the assistant fish guy, filleting salmon, gutting squid, delivering halibut bones to the assistant to the assistant of the *saucier*, the guy who made sauces. I wasn't remotely ready to run a whole restaurant on my own, much less a restaurant group, even if an old friend thought investing in such a thing might be a good idea. And no way was anyone, for a long time yet, going to be calling me *Chef.* And not in one or two more years either.

"Take three years," Magnus had said.

"Five," I said. "Maybe."

"Four," Magnus said, as if he were concluding a negotiation.

I had no idea if four years, or five, or even ten would make sense or not. I just knew my limits well enough to know I had to stay in France to get past them. The commercial kitchen instructed you on this topic. The books I carried with me were a pressing reminder: my Larousse, my L'Escoffier, my *Great Chefs of France* with its paeans to Bocuse and Pic, Thuilier and the Troisgros. Not much of the world really mattered beyond the borders of my own just then. And in all of France, there was no culinary crucible in which harder stuff was smelted than in the notorious kitchens of *La Ville Lumière.*

Paris was making me, I believed. And that was really the same thing as saying that François Coté was making me. Frankie, who'd given me my crazy chance. And it was crazy. You don't walk into a slammed Parisian favourite, recently awarded its first Bib Gourmand by Michelin, show them a CV with a summer job at Danny's Diner on it, and land a job. The *chefs patrons* on their bad days would stab you with a fork for suggesting anything so stupid.

If you had any sense, you didn't do that. But Frankie Coté did that. And he made it happen.

"Quel âge?" said Chef Marcel when I had shown up that day, inspecting me up and down, squinting in disbelief.

Chef Denis leaned forward in a way that suggested he was smelling me. "Très vieux," he said, despite me being just twenty-three at the time. "Mais Frankie a dit …"

We were standing next to the range. I was sweating like a wheel of cheese.

But Frankie said … I didn't know what exactly Frankie had said only that he must have said something because the *chefs patrons* took a long time looking me over that day before all at once setting aside their reservations, releasing long Gallic sighs, tossing my resumé into the coals under the grill, and telling me to come back the next morning at 6:30 a.m. sharp.

Ne soyez pas en retard ou je vais vous botter le cul!

So Frankie had pull with the *chefs patrons*. They still made fun of his Quebec accent and his movie-star good looks. *Comme une salope de Belgique*. Like a Belgian whore. No matter that Frankie was Canadian. But beyond that they listened to him. *Frankie Formidable*, as he was known, a joke about his ferocity in the kitchen.

Frankie wasn't a physically imposing guy despite his good looks. Medium height, medium build. But he had a canny kind of charm I associate with people who look very good on camera, a controlled intensity that drew the gaze. Jet-black hair, cloud-grey eyes. Zealously committed to his cuisine, Frankie had worked every *chef de partie* position other than pastry by the time I came knocking. Grill, fish, sauces, pantry, the bakery. He'd been made sous chef a couple of years before, a real distinction for a North American cooking in Paris at that time. So at service, you'd see Frankie all over the kitchen. And in the heat of things, he unfurled somehow, expanding in reach and size, until at times he'd seem like one of those many-armed auto-assembly robots, a whirling thing of crushing strength, blinding speed, and micrometre precision. I'd seen Frankie gut and bone out a dozen poulets de bresse in less than fifteen minutes, perfectly chargrill baby octopus for piling onto pommes purée, tweezer into place a single quivering marigold between a fried lobe of foie gras and a brandy-poached pear. Frankie had touch. He had grace. And everybody at Le Dauphin knew — from the men and women serving out front, to the apprentice folding whites in the *vestiaire*, to even Marcel and Denis themselves — that if any one person deserved credit for that Bib Gourmand, it had to be Frankie.

"I heard you won some kind of big award," I said to him, that very first night I'd been given the job, before I'd laid hand to a tool in the Le Dauphin kitchen.

Frankie took a long drink of beer, lit a cigarette, and made a face. "Were you really born in Venezuela?"

"The Bib Gourmand," I said.

"I just find this very strange. You know?" And here Frankie fingered my red hair to make his point.

"Dad was a traveller," I said. "An adventurer."

"And you really had a pet ocelot?"

I wish I could remember who I told this story to first. Whoever it was, it spread. Not a pet, really. My dad rescued this ocelot from farmers who were going to kill it. He kept it in a cage out behind our house in San Tomé, fed it live chickens, a detail that Frankie enjoyed hearing.

"Badass!" he said. "And now you know how to make ceviche. Also roulade de boeuf. And poulet au champagne."

"Yeah, well, I inherited a pretty strange recipe box."

"I like this," Frankie said, with a grin. Then, "But listen, they don't give the Bib Gourmand to me. They gave it to everyone working there. They gave it to Marcel and Denis. *Les commis. Les plongeurs.*"

"Frankie, I'm curious," I said to him. "What did you say?"

"To who?"

"To Chefs Marcel and Denis."

"To the Pricks?" Frankie said. Then he smiled again and put his arm around my shoulders, gave me a squeeze. "I vouched for you, mon ami," he said.

It was midnight. One in the morning. A few hours of sleep between us and morning duties.

Frankie could have said anything and I would have believed him. After all the manic kitchen intensity, Frankie became someone else after the counters were wiped down with bleach and the stations were cleaned, all the food stowed back in the lowboys and the walk-in. Frankie stopped running the brigade and became everyone's quiet confidante, the guy who listened, who spotted a round, who gave loose change to panhandlers, who'd be greeted by name in every single Paris café or bar I ever went into with him the entire time I was there.

"Frankie!" Always, someone. A chef or a line cook or a server from somewhere. They all knew him.

"Viens t'asseoir." Someone patting the chair beside them.

Frankie post-service was approachable and appealing with his untucked shirt over jeans, sleeves rolled up revealing the burns. He had a motorcycle, a Moto Guzzi racing bike from the early '70s. He had style, Frankie did. And I saw it a lot. Glances from people, men and women of all persuasions who knew who he was, whose attention lingered, who looked as if they wanted to pick Frankie up and pop him into their pocket for later use.

Frankie greeted everyone. He always took the time. And from the very first night we drank together along the sidewalks in Pigalle, he introduced me as if I were a long-time friend.

"Mon ami Matthew," he'd say. "We call him Teo. Born in Venezuela. Right? You can tell, yeah? Ask him about his pet ocelot."

People would be laughing, leaning in to listen, to get a glimpse of me, the new face. Frankie with his arm around my shoulder. "Teo is one to watch, I tell you. Going to be a great cook one day. He's going to have his own place and be a big star."

Exaggerating, clearly. But I still stood a little taller hearing it. Frankie in the fizzing lights with his arm through mine. Ten crucial years older than me. I saw all those wide eyes taking him in.

Of course, Magnus had wanted me to believe something similar about myself and I'd been flattered when he'd said it. But that was my old friend Magnus with his abstractly successful life, his wife and kids and a house in Essex, his vintage Bentley and his stocked trout pond. From Frankie, who sweated beside me in the kitchen, who toured me around Pigalle in those early days and introduced me to his friends, it meant so much more. And I know why, at least I know now. Because on arrival in Paris, on settling down in the basement suite he'd found for me in Père-Lachaise, on beginning at Le Dauphin and settling into those grooves, on watching him day after day and seeing others watch him, too, there was quite a lot of Frankie that I wanted to be myself.

———

Le Dauphin was just off Rue de Rennes near the Saint-Placide metro. The restaurant was on the corner where Rue de Vaugirard rakes away at an eastward angle from the main street. So the dining room was a large triangle, with high windows opening onto tables that lined the sidewalks on either side, shaded by a wide red-and-white striped awning. Always a rank of scooters parked out front: Vespas, Lambrettas, Peugeots.

In the main floor dining room, Le Dauphin had brightly patterned floor tiling and wood panelling that was decorated with dozens of small etchings and watercolour paintings of the produce and game of the French regions: Charolais cattle, Flemish Giants, brill, sole, bundles of white asparagus, and bright red Saint-Martin apples still hanging on the bough. There were dark burgundy leather banquettes on the back wall, wicker-backed chairs pulled tight in around wood tables that filled the rest of the room, each covered in a red-and-white checkered cloth to match the awning outside, only marked there with the Dauphin symbol in deep navy blue, a sea creature mounted on a cresting wave, with curling tail fin, bulging eyes, and pursed lips, sporting a chef's toque where the princely crown might otherwise have been worn. The circular image of the fish and the wave — universally referred to as *le surf guppy* by those who worked at Le Dauphin, though it looked more like a carp than either a guppy or a dolphin — was also found on the restaurant's crockery and cutlery, as well as on the aprons of the servers and the breast pockets of the white tunics worn by everyone who worked behind the twin swinging doors that gated the dining room off from the restaurant's engine room, which was, of course, the kitchen.

Le Dauphin was a big place: Forty-eight seats on the terrace. Another one hundred and twenty in the main floor dining room and eighty more on the second floor, which was accessed by a spiral staircase with floating dark wood treads that rose from the centre of the big room, encased in a deco iron cage, itself patterned with a rising cascade of waves and surf guppies. The kitchen was staffed to match. There would be as many as thirty cooks in the kitchen at points during the day, handling three service tides that crested at eight in the morning, one in the afternoon, and then a long and late-breaking surge that went from around seven each evening until the place finally shuttered at eleven. If you were apprenticing in such a place — as I did along with half a dozen others ranging from my age down to the *métiers* who started full time at age fourteen — you arrived at 6:30 a.m. to support the morning cooks, you took family meal with everyone else at eleven then worked through lunch, you took an hour from three to four, most typically to sleep on the grassy median in the middle of Boulevard Raspail, then you returned and worked dinner service. Le Dauphin had cleaners who came in to do the common areas, so apprentices only had to scrub down their own station areas and stow their supplies, meaning departure by midnight was typically possible. That left you six and half hours to unwind, sleep, then return to the fray. Repeat that from Monday to Saturday. Then Sundays repeat it again only there was no dinner service so you could head home at three in the afternoon.

Knowing Frankie from day one gave me mixed status. Since I was also Canadian, and since from early on Frankie took me with him to the Pigalle bars where cooks and servers went after service, the youngest apprentices assumed Frankie and I were tight friends who knew each other from home. As that implied I must surely have access to favours, I was helped out in ways I might not have been otherwise. The other cooks and *chefs de parti*, to whom Frankie was an impossible riddle himself — a foreigner who spoke a fluent but unfamiliar French, and who was also their ever-hovering and fanatically attentive boss — I was considered doubly strange, coming into a French kitchen at the very bottom of the brigade, obviously far too late in life for there not to be more to my story. It was openly speculated that I'd just been released from prison, or that perhaps I was married to Frankie's sister or his mother, or that Frankie might have brought me in as some kind of quality control spy. Since I only ever smiled and went along with these stories, never saying a word, I was taken to be a man of tremendous sangfroid despite this never being remotely true. And that's no doubt where the nickname came from, one that I don't remember ever hearing any one first time. It was just suddenly there, my kitchen name. And so it remained for all my time in Paris. *Teo Tranquille.*

Teo Tranquille and *Frankie Formidable.* It was in a strange way exactly the relationship into which Frankie and I then settled. Though that first morning of service I remember being anything but cool. I'd mapped out my metro plan before crashing into bed around two the morning before. But operating on four hours of sleep, I managed to get on the train going the wrong direction at Châtelet, only catching it two stops north at Étienne Marcel. I got turned around and sprinted up the steps at Saint-Placide but still ended up bursting in the staff entrance at six forty-five. Having been assured already by Frankie that Chefs Marcel and Denis were exactly as foul as they sounded and typically smelled, I fully expected one of them to be waiting, ready to kick my ass just as they'd promised.

Fortunately, the *chefs patrons* were nowhere to be seen, which would turn out to be the normal order of things. They lived together in a large apartment five floors above the restaurant. They'd shop the markets, often before anyone had arrived in the kitchen below. They'd inspect the produce and protein deliveries. Then they'd retire for most of the day. We'd send them breakfast around ten and lunch around two using a steel dumb waiter that exclusively serviced their suite. They'd officially come down and preside only starting at about four in the afternoon, whereupon they'd brief dinner service with Frankie, maybe wander into the back to stick their thumbs in the sauces and critique the apprentices with oaths and threats. Otherwise, they'd keep to the bar area out front where they'd greet regulars and work their way through a shared bottle of Belle de Brillet pear liqueur or Janneau Armagnac.

That morning, panting and sweating and foggy from too many *demi en pression* with Frankie the night before, I certainly did not feel tranquil about anything. I was bleary and nervous and my hands were trembling as Frankie beckoned me to the front of the kitchen to where he was standing at the pass, calling into the dining room.

"Café pour la gueule de bois. Vite." And when it arrived in the pass, he swivelled and handed it to me, his expression one of similar skepticism to that which the *chefs patrons* had shown me the day before. "You're late," he said, leaning in to inspect my eyes. "Don't be late again. You ever hear of eye drops?"

He looked great himself. Those grey eyes perfectly calm and clear. His body set in place, steady as a runner's body might be before the launch, like a coiled spring, just as the kitchen seemed similarly poised around him as the breakfast hour approached. I saw that the bakery station was going full out already, the *boulanger* working with two *commis* as they produced sheet trays of fresh croissants and pains au chocolat and chaussons aux pommes. Over at the *garde manger* station, the first shift cooks were prepping for the morning egg dishes Le Dauphin offered: the bistro classic oeufs mayonnaise; oeufs Americains, which were fried eggs served with brioche toast; and an in-house specialty known as *oeufs de maman*, named for one or the other of *les patrons'* mothers, or simply "ovo" as Frankie would call it from the pass, where finished dishes were handed over to waiting servers.

"Where do you want me?" I said to Frankie. "Should I help with the eggs?"

I had no idea just how ridiculous this suggestion was, like an utterly green apprentice in a kitchen cranking hundreds of covers a day just plugged into a station of their choosing. I had no idea that the coffee I was unsteadily sipping was the last Frankie would ever pour for me, that this little *tête à tête* between us at seven in the morning was going to be one of a kind. This was all a courtesy, a one-off for the new Canadian, friend of a friend. From that day forward, I was going to have an assigned place in the rigid structure of the brigade with someone above me, and someone above them, and a *chef de parti* above both of those guys, and Frankie himself sitting at the distant tip of the pyramid. Beyond the moments when the *chefs patrons* came back for a visit, Frankie was the supreme being in the kitchen at Le Dauphin where there had been no executive chef since the last one, named Clémente, had stabbed himself in the throat with his filleting knife and bled to death on the tiles near the vegetable station.

"Since Gauthier's been handling the eggs for the past ten years," Frankie said. "I think I'll leave him to it." Not unkind, but a comment made dryly, Frankie seeing something that I couldn't then, that I had in front of me every single lesson in cooking that I would need to learn. Then he went on to explain very briefly, with a crack of his head toward the ceiling as if to signal the Pricks above in their suite, that no new apprentice touched customer food until they'd proven themselves. Sometimes it took a month. Sometimes a year. House rule. Very firm rule.

"You're on family meal," he said. "Go get your whites and Gauthier will sort you."

Then he was back to the pass as the orders began to arrive. *Mayo. Mayo. Croissant. Deux Pains.*

Deux ovos!

Gauthier was our Belgian-born *chef de garde manger* handling all the kitchen's cold preparations, everything from salads to hors d'oeuvres, appetizers, canapés, amuse-bouches, even sometimes one of those old-school aspic-covered sides of salmon with vegetable garnishes cut fastidiously to look like tulips and roses. *Chef de garde manger* wasn't exactly a glamour spot in the kitchen. But it was a role that touched on virtually every meal eaten by every diner who came through the place. So Gauthier was important. And the *chefs patrons* clearly knew it.

Gauthier himself was a soft-spoken man, though he had a distinct air of menace about him. He had a hard, small frame and flint-green eyes. He had the words *Legio Patria Nostra* tattooed in gothic text down one muscled forearm and *More Majorum* down the other.

"Legionnaire," he said to me, catching my glance. "Don't worry, I don't kill anyone for a long time. Vous étiez en prison?"

I'd learn in time that this question was meaningful for Gauthier, who as a younger man had moved in circles where prison was always close. His own nearest brush came after a calamitous bar fight. Madame la Juge seemed to take into account Gauthier's recent enlistment. So off he went to Zaire and Lebanon instead of La Santé Prison, returning five years later looking for a means to pay the bills and somehow finding his way to the protective attentions of Marcel and Denis, who gave him an apprenticeship at the restaurant they'd only recently opened, where he'd worked devotedly ever since, rising to his present position.

Frankie didn't seem to enjoy answering questions about Gauthier. And observing Gauthier's terse following of his sous che's instructions to the letter, I figured Gauthier didn't care much for Frankie either. The chill might have had to do with Frankie's stellar rise through all the stations to run the kitchen in just a few years, passing Gauthier to become his boss. But there were also personalities involved. Gauthier had this essential toughness, a reserve of legionnaire death-readiness he still carried around with him. Frankie, for all his intensity in the kitchen, was a *bon vivant* at heart, prone to flourishes and extravagance and nightly drunkenness. Gauthier certainly could drink — I'd see this on a few notable occasions. Only, I would never see the two of them drink together.

On that first morning, I didn't know any of this, of course. So I prattled on, telling Gauthier that I hadn't been in jail although I was plenty glad to be gone from Canada and living in Paris, working at Le Dauphin, only realizing while speaking that Gauthier hadn't expected an answer to his question much less a detailed and personal one. So I stopped and waited. *Chef?* And Gauthier cracked his neck by rolling it to one side then the other, then spoke very quickly in the scrambled Franglais that was the kitchen patois. "Faire du chicken. Roast, pan sauce. Haricots verts à la vinaigrette. Pommes purées. Un peu Comté. Cheese, yes? Comme une pomme aligot. Ricky will help for find these."

"Yes, Chef!"

Twenty-seven cooks for lunch service. Gauthier said cook for thirty. Then he was lost immediately in the next of his many tasks, dicing celeriac at blinding speed, his chef's knife sounding like a woodpecker.

Thinking back, I have to wonder if I would've lasted even that one shift working at Le Dauphin had Frankie not called in a coffee for me that morning. But he had. And the young apprentice Ricky had seen it. Ricky was fifteen years old and no doubt figured a coffee with the sous was something he wouldn't rate himself for fifteen more. Somehow that impressed him. So he kept an eye on me while dealing with his own work, watching me stumble around the back looking for the chicken that he'd told me was there. Then he sidled over. "What do you do?" he asked.

"Chicken," I said. "Je cherche le chicken."

"C'est là," he said, gesturing to the walk-in fridge from which I'd just emerged.

We went back in and he gestured again. Chickens. Of course, I hadn't seen them because to me a chicken was pink and came on Styrofoam wrapped in cellophane. But there they were. On having them pointed out to me, hanging right there by their necks, I could not deny it: These white feathered things with their strawberry combs were indeed chickens.

"I see," I said. "Like whole."

"Entiers," he said. "Comme Dieu les a faits."

"How many for thirty?"

"Un poulet, quatre personnes," Ricky said, holding up one finger on one hand and four on the other.

"So eight poulet au total?" I asked.

"Très bien," said Ricky, shaking his head and leaving.

It wouldn't be the last time we spoke that day. I knew nothing. And Ricky could see it, all the while he banged out plastic buckets full of mirepoix for other station cooks, powering through mesh bags of onions and stacks of celery heads and bushels of thick orange carrots. If I'd had the time and presence of mind to actually watch him, I would have seen that Ricky's speed and precision were similar to Gauthier's. I would have seen how Gauthier looked out for Ricky in a stern but protective way. I'd have seen that Ricky himself kept an eye on his mentor, ever watchful for the nod or short word of instruction. What passed between the two was a perfect display of what a year of apprenticeship did to you, how it honed and shaped you, how it smoothed your movement until the peeling and dicing of a carrot became an absolutely uniform procedure with no variation at all from carrot to carrot. I might also have noticed that Ricky was watching me, that he'd glance over from time to time and take note of whatever task I was failing to do properly. He'd notice the failing, let me fail for several minutes, and only then, with a glance to the clock and an almost imperceptible nod from Gauthier, would Ricky slip away from his own chopping and dicing and be at my elbow to show me how to do things correctly. How to use a torch for removing the feathers. How to reach a hand into the cavity of the bird and grip and twist the entrails, drawing them free in one motion. And when I'd done all that and trussed and seasoned and buttered the birds, time now pushing on toward 9:30 a.m. and the birds needing to get into the roasting ovens, there was Ricky again to stop me, showing me again how I was doing even this part wrong, untrussing one bird and rolling it under his palms on the worktable, cracking the ribs near the spine, then re-trussing it so it sat quite differently, with a higher profile, so that the *rotissoire* could cook it more evenly on all sides.

"Celui-là," he said, pointing at one of the birds I'd trussed myself. "C'est un blob."

"Okay," I said.

"Celui-ci," Ricky said, pointing at the one he'd done. "C'est exact. C'est bien."

So it went. My day aligned in what would be the direction of every shift going forward, the pursuit of what was correct, and therefore what was good.

The family meal went down well. Or, at least, I didn't get any complaints. Gauthier didn't say much.

Neither did Ricky, though when he took a plate off the counter when I was handing them out, he did a perfect impersonation of the *chefs patrons* on their kitchen visits. He dropped the corners of his mouth into a deep frown. He furrowed his brow as if greatly perturbed. Then he dragged one thumb through the buttery wine sauce I'd made, stuck it in his mouth, and slurped at it while eyeing me with mock suspicion.

Then, finally, mimicking Chef Marcel's deep voice perfectly, he said, "Pas mal." Then he winked and disappeared down the line to eat.

Later, after a half dozen beers in Pigalle during which Frankie talked almost exclusively about the rabbit stuffed with foie gras we were apparently going to cook together that Sunday night at his apartment in Belleville, I finally asked the question directly. I finally just came out with it because I really needed to know: *How'd I do, Frankie? Was it good? Did I do it right?*

To this day I don't know what he would have said had he responded. I only remember how anxious I was to know what he thought, how I waited in agony for him to tell me that I wasn't a complete failure, only realizing after several seconds that he hadn't heard the question at all because he was distracted. His eyes had flickered up over my shoulder, over to the entrance of the bar, where someone had evidently just come in. Frankie's expression was brightening, those grey eyes widening, his hand now going up above his head to beckon someone over.

So I turned, of course. And that was the first time I saw her, head down, closing an umbrella.

Then, on noticing Frankie's wave, her sharp chin came up and a scarf was swept free of her golden hair. The orange light of the bar found her. He'd mentioned someone would join us. A friend, he'd said. A brilliant cook herself. But he hadn't said anything more. And I hadn't thought further about it until just then, when it seemed that I knew in an instant all that Frankie had decided to leave unsaid.

Stephanie, Stephanie. I saw it was you. I had no doubt. And you saw me too. Your eyes flickered and held. That first time, you did not look away, as if you had been expecting me there. As if you knew something already about me. I was frozen. You were to me that moment like the distant puff of smoke and geyser of flame from across a slammed kitchen. And I was the one standing there dumbly at my station, waiting for the crash of pots, the sound of breaking glass, and the yelling to begin.

Tomato Toast

Before she died my mother told me a few things about her time in Paris. My decision to go seemed to spring these stories free from within her. I could see that at the time, how she responded to the idea that I would go there, this city where she'd once been herself under very different postwar circumstances. What shames me now is to think how I failed to give her credit for inspiring me to go in the first place. That much I always seemed to pin more on my dad, which I suppose is the peculiar and clichéd attraction of distant fathers.

Of course, it's a cliché. But it's a cliché for a reason. It happens a lot.

That said, I do remember the stories she told me before I left. And they stay with me because they weren't your typical City of Light stories. She'd been a refugee in Paris after the war, not a tourist. So nothing about discovering herself as an artist or loving life in the city's famous cafés. I never heard about Brasserie Lipp or Café de Flore, much less Lasserre or Maxim's or La Tour d'Argent, or any of the other legendary white-tablecloth places with that constellation of Michelin stars among them.

I heard instead about how they'd been passing through, courtesy of the International Refugee Organization, and how the day they were supposed to pick up their visas from the Ecuadorian Embassy it had been closed due to Simón Bolívar Day, which meant a three-month delay until the next boat to South America out of Genoa.

"My father had fled Germany to Ecuador in 1940, just after my grandparents were killed by the Nazis," she told me. "All those years later, the war is over, and we are finally supposed to be joining him. Only we missed our boat. So we had to wait."

I was sitting on the edge of her bed when she told me these details. She'd cough into a handkerchief from time to time. Otherwise, she'd just keep on talking as if some of the details she felt were particularly important. I heard about the bugs in the Hôtel Véron in Pigalle where they'd stayed. If you woke at night to pee, my mother told me, you'd see them marching up and down the walls. Not cockroaches, fortunately. But some kind of carpet beetle with the odd centipede joining the parade. I heard about the neighbourhood, sketchy back then, not campy Pigalle as I'd find it when I arrived, but a place where you really watched your step. Down Boulevard de Clichy, around Place Blanche. Especially women, with all those drunken servicemen rolling through, packs of them in a mood, fights spilling out of the cafés and bars, catcalls and spitting in the streets.

"We'd seen enough violent goons for one lifetime," my mother told me, holding my hand. "But we weren't scared of them either because we had Madame Delisle!"

Madame Delisle was their host. And she took one look at my mother and her sister, seventeen and twenty years old, and she pulled my grandmother aside. *Faites attention!* It was urgent. You watch these two! There are men in Pigalle who would take them. *Vous comprenez?*

"She sounds fierce," I said.

Delisle was fierce. A big woman who took no guff from guest or stranger or passing gendarme. She had to be that way, my mother said. Quite a few working women used the hotel and she was herself looked on as something of a guardian.

"Working women?"

"Pigalle, Teo. The red-light district. Some of those ladies did more than dance."

Have you eaten? my mother remembered Madame Delisle asking them after they'd traipsed all the way back across the city from the Ecuadorian Embassy and told her the bad news. They were famished, of course. So Madame Delisle disappeared into her office behind the front counter, returning with a baguette and tomatoes.

"The famous baguette and tomatoes," I said, because she'd told me this much before, even when I was very small. I knew there had been a meal in Paris, a monumentally satisfying meal, now finally presented in its proper context, no restaurant involved at all.

"With butter!" my mother said, smiling. "I thought I'd never tasted anything so good in my life. She had a little jar of crystal salt she gave to us. We ate in our room with the front window open. It was heavenly."

My father called at his regular time, Sunday mid-afternoon Paris time, first thing in the morning for him. He rose earlier and earlier, it seemed. But when I asked him about his time in Paris, because I knew he'd been there only a few years after my mother, he claimed only to remember that all the cafés had been overflowing with Americans.

"And people who wanted to be writers," he added, deeply unimpressed.

That's about all I could get out of him. So I'd try to draw him out about other parts of his history, about his childhood in Toronto. Five children originally, though two sisters died of influenza when my father was just four years old. That left the three boys: Arthur; his older brother, Michael; and then baby Hugh. Not much forthcoming about his mother, Kate, though he'd occasionally talk about his own father, Jack.

"He taught me to box," my father told me. I remember that particular conversation — I was lying in bed in my apartment having burned myself pretty badly that morning. The *chefs patrons* had cursed me out before Frankie pulled me out of the line and sent me to back to the storeroom to find bandages. So I was lying there listening to my father talk about boxing, my own hand wrapped up in a puffy mitt of gauze.

"So what do you remember?" I asked him. "From the boxing lessons."

"Step left," he said, chuckling. "Though for the life of me I can't remember why that was so important."

Grandpa Jack had been a blacksmith for the Toronto Fire Department after immigrating from Ireland. He was a hero and a legend, I'd always heard. So I got some of that material again on the call that day. How Jack had stopped a runaway coach with four horses and saved the lives of a crowd of children who would have otherwise been in the way. How Jack hauled seven children out of a burning building on Yonge. And then the one about Grandpa Jack fighting four policemen at once after some dispute about windows broken at a warehouse down Rutland Street that Jack felt was being blamed unfairly on his boys.

He got in a few licks, my dad said. But then they hit him with batons until he lay unconscious in the driveway of their house. Then the police gave my dad a lime-flavoured sucker and told him to go next door to Mrs. Ricci's house for a towel to clean up his dad.

"Jesus H," I said on the phone that day, although I'd heard less detailed versions of the story before.

"You know," he said, after a pause. "Here's something I never told anyone."

I waited.

"Your mother," he said, "she was a beautiful cook. Always such wonderful food in our house when you kids were small."

"Oh, I remember," I said.

"My mother didn't exactly have those skills," he said. "She made Irish food. Boiled beef with carrots and potatoes. Cabbage soup. My brother Mike could eat a table full of that sort of thing. But most of the time, I went next door to eat."

"What? The Riccis'?"

"Yes," my father said, laughing, remembering. "They were Italian, you know. They could really cook. Spaghetti with meat-balls. Lasagna. Rabbit with olives."

"So you'd just bail on dinner and go next door and they'd feed you?"

"I'd just tell my mother I was going out," my father said. "I had nerve."

Platters of pasta, bowls of bread, tumblers of homemade wine. I imagined my dad as a boy being fed by the neighbour. *Was he half out the door already by then?* There was tragedy lingering in that house, I knew. The sisters lost to influenza. Baby Hugh hit by a tramcar in Dufferin Street, killed on the spot. And the parents fought, probably not unrelated. Pots and knives were thrown. Bottles and fists too. Part of me wanted to tell my father that I saw some of that around me now, that my hand was burned not because I'd stupidly grabbed a pot off the stove without a towel, or that I'd accidentally dunked my hand in the fryer, nothing like that. I'd got a torch across the knuckles. Chef Marcel, screaming epithets about something. Out came the torch and I could smell the hair burning just before I smelled the flesh.

Would that have been a meaningful point of connection between us? Would he have seen me more clearly as trying to follow in his footsteps? I wonder now at how badly I wanted that to be true. As if violence simmered through the generations and *that* was the connection between us, not the lengths to which my mother had gone to escape it.

But I'll never know what he thought about any of that because I never told him about my hand, which was suddenly throbbing badly again as I was lying there.

"That's funny," is all I said, "you eating next door. Is that why you wanted to travel so much? Because you wanted to eat food from different countries?"

All those meals we ate out in Chinatown and Japantown. The strange home cuisine with all those Latin dishes mixed in with German ones: ceviche, arroz con pollo, spaetzle, pot roast.

But my dad didn't pick up on that at all. "A guy had to work," is all he said. "I needed the money. There were jobs overseas."

Which I took to mean that he'd had his own moments of desperately wanting away, wanting adventure. And that version of things stayed in my mind for very long time, dominating my thoughts, working on me.

Belleville

The fact was I fancied myself on an adventure. And so I favoured this reading of his life, adopting it as an inspiration, no matter that it was the oldest cliché, the surest romance to ultimately disappoint you. No way was I seeing that at the time. At Le Dauphin the routine was utterly gruelling. And yet — as I imagined was the case crossing the Pacific on a freighter or chopping your way through the Philippine jungle — surviving the experience was a significant part of the appeal.

Surviving and to be seen surviving by those who understood. Because everyone around you was putting in the same long hours — sixteen, seventeen hours daily. Frankie never left early. Neither did Gauthier or any of the other *chefs de parti*. We surfed those three long service waves. We handled the slams, the weeds, the times when the board was so thick with yellow tickets it looked like a field of canola rippling in a hot wind. We handled the near disasters too. The main range gas line failing at eight thirty one night. The *commis* on grill setting the sleeve of his tunic on fire. The dreaded visits from the Pricks that got worse through the dinner service as the *chefs patrons*' bottle of brandy steadily emptied.

"Qui est-ce branleur, Frankie?" they'd ask their sous. But the abuse was almost always aimed lower, their comments striking at a *commis* or an *apprentice*. "Qu'est-ce que cette merde?"

Not metaphorically either. They'd actually strike you. They had no hesitation or any apparent sense that in other settings the behaviour might be criminal. They liked rolling pins. You'd see them go for one in the bakery and you'd wince for whoever got it across the shoulder blades. A cuff to the ear for the younger ones, a cupped hand smacked home. You're a fourteen-year-old kid from Perpignan and you're smacked in the side of the head by this enormous, reeking man in whites and you stepped back up to your station. *Oui, Chef.*

They'd throw plates. I hadn't been kidding Magnus about that part of the story either. "Recommencez!"

Nobody yelled in the Le Dauphin kitchen except the Pricks. Frankie never yelled. That dish hit the floor and you heard a ripple of voices through the room. Frankie first, calling out what we needed to replace. *Confit de canard. Frisée. Plus de pommes de terre. Tout de suite s'il vous plaît.*

And then the voices in reply. *Oui, Chef.*

Oui, Chef.

Oui, Chef.

Frankie didn't have to direct these orders to particular people. In the kitchen you listened. You worked at the order in front of you. You tracked the new orders coming in as Frankie called from the pass. And when that plate hit the floor and Frankie called out for its constituent parts to be refired, the chefs in the kitchen who owned those tasks heard the call and did it.

For the first year of this, it seemed to me that nobody escaped the violence. I certainly didn't have the time or brain space to register otherwise. I got it. Ricky got it. The other apprentices. The butcher, the fry chef, the confectioner, Frankie. *Everyone.* Until on one occasion, I finally picked up on an important hidden truth about these rituals. A chubby pink finger dragged angrily through a mornay sauce pooled under a filet of sea bream. I don't even remember the technical mistake. I just remember the plate flying across that tight space toward the saucier, and then the fish and sauce splattering, the plate shattering all over the hot grill, shards of white porcelain everywhere. And as bodies recoiled, a spouted copper pot full of brandy was toppled into the fire, where it geysered flame instantly, blue and yellow.

They got the fire out with baking soda quick enough. But in his fury Chef Marcel had ground an entire section of his own kitchen to a halt, cooks and apprentices running around and cleaning up and replacing not just the one flawed dish, but the five or ten others that had been burned in the flame or spackled with shards of plate or bits of bream or mornay or all three. But not even that chaos is what struck me the most, thinking back. It wasn't the way Chef Marcel stormed out entirely uncaring about the way he'd addressed one problem plate by destroying ten others. It was instead the fact that every head in the kitchen came up for that occasion, every pan being shaken on the flame, every pot being stirred, every joint on the grill being flipped with tongs, all that stopped for a good five shocked seconds before the cleanup began. One, two, three … and during that time I looked around and saw Gauthier at his station, continuing as if nothing whatsoever had happened.

Gauthier was unaffected. Gauthier was immune. I didn't know how he'd earned this status, how it was that the Pricks never once threw something that came from his station, never once even dressed him down. He just continued what he was doing, assembling a niçoise salad, focused, unconcerned.

We moved onward. For the rest of us, it was always onward, pressing and pressing. Pushing it all forward. We hardly spoke. We barely lifted our heads from our respective tasks. And when on those rare occasions that I did — to stretch my back, to steal a glance at the clock, to wipe sweat from my forehead because it was starting to drip onto the plates — it was always Frankie and Gauthier I'd notice first. Frankie in auto-assembly robot mode, zipping up and down the lines, leaning in, fixing something, zipping back to the pass for more orders and more orders. Gauthier a *pilon* of culinary rigour, body hardly moving, hands a blur. But either way, either approach, I never saw either of those two men sweat in that kitchen.

Then it was over and we cleaned together. We scrubbed counters with bleach. We stowed our supplies in the station lowboys, in the walk-in. You muttered words to each other. *Fucking crazy, man. Ready for a drink? Peut-être cinq?*

Seventeen hours. I've heard that French labour laws have since changed. There were no laws then. Or maybe they forgot to tell us. Morning to midnight. And then we were filing out that staff door and onto the cobblestones. I would occasionally think that I saw the whole thing in those moments, the whole project. Why I was there. What I was doing. We'd all be milling around, sparking up smokes. I'd look back at those red awnings. And if the lights inside had not yet been turned down, you'd see the sky gone deep blue, and Le Dauphin would glow orange against that dense colour. In that blue I could see the place we'd all made. These young men and women standing around me, smoking. Just a bunch of people who'd worked hard all day and we'd made something. But such intimacy we shared. We'd made that room glowing in the dark. We'd made the evening for all who'd dined with us from the tourists to the neighbourhood families who used Le Dauphin like an extension of their living rooms. People so well known to the restaurant that the *chefs patrons* would order for them.

Civet de Canard au Sauternes, Madame. Oui. Délicieux. Et pour vous Monsieur … poulet aux morilles. Oui? D'accord.

"What do you see, Red?" Her name was Ines and she'd grown up in Le Havre in Normandy. She bused tables front of house. A tiny girl with a slightly crooked nose, very pretty but also very young. I would have guessed about fifteen, but never asked. I might never have known Ines worked at Le Dauphin at all given we junior galley slaves were buried in the back of the kitchen and never saw the front of the house. But of course Frankie knew her because Frankie knew everyone. And he knew her well enough that he'd wave her over for drinks in Pigalle whenever we saw her. So Ines and I ended up at the same table fairly often. Her English was as rough as my French at first. But she took a sisterly shine to me from early on, sometimes tucking herself in at my end of the table and pulling one of my arms around her shoulder as if for warmth. She also called me Red from the first time we met because of my hair. It was another thing I never asked about, but I'd wager she had a redheaded older brother at home.

"That colour," I said, gesturing down the street, up to the sky. "So beautiful."

She took my arm and hugged it in the chill. "Viens-tu à Pigalle?" she said.

Most of the time, that's where I'd go along with the rest of them. Though sometimes, brutally fatigued, mind still spinning, I'd walk the streets by myself instead, all the way from Montparnasse to my basement in Belleville. It took over an hour, more if I meandered. And my feet would be sore by the end of it. I'd collapse into bed often still in my clothes. But I'd also see the stars swirling along the way. I'd see the long spinning arms of the streets stretching away from Place Edmond Rostand next to the gardens, from Place de la République. I'd hear the voices drifting out of the cafés, smell the coffee, the cigarettes, the fat from the fryer, the char on a steak. Once, I passed close to a small and somewhat shabby café near the canal — Le Mouton Noir — and saw Gauthier in the window table with a bottle of Auxerrois and a plate of boudin noir, the ubiquitous blood sausage of Normandy. I wouldn't have stopped. I would have turned my head and kept walking. I was almost home. But he saw me first and held up a hand, beckoning. So I went in and he poured me a glass and we had a conversation I could never have expected. Belgium and Alberta. I pretended to love my prairie memories on his behalf, since he was so obviously fond of the farm memories he had from his own home. I told him I'd learned to ride at school, which greatly impressed him, the son of a man who'd bred championship Belgian drafts. We talked about horses for a while, the warm pleasures of grooming, of sharing an apple or a carrot with this enormous creature who regarded you with such intelligence and knowing.

"Tell me something," Gauthier said, in what I see now was a test. "Mangerais-tu du cheval?"

My French was not good enough to pick up the conditional here. *Would you eat …* I heard the simple form, and I hadn't eaten horse at that point, so I said no, perhaps emphasizing it more than I truly felt because the man had grown up raising champions and had, one suspected, strong feelings.

"No," I said. "Never."

Gauthier didn't clap my shoulder in congratulations or anything. But I could see I'd scored a point. The man did not eat horse and he never would. And he thought that's what I'd just said. So the conversation rolled on easily, and on my second test, I scored even higher. Where did you learn to cook? I said my mother, of course. Lilly Kuppenheim was her name. And Gauthier cocked his head with interest at that.

"You are Jewish," he said.

Mother was half-Jewish, I explained. She was born to a Jewish father and a gentile mother. "Enough for the Nazis," I said.

"This I know," Gauthier said. "Jewish enough. This is my father too."

And I waited for more. But the ex-legionnaire only clapped the table with one hand and leaned forward. "So we both learn from Maman. This is good."

And he raised his glass so I did the same. And he added, "We are a bit alike, yes?"

I wasn't really sure about that. He had warrior blood. I was an English studies dropout, a bookish sort prone to quiet observation and private anxiety. But I think what Gauthier meant was that we were both outsiders to the trade in the way that the French brigade was viewed to those who picked up a paring knife for the first time at age twelve and streamed directly into a commercial kitchen. We'd chosen our respective ways in, later in life, however different our reasons for escaping the life path we'd originally chosen.

Maybe I'd see that a little later. At the time I just accepted that the man with the tattoos advertising his lingering allegiance to a much different world had seen enough that was familiar in me to raise his glass. So I did the same, another small action taken that tipped me forward. The sound of glass to glass, the aroma of that wine as it swept to my nose — linden, peach, ginger. Gauthier had seen me and I would not be unseen.

That evening notwithstanding, Pigalle was my usual after-work destination along with all the others. That milling crowd of servers and cooks would stir suddenly, a clustering of intent. Ines hugging and pulling my arm. And off we'd go into the cycle of things. Fourteen, fifteen hours together and then you'd hit the bar, packed in close and letting the tension run out of you. I think it was a statement of ownership and separation made at the same time, those Pigalle hours. We'd created this thing but it wasn't made for ourselves. We shared something with stage actors in those moments, standing outside after a performance, seeing the theatre in its place. There was real pride there. Frankie at the bar afterward buying rounds was proud of what we'd done together. And for those precious hours, midnight until two in the morning, maybe three, until we collapsed into our beds either alone or with one another, we were able to celebrate our survival and our savvy in surfing such a treacherous wave.

"Red thinks very much," Ines would say.

"Right?" Frankie would say from my other side. "He doesn't say much. But Tranquille is always *thinking*." And he leaned over to tap my forehead with his finger. *Tap tap*.

Ines laughed. I laughed. Everyone would always laugh when Frankie did his thing, eyes shifting to him. When she was there, even Stephanie would crack a smile and shake her head at these moments and Frankie would slip his arm around her and give a squeeze. She sipped a glass of Sauvignon Blanc on those evenings she came. And for a time after our first meeting, when our eyes had met and held across the room, she seemed to avoid my gaze. I didn't understand it. But I noticed. Then I finally said something, a few months into my Paris time, Frankie over at the jukebox singing "More Than a Feeling" with a cook from La Rotonde. I looked over at her and she nodded and looked away. So I slid on down and tapped her arm.

"It occurs to me I never actually said thanks to you directly for talking to Frankie."

Stephanie looked at me like she didn't remember this detail, which to me was a rather huge detail given I wouldn't have been standing there if she hadn't.

"You vouched for me because you knew my old girlfriend," I said. "You went to high school together. I heard you played rugby."

Stephanie laughed. "Of course I remember. I love Angela. How is she?"

"Uh, well ..." I started.

"Oh right, you dumped her and came to Paris," Stephanie said. Then: "Relax, kidding. You're welcome. Assuming you still think I did you a favour."

"Of course you did. Frankie really helped me out."

"Teaching you everything he knows?" Stephanie said.

"Kind of, yeah."

"Well, all right then," Stephanie said.

She had me off-balance. The first time she saw me, I'd sensed she was somehow intrigued. Here, I was no longer quite so sure. And still she did not break her eye contact with me, as if waiting and wondering where I might think to take this next.

"So how long in Paris for you?" I asked her.

Five years, she said. She had a furnished place in the Nineteenth, north of Parc des Buttes-Chaumont. I asked her if it was nice and she pretended to think about this. Then, "No. Not at all. But I'm kind of broke."

"Right," I said. "Me too. So where's work for you?"

She told me she cooked in a *rijsttafel* at a place over on Rue Coustou, not far from us, which surprised me because from Frankie's description I'd imagined her in a French kitchen somewhere fancy, down on Île de la Cité or Rue de Rivoli. And apparently, I didn't conceal this surprise very well because Stephanie then said, "What? Oh, I get it. You're wondering why a top-ranked CIA grad isn't cooking for Gérard Besson or Guy Savoy or Jacques Cagna. Am I right?"

She had this dubious, amused expression. I'd seen her use it with Frankie before. Thinking back now, I'm surprised it didn't scare me away when I saw her immediately start using it with me. But in Paris that wet spring, in that bar in Pigalle, the reverse was somehow true. I was drawn toward her instead. Sometimes, in those early conversations, I'd see Frankie watching us across the bar at these moments, Stephanie shaking her head and laughing about something I'd said, quite often laughing more *at* me than *with* me. I'd see Frankie trying to make out what was going on, and I'd lean in closer to guard the whole experience for myself.

So here she was in our first real conversation, amused at me not understanding the single most dominating factor of life in Paris kitchens for the women who tried to work there.

"I get it," I said. "Sorry."

"Do you get it?" she asked. "Seen any women get past *apprentice* at Le Dauphin since you arrived, Teo?"

"No," I said. "Not one. I hear you. Sorry."

She butted her smoke. "It's all good. So you seriously dropped out of university for this?"

English, I told her. I was in an honours program thinking about grad school. And there went the eyes again, narrowing, curious. She had an elbow on the bar. And at this point she put her chin in her hand, listening, her hair sweeping forward. Reading what she wanted to know.

So I took myself back to that business that had so absorbed me before my mother got sick. Mordecai Richler, Philip Roth, Saul Bellow. Mann, Merton, Gunter Grass. Sakaguchi Ango, Dazai Osamu.

"I wasn't super focused," I said.

"I don't know," Stephanie said, lighting a cigarette. "You skipped your Ayn Rand phase, that's good, right? Plus Jewish and Japanese writers is a focus."

So I told her a bit about that. My parents: the nomad in Asia and the Jewish refugee, the travelling around. Ecuador, Venezuela. The weird family recipe box with ceviche, mole, roulade, langue de boeuf à la moutarde.

"Plus an ocelot," Stephanie said.

"You heard that," I said, laughing.

"Thought for sure Frankie was bullshitting."

"Nope," I said. "The ocelot that ate live chickens was real."

"That's a surprising detail," she said. "Although Angela did tell me a few things about you."

"Did she really?" I said. "Anything I should know?"

"Nah," Stephanie said. Then she looked at me squarely. She said, "Ask me why I'm cooking rijsttafel since I'm neither Indonesian nor am I Dutch."

"Why are you cook—"

"I am cooking rijsttafel," she said, "because of Chef Femke De Vries."

"Who's he?"

"Oh dear," she said. "*Femke.*"

"Sorry," I said. "Who is *she*?"

Femke De Vries was a CIA graduate from ten years before Stephanie, who had pioneered her way to Paris only to find the same barriers in those all-male brigades. She'd saved enough from work in the U.S. to lease and fix up a space in Pigalle that had been an Algerian restaurant. She'd never eaten much rijsttafel prior, despite actually having Dutch ancestry. So she did her research and came up with a menu, refined and refined. And there she was running strong fifteen years later.

"It's superb," Stephanie said. "Like, exceptional. You like babi kecap? Pork belly? Beef rendang? It's delicious without being up its own ass."

"Okay, well," I said. "I guess I should try it."

"Tricky though," Stephanie said. "We have the same hours."

"Maybe some Sunday afternoon," I tried.

Stephanie was pulling on her coat. "You know what's cool about *Femke*?"

"Tell me," I said.

"All girls. Exec through plongeur. We are a chick brigade." Stephanie's coat was on, her scarf too. "That's Femke De Vries," she said. "Nice talking."

She was still smiling. And I thought about offering to walk her to the metro or wherever she was going. But I didn't in the end because it seemed to me all at once like Stephanie was smiling then mainly to tell those in the bar, and perhaps one person in particular, that we'd just had the most ordinary of chats, and that she'd just said something very ordinary and friendly in the way of goodbye.

"All right," I said. And at that point, I didn't turn around to check who might have been watching because I thought I knew. I just watched Stephanie pull on her leather jacket, tie her scarf tight to hold her hair. She cracked the hint of a smile at me. Then I pretended to read a poster plastered onto the wall next to me while she navigated the crowd toward the door, high-fiving the doorman as she went out.

———

If the anchor of each day was that bar in Pigalle, the anchor of each week became those dinners that Frankie would host on Sundays at his apartment in Belleville. He had a beautiful and unusual place up there in the Twentieth, back before anyone could have predicted the area would become remotely fashionable. The streets were mostly shabby then and at night you walked there with one eye looking behind you. Nevertheless, Frankie lived in rare style, not in an apartment or a flat, but in an actual house. This was a freak find in Paris at the time and the price. In Rue des Envierges, just above the park, the house was found at the back of a wide lot that had once been the location of a large seamstress operation, closed decades prior. There was a narrow lane from the front gate lined with cottages where the different seamstresses had worked. The house, Frankie told us, had long ago belonged to the foreman. Various people came and went in the cottages. But for over five years, Frankie had rented that small house at the end of the lane. It was wide open inside, from the kitchen Frankie had installed on one wall, across the concrete floor to a sitting area with bookshelves on the other, where Frankie had also set up a long dining table. To the front of the house were glass doors that opened this space to a garden, where there were rubber trees and wildflowers, where the dining table could be moved when the weather was fine, and where Frankie parked his prized Motto Guzzi until a year or so into my time in Paris when he upgraded to a Ducati café racer.

These dinners didn't normally involve people who worked at Le Dauphin, though I'd see some of the women who served out front show up from time to time. But others came from all over the city's food world, cooks and chefs, butchers and bakers and fishmongers, even the odd farmer who'd come to town. The fact that Frankie knew them all is more remarkable to me now than it was even then. Young and new to everything, I just assumed someone in Frankie's position would have such a network. And it's possible I didn't think any further about it in part because I was so glad to be included.

These evenings were exhilarating and refreshing in those early years. Everyone would be exhausted from service when we assembled. This much was the same as when we saw each other up in Pigalle. But at Frankie's, the cycle of an entire week was complete. You felt the calendar fall forward as you pulled a cold bottle of La Choulette Blonde out of the ice chest, or popped the cork of a chilled Saumur-Champigny you might just have "borrowed" from the sommelier at whatever restaurant you came from.

It was my absorption into Frankie's circle, such that I became a regular at these Sunday dinners, that gave me a first glimpse of the man's inner complications. In the Le Dauphin kitchen, he cooked like a machine, always calm, always precise, always very fast. At home he was expansive. He chatted and joked; he was spontaneous in the menus he chose. There was no formula to Frankie's home cooking, as it did sometimes seem at the bistro. At home he had stunning range, from exquisite white tablecloth dishes, on through the whole bistro repertoire, and from there, on occasion, down to an earthy, farm-gate cuisine that Frankie remembered from personal history growing up around Trois-Pistoles in the eastern Quebec region of Bas-Saint-Laurent.

But no matter what Frankie was making on Sundays, you could feel him pushing outward, gesturing the diner along with him, aspiring to do something that I have to assume eluded him at the helm of Le Dauphin. These feasts he'd lay out along that long pine table — and they were feasts, never one or two dishes where six were possible — these were Frankie's expression of what he wanted us to know he was capable of doing, a broad, enthusiastic cuisine that was the truer essence of the chef in total than I think the *chefs patrons* had ever known to taste themselves.

In refined white-tablecloth mode, cooking out of the Michelin playbook, Frankie hit exquisite flavours with maniacally precise technique. I remember these dishes for their poise and strength, like ballet on the plate. I remember escalope de saumon for which Frankie would bone out filets, flatten them between oiled parchment, then sear for a single minute a side. You sauced that with a reduced fumet made with shallots, white wine, and vermouth, flavoured with lemon and sorrel before enriching with butter. But Frankie could go elaborate just as freely. I remember a roast duck dish, the breasts sliced thin into aiguillettes, napped with a sauce made from the roasted carcasses, flamed with brandy, then simmered in red wine reduction and demi-glace with shallots and thyme, strained off, reduced even more, then finished with crème fraiche and shaved truffles. These were the classics that would have been on menus in the most prestigious restaurants in France at that time, prepared here by a man in a red plaid shirt and denims, cooked with casual elegance and served to chefs and servers, wine sellers and favourite vendors, line cooks, even the odd dishwasher.

I remember one day sitting at Frankie's kitchen counter with a glass of the least expensive Côte de Nuits I'd been able to find, sitting and sipping and watching as Frankie did his version of stuffed hare. He boned out three large ones, browned off the carcasses, then simmered them with bacon, herbs, and a couple of entire bottles of sweet Coteaux du Layon. In another pot he reduced a third bottle of the same wine to a syrup, then made a forcemeat with bread, caramelized shallots, mushrooms, eggs, cloves, cinnamon, a shot of Irish whisky, and a pile of blanched and minced lamb sweetbreads. I remember Frankie tasting the raw mixture with a silver spoon, then swivelling to a basket of Périgord truffles, three of which he then grated into the mixture as well.

All the while he did this, Frankie talked non-stop, so different from his low-voiced persona in the Le Dauphin kitchen. Here he was animated. He asked a lot of questions. About my family. About where I'd grown up. About the food I ate as a child.

"Beef tongue!" he said. "I love beef tongue. My mom used to smoke it. Slice it thin and serve it on dark bread with mustard and raw onion."

"We did the long braise," I said. "Then rice and mustard sauce. Yellow mustard, of course."

"Right on," Frankie said. "My mother used to braise pigs' feet in pork stock spiked with maple syrup and Coca-Cola. Kickass good."

From food to family, back to food, and then to men and women, sex. It seemed an ordinary progression as Frankie pulled squares of pork caul out of the refrigerator and laid them out on the cutting board.

So I told him briefly about my ex when it came to answering his question about last love interests. "She was a rugby player."

"That's cool," he said. "J'aime une femme dure. Was she hard?"

I wasn't immediately sure what he meant by that.

"Big muscles in her legs," Frankie said, looking up as if the detail really interested him.

I didn't think Angela's legs had been unusually muscled. "She played wing," I said. "Super fast. High pain threshold. Runners' legs, I guess."

"Did she have tattoos?" Frankie asked, back to his work. "Rugby players are known for that."

"Are they?" I said. "I mean, she did actually. One."

"Where was it?" he asked.

"Hey," I said. "Kinda personal."

"Tranquille," Frankie said, spreading his hands. "We're friends!"

I shook my head. "It was on her right butt cheek if you gotta know. A rugby ball."

"Oh là là!" he said. "Teo, Teo."

I sipped my wine, unsure what to say next. But Frankie was rolling, so no need to say anything.

"Tell me about Ines," he said.

"What about her? Good kid."

"She likes you."

"She's funny," I said. "Very smart."

"Maybe you like her too, yeah?" Frankie said. He'd now laid out the boned-out rabbits on the caul fat and was spooning out a layer of forcemeat I'd watched him make earlier.

I shrugged. "She's like a kid sister."

"Really?" Frankie seemed incredulous. "She's pretty cute. What? Is that wrong to say?"

"She's fifteen," I said. "And you're kind of her boss, yeah?"

I don't remember if I asked that last bit exactly. I describe the scene now — Frankie laying out lobes of foie gras along the rabbits with their forcemeat stuffing, rolling these up in the caul fat to make ballotine and tying them off with butcher's twine, loading them into the freezer for a quick chill — and I want to remember that I registered some kind of ethical caution or objection, pouring myself another glass of that Côte de Nuits and tracking Frankie's technique as he now reduced that stock and enriched it with reserved blood from the rabbit.

But maybe I didn't. Maybe all the moral compromise I see in the situation now is hindsight. Maybe at the time I was blinded. Frankie was a complete disciple of the kitchen, consumed with this thing we were doing, doing it better than anyone I knew. That was his magnetism, why people looked at him, all those possessive glances. Was I just failing to sync that vision of Frankie as the centre of attention with a guy whose eye would snag on a young woman who seated people and bused tables at his restaurant and didn't even show up at the pass?

Or was my silence the product of a more cynical calculus, a sense that if Ines had caught Frankie's attention, he might be distracted from other infatuations?

"What about Stephanie?" I asked him.

He seemed to intensify his focus on the vinaigrette he was making, the whisk a blur in the aluminum bowl as the oil drizzled down, the whir of metal on metal like the sound of locust wings. Only when the emulsion was perfect did he set the vinaigrette aside and turn to the cooler for greens and radishes and address the question with his back to me.

"Stephanie is a funny one, you know this?"

I shrugged. "Funny how?"

"So beautiful," he continued. "But so much in her mind."

He was rummaging, hunting around in the cooler, pulling up items and putting them in a square basket on the far counter. Baby gem lettuces, hard-boiled eggs, slab bacon for lardons. He turned finally, holding the basket, looking down and beaming. "Simple food tonight, yeah?"

"Looks great, Frankie."

Then he set the basket down and looked at me. "You want to fuck her."

"Come on," I said.

Frankie laughed, leaning back with his hands on his hips. "It's not so strange," he said. "She's super hot. She's tough. But I tell you something, she can see right through you."

"Me?" I asked.

"Anyone," he said. "She told me once, 'At some time in my life, this is very important, I want to walk the Camino.'"

"What are we talking about here, Frankie?"

"That thing in Spain."

"I know the Camino."

"Right. So I said to her, 'Sure, let's you and I do that. We walk across Spain. We go next year, okay?'"

I waited.

Frankie started laughing. "And she saw right through me. No way I ever do that. She knows this right away. So we go out to dinner at Tour d'Argent instead, which was also pretty nice."

"Right," I said, impressed. I wasn't sure I knew anyone else working in the food world who could afford Tour d'Argent.

"Canard au sang," he said, thinking back. "Very fancy. You know this dish?"

"Sure," I said. "I mean, never had it."

So you roast a duck and carve it, Frankie explained, keep the breast and the leg meat warm. Then you put the carcass through this machine like a potato ricer only so big it has a wheel crank handle. You load the carcass into the container of the press, you crank that handle down, crushing the carcass and out come all the juice and blood and marrow. "Oh là là! Delicieux," Frankie said, doing the chef's kiss with his fingers. "Very rich. Very decadent, right?"

I nodded. "Which is the point, I suppose."

"Before we eat that night," Frankie said. "Stephanie, she do this." And here he nodded his head just slightly, then with his right hand cupped and his thumb extended half an inch, he touched his forehead, his lips, then his heart in quick succession.

"So she's Catholic," I said.

"Right?" he said. "You didn't expect it. So much passion. So much lust and appetite. She ate that duck like … I don't know. Like she is a starving person. I watched. I was like … wow. Such hunger is sexy, right?"

"She's Catholic and she enjoys her food," I said.

Which is why she didn't come often on Sundays, Frankie explained. She had her private and peculiar habits. Evening mass on some occasions. Or surfing the *bouqinistes*, he said.

"She likes old cookbooks," Frankie said. "She writes her own book one day. That's what she told me."

"A cookbook?"

"No!" he said. "Like a story about her life in Paris."

"A book," I said. "Wow."

"Isn't it great? She reads. She writes a book. She prays to God. She even believes in God I think, I never ask her. A perplexing, beautiful woman, very hungry for life and all things. So maybe she walks that Camino one day with someone who feels the same. That night we were together and we have a very special night."

I sipped my wine.

"And now," he said, gesturing to the room with a sweeping arm. "Here we are for another!"

I remember that people began to trickle in shortly after those comments. And I was eventually pulled away from the kitchen by conversations with others as they arrived. A couple of cooks from a big hotel on Rue de Rivoli. A group of young women who worked together in a patisserie in the Marché des Enfants Rouges. One of the hotel guys had brought a case of decent champagne. An entire case, almost certainly lifted. But it was open and we were drinking it. Frankie sipping a flute and singing in the kitchen. And then the food came out and I remember a brief silence falling. The ballotines of rabbit had been roasting for several hours by that point, the outsides caramelized to mahogany brown. They'd been cut into thick round slices to reveal the stuffing inside, the lobe of foie in the middle, each slice plated in pool of that reduced sauce, so dark that it was almost black. A dusting of red espellette.

The silence did not last. We fell onto that food. And when I left that evening, one of the market girls had stayed behind, the one who I recall being told made legendary macarons. She was lying back on the chaise longue in the terrace outside the house, an empty glass of wine set aside. She was looking up to the Parisian sky, one strap of her summer dress off her shoulder. I found myself following her gaze, up and up to the constellations there. One star moving. A satellite, I suppose. But I was drunk and I found myself vividly imagining the silver orb overhead, looking down. I felt seen. And I don't mind admitting that in the same instant I envied the macaron girl for being the one chosen to stay behind.

There was one element of our kitchen slang at Le Dauphin that was unique as far as I'm aware. When tickets came in, servers would append to the table number a note indicating what sort of diners were at the table in question. These nicknames corresponded to the suits in a deck of cards. *Les trèfles* (clovers or clubs) were tourists. *Les carreaux* (tiles or diamonds) were locals. *Les coeurs* (hearts) were attractive diners, women or men the cooks might wish to check out based on preference. And the last suit, *les piques* (pikes or spades) was reserved for VIPs. There could have been other categories when you think of all possible types of diners. But there were only four suits in a deck of cards. So those were the names that servers and cooks used. And at any given moment, it seemed to explain the Le Dauphin front room pretty well.

"It started with piques," Frankie explained when I asked. "*Les personnes extraordinaires* was shortened to the letters *P* and *X*. From *pay-eex* came *piques* and there you are."

As for who came up with the system, Frankie credited a server now departed. Others said Frankie himself. However it happened, it was agreed that the practice had begun around the time Frankie arrived. Gauthier said the same when I asked him about it.

"Frankie likes this children's game," he told me on an evening when I had again spied him through the front glass at Le Mouton Noir, and he had again waved me over. "Piques. Trèfles. Maybe he brings this from his fancy school, CIA."

"Frankie went to the CIA?" I asked him. Frankie had told me that Stephanie had gone there. But he'd somehow never thought to mention he'd been there himself.

But Gauthier didn't seem to hear the question. I could see a muscle in his jaw tensing and relaxing and his eyes went to the window while, I assume, he waited for some fleeting thought on the topic of Frankie to pass on through. And then he changed course rather suddenly, surprising me with a detailed description of the bar fight that had nearly gotten him incarcerated all those years prior.

Some insult or other had been given. That part didn't interest Gauthier to retell. What he seemed most keen to communicate is that after getting sucker-punched in that famous fight that very nearly landed Gauthier in jail — *tête de noeud*, he said, remembering the man in question — he'd lain in wait to exact his revenge. He'd slipped out the side door of the bar, bleeding from the head where the man had hit him with an empty glass. He tucked in behind a garbage bin near the rank of scooters. Then, when the man had mounted up on his Lambretta and gained some speed toward the mouth of the alley, Gauthier had clotheslined him out of the saddle with the swipe of a pool cue. The man wasn't wearing a helmet. His head crunched to the stones. Much more blood and trouble ensued.

"J'étais en colère," Gauthier said that night in Le Mouton Noir. Then, after a long pause, an ironic laugh. "Mais pas de problème, il n'était pas un pique."

Of all the piques who came to Le Dauphin, and there were many in that busy and popular part of Paris, one stands out far above all the others for the utter deference *les chefs patrons* paid to him. I could reveal his name, but I'd rather not get sued. He was (is) an actor from Los Angeles, meaning he might have qualified as a *trèfle* were he less famous. But we're talking a big name here. I'll go as far as whispering that he was known for very gritty, violent films in which his morally compromised heroes yet strained toward justice. And he seemed to spend so much time in Paris, and so much time at Le Dauphin, that despite not speaking a workable word of French, neither could he really be described as a tourist.

Setting the man's fame aside, his legendary crooked smile and gravelly voice, his beautiful wife who was from Algeria, the most notable thing about *Pique 22* — as we all came to know him because of the banquette near the back right corner that was always his when he came in — was the fact that Frankie loathed him so.

"This man," Frankie once said to me, well after service and out of the earshot of the *chefs patrons*. "This man makes us into a cartoon, you see?"

I didn't really.

"The neighbours," Frankie said. "These people I love. They come to eat what they've always eaten. It's an honour to serve them. It's an honour to get those meals just right."

"But dude from LA …"

"Dude from LA," Frankie said, elaborately gesturing. "He comes to see an act, a play, or a movie called *Paris*, yeah? He comes and says like, *Do Paris for me.* He orders us and we jump around and do our Paris dance for him. It's because of him we can never change. *Deux brandies, s'il vous plaît!*"

The drinks arrived. I checked my watch but no point objecting. "You said the locals want to eat things they've always eaten," I said to Frankie. "So isn't that the same thing?"

"Oh, for fuck," Frankie said. "You've seen his tickets."

He had a point. Pique 22 might not have been a typical tourist, but he shared something with the *trèfles* that even with limited experience I could see. He ordered the way they did. Always the foie gras, never the Burgundian snails. Charcuterie plates but no calf's head salad. Steak frites over boudin with apples, fifty to one easy. And if a *trèfle* ever ordered the andouillette plate by mistake, you could count on that coming back nine times out of ten from those who thought they were ordering Cajun andouille and accidentally ended up with a tube of barnyard on their plate. Coq au vin, duck confit, dover sole. These all sold to the *trèfles.* Sweetbreads, pig cheeks, beef tongue, not so much.

"Still," I said. "They're reading the same menu."

"They read it differently!" Frankie said. "The neighbours read the whole thing. These other people, they read the carte like they're trying to find the food from *An American in Paris.*"

"I don't think they ate much food in *An American in Paris,*" I said.

"Ah!" Frankie let out a gasp of exasperation. Then, looking around, "You seen Stephanie tonight?"

I shrugged and shook my head.

Pique 22 would never have known any of this, of course. He wouldn't even have known he had a nickname in the back. He'd never laid eyes on Frankie and would have had no idea that the sous was a person of note at Le Dauphin, largely responsible for the popularity of the place, which was in turn responsible for the Parisian costume drama that Pique 22 seemed so much to enjoy. Frankie, just as obviously, was well aware of his invisibility to the man, which only made things worse. Because while Frankie was unknown to his nemesis, he was forced to know Pique 22 in every detail. He was forced to execute every order from the man when it came to the pass, always delivered by one of the *chefs patrons* personally, so visibly pleased with themselves at having chatted with the great actor. Then Frankie would have to relay that order back to his brigade, involving all of us in what he saw as a great charade.

And if that weren't enough, each of these orders — forget the fetish this actor might have had with Le Dauphin and its quintessential *Parisian vibe* — was slightly skewed from the menu, with addendums and eliminations and swapped items, which no other patron at Le Dauphin would ever have been allowed, including other famous people.

Frankie never wavered in accommodating these requests. Though once you'd worked there a while, you'd hear the flint in his voice as he relayed the details.

"Pique 22," Frankie would say, in a cadence that announced: *Here it comes.* "Coq au vin. Steak frites. Salade frisée mais pas de lardons. Oeufs pochés sans sauce. Et … toast."

"*Toast*, Chef?"

"Oui. Oui. Toast. Like out of a toaster. Griller du pain. Rapidement."

So it went. We'd all hop to it and get it done. But I noticed this simmering resentment more and more every time Pique 22 dined at Le Dauphin over that first year, and then into my second year. And I count it as one of my life's more dubious honours that I then witnessed the event, almost two full years into my time at the restaurant, that brought this resentment to the boil when, as with milk left unattended on the stove, there was a sudden scorching, overflowing, along with a mess and subsequently necessary cleanup.

It was again one of the *chefs patrons* at the pass, which was as good a sign as any that an order from Pique 22 was incoming. So in it came with all of its usual adornments and negations, nothing particularly more tiresome and *trèfle* about the order than any other from the banquette in the back right corner until the last item, when Chef Marcel asked for tuna salad.

"Niçoise?" asked Frankie.

"Non, non!" Chef Marcel snapped. "Comme les Américains. Mayonnaise. Like that."

Tuna salad.

"On a sandwich?" Frankie asked.

And here Chef Marcel became angry, raising his voice with his own highly valued sous.

"Oaf stupide!" Marcel said, leaning through the pass and putting his finger to Frankie's lapel. "Comme ta mère américaine la ferait. *Thon. Salade.*"

As your American mother would make it. I winced at the *commis* station near the grill, to which I had by that point been promoted. I can't remember what exactly I was doing. Trimming duck breasts for the *grillardin*. Cleaning langoustine for the fryer so we could garnish the bouillabaisse. I was doing something and I stopped, which you generally didn't do. I stopped and watched Frankie blanch white. Then I heard the "Oui, Chef" and he was in action. Jumping from the pass and back into the room. And he made that tuna salad himself. He didn't bother Gauthier or either of his *commis.* He didn't ask me to help him remember how a North American tuna salad went together. He stepped back to a cold station. He issued forth a few short orders. One of the other *chefs de parti* stepped to the pass to expedite. And in four short minutes Frankie had himself a tuna salad for whomever it was with Pique 22 who would travel all the way to Paris to visit with the famous actor and order it.

I went back to my job. But I was watching him. Spanish tuna from a can. Mayonnaise he whipped up from scratch. Celery finely diced. Shallot and capers likewise. A grind of black pepper and a generous pinch of salt. Frankie folded all this together into the familiar mix. Then he pressed it gently into a ring mold and plated it with microgreens and lavender chicory petals. And just as he reached for the espellette pepper, a dusting of which would have nicely jacked the dish with flavour and colour, Chef Marcel appeared and snatched the plate from under Frankie's nose.

"Pas de poivre!" he roared. "C'est pour un chien."

Which brought several heads up at their stations, though nobody said a word. And perhaps it was because Chef Marcel sensed the attention swivel onto him, and the humiliation of the moment for Frankie, that he said it again in the best English that he had.

"No pepper," he repeated. "It is for *un dewg*."

How many chefs would be driven to a violent fury on learning they'd just prepped a thirty-dollar plate for a Brittany spaniel? I've been around kitchens for a few decades now and I'm just going to tell you: only a fanatical few. But that was Frankie as I was getting to know him. I saw it right away. Frankie in a state. First, a quivering silent rage that, to his credit, he did not let out on any member of his brigade. Then later, after service, where it spilled out in all the more ordinary ways. We got to the bar in Pigalle. There was an order of brandy shots for the bar. Then there were the repeated orders for himself. Courvoisier after Courvoisier, washed down with glasses of Pelforth draft. All the while, the torrent of words. I might have been sitting there, but it wasn't really a conversation. It was a rant about everything bothering Frankie, all of which appeared to have collided at once that evening: toxic celebrity, sucking up to the rich, being held back creatively, what it meant to be original, what it meant to be authentic, what it meant to strive for genius in the pursuit of which one found the only viable approach to personal truth.

"A circus!" he shouted at one point, as if this single word had popped to mind and answered all outstanding questions. And he stood for this part, facing the bar, seeming to address the vast array of colourful bottles there and, perhaps, his own reflection behind them. "We're not acting in a movie or a play!" he shouted. "This man would have us all be dancing bears in the circus!"

And here he spun from the bar to impersonate a dancing bear, his arms hanging out from his side, his back hunched, his face collapsed to what I suppose Frankie thought was an expression of bearlike benignity, but which, after only a spin or two, brought him crashing into a cook we knew from Polidor who was just then passing behind, squeezing through the crowd toward the door.

"Derrière," the man said, holding up his hands.

"Va te faire voir!"

"Calme-toi, *Montreal*," the cook said, in good humour.

"Es-tu un ours?" Frankie said, trying to puff himself up in height. "Un ours dansant?"

"No Frankie, I'm not a dancing bear." The man was laughing.

"Frankie," I said. "Come on."

"Take him home," the cook said, still smiling.

"Va te faire enculer," Frankie said, surging forward.

"Frankie, Frankie, no." I grabbed him by the shoulders.

"Frankie," said the bartender. "Asseyez-vous ou sortez. Okay?"

"Nique ta mère!"

So I wheeled him out, guiding him through the crowd who cheered him on his way.

"Formidable!" shouted someone. Which really didn't help.

I sprang for a taxi to avoid having to navigate the metro with him. And then I had to listen to him continue to rant all the way back to Belleville on the topics of the moment, only now with more focus on his immediate future plans. He was quitting that stupid job at Le Dauphin. He was heading back to Montreal. He was going to show people what might really be done by a person with blood and true heart and commitment to a vision. And then he swerved, he veered into a different lane of torment. "And I'm taking Stephanie with me," he said.

I looked over at him, unravelling there against the window. "Have you told her yet?"

"I don't have to!" he shouted. "She's brilliant! She's beautiful! She deserves it! She'll be sous to my chef de cuisine and we will make beautiful food together."

"Easy now," I said. "Just take it easy, okay?"

"What kind of gross piggery is it anyway that she's cooking rijsttafel?" Frankie was still going, voice raised. "She's making fucking curry for the Néerlandais, Teo. How is that right?"

"I think a lot of people go there, Frankie."

"But she only has to cook rijsttafel because these French assholes don't like a woman in the kitchen? You don't see the wrong in that?"

"Sure, Frankie," I said. "Sure I do."

"Because I do," Frankie said, his voice cracking. "I see this brilliant woman. And I've loved her since we were in culinary. I love her like oysters and truffles and I love her even though she hates me now."

I turned my face to the other window. I wanted him to say more, which was like wanting to cut myself.

"Why do you need a penis to work in a decent kitchen in this country?" Frankie was saying. "How does this even make sense?"

I didn't say anything. I clenched and unclenched my fists.

"You seen how beautiful she is?"

"Sure, Frankie," I said. "Sure I have."

"And Pique 22?" Frankie went on. "This isn't over yet."

"Jesus, man," I said. "Don't say that."

"No way this is over." It sounded as if he might start crying.

I kept my eyes to the side window and on the swimming streets. It had rained. The pavement was chromed and coloured by the lights along Boulevard de la Villette. I waited and didn't look back at Frankie because I both wanted him to tell me more as well as dying inside at the thought of hearing more, taking on more information that I'd never be able to forget in the morning.

We'd turned left by that point, off the boulevard, heading up the hill along Rue des Couronnes, just now passing under the black trees of Parc de Belleville. I finally turned to see how he was doing. And of course he'd burned himself out. His head was on the side window glass, vibrating with the paving stones. His hand had fallen between his legs and was hanging there, limp and white in the silver darkness.

Oyakodon

That August holiday in Paris, after we shut down the Le Dauphin kitchen, I listened to people talk about their plans to escape the city and realized I hadn't thought to make any myself. Frankie was heading back to visit family in Quebec. "Bas-Saint-Laurent, baby," he said. "You want to come? I have cute cousins."

Which might have been true, but I said no. For a couple of days I tried to work up the nerve to call Stephanie, maybe ask what she had planned. When I finally did swing by her work, Chef Femke herself was the only one there. She told me with a grin that Stephanie had gone back to the States. But she didn't volunteer any further information.

I was thinking about Frankie's meltdown in the taxi those few nights before. So I decided maybe I should call home myself, at which point my father explained that the farmhouse wasn't really ready to host guests just that moment. So I called my sister Simone instead and she said no problem, which is how I ended up in one of the bedrooms of the sprawling suburban place in west Edmonton where she lived with her husband, Greg, and their twin girls. The place had a big pool and a backyard grill and wet bar set-up that was quite a bit nicer than a lot of commercial kitchens I'd seen.

"We try to help him keep the farmhouse clean," Simone said, warning me what I might find out there. "Greg goes out and does dishes. I run the vacuum around. But you know what he's like."

I wouldn't say my father was visibly ailing by this point exactly. He was still driving his skid-steer around, cutting the half acre of grass around the main house, digging trenches for new drainage, tearing down outbuildings on the farm that got in the way of his view down toward the lake. But running errands into town with him, you couldn't help but notice him driving this enormous truck — he had a black Dodge Ram by then, the black Mercedes long since sold — and he'd be doing the speed limit plus about 30 percent, straddling the centre line at points, then swinging over until I'd hear the huge tires kicking up gravel along the verge. He'd be talking and gesturing the whole time, too, telling me which farmer lived where, how to get to the post office in the little town nearby, directions to the dump, all these local things he seemed keen to share. He was obviously glad to see me. He even apologized at one point for not having had time to clear out one of the bedrooms so I could stay out there with him. But when I poked around later, it was pretty obvious no quick tidy-up would do it. Every spare room in the house was stacked with boxes, old tools, plumbing supplies, file cabinets full of papers and, in the case of one drawer that I opened, eight or ten pairs of old leather shoes.

"I'm going to get you groceries," I announced. "We're going to leave you with some frozen meals, stuff like Mom used to make."

He didn't exactly jump at the offer. He told me he mostly ate at roadside restaurants, grabbing things on the go. But when he took me to one of his favourites and it turned out to be a Subway off the highway, I doubled down.

"I'm filling your freezer with food," I told him, which meant first thing we had to go buy storage tubs and every basic kind of supply imaginable.

I asked him to name any dish he'd love to eat and hadn't in a long time. And he thought for a second, then, "What's the one with eggs and chicken?"

Nothing I recognized. "Like battered fried chicken?" I tried.

"No!" he said, sounding annoyed, then struggling to remember. "On rice. In a bowl."

I had to think about that. Then, finally, "You mean Japanese?"

"Yes!"

"Oyakodon?"

"Yes!"

Which was a surprise because Japanese rice bowls had never been in my mother's repertoire.

"No one taught you that one?" he said, seemingly incredulous. "Por Dios y los santos."

Well no. Not in France, clearly. But I'd done my own reading over the years. All those family visits to Japanese restaurants hadn't been forgotten. So off we went to the grocery store to buy a chicken and eggs and rice. No way we were finding dashi fixings out in the country around where he lived. But I did find dried mushrooms, green onions, ginger, garlic, soy. And I knew my mother would have had a pressure cooker somewhere, which she did. And with that cleaned up and scrubbed free of rust, we had everything necessary to make a chicken broth with a real punch of umami. So I made that, and I made rice, and I simmered the chicken with onion and then poured in the eggs.

"I really like this with sesame oil," I told him, which we hadn't been able to find. But he didn't seem to notice. He ate two enormous bowls, sprinkled with green onions. He looked amazed, like all those hours before when the word *oyakodon* had just popped into his head but that he'd had no expectation that I could make it real.

"What're you thinking?" I asked him when he was finished that second bowl. And he sat for a long time, leading me to believe that maybe I was going to get some more detail on his travels, some nuance to the motives and drives that made him travel those tens of thousands of miles by himself, from bomb-damaged power stations to crumpled dams, fixing what the war had left behind.

But instead he told me about getting into a fight on Dufferin Street when he was twenty, just back from the war, jumped by a couple of U of T Aggies looking to cut off his tie.

Necktie. It's what they did, apparently. Guys from the colleges would go around with scissors attacking each other and cutting off their ties.

"Crazy," I said.

"Buncha college bullshit," my dad said.

What annoyed him most when he remembered it was that he wasn't even in university anymore. He'd done tours in the Mediterranean by then. He'd seen those geysers of water from the depth charges and the slicks of oil. Plus, he was wearing a new suit. I still have a picture of him in what I imagine might have been that same suit with its high waist and baggy four-pleat trouser legs ending in two-and-a-half-inch cuffs. In the photo, which was snapped by a street photographer, my dad's tie is flapping over his shoulder in the wind. And he's walking with his eyes narrowed, which was more or less his resting face in all his later years: skeptical, suspicious, thinking one step ahead.

"So what happened?" I asked him. Which is how I heard about that fight, very short in the end. My dad had the guy on the ground in about five seconds. Then he was slamming fists downward into the young man's face, right then left, right then left. And only when he saw the man's hands had fallen to either side and that there was blood on the sidewalk, he stopped.

Which left me speechless, honestly. Finally, I managed, "I guess Grandpa Jack's boxing lessons worked, hey?"

But his face only darkened on hearing that, his mouth firming. His father had been quite ill by that point, he told me. "I kept my stupid stories to myself. Tried not to bother him."

I waited. But there would never be anything more if I didn't ask for it. "Died in his sleep," I said.

"That's it," my father said. Then after a long pause, "*But the souls of the righteous are in the hand of God, and there shall no torment touch them.*"

I'd never heard him quote anything before. Don't think I ever did after that moment either. Outside, the shadows were stretching, the prairie sun burning furious orange to the west. I saw bird shadows on the window, dark shapes that strobed across the panes.

I made him a dozen meals of stroganoff and another dozen of Königsberger Klopse, stacking the containers carefully in his chest freezer. I returned the next day, and the next. Hasenpfeffer, beef tongue in mustard sauce. I worked my way around the world with him that August, visiting the places he'd been, faithfully repeating the food memories that Lilly had brought to the dinner table over all those subsequent years. The north European and French bistro classics. The Spanish dishes. I froze him small portions of mole, adobo, salsa, labelling things and dating them. I drew up a wall chart for him to track what he had and eat things in the order of his choosing.

And at some point while I did all that, cracking him the odd Becks lager and carrying it on over to the dining room table for him, he surprised me with another story that was connected to the first: This one about his departure from Toronto, which was tinged with a base note of shame that it seemed all the years had not quite extinguished.

"My finger," my father said from the table.

I thought he'd hurt himself, so I went over to help.

"No, no!" he said, annoyed. "That kid!"

I was lost. "What kid?"

"On Dufferin Street, that Aggie!"

Oh. The fight. Right.

"Yeah, well I broke my finger on that kid's face," my dad said, wincing again. "And I never told Jeanie a word about what happened, but she sure noticed that finger."

Jeanie. So this was also new. But I didn't immediately press with questions. I kept on prepping the flank steak I was working on for his dinner instead. I let him prepare himself for disclosure.

Jeanie was the girlfriend, he said. They'd been dating a year. They were getting pretty serious.

And here he looked at me across the room like, *Do I have to explain this?* Which he didn't. They'd had sex is what he meant. So I just nodded and waved like he should go on. And so he told me the rest. They used to walk together in High Park, Jeanie and Arthur. And that's where she first noticed him favouring his right hand. So she stopped on the path and took his hand in both of hers, moving the fingers, seeing those bruised knuckles. She saw Arthur wince in pain. She knew him well enough. She knew the truth.

She had on a flowered dress that hugged her figure that day. He thought she was as pretty a girl as would ever go for a mug like him, in his Navy crewcut, with his small frame and wiry arms. Irish kid from Rutland Street. She lived over in Forest Hill in a house with a garage, which was fancy. And there she was holding his hand and looking up at him, forgiving him for the fight all in the same instant that she'd found out about it, and all without him even confessing, without him saying a word.

Something about that just made him blurt out the question, he said. Maybe it was guilt. Or maybe it was just because Jeanie was a nice girl who deserved some certainty. So as she finished inspecting his swollen finger, he just came out with it: "Jeanie, my girl. What comes next for us now?"

Of course, she replied without a moment's hesitation. She said, "Well, Arthur, since we've now been together in the fullest way, I suppose we should be married."

It was Pabellón criollo I was making, I remember. Black beans cooked in beer, flank steak, and rice all served topped with a big fried egg.

Of course, my father knew what she was going to say before she said it. He'd only wondered how it might make him feel to hear it. So there it was. And it did make him feel something very distinct indeed. It made him feel that everything around him — the foot traffic, the picnics on the grass, the man playing trumpet near the tennis club, the sound of traffic on Parkside Drive, indeed this very pretty girl herself who he had wanted physically and urgently — were all suddenly objects seen as if from the window of a speeding train, brilliantly coloured, vibrantly scored, passing in a flickering instant.

"Well, you sure got quiet," Jeanie said, pressing her cheek again to his shoulder. "What do you think, Arthur? Should we be married?"

My father sat remembering these things that August. And as I listened, he took his napkin and began to twist it in his hand.

"That's a big moment," I said, finally. "What'd you say?"

"I told her we really should," he said to me. "Then six weeks later, I was in San Francisco. Six months after that, I was in Japan."

Not so much as a note under her door. Not so much as a postcard from SF or Tokyo, or Baguio, Olangapo, Subic, Hong Kong, and all the way around. Of course, there would have been many chances. None were taken. And when he saw my expression, my father said only, "Well, I'm not proud of myself."

I wasn't judging him. I just found myself thinking how surely Jeanie had stayed with him all those years, how she had invisibly haunted his days.

But I was in the air by then, trying to sleep near the back of the plane in my seat that did not recline. I twisted and turned and thought of Stephanie and Jeanie, my father and the legend of Jack.

I thought of a freezer loaded up with weeks and weeks of food that would remind him of better times, assuming he ever got around to eating it.

Then, thirty thousand feet over the Atlantic and in a posture that would leave me with a crick in my neck for days after, sleep finally and mercifully took me down.

Les Bouqinistes

"How were the holidays?"

Stephanie had been in New York, she told me. Friends in Brooklyn were running an organic farm on a warehouse rooftop in Greenpoint. Beets and arugula and eight varieties of chard.

"So I got blisters," Stephanie said. "How was … Where did you go?"

"Alberta. To see my dad."

"And how was that?"

I told her a short version. Many, many hours of cooking. A brimming chest freezer full of food that just possibly might never be touched.

"Since my mom," I told her, "I think he actually prefers fast food."

"That could happen," Stephanie said, looking at me closely.

In what crack did we squeeze in this conversation? When she was in Pigalle, Frankie would always monopolize her. Maybe he was in the bathroom.

"So all refreshed and ready to get back to work then?" I said.

"Not at all," she said. "I'm completely exhausted."

"Me too," I said.

And somehow that's as far as we got, whenever this exchange did happen. Stephanie with her jacket pulled tight around her. Stephanie heading toward the door to bed. I'd watch her go. I'd suppress the urge to follow her, not at all sure what would happen, but feeling Frankie's eyes on us both.

So the cycle continued. We'd work. We'd drink in Pigalle. And in the mornings, Frankie would look as fresh as the very first day I'd arrived at Le Dauphin with my own brutal hangover. This pattern refused to budge. The man was seemingly impervious to any of alcohol's famous downsides despite often drinking enough to forget key details of what had happened the night before. He'd wink as he passed my station quite frequently, leaning in with a question, "Remind me. Was Stephanie in Pigalle last night, my friend?"

She was rarely around after service during those months, as I recall. Stephanie held herself at a distance however popular she was, however much Frankie would burst out himself on her arrival, leaping to his feet, calling out for a glass of house white, launching in on one of his stories.

So I'd shrug and say something like, *Nah, don't worry, Chef.*

And he'd pretend to mop his brow. *Phew.*

And then we'd be slammed again.

Which is how we moved on. The days crested and broke. Then the next day and the next. And punctuating the organized cyclone of Le Dauphin service and the debauchery of nights in Pigalle, Sunday dinners at Frankie's remained the weekly pivot. Maybe I learned as much up in Belleville as I did in the Le Dauphin kitchen. Or maybe I just learned a different category of things. I'd sit across the counter from Frankie and watch him work from one end of his own culinary spectrum to the other. We'd have a fricassée de poulet à l'angevine in its gorgeous creamy sauce with pearl onions.

There'd be an enormous choucroute garnie one Sunday, the room steaming from the sauerkraut from which protruded pork sausages and frankfurters, veal bratwurst and chicken liver dumplings. Another night, a simple tomato and zucchini gratin with breast of veal simmered in Sauvignon Blanc. Tourtière once, which had to be explained.

"Is it ground meat in a pie?" asked someone.

"It's ground meat in a pie!" Frankie said, pouring cheap Burgundy all around.

Frankie in high gear. Frankie serving endless glasses of wine. The cadence of the ritual took on a familiar swell. Chatter on arrival. Silence as the food arrived. Then an explosion of conversation as the eating began. And it was all so easy with Frankie in charge. We were all so much more intelligent when we were eating crab fondant and sipping Pouilly Fumé. We all had more interesting things to say to each other when Frankie slid the platters of chanterelle-stuffed quail onto the table and produced the two magnums of Pinot from Vosne-Romanée. Maybe others saw the costumery in it. Not me. I was entirely seduced. I thought we were the culinary intelligentsia out there under the rubber trees with the short glasses of cognac and the rising tendrils of Gauloises and Gitanes and Marlboros.

Of course, I was also reminded endlessly that I was the least in these affairs. Even those who hadn't risen much in their own kitchens had known Frankie longer. With few exceptions they were French. I was this red-headed North American who spoke the language poorly, haltingly at best. Any number of women I'd approach in conversation would engage, only to fade away as the conversation grew stilted because I couldn't follow what they were saying, or when the host entered the room and attentions naturally turned. But I think back and I know that I didn't really mind. I was glad to be there. Because at Frankie's place on Sundays, there hovered always the sense of something more, always another course, always something just waiting to happen. After the amuse-gueules and cocktails, after the first sips of wine, after the groaning table and the magnums and then the glazed apple tart and then the brandy, after the espresso, there was always more. Weed. Cocaine. A tornado of voices. I took my share of each thing offered. And sometimes the evening would arrive at a place where I felt some levelling off, some place of equivalence.

"You are his oldest friend," someone said in one such moment, turning an enormous eyeshadowed gaze on me. Perhaps the evening was guttering out. Perhaps most people had gone. Perhaps Frankie had disappeared into the back and there was laughter coming from the bedroom.

"Not the oldest," I said. I remember very bright red lipstick and both of us being very drunk.

"Special friend." And they were leaning forward, touching my lips with a finger that smelled of cigarette smoke and cinnamon.

"Don't know about special," I said. But it was all smudging around the edges. The face, the room, the whole evening.

I would later ask Stephanie about this period, those months of the new year when she seemed to go into hiding. I asked her years later about the absence and she couldn't even remember it.

"Maybe I was working?" she said, shrugging.

"Did you quit drinking maybe?" I asked her.

"Jesus, Teo. Like I was the one who needed to quit."

But I remember that she did reappear eventually, later that spring, coming into the bar about an hour after us. Frankie was at the counter, long since best friends again with the cook from Polidor. But he spun free of that engagement as soon as he saw her. He was suffused in such happiness, so immediately, that I felt a tug in my stomach. It was incredible to me that he could grow yet brighter. But there was Frankie, beaming, pulling out a stool at the bar for her, gesturing her over with big comic sweeps of his arm. And so she drifted in that direction, floating in what seemed to me like a sparkling cloud.

"Hey Steph," I said, as she passed.

"Hey you," she answered, looking at me, squeezing my arm, then gliding by.

I watched. I had no illusions. He was magnetic, like I didn't know. So over there at the bar they embraced, Frankie holding her tightly, rocking her back and forth, her hand patting the middle of his back as if she was for some reason consoling him.

Then he called for her drink — *Sauvignon Blanc maison, s'il vous plaît!* — and stood next to her for the next hour while she sipped it, drinking multiple drinks of his own in that time. How can I report this? Because I watched from the far wall and didn't disturb what I knew was a relished moment for Frankie. I could have gone over. Of course I could. I remember she even glanced my direction in the middle of some long thing Frankie was telling her. He was gesturing. She cracked her eyes over an inch and there we were locked for a microsecond across the smoke and noise. She was asking me to come over. But instead something rose in me that was brittle, petty, even angry. Of course, we didn't know each other that well. We'd barely been able to get to know one another for all the attention Frankie paid, the way he gated out others with his enthusiasm and his social largeness.

But I don't think I was really angry with Frankie, not at that point. Certainly not Stephanie. I was angry with myself. So I found myself turning sharply to talk to Ines, who was at my elbow. Ines, my true friend. That's what I thought in the moment. Ines was genuinely familiar to me. I knew the feel of her body tucked under my arm, the smell of her hair. So I turned to her, feeling Stephanie's eyes linger. Feeling and relishing the gaze as Ines the teenager and I drank those small *demi* glasses of beer. One after another. Ines could hold her drink.

"How many is that for you?" I asked her, Frankie bellowing for more brandy across the way.

"Are you watching out for me?" she asked. "Five."

"Five! Maybe enough, hey?"

She leaned her head into my shoulder as she sometimes did. She said, "Red?"

"Yes?" I said.

"There is a man who asked me to go to dinner," she said.

I nodded, waiting. The idea of Ines at dinner with a man didn't thrill me, speaking honestly. Ines with her wide brown eyes and cutely crooked nose. Ines who was small and quiet and about whom I felt protective. "Who is he?" I asked.

This bothered her. And I saw her bite her lip.

"Do I know him?" I asked.

"Well, you might!" she said, covering her mouth.

"Tell me who," I said. "Someone here tonight?"

But she only looked away and made a face, wrinkling her nose very much as a kid might. But so much not a kid. Le Havre had been tough, she'd told me. She'd jumped at the chance to be free, to go to Paris, to be introduced at a restaurant where she might have a stable job that grew into a career. I remember when she told me about her hometown I wanted to imagine that I identified, that we'd both broken out of prison to come to this place, to embark on this life. Only when on those occasions we really connected, when her eyes met mine and I looked into that deep velvet brown there, when I really *saw* her, I knew that our friendship didn't give us similar backgrounds or equivalent privileges or immunities. Something burned in Ines that she'd keep to herself and that I knew I shouldn't attempt to dislodge or disturb, much less try to share.

"So what are you asking me then?"

"Well," Ines said. "Il est un peu plus âgé que moi."

I processed this a moment. "How much older?"

She shrugged. "Older."

"How'd you meet him?"

"Ah," Ines said, and looked around, making that same face.

"Should you speak with someone in your family maybe?" I asked.

"Oh no!" she said, eyes wide. "My family is small. Everybody knows everything."

"So your parents wouldn't approve."

Ines rolled her eyes and sipped her beer. "My parents ..." she said, but didn't finish.

"Where does he want to take you?"

"Dinner at his place," Ines said.

"Okay," I said to her, "listen —"

"But with people there!" she said. "I'm sorry. I didn't say this. It's a dinner party."

I looked at her carefully. "Sunday night?" I said.

"Yes, of course. It's my only night off."

"Ines," I said, but I couldn't continue. There was an ache forming, a sense of shortened breath. "Let's go. I'll walk you home."

I glanced across the bar. But Frankie had taken no notice. He had his back to us and was, as usual, regaling those assembled with a story. So Ines drained her beer and we slipped out unseen and walked the cobblestones in silence, up and around the corner a block north of the boulevard where I felt the quiver of history, where I thought of my mother as a scared young woman in these same streets. And when I left Ines at her door — she shared an apartment in Rue Véron with a cousin in whom she apparently could not confide — while I could have said any of the dozen things swimming through my mind just then, I only said "see you tomorrow," and she pecked my cheek and said the same.

"À demain, Red." And then a key in the lock, a creak of old hinges, shoes on the stair, and Ines was gone.

I didn't go back to the bar, as I'd originally thought I might. I didn't go back and insert myself into the group of them, maybe even try to get Stephanie alone for a second to tell her Ines was like a kid sister to me. And I never raised Ines with Frankie either. I planned to do that as well, thinking that a friendly question might be all that was required. *Frankie, you really think bringing Ines to Sunday dinner is a good idea? I mean, there's an awful lot of drinking and there's drugs and she works for you and she's also really young.* Nothing confrontational, more of a request for an exchange of views.

But none of it was ever quite said. And that Sunday, I had to go to Le Dauphin to supervise a deep clean of the grill and roasting ovens. So I was black with grease and soot to the elbows while Frankie was doing his weekly entertaining. It occurred to me as I was scrubbing an iron grate down with steel wool out in the side street that I hadn't missed a Sunday dinner in Belleville in many months, even a year at that point. It was a hinge in the week-to-week of my life in Paris. And I won't lie, I was hungry imagining it, thinking of the donair that was probably the only dinner in my future. There was Frankie up in Belleville at his beneficent best, doling out amuse-gueules and cocktails du jour, endlessly chatty, and inspiring the same in all who attended. And that's how hungry I must have been, remembering all those Sunday meals, how self-pitying I was there sitting on the curbstone watching the blackened soapy water disappear into the sewer grate, that I thought only of what I was missing and Ines slipped from my mind entirely, not returning until I was on the metro home.

I didn't pick up a bottle from the late-night. I felt like it, but didn't. And if the Parisian kitchen had taught me anything, it's that the deprivations were handled in one reliable way: You faced up. You did what you had to do. Then you sipped and sipped until the morning came. Then you did it again however you felt. You worked it through in your duxelles or your brunois, you made that hollandaise you'd been tasked with making. You trimmed those halibut, laid out the duck legs in the fat, and put them in the slow oven. You took the rolling pin to the back. *Oui, Chef.* Picked up the pieces of shattered plate and scattered food from the floor. *Oui, Chef.* You carried on. Pushed on. You did not stop for any feeling or anybody.

But I didn't feel like drinking just then. I felt instead a kind of fury rising.

"Can we speak?" I said. And even so, without a hangover for the first morning in what seemed like months, I waited until Frankie passed my station before asking. I'd long learned what the coffee together on morning one had meant, a signal to me of all that would not follow.

He looked at me prepping chickens, perfectly trussing them as I'd learned two and half years prior from young Ricky. He looked red around the eyes, in what I thought might be a first, a rosy tint in the whites that surrounded those grey irises, the wide black pupils. He gestured with his head and we walked back toward the walk-in.

"I gotta ask, man," I started.

"Chef, please," he said.

"Sorry, Frankie. Chef."

He leaned in close and smacked my arm. "Fuckin' with ya. Can't this wait 'til we're drunk?"

"I don't think so, Frankie."

He straightened, gestured again. *All right then.*

"Did you have Ines to dinner last night?"

And his eyes went wide. He stepped back. He spread his arms at the elbows, fingers splayed, like someone who's just opened the door to his apartment to find all his friends assembled, balloons descending. *Surprise!*

Then he stepped forward, real concern in his eyes. He put one hand on either of my shoulders and looked at me, slightly upward as was our relative size. "Is that what's bothering you?" he asked. "Brother Teo, tell me true. You think this?"

"Ah, shit," I said. "I'm really sorry."

"No, sorry! You've been carrying this worry since last night, shovelling shit out of the grill box. Ah, Teo. No, it's I who will be sorry here."

"So …" I started, but I had nothing.

"No!" Frankie said, hands still on my shoulders, eyes holding mine. "She is too young. I know this, mon ami."

I heard the words. I let them sink home.

"You're not sure," he said.

"No, listen. It's crazy. She told me something."

"What did she tell you? Did she say she visit with me?"

"No, she didn't."

"Ask her tonight. Don't worry. It's all good. Last night was a special night, but it was not Ines. I swear."

"Last night?"

"Special," he said. "Very special."

I looked at him and he was smiling. But the feeling in me was one of sudden unravelling. From one moment to the next, relief to dread. Renewed health, my breath back, my spine straightening. And suddenly sickness. I felt sick. I wanted to puke and very nearly did.

"Tranquille, relax," Frankie said, looking at me. "Someone you don't know. I hardly know her."

That night I saw Ines again in Pigalle and again we drank together. Stephanie once again didn't show but this time I was in agony somehow. Frankie, for his part, was unaffected by whatever had gone down. He held court at the bar as he always did. It was all normal. It was all desperately normal and before I knew it the room was spinning and I staggered outside to lean on a wall, to take some air. And Ines was there, speaking from very close, saying, *I'm going to take you home this time.*

"Nah, nah. I'm way up in Père-Lachaise, forget it."

"What, Teo? What, my Red? Why did you drink so much?"

She had her hands on my face now, up on her toes, her lips very close. I touched her hair.

"Ines," I said. But nothing else came out. She was looking at me from so close. Then she let me lean on her shoulder as she walked me inside and over to Frankie at the bar. There was some negotiation here as Frankie agreed to pile me into a taxi for the purpose.

"Il est saoul!" Frankie said. "Atta boy, Tranquille!"

"You get him home," Ines said to Frankie, who bowed at the waist in response to the command from the young service girl. Then I felt the peck of those small lips to my cheek. And her laughter, not harsh but happy to my ear. I remember her happy laughter dwindling behind me as Frankie helped me toward the door.

The following week, Frankie asked if I wanted to help him prepare the weekly meal for friends. And I remember how much that pleased me, how I rushed home and cleaned up, put on a fresh shirt and clean jeans. I jogged up the hill to his place in Rue des Envierges where I arrived just in time to help the Le Dauphin butcher carry in the supplies Frankie had laid on. Six stewing hens, a bag of marrow bones, two whole foie gras, a beef tenderloin for tartare, some pork loin, and a couple of litres of pig's blood in a plastic bucket.

Frankie blindfolded could cook the menus from Alain Chapel or Jacques Pic. But that day he showed us his home food: coordinates *Trois-Pistoles, Région du Bas-Saint-Laurent, Québec.* So we made boudin noir. And we stewed the hens in red wine with heads of garlic. We made ploye buckwheat pancakes that we topped with thick slices of browned foie and crisp bacon garnish, served with a reduced maple syrup sauce. We stuffed a half dozen small pig's stomachs with a mixture of ground pork and grated potatoes, cockles and clams cooked in Barsac, all flavoured with garlic and sage. We cooked these with langoustine shells, tomatoes, and pork stock, then brought them to the table in tureens, bathed in a reduction of the cooking liquid and garnished with the shellfish meat. I don't remember people actually arriving. It seemed that all at once the table was loaded with food and the room was full. I was carrying out those stewed hens on platters, each bird plated between roasted marrow bones that were each topped with a thick slice of boudin noir. Frankie was handing out his amuse-gueules — crispy fried smelt in baskets, little discs of aspic in each of which was suspended some spider crab meat and a dill flower. The tartare was on the table with mustard and pickles and crusty bread. The cocktail that night, because the weather was fine, was an English gin and tonic, and there were pitchers of these along the sideboard and on tables in the garden.

I remember that evening unrolling in familiar fashion. Although I do see now that something different was afoot with Frankie. He was bringing us to his family. I could have asked why. What was it in the moment that made Frankie want to draw us close? But for the first time since my mother's death, I found myself thinking of home and not immediately of either her or my father. There was another person hovering there, significant for their absence.

Dinner was over. The cigarettes were out on the table. Frankie was dancing with a woman near the turntable to an old Chet Baker record. I remember the moment it snapped into place. I wasn't thinking of my mother or Frankie's mother or Ines for that matter. I was thinking of a glaringly obvious hole in the centre of this thing no matter how you looked at it, visible from every angle: Stephanie. She moved in the shadows of the book stalls, she leafed pages, she read lines. And she was everything and the only thing I could think of that moment, everything and the only thing I desired.

It was early for me to leave, only nine o'clock. But I knew how to find her if not quite where. I was down at the bouquinistes inside thirty minutes. I surfed the quays, but most of the vendors were closed. Then I went looking in the nearest likely spot I knew. First time lucky. The church of Saint-Germain-l'Auxerrois. In the very last pew. Evening prayers. I noticed she wasn't kneeling or even moving her lips with the echoing words from the distant front of the nave. I slipped in beside her and she didn't startle. I saw an old copy of MFK Fisher's *Consider the Oyster.* She turned and looked at me steadily.

We didn't say a word to one another for over thirty minutes. I opened my mouth to say something in the church and she put a finger to her lips. So I stayed quiet until the service was over and we'd walked all the way back to Quai du Louvre. Then she spoke: "Kinda wondered when you might show up."

The Seine was black. The *bateaux-mouches* were bristling with tourists, plying the waters up and down and beaming their white searchlights on Notre Dame and at the picaresque bridges. We leaned against a railing and Stephanie lit a cigarette. She had a way of smoking that stayed with her all the days that I knew her as a smoker. Instead of holding it between the first joints of the index and middle finger, she pinched it between the tip of the index finger and thumb, as if from the first puff she were readying the thing to be flicked away in a long arc of embers.

"I've been thinking about you," I said, finally.

She exhaled smoke straight upward past her nose. "And you came all the way down here from Frankie's before the totally drunk part of the evening to tell me?"

We went to a café at the corner of Rue du Pont Neuf where we found a table at the rear of the terrace under the awning where the light was yellow and a dense laurel bush closed in from the street side and gave us some privacy. Coffee and Calvados arrived. Then a plate of baguette with rillettes and cheese and apricot preserves because Stephanie said she was starving. We worked on that together — spreading rillette and Saint-Marcellin, sipping rich coffee, clinking brandy glasses before the first sip — and I pretended not to notice that we were crammed in that corner, our legs touching whenever we moved, that I could smell her — green apple, lavender — and that she hardly said a word while eating and I felt no particular need to fill the silence.

After that — when the second glass of Calvados arrived without me ordering it, around the same point I realized that Stephanie knew the waiter, that he was paying close attention to her, that she was entirely in control of our evening — only then did we really talk. But I remember only snips of it. Families and personal history. Where we spent our childhoods. For Stephanie it was outside Seattle, only child to her father, George, and his third wife, Theresa.

"Who I called Tess," Stephanie said. "Like from age six, no idea how that started."

"And what were Tess and George all about?" I asked.

Love, she said. Tess and George had truly loved each other despite everything. Despite George's first two marriages, which hadn't worked out well at all. The first lasted weeks, apparently. They were young. The second ran long enough for George to have two daughters who now didn't speak to Stephanie.

"Not a great divorce," she said. "Neither of them. But George and Tess are both dead so can we maybe talk about your family now?"

Of course, of course.

"Siblings?"

"Two," I said.

"Kind or cruel?"

One of each, was the truthful answer. Simone had always looked out for me in her quiet way. A brilliant student, determined and loyal. She'd wanted to be a doctor as long as I could remember because that's what my mother had wanted to be before the Nazis took all ambitions from her. Jonah was our rebel, always fighting with our parents or teachers. He'd wanted out of the family from the time he was about twelve, I figured. He was in a lot of fights at school and pummelled me at home, maybe for practice.

Meals too. I remember talking about the ones we remembered from our earliest years, others that we'd made for parents when we were in our teens. Stephanie had produced a meal of quail at one point, bought whole and alive from a farmer down the road, plucked and spit-roasted all on her own. I remembered making ceviche out of prawns bought from a fisherman in Horseshoe Bay, buckets of shellfish and onions, tabasco and lime.

Parents, siblings, dogs.

Why vespers? I might have asked her or Stephanie might have posed the question herself. To repeat something, to steady oneself for the insanity of what we were doing every week. I thought I understood.

"So … Frankie," Stephanie said. "Do we need to talk about that?"

"You were at CIA together."

"We were," Stephanie said. "We came to France together."

"Okay," I said. "I see."

"No, you don't see," Stephanie said.

"Tell me then."

"My dad drove a forklift most of his life," she said.

I waited.

"I needed a scholarship or no way I go to culinary. So I get one. I do culinary. And I have this friend at CIA, Frankie. He's going to France after graduation."

"To work at Le Dauphin."

"He didn't even have a job lined up. He just announces he's going and he's going to find work. That's what Frankie was like. I was dying to get out of there. So I travelled with him because Frankie offered to pay my flight. When we got here, we were roommates. Together but not together. He'd found this amazing place, which you've seen. He wanted me to stay. But I didn't."

"Then you started at Femke?"

"No," she said, blowing out a thin stream of smoke, up over the hedge, into the hanging lights. "Is it a bit early for war stories?"

"No," I said. "No, it's not."

So I heard. She started in a French kitchen. She'd started at Jardin Jardine, which was high end. No stars, but run by a chef from the U.K., a bright light coming out of the Marco Pierre White constellation. I didn't know the guy and Stephanie didn't even want to say his name. She got in a month of shifts before the hands started. Stroked across the ass. Full grab over a breast. From behind across her stomach, pulling her back into him so she could feel his erection. The day he got her in the walk in was the last incident, less than a year after she started. No worse than the others, just final. He pressed his face to hers, kissing her cheeks and down her neck. He was wasted on something — crystal, coke, didn't really matter. She hit him with a closed fist. He fell. Then he fired her in a torrent of screams, being held back by apprentices while doing so. But her apron was on the floor already. She was out the door.

"You look shocked," she said to me.

"I'm just sorry that happened to you," I said.

"It wasn't a freak thing, you realize," Stephanie said. "I struggle to think of a single woman I've known well enough to talk to in any depth at all who hasn't had some story like that."

"In Paris," I said.

"Anywhere, man," she said. "Not just here. Not just *kitchens*."

On another day, in another mood maybe, Stephanie might have bailed on me right there, just another guy who thinks he's been taken into a very special confidence having learned of something like this in a woman's past. But she only sighed and looked away a moment, then back.

"Frankie had heard of Femke and made the intro," she said, finally. "I'll give him that much. So she gave me a job and that's when I got my own apartment."

I was staring at her, not sure what to say. Not wanting to follow what she'd said with something stupid.

"Your turn," she said.

"Got grabbed by the balls once," I said. "One of the Pellerey Pricks. Which is not quite the same I realize."

"Not great though."

"Question?"

She butted her smoke.

"Once, early on," I said, "you said Angela had told you about me."

I waited. And here Stephanie shook her hair back. She did this in a way I can close my eyes and see. Chin up just a fraction, her green eyes still on me. Then the tiniest of shakes, right, left. And the ringlets of gold fell away to the side of her forehead. A stroke of the finger and these were tucked behind her ear.

I didn't actually get any answer in the café over third glasses of Calvados and a plateful of breadcrumbs and smears of cheese and jam. Walking later, nothing definitive. Not on the midnight cobbles between the quay and the street outside Stephanie's apartment. Not between the street and the courtyard inside with the garbage bins, on the worn marble stairs, the wooden treads winding up to the very top floor. In the narrow hallway, in rumpled sheets on an unmade bed. In between breaths that I could feel on my neck and my chest.

"Are you sure you want this?"

Who said that? Was that me or you, Stephanie? Who wondered if the next move, which would change everything, had really been properly considered? Maybe it was, in the end, both of us speaking the same things in the same moment, merging. I wanted nothing else. I wanted the world. But the world was only you.

"Yes."

"Me too."

There was a space pried open by those spoken words, a space that we then wordlessly closed with the very same lips that had spoken them. We closed the space, fused, and afterwards in the silver light there were slate-grey motes of dust and a tiny spider on the lampshade, still and perfect, as if it were watching. That's when you finally answered.

"She said you were very romantic."

Up on an elbow in stripes of blue. A clatter of traffic rose and fell outside the window, rain came.

"Something else."

"That you're sweet. That you worry too much."

I waited. Something else. There was something else there, darkening the corners.

April in Paris. It actually was. I was cooking in France, brigade at Le Dauphin. Twenty-four years old, my future unfolding on the top floor in the Nineteenth near Parc des Buttes-Chaumont. I had no idea that I was passing through a window, that I was floating free of things that had come before. You up on one elbow beside me, leaning over now. At the time I knew only that you were the sound arriving, Stephanie. I knew only that you were carrying the truth. I wanted the whole truth.

Right next to my ear. You at a bare whisper: "She said I might regret it."

Hangtown Fry

Hurry up and wait. That's what the military guys said. So Arthur had his big inspiration and takes the job and hits the road, leaves the girl behind with her fuming father. Then he gets to San Francisco to discover there's a dock strike well in progress and the whole west coast is frozen like the Northwest Passage used to be frozen in January.

"Fuming father?" Stephanie said.

"That's what he told me," I said. "He splits for San Francisco and leaves this girl behind. I guess her dad was pretty pissed."

"He would be," Stephanie said. "Your dad deflowers the man's daughter then ghosts her."

"I guess that's one way to look at it," I said.

"Yeah it is," Stephanie said.

"So then he gets to SF and there's this dock strike and he's stuck there for three months."

"Poor him," Stephanie said. "Meanwhile, Jeanie's back in Toronto probably getting married off to some dork who works for a bank."

It was Sunday afternoon after both our workdays were done. My dad had just phoned at his regular time. Stephanie lay smoking next to me, having listened to my conversation with my dad, a neutral but seemingly peaceful expression on her face and she drew in that Gauloises smoke and released it in slender streams toward the low ceiling.

It did sound pretty good, I thought, the whole SF delay business. My dad was working for Hessen Worldwide in those first postwar years, a construction consulting firm doing postwar cleanup in countries around the world. Buildings, infrastructure. Dams and power stations. But during the dock strike, as my father described it, all the Hessen guys in San Francisco seemed to do was go to lunch. Crab sandwiches at Joe's near Fisherman's Wharf, Rico's for oysters on the half shell washed down with ice-cold beer, Connie's diner on Eddy Street for overloaded blue-plate specials of meatloaf smothered in mushroom gravy.

I'd told him that on the phone too. "That sounds pretty great."

But he just grumbled about being ready to get to work. About being impatient to get to Asia.

"And what was the gig there?" I asked him, as Stephanie passed over the cigarette, then slid off the bed to go to the bathroom. I watched her cross the room, T-shirt, no panties, bare feet whispering on the hardwood.

My father never told me much about the work lined up in Tokyo. There were U.S. Army people involved, a power station off in the jungle somewhere that had to be rebuilt, two other guys who'd be his crew: Maitland and Simms. Like out of a movie, yes. Only a bad movie.

"Bad movie how?"

"Oh, they were jackasses," my father said that day. "Coulda gotten me killed."

"What? How?" I said. But then my dad got shy about the details.

"You with your new girl there?" he asked me.

"Well, as a matter of fact, yes I am."

"Why don't you put her on the phone? She sounds sensible. Maybe she won't have so many questions."

He liked Stephanie from the get-go, long before he even met her. If I'd done a runner on Stephanie like my dad had on Jeanie, he probably would have flown to Paris to intervene. But no way was I doing that. I was infatuated. Plus, I didn't have that kind of stuff in me, I didn't think. And I glanced over to the bathroom door with that thought, willing her back into the bed.

Maitland and Simms took my dad out to International Settlement, he remembered. That was the entertainment district along Pacific Avenue east of Columbus. Maitland wore a brown leather jacket with aviation patches. He'd apparently flown Hellcats off the USS *Essex*. His friend was Simms, some sort of mechanic who came out dressed in one of those shirts from Hawaii patterned over with girls in hula skirts playing ukuleles.

"Strictly contractors," he said. "They had guys like this around. Bored ex-pilots, stokers who weren't socialized outside an engine room. A lot of those guys were into motorcycles, I discovered."

"Hessen was linked to the CIA," I said. "Or that's what I read."

"Oh, I didn't know anything about any of that," my father said, exasperated. "I was an electrical engineer! That's all I was! Anyway, I avoided them after that. Stuck to sightseeing and hanging out with Bella."

"So tell me all about Bella then."

"Don't get any ideas," my father said. "She was married. Boston married."

"To a guy from Boston."

"To a *woman*," my father said. "Mina was her name. You never read Henry James?"

I hadn't, actually. But on he went. Bella ran a shoeshine down at the corner of Market and O'Farrell. Arthur, who spent his days and nights being ready to leave, would stop every few days for a shine. He hardly had anything else to do. So the day he heard the strike was over, Bella was the first person he went to see about the matter.

Bella in her San Francisco Seals ball cap and white T-shirt with the sleeves rolled up showing a bicep tattoo that read *One Sweet Girl.*

"I got my berth assignment," Arthur told her.

"Oh yeah?" Bella said. "So who's your mother?"

"Very funny," he said. "SS *Fortune* out of Pier Thirty-one. Got an officer's stateroom on the boat deck, my own head and everything."

"Fancy," Bella said. "Where to?"

He was sure as far as Japan, only not so sure after that. Bella was squinting up at him, bemused. And that was when she had her big idea to take Arthur swimming.

"I didn't know how to swim," my dad told me. But Bella insisted.

"We're going to dunk you in the Pacific Ocean briny we are, Mr. Wolf. Then we'll go to The Tadich Grill for Hangtown fry. Game?"

And he was too. He was game to go and game remembering. And I could hear it in his voice as he told me that day, Stephanie now tucked back into bed in the crook of my elbow. My father just then rolling on down to Ocean Beach, sunny Saturday in June, the three of them.

One thing in particular he remembered of that day: these four kids on a homemade raft making their way out into the bay. They'd lashed together some fair-sized timbers and nailed down a piece of plywood as a deck. They had a big sheet for a sail, rigged up on a mast and a stay made out of old brooms. They were using an oar as a tiller. They were moving, too, they really were. Shirtless and barefooted. Their expressions so serious. They were trimming the sail and catching the breeze that was flowing offshore, carrying the smells of the midway, the popcorn and sweat, girls' perfume and sugar candy.

My father remembered those boys as they worked their raft out into the swells. They were heading somewhere and he felt it pull on his heart.

Then I heard his steady breathing on the phone. And I realized my father had fallen asleep.

Trois-Pistoles

When the word was finally out about me and Stephanie, I felt new things flourish, growing like spring grass between the paving stones, greening suddenly the spaces between objects and people.

That's what it felt like to me anyway. We started very fast. Matthew Wolf and Stephanie Bell. Teo and Steph. I'd catch our reflection in café windows and say our names aloud.

"We look good together."

"Teo, shhh," she'd say.

I'd rush to see her on Sundays. Those afternoons, I'd wipe down my station and stow my tubs and jars and squirt bottles in the lowboy. I'd dump my whites in the *vestiaire* laundry sacks and pull on my street clothes, practically run for the alley and my scooter. Ah yes, the scooter. *The Ostrich*, we called it. I'd saved just enough. Dented but not defeated, the Ostrich was a thirty-year-old Vespa Struzzo, once mint green, faded to a mottled patina of rust and mouldy grey. It had a one-cylinder two-stroke that popped and farted. But it ran. And I'd push it hard out of Montparnasse to pick up Stephanie at her restaurant, crossing the river at Pont

Royal, rattling through the Tuileries where the berries were already emerging on the mulberry trees. I remember that when I'd wrap her in a hug on those days that spring, she'd smell like coconut and chilies, tamarind, five spice. The women of Femke would chuckle at me. I didn't mind. Femke De Vries herself said at one point, "a regular Latin lover, our Teo."

Then she'd haul out tubs of family meal and serve me a cold plate: pork skewers, this hard-boiled egg thing they did in chili sauce and coconut. The food was fantastic.

But I also remember during those early months that work generally became the least of topics between us. Two young people in love in Paris, we had no money, we were exhausted from our shifts, from our weeks. It was almost like the time that had accumulated since we'd met, the great journey to that moment had been itself exhausting. Which was romantic, but glorious too. And on those Sunday afternoons with the powder-blue sky and horsetail clouds above, if we needed dinner at all, a baguette and a round of Saint-Marcellin crémeux, a coffee made in a Zulay on Stephanie's one-ring burner kept us going long into the night.

Everything was new, like the world had been upended, the scales falling from our eyes so that we could really see this new place that stretched around us. Plus it was spring — new shoots, new buds, as if the earth were acting it out for us alone. Stephanie's father had been a gardener in the day, and she knew her flower and foliage from many forest walks and talks. So Sunday afternoons we'd ride from her apartment to look at the cherry blossoms exploding around Notre Dame or in Trocadéro, and she'd take pictures of the ranks of tulips, daffodils, and peonies in the Jardin des Plantes.

"Peonies make me kind of sad," she told me. "Can't explain it." Then we scootered over to the Luxembourg Gardens, into the orchard near the Pavillon Davioud where we could see the fruit coming out. By harvest time these would be plump green Comptesse de Paris pears or brilliant yellow Reinette apples, which Stephanie told me tasted like pineapple. And I pulled her to me to kiss her again.

Walking the bridges. Lining up the Arc de Triomphe for a photo. The Porte de Vanves flea market, where we never bought anything for not having the money or any place in our tiny, furnished apartments to even keep our own stuff. Perhaps we were playing at being a couple, acting out what it might be like to one day have a house or an apartment to fill with our things. Did we know it that early? I wanted it already then. I'd catch our reflection in a gilt-framed mirror, Stephanie bent over a box of old vinyl records, me standing holding her left hand in my right. She had a way of doing this where she interlocked her pinky finger with mine, like a secret handshake. First time our hands went together, that was the woven shape they found.

That's the way it was, our first spring and summer. In the gardens and flea markets and browsing the bouqinistes. We were *trèfles* together, wanting no local that extended beyond us. And I remember one evening wandering into Place Saint-Germain-des-Prés, following the sound of a jazz quintet playing "Parlez-moi d'amour," rounding the corner out of Rue de l'Abbaye into a crowd enjoying a public concert. And the band segued as if on cue to "C'est si bon."

Arm in arm. Singing songs. Whispering sweet nothings.

And there we were, two *trèfles* in Paris, dancing inexpertly across the paving stones, spinning and dipping and laughing.

We walked down the Quai du Louvre later, up the arc of the Pont Neuf. I'd had a nice find at the stalls that day and bought it for her: a dog-eared, food-stained copy of Saulnier's *Le Répertoire de la Cuisine* in paper, in French. She was holding it in both arms across her chest as she walked. She was smiling, not looking at me. I don't know what exactly she was thinking about just then, but she suddenly swivelled there to face me, right near the apex of the bridge. I remember her rising on her toes, one hand sliding to the back of my neck and pulling me down. Our lips were together. And just then a bright, white spotlight found us, shining up from a river below. A hot white light from a *bateau-mouche* approaching the bridge, pinning us there at the railing. And from the top deck of the ship, from a hundred tourists assembled with their glasses of wine and canapés, a single low voice as Stephanie and I stood blinded. The voice said: *Awwwwww.*

We were seen. We felt ourselves being seen. We were kids happily enacting a cliché, for sure. But we felt like the perfume of Paris, we two just then. The fragrance of love floating above the black water, hovered over by those gothic spires.

And so began my very happiest time in Paris, things settling into pleasant grooves. I honestly lost track of time because I was, for the first moment in my life, precisely where I wanted to be. Work was going tolerably well as my skills increased. Stephanie and I were together almost every night. No point denying it, I'd been anxious how Frankie would react to our relationship. Everyone knew he adored Stephanie. I figured he might be upset by us not only suddenly together, but then inseparable. Upset, jealous. Angry even.

But any worrying along these lines proved to be foolish. What I failed to factor in was that Frankie was still Frankie, still the man at the centre of attention, still the one to whom the room's gaze would pivot when he raised his voice. Frankie whirring up and down the lines at Le Dauphin, whisking a sauce, poking a bavette on the grill with his finger; Frankie in Pigalle raising a glass and making a speech. Frankie didn't need the world quite as much as the world needed him. Or at least, that was an important part of the role that Frankie played for the world. So no way was Frankie going to act jealous even if he felt it. And if I didn't show up for Sunday dinner in Belleville as regularly as I used to, no way Frankie was going to mention it because he just wouldn't.

During the rest of that year and the following, if anything, he rewarded me with more serious attention in the kitchen, and increasing trust. He began to treat me as a colleague, as a peer. By the time I'd been there four years, I'd apprenticed and had been *commis* all over the kitchen. I'd done well. *Les patrons* seemed to notice in their suspicious way. Now Frankie started to really place me, giving me control of different stations for a few days at a time, a week, even a month. I did time on grill and fry. I worked with the butcher breaking down beef sides and whole pigs, ran charcuterie for a stretch, making rillettes, and logs of pâté de foie, boudin noir, tête de veau, and pickled lamb's tongue. I ran the bakery for several months. And eventually, getting on toward the middle of my fifth year, I was promoted to *chef tournant*. This was a special role in a big place like Le Dauphin. The *tournant* was an all-stations chef, expected to step in and cover virtually any role in the kitchen as needed outside pastry. The *tournant* reported directly to the sous, rising to a special place in the hierarchy, above even the various *chefs de parti*. There was one other *tournant* at Le Dauphin. His name was Bozonnet and he looked to me to be about seventy. I'd always assumed he'd been given that role as a reward for years of service, a last pre-retirement posting because sometimes there really wasn't anything urgent for the *tournant* to do. Maybe for Bozonnet that was the arrangement. Frankie made sure I knew my assignment was different. He'd promoted me past the *chefs de parti* to make me his second-in-command. On occasion, he would himself now even step out of the kitchen on business, leaving me as the deputy sous. I'd be busy but I loved it, the evidence of progress, sure, but maybe even more the way it showed how Frankie had seen and acknowledged my work.

"Attention! Attention!" I remember him shouting at the bar, the evening that he gave me the promotion. Here he climbed up on a chair, pulling me up to stand next to him on another, the conversation that roared in the room at that hour slowly fading, heads turning toward us.

After Frankie had the room's attention, he continued, one hand placed in comradely fashion on my shoulder. "You all know this guy," he continued in French. "Matthew to some. Mateo to others. To me, always Teo Tranquille."

The was a smattering of applause. And I heard someone begin a chant: *Tranquille, Tranquille.* But Frankie raised both his hands now and the room grew quiet again. Even the bartender set down a glass that he'd been polishing.

"But one thing nobody here knows better than I do," Frankie went on, "is that Teo is also a great person, and a great friend. A true friend."

Murmurs in the crowd. Frankie stood silent, unsmiling. Then, hand up. "My best friend," he said. He wasn't done. He spoke for several more minutes about the cook that I'd become. The *chef.* How I'd worked my way through every part of his kitchen, how important I'd become to the Le Dauphin family. Not bad given how terrible I'd been at the beginning.

People laughed. Frankie was having fun now. "It's true," Frankie said. "He was truly horrible. Les patrons … oh man … they do *not* want to hire him when he come."

Much laughter here.

"But I have another friend," Frankie said, growing more serious.

"Hey Frankie, it's all good," I whispered. "I appreciate it …"

"And that friend, she is special. She has all my respect, you know? We go to culinary in the U.S. together. Some of us graduate and we're good. Some are very good. Some are even excellent. But this friend, she is *superbe.*"

"Stephanie!" someone yelled.

"And she said I had to hire him!" Frankie said, as the crowd, sensing the end of this toast, began to cheer and chant. "So of course, I did! Because she say so! And here we are! Please welcome Le Dauphin's new Tournant Tranquille!"

At which point the cheers overwhelmed everything and we finally stepped off those chairs and raised our glasses. I saw familiar faces all around. Friends from La Rotonde and Polidor, Closerie and La Çoupole. Ines was there too. She smiled at me, a little shyly, put her arm around my waist and leaned her head on my shoulder.

"Frankie," I said.

And he turned to me with a half smile, an odd smile. He was, I noticed, not a quarter as drunk as he typically was by those dwindling moments in the Pigalle evening. Frankie looked at me with a mix of sadness and pride, not that I saw it in the moment. But I see it so clearly now. Standing there with Ines on my shoulder, I see Frankie controlling the room as always. But I see him also as full of sorrow. And with that thought, he reached out a hand and put it to my cheek. He said: "And now, my fine friend, I'm going to borrow your sister for a drink. Or three!"

And he twirled Ines away into the crowd, a hand to her hip. She was smiling, proud. Ines with the chef and his new second-in-command. Ines from Le Havre out on the town.

I was on my Vespa already before thinking any other thoughts. Pushing the Ostrich down over the paving stones. I didn't actually know where I was going. Stephanie would be long asleep. Maybe I'd wake her. Maybe I'd throw pebbles at her window, no matter that it was two storeys up. Maybe I'd bang on the drainpipe or I'd rattle the front gate. I needed her more than anything in that moment. And that need just swelled and swelled as spring unfolded and the summer advanced. I needed my Stephanie awake and with me. I was learning that intensely as my time in Paris slowly reached its peak.

I hadn't been sure what to expect from Gauthier with my promotion. I'd pretty much accepted by that point that our *garde manger* really didn't like Frankie, maybe even hated him. But I'd assumed that was about Frankie soaring past him in the kitchen hierarchy when he arrived despite Gauthier's own decades of service. So I worried that same resentment might extend to me.

Stephanie thought I worried too much. And she was, of course, entirely right. I needn't have. If anything, my ascendency seemed to amuse and please Gauthier. When Frankie made the announcement at afternoon briefing at Le Dauphin, Gauthier merely turned his head in my direction and nodded with mock gravity. And a week or so after the announcement, some days after Frankie's toast in Pigalle, I walked the long way home instead of going to the bar after service and found Gauthier in his regular late-night spot at Le Mouton Noir. He didn't even beckon me over. I just saw him reach for the bottle on the table, and by the time I was inside and my jacket off, there was a nice glass of cold Auxerrois already poured and waiting. When I sat, Gauthier raised his glass and I did the same.

It certainly didn't change anything in the kitchen between us. Gauthier was always going to be the hard man to me. *Legio Patria Nostra.* His homeland lay elsewhere. And at Le Dauphin, unlike most of the rest of us, Gauthier was implacable, immune, impossibly tough.

I thought this all the more as June unwound and July began. It had grown very hot in Paris. Thirty-five degrees Celsius by noon outside and many more in the kitchen at Le Dauphin. With the roaring grill flames and glowing ovens, I was soaking with sweat in my whites before dinner service even began. Gauthier himself would glisten and grow red-faced but never complain.

"Visitez le Liban," he would say to Ricky, if the young man would sigh or indicate discomfort in any way.

During those weeks Stephanie and I would sleep at my place, which was cramped and had low ceilings, but was cooler than her place at night for being half underground. We'd lie and smoke in the darkness, waiting for temperatures to fall below thirty. Families would be the topic, often, because they always somehow cycled back into view.

She spoke of her father's struggle after the war. The first marriage that dissolved. The second that he left and which she didn't know anything about for many years. Then Tess.

"Which was love," I said.

Stephanie smoked and looked straight up to the ceiling. "Mostly," she said.

"How'd they die?" I asked. "You know, you never told me."

Well, not great stories, Stephanie said. For Tess it was probably addiction. Alcohol, painkillers, eventually cardiac arrest. That was back when Stephanie was only ten. Her father quit drinking and lived a quiet life after Tess was gone. Then he drove off the road on an overnight trip to Austin. Missed a turn and went into a ravine fifty feet deep.

"I was in France at that point," Stephanie said. "I'd just arrived here."

"Holy shit," I said.

She said, "Tell me something you've never told me about your mother."

So I told her about the one and only time I'd seen her cry. We were passing Pacific National Exhibition at night, returning from a visit with family friends in Burnaby, coming westbound down Hastings Street. And when we saw the searchlights painting the clouds above the midway, white pencil beams criss-crossing, my mother suddenly covered her eyes and began sobbing quietly.

"Remembering the war?" Stephanie asked.

"I guess," I told her. "She didn't ever talk about it. The Holocaust and the war and what all that meant. You just didn't back then.

But I guess she'd seen searchlights from the ground in Münster when the bombs were falling every second night."

My father with his hand on her back between the shoulder blades. We kids suddenly frozen in the backseat of that Volvo wagon. A five-year-old doesn't know why a parent is in distress. They know only that distress is present, and they feel it as a shortness of their own breath.

"I've been thinking," Stephanie said, after a moment.

The summer break was coming. Le Dauphin would close on the Saturday night of the last week of July, which also happened to be the thirty-first of the month. Three weeks off. Stephanie had the same schedule. We'd talked already about going to the South. Nice for the beaches. Cassis maybe, to sip rosé and look at the fishing boats. We didn't have much money so I'd been looking into renting a camper van. But there in the darkness that night, two or three in the morning on a Saturday night, early July, I could read in those shadowed eyes that another thought was blooming.

"Maybe we just go home," she said.

We, she said. *Home*. And I knew she wasn't talking about returning to be with family. She meant an end to this, to Paris. She meant finding somewhere for ourselves back in the Pacific Northwest, somewhere among the deep green trees, the salty breeze, warm sun, lichened rocks, gulls and eagles wheeling.

"Did you hear about Ines?" I asked Stephanie, suddenly thinking of it.

She looked over sharply.

"She went home."

"Back to Le Havre? Why?"

I didn't know. She hadn't said a word to me. She hadn't said a word to anyone as far as I knew. Frankie said he had no idea.

"That's odd," Stephanie said. "She loved being in Paris."

"I know. I thought she'd tell me if something were wrong."

Which was true. I was confused by her leaving without a word. But I also felt guilty. Whatever reason had driven her back to the confines of Le Havre must have been a good one. I might have liked the chance to offer support. But I hadn't. And worse, I hadn't even noticed when she left. A week passed. Maybe ten days. Ines not in the dining room. Ines not in Pigalle. I was distracted, of course. Stephanie, new growth, new shoots. How useless was I as a friend, as a so-called brother? Frankie knew nothing and seemed himself confused by the sudden departure. And I got nothing from asking around either, shrugs and glances away. She left and it seemed as if Ines was suddenly not supposed to be remembered.

At Le Dauphin, meanwhile, the summer heat was taking its toll on everyone. Gauthier would never talk smack to Frankie in the kitchen in front of the others, but he'd slam down his knife after taking an order or wait a passive aggressive three seconds before saying *Oui, Chef.* Frankie noticed and asked me about it after work. I could only shrug.

"You know him, yes?"

I didn't really *know* Gauthier. We have a drink together once in a while.

"That's knowing him!" Frankie said. "So talk to him!"

"It's the heat," I said to Frankie. "Let's just get to August, take a break. Then we start again in September."

But Frankie didn't think it was the heat. Something else, though he wouldn't say. "He's violent," Frankie said.

"Gauthier? Come on."

"He's dangerous. You hear about this fight?"

The scooter and the pool cue. Yes, I had heard.

"Not that," Frankie said. "I mean Clémente."

So now Gauthier was somehow responsible for the death of the last executive chef. I laughed at Frankie, sitting there in the bar. He was red-faced, ranting, ordering more beer and brandy.

"You weren't even in Paris when it happened," I pointed out.

"I hear," Frankie said. "They say *accident*. Ha."

I changed the subject because the brandy arriving just then was at least his seventh. I'd been trying to cut down after my conversation with Stephanie, who never said a word, who hung out at bars on occasion, but who I knew did not like me drunk or hungover. That didn't stop Frankie, who'd just lap me on rounds, then lap me again as necessary. His drinking was up, if anything. And maybe that, too, was heat. The tension in the air. Ines gone and Gauthier and Frankie seeming to be at one another. So it was with brutally imperfect timing — second last week of July, just over a week until we closed for the much-needed August break, daytime temperatures sneaking up over forty — that Pique 22 decided it was the moment to walk in the door.

He sent his personal assistant, a young man who came into the restaurant midday on the twenty-third. Not by the front door, naturally. He came in through the alley, through the staff entrance, so that Frankie personally had to fetch the *chefs patrons*, that they might assist in this reservation for two dozen people that Pique 22 wanted for the following Saturday, our final night of the season.

This was all notable for playing out in the kitchen itself and not at the front desk. So the whole brigade could see the bowing and scraping that the owners did in front of this tanned elf with his turquoise framed glasses and trim Brioni suit. It was also unusual for the very fact of a reservation, something Pique 22 had never made at Le Dauphin previously as far as I was aware. But so, too, was the size of the party. Certainly, the favoured banquette would not accommodate, so it was agreed that we would empty the entire upstairs dining room and set up a long table where Pique 22 and his group could dine in privacy.

But not even these features of the transaction were as notable as the PA's last inquiry, which was about the menu.

Was there some way to make it very special that night? Very French. Very … white tablecloth?

Frankie was livid when the young man had secured agreement for all of this and left the kitchen the way he'd come in. "Oh, so now our whole menu isn't French enough?" he raged. "And *white tablecloth*? Was does that even mean? We're a Bib Gourmand bistro!"

"Frankie, Frankie," said Chef Marcel, who was now clearly sweating the prospect that his sous wouldn't play along. "L'ensemble du menu est à toi. It is for you to be … créatif."

"Like I'm not creative every day?" he fumed after the *chefs patrons* had pulled back to the bar in the dining room.

Gauthier, I observed, had been watching all this with a sour look on his face. I wondered briefly if this might be the odd occasion when Frankie and Gauthier were truly allied in their scorn. The *garde manger* had no reason to love Pique 22 or any of his crew, who'd never scorched off a fingerprint on a pan handle just out of the oven much less fought in the Battle of Kolwezi or been shot at in the streets of Beirut. Nevertheless, Gauthier warmed immediately to the upcoming special occasion as if to deliberately remain opposed to his sous. Gauthier even asked if he could help create the menu.

"What an honour!" he said, with elaborate courtesy, which made Ricky snort and snicker and cover his mouth.

"Don't you have anything to do?" Frankie barked at the boy, in a rare show of anger toward anyone in the brigade.

But Frankie wasn't letting this whole assignment go to his *garde manger*. He put me and Bozonnet on it, allowing that Gauthier could have input. But then he was all over us at the kitchen whiteboard as we mapped out the meal, questioning every idea.

"Pheasant?" he said over my shoulder. "Pheasant is so 1980s."

"Mais Chef," Bozonnet said patiently, "it is a Pique 22 favourite."

"Fuck his favourites. He wants *white tablecloth* I'm not serving pheasant chasseur."

"What about a roulade?" Gauthier said. "Stuff with truffle and foie."

Frankie scowled. "I'm thinking offal."

Bozonnet looked away and sighed. Gauthier shook his head.

"Calf's head ravigote," Frankie said.

Bozonnet was sweating now. "Mais Chef, s'il vous plaît ..."

"Why be a prick about it?" Gauthier said to Frankie. "Give the guy his pheasant with mushrooms, his frisée-lardon and steak frites."

I'd never seen Gauthier speak as directly to Frankie before. But Frankie just stood looking at the whiteboard, hand on his chin as if he hadn't heard. Of course, both Bozonnet and Gauthier knew very well why Frankie was proposing the calf's head. It was a lavish, old-world preparation they all knew was from a Burgundian one-star called Chez Madelaine. I had to look this up later, at which point I learned that the dish involved slow simmering a whole calf's head, then serving the entire thing on a platter — snout and ears intact — arranged next to the cubed meat, the tongue, and the brain, which had itself been simmered more briefly in vinegared water. The picture I found showed a Chez Madelaine chef hefting this all on a silver platter, the calf's death-grey forehead crowned with a pleated garland of parsley.

"What about a terrine of veal sweetbreads?" I suggested, thinking of ways to get offal on the table without revolting our guests from Hollywood.

"Or tripe Lyonnaise," Frankie said.

The argument about tripe lasted the better part of thirty minutes going back and forth on whether this was exactly what Pique 22 would want for being essentially French or whether his party might well find it flat disgusting. And again I noted I'd never seen anything like this kind of open disagreement. Normally, Frankie spoke and it was done. Here Gauthier, even Bozonnet in his own quiet, supplicating way, were both opposing the sous. And as a result, Frankie was raising his voice in a way that was not typically his habit. Gauthier, too, was very close to losing his cool, at one point turning away and muttering.

"What did you say?" Frankie snapped.

"I say maybe … tuna salad?"

"I know," Frankie said. "Postier Breton tartare. Bozonnet, write that down."

The Postier Breton was a draft horse. Even I knew that. *Cheval.* Gauthier had appeared heated before this was said. With the words, went instantly, utterly cold. "If you bring the flesh of a horse anywhere near me, Chef—"

"Easy, easy," I said.

"What? What'll you do, *Chef*?" Frankie spat the question.

"CIA should remember Clémente," Gauthier said, recalling Le Dauphin's last executive chef and his gruesome end. "Accidents happen."

Then he left, which was a problem because dinner service was hard on us. But Gauthier balled up his apron and threw it on the floor. He stripped off his whites and tossed them down too. He stood there several seconds in his briefs, hairy legs dropping down to his clogs. It was a striking moment, to suddenly see all the other tattoos patterning Gauthier's tanned and densely muscled body. It all happened so fast I wouldn't have seen a quarter of them. But I remember arcs and tendrils of script, spiderwebs and black stars, a cigar-smoking skull wearing a crown in the middle of Gauthier's chest. He swelled briefly in place, projecting a turgid ill will. Then he turned and left us, back to the *vestiaire* to put on his street clothes, then out the alley door into the humid and scorching night.

Frankie knew he couldn't do anything about it. I think most people in the Le Dauphin kitchen knew that Gauthier was untouchable even if no one knew exactly why. So Gauthier took a service off and I covered, Bozonnet and Ricky covered. We got it done.

"I'll talk to him," I said.

"You better," Frankie said, gulping his beer.

"We should talk about dinner," I said.

"Fucking threatening me. I should fire his ass."

"But you can't and you won't. Because the Pricks."

"Exactly. And why is that? Why do they treat him special?"

"Maybe they're scared of him," I said, not sure if I was joking. *"Remember Clémente."*

"We should talk about the thirty-first. Our special guest."

Frankie did ultimately decide on that. And it was an unexpected gesture after the confrontation with Gauthier, but he suggested we make it a meal about ourselves as cooks, each of us, drawing on dishes that reminded us of how we'd come up from childhood and through the culinary world, all the way to Le Dauphin. "If we don't cook from our own carte, then we will cook from our own heart, yes?"

Poetic, for Frankie. But it did at least temporarily calm both his and Gauthier's rage. No diet-friendly tasting menu, this one. We drew our dishes from the white tablecloth canon that was already then beginning to fade. That and our memories simultaneously, those elements of our own history in food that were themselves perhaps faded at the edges with usage and time. All this still paying respect to what Le Dauphin under Frankie had been about all along: a vivid and hearty filling of the senses and the stomach. So we settled on stuffed clams that Bozonnet had eaten as a child; sweetbread brioche by Frankie; a cold calf's tongue inspired by my mother; filets of mullet in a red wine sauce and thrushes with foie gras, both from Gauthier; the stuffed rabbit dish I'd seen Frankie make in Belleville a seeming lifetime prior; a cleansing crab sorbet I'd proposed; all closing with an elaborate round roast of veal Brillat-Savarin that Bozonnet remembered from a meal thirty years prior at L'Hôtel de la coté-d'Or in Saulieu in Bourgogne.

"Magnifique!" Bozonnet promised.

Gratin Savoyard and the house Dauphinoise potatoes. Cheese board. Then we'd let the pastry geeks take us home with dessert.

"We're going to kill him," Frankie said.

And that was the spirit of the undertaking as I now think back on it. It was all far too much and excessive as a matter of intent. We could have devoted the entire brigade to the project, though in the end Bozonnet and I carried the bulk of it over three days, with Gauthier and Ricky subbing in to help. When I think back on those days, I feel real darkness in the project, all that intensity and richness, all that refinement simmering alongside knucklebones of hostility and aggression. *You can't bake with anger*, my mother had told me when I was a boy. As it turns out, you can. I remember in the run up to that meal how the Le Dauphin kitchen even sounded different. Gauthier singing as he worked, which was unusual. And Frankie saying nothing to stop him as he returned again and again to a dirge-like, mournful melody — an old Legion song, he explained, about singing while marching to your death, or something along these lines — all the while powering through the prep we needed for the mullet's red wine reduction. Gauthier and I lifting the largest stockpot we had in the kitchen, three feet deep and wide, swinging it up onto a gas ring in the back corner, adding the halibut bones; food processor–loads of garlic, celery, carrot, shallot; branches of thyme; and handfuls of bay and peppercorns.

My forehead glistening with sweat.

And then the wine. It was a mid-range Côtes du Rhône that we used with our family meal. Bottles and bottles of it. I lost track after four cases were gone as I uncorked them and handed them over, Gauthier dumping in two at a time as the flame roared.

"Three days," Gauthier said to me with a flinty grin. "Like Christ in the tomb."

Three days while the kitchen hummed around us with its regular service. Each morning I'd check that pot, which would have reduced overnight, pouring in more wine, then glaçe de viande on the final day, mopping down the sides of the pot with a wet brush so as not to waste a drop. By the end of that time, we'd reduced 150 litres of wine down to exactly four liters of syrup, red-black in colour, like dried blood. And when we'd portioned the sticky sauce, it hardened to pucks in the walk-in, ready for use at service.

Gauthier showed me how to make the garnish for that same dish. I remember the fanatical precision. Compound butter with garlic, shallots, and herbs. We piped this, finger-width, onto sheet trays and froze them. Then we broke them into five-inch batons, which were breaded and deep-fried. When they were perfectly golden, Gauthier showed me how you could scissor off the tip of one of these sticks, pour out the melted butter for another use, and fill the crisp tube with a purée of fennel and apple.

At service two crisp, fried filets of mullet would hit the plate on a puddle of that three-day red wine reduction mounted with six parts butter. Two crisp batons de pomme et fenouil. I ate a lot of fantastic preparations during my time at Le Dauphin and in Frankie's own kitchen. What Gauthier showed me how to pull together that day was on another planet. A mouthful of fish and sauce, a bit of that crisp baton, these seemed to act on every part of your mouth at once, every one of your senses alive as you ate. I stood at a side counter when we'd run the first test plate, Gauthier and I shoulder to shoulder, leaning in over the dish, eyes closed and chewing.

"How you like?" he said.

The hairs on my arms were standing on end. I pointed at them and looked at Gauthier. I remember his chiselled jaw, now clenching and unclenching with satisfaction.

We're going to kill him. All the finery, the madness of that particular service. We shipped those plates upstairs where I could hear the guests talking and laughing. It was a level of slammed that I do not remember having been prior, a degree of focus that utterly consumed me. I remember snippets of the evening, fractional moments. The plated calves' tongue, smoked and thinly sliced, wrapped around a port-flavoured stuffing of foie gras, truffles, and butter, nestled under a shimmering glaze of aspic. Thrushes on long skewers, grilled with slices of baguette soaked in duck fat. A lot of details are now lost in the blur. I don't even remember making the crab sorbet, though I must have because there is one particular moment in the evening I remember with vivid clarity: Chef Patron Marcel bursting into the kitchen, eyes wide, face red, and as the kitchen grew still, everyone expecting a tirade, his eyes found me, his expression one of surprise, even wonder, one finger pointing at me, then beckoning.

I remember climbing the spiral stairs, all eyes in the main floor dining room pivoting to me, my hand on that railing, those ironwork *surf guppies*. When I entered the upstairs room, the assembled group applauded, the famous man himself rising to his feet, shaking my hand with both of his clasped over mine, which was the very first moment I registered that Frankie was not in the room. And he hadn't been in the kitchen either when Marcel had entered before.

I don't remember exactly what was my final sight of Frankie in Le Dauphin that evening. I wish I had that. It seems right that there be some final moment, given all that had happened and still was to happen between us, a closing image of Paris and that particularly important kitchen. Perhaps it was him slicing off rounds of that stuffed rabbit dish and plating these in their pool of sauce. Perhaps it was him washing his hands over at the side counter. Did

I see him do that? Wash his hands and close the chapter, slip out the side way? He must have. Whatever was on his mind that evening as it unfolded, the effect was undeniable. Frankie was there. Frankie was everywhere in his kitchen. And then, at some point that I seem not to have noticed, Frankie vanished.

Gauthier, I have to assume now, knew all about what happened but wouldn't say a word. He was both exultant and full of fury somehow, though I couldn't see it then. All I knew was that after service, when we were all scrubbed down and stored away, August now upon us and three luxurious weeks to ourselves, to do nothing, to sleep, to make love to our lovers, to dream, Gauthier took me by the arm and escorted me to a bar where I'd never been before, a low-ceilinged basement with men in leather jackets and women in skirts with long cigarettes. *Bar America*, said the sign. Gauthier drinking whiskey and Budweiser long necks, laughing hard. *Formidable*, he roared at one point, his bottle sarcastically hoisted in a toast. And of course the evening ended just as poorly as all this might suggest. Some imagined slight from a man passing by in the crowded bar. A bump. An incautious word. Some tough guy in the wrong place at the wrong time. And Gauthier in an instant fury. Gauthier in the alley, fists flying. Dead sober I could never have stopped him. Drunk I was less than useless. Gauthier hitting the man again and again, his fists an expert bloodied blur. I remember the man falling. I remember his head hitting the stones and bouncing. I remember he didn't move after that and Gauthier spat down at him, a treacly wad of phlegm. I pulled him away, found us a taxi. I have no idea what damage we caused. But I knew even then that it was *we* and not only him. Teo and Gauthier together, not just an enraged veteran legionnaire with the white heat of all the anger he still carried. Without raising a fist I was complicit, fully involved. And that was the evening as it ended. That was me in Paris as the curtain began to fall, bruised knuckles and a dry mouth, blood on the stones and on my hands.

Continental Breakfast

I dreamt my father's departure at the same time I was dreaming my own. Deeply asleep in twisted sheets, Stephanie up on an elbow, shaking my shoulder: *Teo, Teo.*

Up the gangplank he went, leather heels knocking on the boards. The smell of diesel in the morning, the cry of birds under the pillowy seam of clouds, lacy strands above. Gulls screaming in the updraft as the turbines thrum below. I dreamt these things as if they were in my own memories as well as my future. A great rotation of gears and the thrust of pistons, and the roll of the earth. Arthur felt the vibration in his hand on the steel railing, all that movement above and below. Duffel bag thrown down in his state room, back on deck. That feeling at the precise moment of slipping, the big ship shuddering as they slipped the slip, the sagging chains and rising gantries, men waving from overhead. Arthur waved back, one arm high over his head. Green algae and blue mussels along the piles. Three short blasts from the horn. I am moving under sternward propulsion.

Teo, Teo!

I gasp to the surface and find her there, that furrow down between the eyes, one hand holding back her own hair.

"I dreamt of my father, leaving," I told her in the dusty light. Four in the morning.

"Okay," she said. "You were kinda yelling."

"Sorry." I laid back, took a deep breath. I didn't remember being anxious in the dream.

But in the pixelated night, there with Stephanie, in the impossible aftermath of that infamous last supper — details now filtering back to consciousness, Gauthier celebrating the absent ghost of Frankie — I couldn't tell what my father had told me of that Pacific crossing and what I might have dreamt entirely, of whole cloth.

At which point I woke up for real and rolled over to realize that Stephanie wasn't there at all.

I never saw Frankie again in Paris. Sunday after my night out with Gauthier I slept and dreamt and then slept more, then woke finally only at ten. Then I phoned Stephanie immediately to see if she knew anything about where he might have disappeared to the night before and she told me Frankie had gone home, back to Montreal.

"Unbelievable," I said, wide awake all at once. "Without a word?"

"Well, he called me and told me to tell you. That was his word."

I was stunned. Frankie had the perfect job in Paris. But he was also my closest friend in the city. And he just leaves without telling me?

"He says he's talked to his landlord," Stephanie said. "If you want it, you can have his apartment. Well, *we*. He said *we*."

"Okay, this is just crazy," I said.

"It's Frankie," Stephanie said. "Man of impulse, man of action."

Which might have been true, but the situation still made no sense to me. Frankie talked about going back to Montreal when he was pissed off with Gauthier or the Pricks. But I never really believed him. We were cooking in Paris. We were living the life.

Stephanie and I agreed to meet the next day. We were both winding down our kitchens for the August break. At Le Dauphin everyone in the back was coming in for the half day to do final clean ups, empty fridges, stow gear. When I got to the restaurant forty minutes later, the place was a low buzz of activity and people moving around to get things done quickly. I noticed Gauthier over at his station, looking pretty fresh given the shit show of the night before. When he saw me looking, he stood up from the sink he was cleaning and waved me over.

"Tout va bien, Tranquille?" he said, a hand closed on my bicep.

I shook my head. "Dude. Last night was not cool."

"I have ..." he looked for the English words. "You say ... anger management."

"Oh, you think?" I said. "The fuck happened? And what do you know about Frankie leaving?" Gauthier was in an inexplicably good mood, it seemed to me. So with this question, he leaned his head over to one side as if he were trying to remember where the information I needed about Frankie might have been misplaced.

Then he said: "Les patrons, they want to see you. To take them breakfast."

That was odd in itself, but Gauthier wasn't offering up any more information. So I just sighed and pulled on whites. "Deux ovos," I said to no one. Then I turned to a station and whipped up our owners some eggs, just as one of their mothers apparently had done for them when they were a child. Two jammy soft-boiled eggs over diced toast in a bowl with a dollop each of grainy and Dijon mustard. As I was prepping the baguette for the crouton, I thought suddenly of my own mother, who would on special Saturdays fry a piece of bread in bacon fat only for me. My brother Jonah would grimace at the prospect. I love it, like a salty pastry. So I fried the crouton bread in bacon fat instead of grilling it with a brush of butter. Garnish with frisée. Then I shot the dishes up the dumbwaiter to the suite of the *chefs patrons*, washed my hands, and jogged up after them using the back stairs.

I'd never been in Marcel and Denis's apartment before. I'd never once imagined being invited. I knew these two for almost nothing but their abuse. And I hadn't forgotten that one of them had once grabbed me by the balls from behind while yelling over my shoulder.

Entrez! I heard one of them call out when I knocked.

So I let myself into a wide front hall leading to my first surprise, a glimpse of what life the Pricks appeared to live in private. The apartment front hall was burnished parquet. The walls creamy white with gilded crown mouldings. There were pictures, etchings, and drawings, one small framed photo of the two of them in much younger years, posed at the grave site of Karl Marx, slouched against the high slab with their arms crossed. *Workers of All Lands Unite.* Oh irony, though this would have been way back in the '80s judging from the zippered moto jackets, the spiked dog collars, the bright slashes of yellow and pink eyeshadow tapering to points.

In the living room, meanwhile: couch and chairs from Louis the something, carved mahogany accents, plump lavender cushions, bookshelves lined with colourful volumes, an ornate mantel filled with plaster busts.

The chefs themselves were already eating when I entered, tucked into their *ovo* at a small round table in front of one of the apartment's many high windows, an expensive view of the rooftops of Paris all the way down to the Eiffel Tower in the distance, the spreading, colonnaded arms of the Museum of Man spread open in welcome behind.

"Chefs," I said, bowing ridiculously, like I was a waiter.

The two of them glanced up with calm detachment, again off-brand. They were red-faced rage robots in the kitchen, saying nothing that couldn't better be yelled and laced with profanity. Here they sat sipping black coffee out of silver-rimmed monogrammed china, nodding gravely to me, both at once, indicating with their gaze that I should sit down on the nearby settee.

I think Chef Marcel went first. But they spoke over one another, trading sentences back in forth. So it was hard to tell one from the other. But the message was simple enough to follow. Two messages, really. The first was that while the bacon-fried croutons in their oeufs de maman that morning had a certain peasanty appeal, it was too bold a flavour gesture.

"In English ..." said one. "Too —"

"Loud," said the other, like they'd ever been known for their delicacy and control.

That dealt with, the second point came quickly. The second point was that the breakfast was otherwise superb, perfect to the details. That they had come to appreciate my dedication to precision and perfection in this regard as I had developed under them over ...

"Five years," I said.

Yes. And so, they wondered aloud, now that Frankie had departed under such regrettable circumstances, would I honour the *chefs patrons* by taking his place?

Regrettable circumstances. That's what they said. And then they quite happily divulged what those circumstances had been. It seems this whole unfortunate affair had to do with Gauthier's niece.

"Niece?" Stephanie said, when I told her later.

"Gauthier has a niece," I said. "About whom he apparently feels very protective."

"And what's that got to do with Frankie?"

"Well, see, Gauthier got it into his head that Frankie was messing around with this niece."

"Messing around?"

"*Sleeping with.* Or trying to … which would have been enough."

"Because Gauthier *hates* Frankie," Stephanie said.

"And because the niece is a teenager working at Le Dauphin."

Stephanie leaned back sharply, her expression was one of a dawning realization, eyebrows high, hand unconsciously up to cover her mouth.

"Someone we both know, this niece," I finished. "Her name is Ines."

Stephanie's hands were now on her cheeks, which were flushed red in what I'd learn was a rare event.

For their part, the *chefs patrons* did not seem particularly scandalized telling me any of this. I observed a glance between them that suggested quite the contrary, that Frankie remained a lovable rogue in their minds. They also quickly noted that maybe none of this had happened at all. The young woman herself denied it. Ines had told her uncle that she'd quit her job at Le Dauphin and returned home to Le Havre because of someone else entirely, a young man whose name she refused to divulge.

But Gauthier was Gauthier. We all knew Gauthier. And when he was convinced of something that was the end of it.

"Gauthier …" the *chefs patrons* said, glancing again at one another. They shrugged, just as they had the day they hired me, Gallic resignation in the face of what had been thrust upon them. Gauthier wasn't changing his mind. And Gauthier wasn't going anywhere. So the *chefs patrons* had spoken to Frankie privately but candidly about his situation. Frankie apparently didn't argue. He knew the risk of staying. Gauthier was angry. And Gauthier was dangerous.

So Frankie left, but not before agreeing with everyone else on the matter of his replacement.

"Frankie, Bozonnet, Gauthier, everyone at Le Dauphin," said Marcel and Denis. "They want you to lead."

And not as sous chef. Marcel and Denis felt it was time for Le Dauphin to have a real executive chef.

Stephanie remained sitting where she was now holding my wrist. "This is terrible," she said.

"It is terrible," I said. "I can't believe it."

"No listen," Stephanie said. "When he called last night, he specifically mentioned Ines. He brought her up. He said: *I need you to know I never touched her.*"

I waited. I waited. But neither of us knew what should properly come next. Did Gauthier's conviction mean he was telling the truth? Did Ines's denial mean she was covering something up? More pressingly: Was Frankie a completely different person than we thought previously, some kind of monster?

We wanted to believe the right thing. But we didn't know anything.

Or maybe we did. Even at the time, in the moment, maybe we knew enough to see that we were hopelessly conflicted, both very fond of Ines, but both indebted to Frankie for all he'd given us. We were imperfect mirrors of Gauthier that way, who was at once fiercely protective of his niece while filled with blind hatred for Frankie. We were in love and wanted nothing more than that the world be peaceful. Gauthier was a man with stars tattooed on his kneecaps who'd evaded prison by agreeing to drop his family name and go get shot at in Lebanon.

Looked at one way, how different were we?

Of course, you don't see your own blind spots. That's why they call them blind spots. So none of this registered at the time. And Stephanie and I both simply acted on instinct. We were caught in this whole thing. We couldn't tell what was truth and what was fiction. And all that winnowed out to a single conclusion that we reached together almost instantly, hardly exchanging a word.

It was time to go. Time to leave. Time to return.

So Stephanie and I head back together toward where we'd both started so long before. And it seems to me, in my mind anyway, we moved with my father in transit somehow. We fly or we enter the harbour by boat, exhausted. We trace a line across a smooth and rounded surface, scattering cloud. The orange light of morning paints the surrounding hills, densely greened with trees, the notes of the sea in our ears and our noses. The waves are capped with white below, the shoreline bristling with its piers, Yokohama is abuzz with boats, the inner harbour guarded by those famous lights.

I squeeze your hand on descent. You wake up and are for a moment unsure of where you are, then you shake your head and laugh. We arc downward, there's an untouched breakfast tray in front of you that the flight attendants are going to remove shortly.

"It's a *continental* breakfast," I say.

"Coffee?" you ask. And I gesture to the cup that is already poured and waiting, as if even the flight attendants know that we've been away a very long time and are suddenly in a great rush, a frenetic rush. My old friend Magnus is waiting. The first friend, the original West Van friend. Magnus, who'd called those many years before on that first anniversary of my mother's death to set all these things in motion.

You and me and Magic Wolf.

Now Magnus was picking us up at the airport. Magnus who couldn't wait to meet you, Stephanie, to introduce you to Zaina and the kids. *There's a fourth on the way!*

Shafts of light below, reflections and shimmers, whorls of grey under the blue clouds over the mountain. Rain would come in a mist later. Welcome to Vancouver.

Arthur, for his part — and this is down to my imagination, almost purely — was in the Port of Yokohama by this point in his journey that I was still trying to interweave with my own. Not quite Tokyo, but close — 1947 or '48. He's at the rail of the ship because no way he's going to miss that crossing come finally to a close. The ship is wheeling slowly to port, nosing in between the twin lighthouses on the end of those two curving breakwaters that shield the inner harbour. There's a man on an outside deck up top of one of these, a speck at that distance. And he raises his arm in a slow swinging greeting. Sharp prowed boats in the water. The sea is green and fragrant, flown over by strange gulls, bright white with black-tipped wings and tail feathers.

Touching down now. A shriek of tires on the tarmac. The scent of rubber burning as the hull slowly grinds along the fenders.

"Are we there yet?" you say, smiling, awake, with coffee inside you, the love of my life. I don't know, truthfully. Maybe not quite there, but closer. Arthur, I think, knew already that his journey was far from ending, with his eye on the Tokyo skyline that laced the horizon to the north, seeing his pathway curve over it and beyond, spiralling out of sight.

2

VANCOUVER

Belmont Farm

We never went back from that August break. That was essentially how it happened. We packed our clothes. We left for our holidays. And since we'd both been living in tiny furnished apartments, we ended up carrying everything we owned. Neither Stephanie nor myself admitted to ourselves we were doing it. After buying the one-way tickets, we said it was because of a seat sale. Even after I mailed a letter to the *chefs patrons* thanking them for the experience, Stephanie and I still talked about it like we could both still get jobs back at Femke or Le Dauphin if we changed our minds.

But we weren't changing our minds. And Frankie was part of that too. He was the door that opened into Paris for both of us. He was also the door we heard closing behind us. So August break somehow turned into the next ten years of our lives. It turned into *Magic Wolf.*

Of course, Magnus was the bigger part of all this than Frankie. This much was an education for me. I remembered Magic as the crazy kid jumping off the cliffs out back of Whytecliff Park into the frigid waves below. Magic setting garbage cans on fire. Now he was some grown-up version of that same fuck-it dead certainty. Magnus decided. And then Magnus got it done.

Stephanie wasn't entirely impressed, which chafed a little at the time. Magnus had been so excited to meet her. Plus, I thought we'd won the most freakish kind of lottery, a couple of young people in the resto trade, leaving decent jobs, changing cities, and getting picked up at the airport by an old friend who'd made a mountain of dough in his business willing to dump a whole bunch of it in ours.

"Your old friend," Stephanie would say, a distinction I didn't think made much difference.

"Yours, too, now," I'd say.

She'd shrug.

Did she wonder if Magnus was just a handy replacement for Frankie in my life? She never said so and I never asked. But I can see how that might have been the reasoning. Like I needed a mentor, a model, an extrovert to complete the fraternal dyad. Certainly, Frankie and Magnus had things in common, both generous, both expansive hosts, born storytellers, both catching the eye in a particular way. I saw people react to Magnus as they had to Frankie. The possessive glance. Though again, like Frankie, Magnus never once revealed himself to be trying for these attentions. At that airport pickup, he didn't arrive in a Mercedes or a Range Rover. He pulled up in a Subaru, a muddy family wagon with a big dent in the front fender. He wore old Adidas sneakers and a faded green hoodie. I'd learn later he went off to meetings with bankers and lawyers one-strapping a purple nylon backpack like a kid going to middle school.

But there were stark differences too. Magnus was a family man. He was a dad, affectionate with his kids, Caleb and Zach, the youngest, Piper, and then baby Eva when she arrived. He got down low on the grass to talk with them, eye to eye. I saw him wipe mud off his son's cheek with a finger, put a Band-Aid on a scraped knee. Fix a bike.

"Here, pass me that," he said, hunched over in the laneway garage of his enormous Point Grey house. And I dutifully handed him a wrench from where it hung on the pegboard with a hundred other tools, marvelling at what the world had become.

As for Magic Wolf, I thought of the project as belonging to Stephanie and me both. At one point I thought we might even work together. But I was the only cook in the family by the time we got settled in Vancouver. Steph had folded her apron and hung up the tongs, having sold a book proposal just a couple of months after our arrival, a food memoir about her experiences as a woman in culinary Paris over almost ten years. *The Femke Years.* She'd been asked to tone down the war stories, the chauvinism and the crotch grabbing. Stress the positives of life at Femke after leaving the French brigades. And of course Stephanie bridled at that.

"Me getting grabbed by the tit is why I ended up at Femke," she said. "You can't deny these things are happening or that they have an impact on people."

But she was still getting it out there, her irreverent and honest version of a chef's life in Paris. I was always impressed by how instinctively she made fun of culinary pretensions. I was occasionally reading the work in draft form and looking for examples of myself fussing over a garnish or stressing the reception to some new dish I'd developed. She was merciful and spared me. But I thought the drunk sous buying drinks for all the young apprentices and utterly absorbed in their adulation had a pretty obvious source. So, too, the tattooed chef who appeared in one piece with scraped and bloodied knuckles that were never explained.

"Did you ever meet Gauthier?" I asked her.

"He ate at Femke once in a while," she told me. "He tipped big. I had no problems with Gauthier."

Some of these pieces — all non-fiction but with the names changed — had started to get attention even before the book deal. Steph had one picked up in the *Best Food Writing* anthology.

Another ran in *Best American Essays. Martha Stewart Living* magazine was running a piece she was writing on collecting old cookbooks. She wasn't retiring on the money, but she was busy and liked this work better than cooking. I also remember the excitement we both felt when the email came with the book deal news. We celebrated in the rented apartment that a real estate friend of Magnus's had found for us at the price we could afford down in Gastown. We bought a jar of salmon roe at one of the Alexander Street tourist gift shops, cracked a bottle of Cava. Stephanie leaned back into me as we held up our glasses to the sunlight streaming through the windows over Victory Square.

"How lucky can an almost-married couple be?" I remember asking. And she turned around slowly in my arms so that she was pressed chest to chest against me, looking up with an amused expression. I could read a question in the wrinkle between those green eyes.

Then she sighed and I felt her relax in my arms. "Not much luckier," she said, yet with a residual trace of skepticism, too, not about marriage, I don't think, maybe more about luck itself, the whimsy and caprice of it. Still, she went up on her toes to kiss me. We made love. We made dinner.

That was the way it began. A new place in a new city, an apartment in a building with a fire escape that spidered down the side into the alley, where the dumpsters overflowed and the graffiti flowered, where an unlikely number of wrecked bicycles spent their final rusting days. Where Stephanie wrote in the mornings, her journals and her cookbooks laid out around her on the one table in the middle of the room. And I'd cross town by bike or transit to meet with Magnus, to define this thing we were actually building together.

Magic Wolf.

"It's a holding company," Magnus said, explaining.

"And you're saying *we* own this holding company, you and me?"

"Legally," Magnus said. "You own one share and I own the rest."

"Okay," I said. "But just to get this out there … I spent literally my last dollar last week on a damage deposit and a futon. So I'd have to owe you for the share, right?"

He waved his hand as if swatting a mosquito. "Your share is what I give you for the rights to use your name. Magic *Wolf*. Like a licensing fee. One time."

I began coughing and had to wait to continue. "Licensing. Listen, I wasn't like this famous person in Paris or anything. I doubt ten people even knew my last name was Wolf. Everybody in Paris called me *Tranquille*."

"It's still your name, Teo. And it's gotta be our name too. Magic Wolf. That's where this all started."

"I'm broke. That's my point. And I'm not Alain Chapel. I'm not remotely a *brand*."

Magnus said, "Well, let's work on that."

Any third party would have thought I was trying to talk Magnus out of it. And I don't think I was. I guess in those swirling moments I wanted Magnus to know that despite the long-ago phone call after my mother passed, I didn't think he'd made me any promises.

Magnus, who I was, in the end, only just getting to know again, certainly hadn't considered it a promise either. It had been a proposal from a guy who'd developed a rare skill set in the matter of making them. Magnus calling me from London — where he'd gone to "make money" as if it were something people just left lying around — had been a salesman for a tech company that sold financial trading systems to banks. No point pretending I even understand what a job like that was all about. I could see Magnus walking into a big glass building in the City of London and after that I wouldn't have a clue what he did all day until the moment he walked out. What I do understand now is that his next move — having picked up a significant amount of the money that apparently was lying around wherever he knew to be looking — was to sign on with the private equity group that had bought the tech company where he'd been working. From there to managing partner inside three years. Right around the time I was watching Frankie prep stuffed rabbits, sipping the least expensive Côte de Nuits I could find, Magnus was buying an airline. He'd long sold it by the time we spoke. He'd also left the London fund and set up his own. Not the point. The point is that Magnus was Smaug the Dragon atop his pile of treasure by the time we got to talking on his rooftop deck in Point Grey, across the way from Trimble Park, where our northward view was nothing but green slope descending to a slate-grey ocean, and across the white caps to that glinting, bristling city of glass that was really starting to crystallize on the downtown peninsula in those years. Towering blue mountains rising behind all that.

"You want me to explain something?" Magnus asked me that day. "You want me to explain to you why this makes sense to me financially? Maybe help you relax so we can just do this thing and have some fun?"

So Magnus explained it to me. Magic Wolf made sense because Magnus's fund had, six months prior, purchased a mid-market "casual fine dining" interest, a restaurant chain called Duke's.

"Cow-print chairs, birdcage lamps, potted ferns," he said, as if of course I'd know the template, which I didn't. I'd been in France, missing all this.

"Chicken fingers, zucchini sticks, French onion soup," he spieled off. "Guacamole burgers, fettucine alfredo, teriyaki steaks."

Right, I thought I got it. American roadhouse fare — not great, but popular and well-priced. Duke's was in sixteen locations across Western Canada and apparently spreading down into the U.S. by then.

"Okay," I said.

Buying power, Magnus explained. It was all about buying power with suppliers. The produce, the protein, the bevvies. The restaurant equipment, furnishings, services. You name it, the Duke Group bought a lot. And buying in volume like that put Magnus in the position to get those supply costs down very low.

If I'd taken the exec job at Le Dauphin, I would have been immediately immersed in buying. As a *chef tournant*, I didn't really deal with vendors. But we all knew that Frankie and the Pricks hovered over every box of oysters and radishes and lamb loin that arrived at the supply bay off Rue Saint-Placide toward the rear of the kitchen. One constant of the very earliest hours of the workday had been the sight of the three of them plucking and picking at things and exchanging frowns about what had been ordered earlier. *Only the best,* Frankie would say, sending back a flat of Brittany sea urchin roe that did not sweetly meet his nose.

"At that scale I guess my questions would be about quality," I said.

But Magnus was ahead of me here, too, as would prove to be typical. Or, his people were. He'd fired the entire top management tier when he'd bought Duke's, installed new people, younger people. He used a word here that I had only recently learned, still vaguely alarming to me. His new young management team, Magnus said. They were all *foodies*. And so the approach would change accordingly. They were moving Duke's up the scale in crucial degrees. The cow-print chairs would be gone, sure. But the menu too.

"Quality, organic, farm-grown," Magnus said, counting off the words on three fingers.

It's hard to get your mind back to when these ideas were new. But they were still new at that time. Magnus was part of a new era that even I couldn't quite see then.

"Those are our group values," he announced. "Those are the words we're using. And that's also where you really come in."

Duke's would still be there to feed the crowds. The Magic Wolf restaurants would come in to feed the critics, and those who care what the critics have to say. Old-world executive chef, new face in town, a menu of rare sophistication at a prodigious price. But a revamped Duke's would be quietly at work in the background, prices slowly rising on those tweaked menus, justified by Duke's proximity to me. "That's basically the play," Magnus said. "Get more profit out of Duke's. Then sell it."

"Sell Duke's," I said.

"Three years tops," Magnus said. "Four maybe. But the Magic Wolf restaurants, those we won't sell. Those are going to be keepers."

Smaug is unfair. That makes Magnus sound greedy and protective of his wealth, which he really wasn't. Magnus didn't need a partner to make all this work. He could have hired anyone he wanted to be chef. Sure, in reaching out to me, as with all his business decisions, there would have been an ordered thought process at work. I just didn't know what it was at the time, assuming instead that I was seeing a side of Magnus I'd never seen before, a part of him that acted on inarticulate passion. There was that priceless resumé of unforgettable meals he'd eaten with Zaina and been telling me about — The Fat Duck, The French Laundry, El Bulli, and Chez Panisse, places hitting all the best in the world lists. There was the way he talked about them, as if these institutions were crucially more than an epic dining experience with all the intrinsic associations: connection, intimacy, sensory pleasure. Every such restaurant was also a story.

Personal, relatable.

Magnus told me all this under what I see now to have been absurd circumstances. At the time I rolled with it, tried to pretend it was all part of the new normal. But it turned out the house where we'd been meeting wasn't even his house, or not his permanent place. He'd bought it to live in just until the bigger one was complete.

"Oh, sure," I said at the time.

"Let's have a look," he said. So he drove me over, climbing down from that spectacular rooftop deck off Trimble and driving a few blocks west toward the university, across Fourth Avenue, over the crest of the Point Grey peninsula and down into the looping streets where apparently the real money lived. Drummond. Belmont. These houses were hidden behind high hedges, stone walls, security gates. You got glimpses from the street. Modernist palaces. French chateaus. Cartel-style haciendas. I saw one with high gable dormer windows and lost count at twelve in a row before the house disappeared behind a bank of purple cherry trees.

"Yup," Magnus said. "Whole lotta money. But I found this one place and Zaina fell in love. Couldn't not buy."

We were pulling into a dirt driveway, no gate, driving through a curtain of trees into an open expanse of meadow. Whatever had been there had been torn down and they hadn't started the build. Still talking to architects, Magnus said. But he wasn't in a rush, because he was really getting into gardening.

"Sure," I said.

Farming, more like it. The lot was almost three acres, the last property before a cliff down to Spanish Banks. Up there on his priceless ledge, Magnus had planted rows of carrots and radishes, heirloom tomatoes, corn. Magnus was growing ancient grains. He was holding a stalk of Kamut when we got the heart of the matter.

"This is Kamut," he said.

"Yeah," I said. "I know what it is."

"I like to bake bread," he said. "Did I tell you that already?"

"No," I said. "No, you never did."

"When we get back to the house, we can try some. Do you make bread?"

"I do," I said. "Yeah, I did learn that."

"Back to us," Magnus said. "The project."

So we came to it. The distillation of all those meals, all those conversations, all that evident thought. Magnus said: Food is a language. We use it to talk about ourselves, what we believe, the places and people we love.

"El Bulli is one story," he said. "Chez Panisse was another."

My mind was wandering as he recounted dish by dish that last meal he'd had at Chez Panisse in Berkeley. Fritto misto of anchovies, sweet onions, and squash blossoms with pickled mushrooms and a liqueur made from wild fennel. I was thinking about Magnus in a rock fight. Magnus rolling tires off a bridge over the railway tracks and almost hitting that guy as he pulled up in his truck. Magnus was talking about the quality of salt Alice Waters favoured. A particular kind of fleur de sel from Guérande in Brittany.

"You know Thomas Keller's story about rabbits?" Magnus asked me, having skipped onward from his knowledge of the founder of Chez Panisse to his knowledge of the founder of The French Laundry.

We'd by this point strolled down his field to stand at the very lip of the land, where it fell away, down to Marine Drive, the Spanish Banks beaches stretching away to either side. That water. That city beyond. Those mountains. Magnus talking about Thomas Keller's rabbits. How the great chef had fumbled his first kill, injuring the animal. How he'd felt terrible at the time. How the experience had changed him. Made him commit to doing it precisely right going forward, every time.

Out of respect for the ingredient, the preparation, the plate, the diner.

Sailboats plying the water, pilots hiked out. Freighters in colourful silence, their immensity in the water at that moment almost overwhelming to me. I was looking over at Lighthouse

Park fringed with white waves, my old neighbourhood out of sight and around the bend. My mother and my father. My sister and brother. Magnus himself. We'd all lived out there once. And staring at that distant shoreline, I flashed on the most improbable memory. Toward the very end of my time in West Van, before Magnus and I lost track of one another for ten years, I remembered that we'd been to a pool party at a house on the water over there. A rich kid, Hugo Sullivan was his name. And I remember that the Sullivan house was impossibly swanky, cantilevered out over the rocks and the waves, the swimming pool hugging the granite shore and illuminated with lights from under the water. At some point in that party, late in the evening, I remembered that Magnus and I had wandered into the back of the house, down dark corridors, finally finding ourselves in one of Hugo's brother's bedrooms. And there on the concrete wall, illuminated by a golden hanging light, was a poster of a naked woman. She was on her knees, facing away from the camera, bum back on her heels. She wore a white cowboy hat and was glancing back over her shoulder toward the viewer. Her brown hair flowed to her shoulders, but had been pulled aside so that the markings on her body were revealed. In what appeared to be a wide black felt pen, she'd been sectioned like a side of beef and labelled. Shank on the arm. Chuck on the shoulder. Rib, then loin. Rump and round. Down her thigh: soup bones.

Top left, in large type: *Break the Dull Steak Habit.*

On the bluff that day, I finally heard Magnus exhale a big breath behind me, as if he'd been waiting for me to say something and had grown impatient.

"So that's Thomas Keller's story," he said, finally. "I guess the pressing question is now *what's yours?*"

Of course, I sort of knew that already. Le Dauphin had been my life for half a decade by that point. All those plates that succeeded and all that were smashed to the floor. The roast chickens badly trussed, the duck confit, the gratin Dauphinoise, the poulet aux morilles. Frankie's foie-stuffed rabbit, Gauthier's crazy mullet in three-day red wine reduction with the baton de pomme et fenouil that made the hair on your arms stand on end. Plus, my parents had both been through Paris. So the first thing Magnus and I did together was always going to have something to do with that city.

"What exactly took you to Paris?" I asked my father. "I mean for Mom, she kind of had to go there. You were just touring around."

First visit up to Edmonton since my return. Stephanie and I were staying with Simone's family. Her husband, Greg, lent me a truck to drive out to the farm. Stephanie and I did a couple of hours' worth of cleaning, then took my dad out for a walk, a slow amble down the berm with his two enormous Anatolian shepherd dogs, now getting quite old.

"Just passing through," he said. "I was coming back from Japan the long way on my way to a job in …"

Here he forgot where he had been going back then.

"Ecuador," I tried.

"No, Venezuela first, then Ecuador."

"Didn't you start in Ecuador before going to Venezuela?" I said, confused.

But then, so was he. So he brushed on by the question. "Anyway. I'd been in Madrid. I guess I thought everyone had to see Paris."

"When was that?" Stephanie asked. "What year?"

He thought a long time, squinting and looking toward the road. The dogs would come close to him and he'd touch their backs or their shoulders. They'd bound off through the grass, down the berm, into the field, watching and watching.

"Nineteen forty-eight?" he said. "Something like that?"

I looked at him when he said that. Because the year couldn't be right. He was in San Francisco en route to Tokyo that year. Or at least, that what I'd always understood. "Same year mom was there?" I asked.

"I guess," he said.

"Wow," Stephanie said. "That's kind of incredible."

I looked at her, but she just very slowly shook her head.

"Are you sure?" I insisted. "Or was it maybe later, like fifty? Fifty-one?"

"No, no," he said. "Nineteen forty-eight."

Down around Place Pigalle there was a hotel, he told us. He couldn't remember the name. But it was simple and clean except for the bugs. "The lady there gave me bread and tomatoes," he said. "There were lots of cafés around. But just that simple thing, bread and butter, fresh tomatoes. I swear it was the best thing I'd ever eaten!"

I was staring at him. Finally: "Mom told me the same thing."

"Oh yeah?"

"Her family stayed in Pigalle too. Mom and her sister, and our Oma. They stayed there waiting for a boat to South America. They stayed at the Hôtel Véron."

"That's the one!"

"But—" I started. But now Stephanie had her hand on my arm, squeezing.

"Don't tell me I'm forgetting things," my father said, squinting in the light. "I'm not forgetting things."

His eyes were toward the horizon now. And there would have been no changing his mind on this one, even if I were to try, then or ever. These were places and experiences that my mother had described from her journey en route to Genoa and Guayaquil beyond. All my father had ever said before about Paris was that the bars and café terraces were jammed up with Americans.

That spring day, perhaps it didn't matter. Horsetail clouds above and the wind picking up, the line of birch trees just beginning to whisper and dance, Stephanie looking at both of us in turn, taking my arm in hers just then, hugging it close. That spring day, my mother Lilly's version was my father Arthur's version. Her history was his as his was hers. Their journeys were joined that moment at the Hôtel Véron over that very meal. They lived there together for a fleeting moment as I watched. And since Magnus was all onside with French-inspired restaurants, clearly he'd get onside with this one too. So I let it be born officially on the berm that day on my father's farm, those dogs hunting mice in the tall grass.

My starting place for a new turn in things would be a restaurant called Rue Véron.

Nigirizushi

By Christmas, at last, my dad was in Ginza.

The grey air scudded with enormous snowflakes, a grainy texture to the light. There were fires burning in spots to the north and smoke wafted over the city. Arthur walked to the Nihonbashi River and looked at a row of wooden buildings there, slumped over toward the water, a tumble of boards down over the railing. The streets were rivers. Nothing he'd ever seen before in Toronto or San Francisco. Humanity in constant flow — charcoal-powered cars belching black; bicycles, rickshaws, people, and more people leaning into the wind.

Arthur wanted to push onward himself. But they were cooling their heels again. Maitland and Simms were off running some side hustle in the black markets. Arthur didn't really want to know.

"Side hustle?" I asked him.

"I told you, I didn't want to know!" my father said. "I kept myself busy exploring the city. I got this red cardboard phrase sheet from the American PX. Konnichiwa. Domo arigato gozaimasu!"

I listened to him say these words and remembered him ordering in Japanese restaurants when we were kids, me and Simone and Jonah. We'd stare at him when he did this like he'd been transformed into a different person. My mother would just keep reading the menu as if she hadn't heard.

He was down from the farm to visit, first time back in Vancouver since my return from France. We'd gone and picked up coffees around the corner, then walked back into Cambie where Magnus and I had found the exact right room for Rue Véron. A huge stroke of luck, that find. It had been a pretty popular place back in the day. Then they'd apparently reno'd and doubled the capacity, then gone spectacularly bust. There was a scandal and a lot of rumours and a chef who'd become a big local star then flamed out and disappeared and existed now as some kind of urban legend. People said he was working at an underground restaurant run out of an empty house near the Dr. Sun Yat-Sen Classical Chinese Garden. Gerriamos was the name of the restaurant that had failed. Terrible name. I never heard the whole story, but they were ultra–high end and overfinanced and they died trying.

Bad karma to choose that spot, maybe. But Magnus didn't care about karma, all sleeves rolled and immersed in this new thing. We'd gutted the room by the time my father came down, plywood and exposed lathe and plaster in the walls. Every surface we stripped led to a new stroke of luck. Great flooring, no rot. Clean sump in the kitchen. Plumbing only a year old, perfect condition, copper still shiny. We could have kept most of the kitchen, but Magnus had heard that convection electric with gas tops was state of the art. So banks of Sub-Zero were sent to auction. Out front, everything was gone: furniture, fixtures, the old wood bar. We were putting in a set of red leather banquettes down the north wall and a zinc bar down the south with a towering mirror. New hanging light orbs had arrived in boxes and were stacked near the kitchen. I remember my dad pushing open one of the kitchen doors, then walking slowly and inspecting as an engineer might, leaning back to review the fire suppression system overhead, snaking its way through the roof beams, tanks linked to burst-proof steel mesh pipes that were themselves linked to lines of spray heads that would drop down through the range hoods. He was nodding. He seemed impressed.

When we'd picked up the coffees, my father had stopped a long time in front of the shop next door. Sushi Sendai. He was staring up and remembering. So when we got back to the restaurant space and sat in the front window at a workbench the carpenters had set up, I wasn't surprised that he mentioned it. He'd been thinking about it. Sushi took him back.

"Only in Tokyo, in those years," he said, "they weren't always fancy like that one up there, with window seats and that big picture menu over the counter."

I was watching his face as those long-ago memories came through.

"How long did you end up staying?" I asked him.

"Tokyo?" he said. "Two months. Maybe three. You know those sushi places would be just a sawhorse and some boxes. Set up in one of those Ginza food alleys, little streets above Chuo-dori."

He remembered street names. Later, I'd look up pictures myself. I'd see the old black-and-white images as if with his eyes, as if they were memories. An ice box and the daily catch from Tsukiji. Prawns, cuttlefish, octopus, tuna.

"I didn't know what anything was called," my dad said. "I just pointed."

He remembered those food alleys, the rain-polished concrete, the thicket of signs. His first piece of raw fish was eaten in a place where he never did catch the name. He'd been mesmerized watching the boy make the nigirizushi, packing the rice into these perfectly uniform balls and squeezing the little piece of fish into place.

"The boy wore a white towel wrapped around his head," my father said, smiling. "White smock. I bet that kid was fourteen."

Arthur would have been considered brave by most Americans for going in for all of this, the steaming noodles in miso and soy, the sushi, the yakitori and yakiniku, the places that sold unagi no kabayaki, butterflied eels in a sweet barbecue sauce. Most of the occupation guys never got past beef sukiyaki, as he recalled. Or they just stayed with burgers, since the PX sold those and every other imaginable type of American fare. Arthur couldn't understand that whole approach to visiting a place. You had to get in there, get involved. You were the stranger. So you should expect to do strange things. He perfected an innocent, inquiring expression and some rudimentary gestures that he'd flash at the door of a restaurant, just inside the fluttering cloth banners. *Okay? Come in? Eat?*

Sometimes he'd try a phrase in Japanese, read carefully from that red cardboard sheet. *Hai, tempura o onegaisimasu?* They'd laugh and wave him inside and most of the time he'd never really have to order things. They just fed him and then counted the coins out of his hand.

He liked Tsukiji in particular, the sprawl and the noise of the market, buckets of jumping live fish. There was a superb little unagi place south across the bridge into Kachidoki. Arthur would walk down, across the slate-grey water, counting the fishing boats and the American cruisers at anchor or alongside the pier past the Hama-rikyū Gardens. The air would be briny, distinctly but not unpleasantly fishy. Then you turned into the second alley on the left, and on the first corner right there was an open-front shop with a simple counter and a grill box. And that smell. They dipped the eels in some kind of sauce, then over the coals they went, sizzling until mahogany brown. Served over a bowl of rice. Heaven.

Of course, there was a lot of evident suffering around him too. "Those people," he said that day in the empty shell of Rue Véron. "They'd had a terrible time."

They'd been starving just a couple of years prior, unthinkable shortages. It was starting to improve by the time he got there. But you still saw it walking around. Then once you saw it, then you really saw it. Entire families living in Ueno Station, huddled against the base of a wall. Men sleeping on straw mats in the shelter of the bridges. Veterans in hospital robes over in Chuo City, shaking tin cups, or standing on double leg prosthetics plucking out songs on the guitar. Arthur dug out a coin, always.

Magnus arrived just then, knapsack slung over his shoulder. He came loping over, big grin on his face. "Mr. Wolf, it's good to see you sir." Extending his hand. "Magnus Anders!"

"Oh yes," my father said. "You're the neighbourhood boy."

My rich friend with his farm on Belmont Avenue beamed like he'd finally been really seen.

"We were just talking about Tokyo," I explained.

"I understand you were there after the war, Mr. Wolf."

My father nodded slowly. Then he said, "I was just admiring your fire suppression system back there."

"You got an engineer's eye, Mr. Wolf," Magnus said. "That's a slick system all right. Sensors cut off the gas if there's an incident, then there's a throttle discharge of wet solution mist."

"Sodium carbonate?" my father asked.

"Potassium," Magnus said. "Automatic release."

"Pretty slick, all right," my dad said. "You made a good choice about your partner here."

At which point we all stood for an awkward moment, not sure if he was complimenting Magnus or me.

———

I borrowed Magnus's car and took my father back to his hotel later. He was staying at the Sylvia down on English Bay where we'd lucked out with a room looking toward the water. He was exhausted but paused outside, face to the ocean.

"You know, those Katzenjammer Kids," he said, as if returning to this matter had been on his mind all along.

I waited. Then I got it. "Maitland and Simms?"

Yeah, them. My dad made a motion we might walk toward the beach. So I took him across Pacific Avenue and we found a bench on the seawall. There was a guy stacking stones into precarious towers down on the sand. We watched him for a while as my dad's story unspooled.

"Black markets," I prompted, because it felt like things were darkening there, despite the high afternoon sun. I felt a breeze pick up and the leaves shiver in the elm trees behind us.

"Worse," my dad said.

The twins had managed to drag Arthur out on the town eventually, he said. In his own defence, he was in a particularly good mood because he'd finally been given his orders, sent down from on high through the folks at the War Damage Commission. So Arthur was carrying plans of a power station in Luzon and maps of how to reach it. He had photos he showed the twins, spread out on the table of a beer hall down Showa-dori Avenue. You could hardly tell that the twisted pile of steel members, crumpled housing boxes, strew cables, and leaning towers had once been a power station at all. But with a magnifying glass, Arthur showed the two of them the circuit boxes and the shattered insulators, the voltage switchgear, and gave them an outline of the work they had to do.

Maitland examined the pictures warily, toothpick bobbing in the corner of his mouth. Simms took it all in with a glance, but seemed not to notice much or care. He wanted to head out to see the sumo, then hit the bars.

"Let's get you up to the Brightness of Shibuya," Simms was saying. "Let's show you the yamaichi, baby. They sell vipers in vinegar up there. Make a man hard as a redwood. You getting any?"

"All of which should have been a big warning to me," my father said that day on the beach, squinting again. He ran his fingers across dry skin and blotches at his hairline, lifetime wounds left by the tropical sun.

Of course, you didn't heed these inner warnings when you were young, overwhelmed as you were by other inner tides. So off they went to see the sumo. My father remembered the shafts of light down through the dusty air, the ritual posturing, the thudding stamp of bare feet, the knuckles in the dirt, the slap of flesh as the wrestlers collided. Simms was drunk on shōchū liquor already from a stall down in Ginza where they'd started the evening, a kiosk more than a bar, a stand-and-sell as they called it, a *tachiuri*. But by the time they'd wandered off into Taito City, Arthur was lost completely. Bar Cherio was the place, a slapped-up wood slat structure about the size of two outhouses conjoined.

"Yatai," Simms hollered to no one. Then leaning in to Arthur, whose education he seemed to have taken on as his personal mission, "Where the real people drink."

Bar Cherio was built onto the side of what appeared to be a pile of rubble, the blackness stretching behind it over what Arthur thought must be a block of similar destruction. There were posters plastered to the outside boards, characters Arthur couldn't read, a small tin cannister by the door in which a belching and spitting coal fire burned. Through the doorway Arthur could make out metal tanks and plastic tubing, gauges and spigots, a glowing yakitori box with skewers laid across it.

Pig guts, Maitland explained. Slices of snout and tongue, rings of intestine and squares of stomach lining. All quite delicious apparently, though it was wise to gird yourself for the farmyard flavours. That, Simms informed, leaning in close again, is where the bakudan came in.

Maitland was standing back over Simms's shoulder, shaking his head, making a motion with his hand, a knife edge across his own throat. *Don't.*

"What was it?" I asked my father. "What was bakudan?"

"Simms," my dad said, almost wistful, not answering. I heard a boat sound a horn in the distance, a mournful tone across the water. I heard gulls scream.

I leaned in to hear him as his voice had dropped. *What happened to Simms?* I wanted to ask, but I didn't say the words.

"Simms died," my father said anyway. "He was always going to croak going on the way he did." Bakudan did kill people on a fairly regular basis, my father explained. Killed or blinded them. The stuff was made with industrial-grade alcohol siphoned out of aerial bombs, sold into the markets. Supposedly, they boiled off the methyl but things happen, mistakes were made.

"Is that what happened to Simms?" I asked.

"No," my father said. "But the bakudan would have killed him if a better way hadn't found him first."

Maitland didn't touch his glass at Bar Cherio that night. Arthur made a motion as if to take his drink in a single shot, but threw it artfully over his shoulder. Only Simms drank, which he did so lustily, with a glinting expression as if he'd grown used to passing this close to the flame. *Aaaah*, he said, pounding his chest with a closed fist, directly over his heart. And that's the moment he decided to disclose the particularly grim black market side game he had going on. Even Maitland looked away with distaste as Simms gloated about the money to be made. He knew people in the army, he said. That was the trick. They lacked ambition so they were happy to leave this stuff to him.

"Leave what stuff, exactly?" Arthur asked.

Canteen garbage.

"Yeah, you heard that right," Maitland said. "Our boy Simms is buying mess hall garbage in bulk."

Arthur shook his head and squinted. *What?* But he knew his explanation was coming. Simms was a talker. So Simms told them that he bought mess hall garbage by the wagonload because G.I.s were like any other greedy bunch of bastards and overloaded their plates in the cafeteria line then ended up throwing half of it out.

"Burgers, hot dogs, potato salad, slices of pie," he said. "You wouldn't believe it."

Arthur was struggling to process this information.

"People need to eat," Simms said, hands spread like: *am I right?*

"And starving poor people will eat practically anything," said Maitland. "I'll cut to the chase here. Simms sells mess hall garbage to a guy mobbed up with this Ozu gang, which is risky right there. Then that guy sells to people paying him for market stalls in Shibuya, which he controls. Then *those* people dump all of Simms's mess hall garbage into giant oil drums where they mash all of it together, boil it up and call it stew."

"Kanpan stew," my father said that day on English Bay in the weakening sun, having just come over by taxi from the front room of what we were hoping would be one of the finest dining rooms in all of Vancouver when it opened.

"*Jesus Christ,*" I said.

"Best not to swear," my father said. "Your mother hated it when I cursed."

"Sorry," I said.

"You know your mother …" my father said. He was watching the sailboats, flecks of white on the steel blue waves.

"Dad?" I tried. "What about Mom?"

He was working on it, something he wanted to say. Then finally, just this: "Simms was a bastard. Kanpan stew was some kind of war crime in my mind. But me seeing that was not suffering, you understand? Around the same time, your mother had it much worse."

And then he told me the whole story about the searchlights that I'd told Stephanie myself only a few months before we left Paris. How we saw them from the car driving down Hastings Street that night. How my mother had cried because she'd seen them before under very different circumstances when her life had been in real danger.

"I never went through something like that," my father said, eyes still out on the sea and those distant sails. "Thank God I never went through something like that."

I'd only ever seen a few photos from this time among my father's things. Simone had all that stuff. And at some point, we must have leafed through them together. The one I remember was a postcard. It had been sent to my Uncle Michael in 1948 and it must have been returned to my father when Michael died. On the front: a picture of American G.I.s watching a girl in a bikini bottom and pasties on a trampoline swing. On the back: my father's unmistakable block cap printing. *Was teamed with a couple eccentric Yanks in SF. They're here now. A heavy duty mechanic and an ex-pilot who operates cranes. We're off to the jungle Sunday, can't say where. Classified. We're off looking for something. Can't say what that is either.*

Stephanie was with me on that visit. I remember specifically because, as the three of us stood there going through those postcards, she said something after seeing that particular image. We all knew strip clubs weren't his thing, that the postcard was a souvenir from strange times. But Stephanie was turning the thing over and over as if looking for clues. She was trying to see out the edges of the picture, past the G.I.s arrayed at that table, looking up at that woman, past the gaze on her, past the woman herself. Stephanie was looking for the man who'd seen the action live, who'd bought the memento, who'd written the note and signed the back.

"Your father in the underworld," she said, lips pursed, brow furrowed.

"Looking for something," I answered. "Wonder what that was?"

At which point she looked at me like I were a little slow, then over to Simone who smiled a half smile and nodded.

"Your mother!" Stephanie said.

Victory Square

The summer before the opening was a blur. But I got to see Magnus in action, which was an education. He'd fly in from New York or Los Angeles, London or Beijing, or wherever he'd been. Then he'd show up at the restaurant and, amid all the chaos of fast-track renovations, he'd always know exactly what was going on, as if he'd been on the phone with the general contractor the entire time he was gone. Which I knew wasn't true. He'd been in meetings with data systems designers, game developers, chip manufacturers, online gambling ventures. The dot-coms were crashing. Or maybe it was biotechs. There was blood on the floor and deals in the wind. That's all Magnus told me, the quick version, over coffee.

Then his attention would snap sharply back to Rue Véron, which by then was swarming with carpenters and upholsterers and electricians stringing lights. And Magnus would be on to the next exciting solution to a problem I hadn't known we had: the most amazing cold and dry storage units, a computerized ordering system that would eliminate that fluttering field of yellow tickets we'd pinned to the board at Le Dauphin.

"Wine storage!" he said in one of these conversations.

"What about wine storage?"

Well, we had issues there. Most of what we'd found on-site had been perfect. The people who'd financed Gerriamos had apparently dumped millions into structural renos. When they sold Magnus the building, they'd tried to jack the price to reflect that, but Vancouver real estate was soft when the tech bubble burst and there were a lot of people selling. So Magnus made his deal and there we were with all those fresh floor beams and shiny plumbing fixtures. No leaks. No squeaks. And yet, for all of that, we still had no workable basement. We could excavate the crawl space that was presently under the floorboards. But the engineers didn't think we had more than a couple of feet before we'd hit clay and bedrock. So that wasn't viable either.

"Which means no cellar, which sucks," Magnus explained. "No below-grade temperature-controlled space suitable for vino inventory."

I'd never been a sommelier, so I didn't know much about wine storage. At Le Dauphin I was aware that Bozonnet climbed down a narrow spiral stair to our cellar with Frankie or one of the Pricks each mid-morning. There they would stand and peruse the racks, shuffling back and forth on the straw-lined floor, pulling out bottles for the board specials and the bar, setting these out at the station where the wine apprentice would send them up in a metal box on a crank chain when they were ordered. I hadn't honestly thought about the Le Dauphin wine program much beyond that.

Magnus, as I might have guessed, had become a hardcore oenophile in the time we'd been apart. His house opposite Trimble had a cellar of four hundred bottles. The drawings for his new place over on Belmont showed a sunken stone room down a ramping corridor off the sports complex — there was going to be a pool and basketball court down there when they got around to building it — where fifteen hundred bottles might be stored. All this was still on paper as Rue Véron came together. But Rue Véron was then infected by these very ideas.

"I kind of thought we might order weekly," I said.

But no way Magnus was doing that. We weren't a pizza joint. The wine was part of the draw. The wine, he explained, was part of the demographic we were targeting. The wine, he said now, opening his arms in that front room, standing over blueprints with the contractors, was a key part of the *impression*.

Magnus was big on impressions. You needed to get a person in the door, sure. But you had to send them home with impressions they'd never forget. Every customer was a potential Magic Wolf brand ambassador. So every detail at a Magic Wolf restaurant had to be perfect, every element of decor, service, and food. At Rue Véron we were going for the impossible refinement and reserve of the French Laundry, the depth and honesty of flavours you'd find at Chez Panisse, the wow factor of the Fat Duck or El Bulli. That was the composite impression Magnus had in mind. And if we did all that, well, then diners wouldn't mind being impressed with the bill when it arrived.

So that was where Magnus's wine storage solution came in.

He showed us pictures. It was by Arctech and was called the Otto, a climate-controlled, customizable glass box build-in that racked your wine cellar in such a way that your bottles were visible from the dining room. Computer controlled by a console at the sommelier station, the Otto not only uploaded bottles at a rate of two cases a minute into the racked display cases, it also silently retrieved specific bottles arranged by varietal and region from their climate zones on order from the sommelier and delivered these silently and speedily to a service window at the bottom of the unit.

Magnus showed me the plans. I stood wide-eyed, nodding. The unit he'd had designed for us would stand in the centre of the room, a glass pillar five feet square rising to the twenty-four-foot ceilings much as the central stairs at Le Dauphin had done, enclosed similarly in a deco grating, only this one not adorned with *surf guppies* but with the Véron emblem — a stylized letter V arrayed with the four suits from a deck of cards.

I'd once told Magnus the story about the nicknames for customers coming from card suits. It had apparently stuck hard.

"I absolutely love that," he said, when I told him. "Let's use it and never explain. Like a house secret."

Magnus loved a secret even if there had been no real secret to begin with. So he adopted those card suits without even knowing how they'd once become so important to me: *les carreaux*, *les coeurs*, *les trèfles*, *les piques*. They went onto our menus and cutlery, our uniforms front and back of house, painted onto the twin windows looking out on Cambie Street and the towering Dominion Building across the way. And yes, it went onto the grate that spiralled up and around the Otto too, twenty-four feet up to the tin-stamped roof, a five-foot square tower of smoky glass in the centre of everything.

One thousand four hundred and forty bottles was the final number. And Magnus had hired a sommelier to fill that thing before I'd hired a single other member of my front staff or kitchen crew. Delphine was her name. And she was on hand before we even had ranges. Delphine had worked at Robert Mondavi, had a Master Sommelier designation at the age of twenty-five, and was on seemingly molecular-level familiarity with every type of fermented bottled grape juice known to man. She was impressive. She was also convinced that most cooks had no real wine nose at all. When she gave me something to sample in our early food pairing sessions, I'd see her watching me suspiciously, her mouth spreading into a flattened frown.

But she was organized. She had wine reps and owners arriving from the Naramata Bench and Napa and beyond. Delphine put out the word. And I'd walk into the front around that time and I'd hear that Otto humming as the bottles were loaded, and I'd think of the constancy of Le Dauphin, the long years during which not much had changed in that restaurant at all, and I'd register how fast we were moving, at what blinding, incomprehensible speed.

After the Otto was installed and Delphine on hand to supervise the program, Magnus did pull back a bit. He was good that way. He knew about start-ups and how to get out of the way of the smart kids. Of course, he was always going to lean back in on menu design. But I expected that. I remember a long discussion of my idea for tomato toast.

"It's not like I don't get old school," he said. "Duck confit. Wrap a boned-out rabbit around something. I love that."

"Foie gras," I said. "From Quebec."

"And that makes sense," Magnus said. "But tomatoes on toast. I just wonder if that's exciting enough."

"It's supposed to be simple."

"Tarte à la tomate is also simple, but elevated. Had that at Ducasse's place."

Sometimes I'd wonder if a non-foodie investor might well have been easier. But those were his dollars pouring in. I'd just seen the range tops installed under those gleaming aluminum hoods. Those were his ceramic surfaces that ran right up to the edge of the flame and stayed cool to the touch when the burners were roaring. The fans we'd installed were silent. The overhead lights were brilliantly bright but cast no shadows and weren't hard on the eyes. The floors were padded under the firm white tile surface, providing an imperceptible cushion as you sprinted back and forth between stations. Magnus's new young people over at Duke's were plugged in, they knew where to find things, in many cases luxury things that I didn't know existed.

"Tomato toast," I started, again. We were going for a sense of what simple food tasted like when you were really hungry. We were going for that eyes-wide wonder that simplicity can on occasion inspire.

It was also the single dish in direct tribute to my mother, I wanted to say. But that would never sell him. So I made him a piece just standing there. We had enough of the kitchen in place. Test ingredients had been arriving at the delivery bay at the back of the kitchen, tucked in behind the dish station. So I cut off thin slices of heirloom tomato and crisped a couple of slices of baguette in a pan with duck fat.

Salt, Espelette pepper. I'm not going to claim I got eyes-wide wonder, but he saw something.

"Your mom ate this in Paris," he said. "Well, that is a good story. We can use that story. Our restaurants need stories."

Restaurants plural, always. He thought number two was a year out, maybe eighteen months. And I knew where he wanted to go with that one too. He'd said it already. Hadn't I always known Magnus was a longtime fan of my father? Magnus was thinking already about following Arthur Wolf to Latin America.

"Maybe we get this one open first," I'd say when this came up in those early months. "See how that goes."

He'd just shake his head. "It's gonna go," he'd tell me. "Trust me: Véron is going to be huge."

I'd take a stroll sometimes in the early afternoon, walk the neighbourhood thinking of Pigalle. Cambie Street down to Cordova, past the bar on the corner in the Cambie Hostel, where the kids gathered early and stayed all day, wafting smoke and the smell of draft beer. Down Cordova the light would seem to fail and there would be people in the dumpsters, in the strewn alleys. There was a guy who played a beaten guitar who'd sit on the corner of Abbott and strum tunelessly, no particular fingering on the guitar neck beyond a vague fluttering of the hand, opening and closing, serving to mute and halt the jangle the of notes, holding and releasing the sound. He had a set of small pastel drawings that he'd set up all around his feet, like a shield. The Virgin Mary. The bleeding body of Christ. The round tombstone rolled away. He never looked at me except the one time I asked if I could buy the Virgin Mary. I was gesturing down, thinking of Stephanie, who might appreciate the spirit of it, the street-level commitment, the non-traditional form.

The man looked up, then past me. Then he went on strumming, not strumming, holding and releasing that one sound he made.

We signed papers at Magnus's lawyer's office on Burrard, up on the thirty-fifth floor of one of those towers. My ears popped the wrong way on the high-speed elevator. Magnus was sitting at the end of the boardroom table, leaned way back in his chair. He'd just signed each of the pages himself where the yellow sticky note arrows marked his name. Then he'd slapped closed the file the papers were in and slid the thing down the whole length of the shiny black table to me like a shuffleboard puck. Swoosh and there it was. And a lawyer was opening it and pointing to spots, and I was signing again and again while Magnus leaned way back in that leather chair, fingers linked behind his head, eyes on the ceiling, a big smile on his face.

"Oysters," he said.

I signed the last three of fifteen signatures. I sat back and took a big breath. I was now on payroll at Magic Wolf Restaurant Group Ltd. I had an income. I realized I was holding my breath, having swivelled in my chair to look out the boardroom window and down through the glassy view corridor to a slice of the sea and Stanley Park beyond. There was a gas station for boats on the water there, and many watercraft coming to and fro. I felt like I'd been launched into flight rather suddenly, like I was gliding through the glass and out into that view.

"Oysters?" I said to Magnus.

Dinner, he meant.

So that evening, Steph and I made our way around the corner from our place to Rodney's Oyster House. Magnus ordered a table of Little Wings and Malpeques, Olympia and Royal Miyagi. We slurped these back with a splash of mignonette or Tabasco or nothing at all but cold, cold Sauv Blanc, light, crisp, acid, and herbs. Magnus told stories from back in our childhood days, our adventures, our near disasters. Those tires we rolled off the bridge, of course.

After that one Zaina and Stephanie exchanged a glance and shook their heads.

"So who was the ringleader in all this mayhem?" Zaina asked. "There's always a ringleader."

Dense curly hair, sharp features, a quick wide smile. Zaina wore a pendant on a thin gold chain that hung over the neck of a black sweater.

"I was the mastermind," I said. "He was the field marshall."

Steph was holding my arm, smiling. It was a fun evening. Magnus kept ordering more wine. And once the oysters were gone, more coconut shrimp, scallop ceviche, crab cakes, a bucket of clams steamed in white wine, butter, and garlic.

"Tell me about your necklace," Stephanie said.

It was a twenty-five-piastre piece from 1933. "A gift when I graduated from high school and went to Oxford," Zaina told us. "Father said it was a tip he'd received on the first day of his first job, bellman at a hotel in Beirut when he was just twelve. He was thrilled because it was from his birth year, though I always wondered about that. He liked a good story, my dad."

She was fingering the gold coin as she spoke just now, holding it out for Stephanie to inspect. It had the famous Lebanon cedar on it, some Arabic script, the words *République libanaise.* I flashed on Gauthier suddenly, a rush of images, speaking to Ricky, *Visitez le Liban*, a scooter, a pool cue, blood spackled over paving stones. Then I realized Zaina was talking to me.

Restaurants. What did I want to do with these restaurants that Magnus was so committed to opening?

She caught me by surprise with the question. And then I surprised myself with the answer too, saying something that hadn't even been on my mind previously. I thought of it right that second, sitting there, remembering Gauthier.

I said, "Stephanie worked in a place called Femke in Paris. They only hired women. I want to do that. Or as many as possible. I want my kitchens run by women."

Magnus thought fall was the best season to open. Media was hungry in the fall, year-end roundups and award lists coming. Plus, who doesn't like the cooler weather, the Norway maple leaves turning golden along Water and Hastings and up into Victory Square? It was the season for warm meals in warm rooms with warm stories. It was the season for Rue Véron, the season for this dream.

I remember the frantic weeks in the lead-up. We were doing a soft open, inviting friends and friendlies. My father came down for the occasion and for the first time agreed to stay with us. We'd moved by then to a bigger place down at the corner of Cordova and Carrall, an eight-storey brick condo with double height lofts and tall windows looking north. We were on the top floor. Magnus had found it. Magnus had arranged an opening bonus to help us with the down payment. I was helping install worktables for food prep at the back of the kitchen, helping stock the tall mirrored shelves of the bar, helping run wires for the ticketing system, gas lines for the range. I was feeling out of my depth in multiple dimensions, in all the dimensions. Stephanie had flown to Toronto to sit down with editors. The *Femke Years* book was coming out soon. Rue Véron was nearly there. I could stand in the front room and be impressed by what we'd done. Red leather banquettes down the north wall, the towering bar with its own seating to the south. The raised section near the front windows with the round four tops. The main room with its sixty seats in twos and fours. There was an enormous glass window opening to the kitchen with a counter and seats for those who liked to watch. The kitchen beyond with its lab-like surfaces, gleaming and clean, that crisp white light and the cooks moving back there, practising their routines. Bell and Linnie, two young women fresh out of culinary school on the East Coast. We had them at the central island on grill and sauté. Our *garde manger* was Gracine, who'd been a U.S. Marine Corpsman until a life change. We had four apprentices who answered to my sous chef, Kiyomi, who'd worked at Chez Panisse, hired by Alice Waters herself.

Kiyomi was going to be crucial, I sensed. One of Alice's favourites, I'd heard. I thought there might be a story to why she'd left Berkeley for this gig north of the border. But I didn't ask and she didn't volunteer it. Early twenties, with her compact frame and her black hair pulled back in a ragged ponytail, she looked like she'd be at home on a skateboard. She had a resting face of complete calm and distance that would then break all at once to ironic amusement when anything happened she found foolish or funny. She was fast and strong in the kitchen, with utterly sure technique. Quite a lot of Frankie in those movements, though also more finesse and control somehow. More intelligence. It was, in any case, immediately clear to me that Kiyomi could lead the line, taking deliberate but gentle control of the people around her. Quick with instructions. Quick with quiet praise.

So everyone in the kitchen began to fit together in Rue Véron surprisingly quickly, so that I'd occasionally lift my head in the kitchen and see them all in action as if they'd been doing it for years. Tasting something at the plating station, Kiyomi and Bell and Linnie huddled, spoons poised. And Kiyomi would wave me in to try and I'd pick up a spoon and taste the sauce and it would be perfect. Chicken with morels and cream. Rabbit in brandy. Black cod with burnt butter. Whatever it was. And I remember one time, some scene playing out almost exactly like these others, when I wandered out into the alley afterward for a cigarette, which I'd started smoking again after quitting in France. And wandering from the delivery entrance and up around through the alley and into Cambie Street, staring up the street past the Dominion Building into the square. That was the moment I saw her again for the first time in what had to be fifteen years. Still, she looked quite the same, I thought, brown hair flowing to her shoulders, that same white cowboy hat. *Break the Dull Steak Habit.*

"So did you know this person?" Stephanie asked, later, on the phone from New York.

"No, no," I was stammering around trying to explain this oddly forceful moment. "She was on a poster back then. It was actually a promo for a steakhouse, believe it or not."

"I'm really struggling to know what you're saying here."

Of course, I'd never told Stephanie the backstory. Never told her why I carried the memory of Magnus and I standing there transfixed, of the naked body marked for meat, of the feeling of guilt and regret just as Hugo Sullivan walked in.

"Like with a Sharpie," I said, after describing her body. Chuck. Shank. Soup bones.

"Yeah I'm getting that part, Teo," Stephanie said. "It's disgusting but I guess it was the disco seventies."

"I don't know," I said finally. "Probably someone else. She was way down the end of the block."

"You're agitated," Stephanie said. "Everything okay?"

"What did they say about your new draft?" I asked her.

So we changed the subject. Or I did. They liked the new manuscript draft, she told me. Things were going well. She'd be back the day after tomorrow, Thursday. The soft open was Friday and she'd be there. It was all good, Stephanie said. Though as it played out, the editors wanted her to meet the publisher, who wasn't free until Thursday afternoon. So she'd be flying out Friday morning, she told me.

She'd be back in time. Not to worry. She'd come straight from the airport. It would all work out fine. *Just relax, Teo.*

Just relax.

My dad flew in the next day and Magnus had him picked up and brought downtown. I hung up my whites in the *vestiaire* around two that afternoon and rounded the corner to our place to be there in time to meet him, to carry his suitcases from the car to the elevator. He looked confused by the trip somehow, as if he couldn't quite place himself.

"This is your place, where you live?" he asked, twice or even three times. I think the neighbourhood threw him, the street people and the overflowing dumpsters, the crowds milling just down the block from my front door at Hastings, a circling, restless, shifting mass of those with and those without. I'd almost started not to see it. But then your father arrives and he notices, and there you are ashamed to have let things slip from view.

"It's cleaning up around here," I said. "Used to be a lot worse."

Stephanie and I had moved out of the upstairs loft and down to a pullout in the living room, near the tall windows that looked north over the harbour and to the mountains beyond. My dad objected at first, saying he loved the view. But I told him he could see it just as well from the loft above, only he'd have more privacy. And he could sleep in if we got up earlier than he wanted to.

"Doubt that," he said, accepting a small pour of scotch. "I get up pretty early. At my age you don't want to sleep away too much of the time remaining."

I left him, having shown him the bathroom up top and helped him lay out his things. Then I walked back down Cordova thinking about Stephanie. Thinking about the slow crush building, everything we'd planned for seeming to arrive at once.

We did a tasting menu for the soft open, a sweeping tour of the Rue Véron menu. I probably needn't have worried about any of that side of things. I took my station at the front of the meal prep island next to the long pass table where the finished plates would go up. Since everyone was eating the same dozen small plates and I didn't have to expedite orders, I tucked in next to Kiyomi and did a couple of the cold plates myself. We had an oyster in a puddle of watercress cream, salmon tartare, terrine of foie, and crisp tomato toast served that night with saffron mayonnaise. We moved on through a lavender sorbet to hot plates: pork tenderloin with mustard, oxtail with green peppercorn, duck breast with grapefruit jelly. It was technical food. It was vibrant. Vivid, I hoped. Did a diner stare at the plate with wonder that food could be so beautiful? Did they taste it and close their eyes, like a famished young woman taking that first bite of baguette and tomato? I think people did experience the plates and flavours that way, even if they could not have known it.

I went out front with the whole brigade afterwards. Tools down. Step up. Take the applause. Magnus stood at the bar with friends, applauding alongside everyone, gesturing toward me: *You! This is for you!*

Kiyomi linked her arm through mine and pulled me close. And I did the same with Bell who was on my left, all the way down the line to Ali and Ivan, who were our dishwashers and the only men in the kitchen other than me. We all linked arms and bowed deeply, like a chorus line at the Moulin Rouge. When I came up I saw my father there, sitting with Stephanie, her arm around his shoulder. She was clapping her left hand into his right. They were applauding as if one person. And after I went over and hugged them both, the room broke down into a conversational roar, people milling through that front room, from the front glass all the way to the back, staring in at the kitchen, up at that enormous tower of wine bottles in the middle of the room, our sommelier, Delphine, and all the white-shirted, black-aproned servers flitting around the room with trays.

Some small and specific things I remember about the unrolling of that night. My conversations up and down the room. Hugo Sullivan was there, that long ago West Van friend with the house on the water. It didn't feel possible that it had been fifteen years. There were others I recognized and some I didn't.

Stephanie took my father home and made a small face. He'd had a few.

"You need help?"

"Stay," she said. "Zaina's coming over for a nightcap. She says talk to Magnus. Make sure he doesn't misbehave."

Magnus leaning on one elbow at the bar with an empty glass. A nod to Delphine and she intercepted me on my way over with two fresh glasses and a bottle on a tray. Chambolle-Musigny, from the Premier Cru vineyard at Les Amoureuses. The lovers. Maybe Delphine's idea of an oenophile joke. She poured the glasses and I carried them over and set the bottle on the bar. I remember the group Magnus was standing with, five or six guys, all in suits, bright ties, light tans, each seeming to have the same unkempt hair that signalled they might have all just come from surfing Long Beach on the island. Magnus was making introductions, I was shaking hands, smiling, accepting congratulations and comments on the food. It was all going down huge. And when someone with a television camera came sliding back through the room, shimmying through the crowd toward us, and a bright light sparked up as they began to shoot, we all acted as if this were to be expected. I'd never had a television camera trained on me in my entire life. I stood there making happy small talk with this ring of guys, everyone joking and laughing loudly, a kind of nonchalance settling into me, as if what was arriving just then — my face as the face of Rue Véron, my personality and story stamped onto it, and Magnus, with his elbow on the bar, the less voluble partner, his ease of manner, his quiet power — as if all that was what I'd seen coming all along, as if that was deserved, meant to be, the just and proper outcome in the sweep of things.

Tell us about your inspirations, the guy was saying from behind the camera. And I could hear myself answering, while at the same time hearing Magnus tell that same old story about the bridge over the railway track, the tires. I was talking into the camera about my mother being a refugee, about my father being a nomad. About their paths around the world and the way they'd finally met. About a strange recipe box that held our family cuisine, about oeufs de maman made with bacon croutons, about tomatoes on toast with the lightest sprinkle of crystal salt. And as I told the man, I was trying to make sense out of that backstory at the same time, trying to make it some organic part of what Rue Véron had become, even if I couldn't put it perfectly into words.

However it came out, when the interview was over, and the camera pulled away to take in other shots of the room, there was Hugo leaning in and congratulating me.

He said, "That's a beautiful story about your mother. I really liked that."

I reached out for a bottle and topped his wine. And I said to him, "You know what's really weird?"

"That Magnus is rich?" Hugo said. "Totally didn't see that coming in high school."

"*Break the Dull Steak Habit*?" I said to him. "Remember that?"

Hugo's eyebrows were raised, his expression amused. The night Magnus and I had seen that poster in the back bedroom of one of Hugo's brothers, Hugo himself had come in as we stood staring. He'd been holding a glowing red glass of Campari on ice, I remember. He was shaking his head. *You straight boys*, he'd said.

"That woman in the poster," I said to him in Rue Véron that night. "I totally saw her the other day. I'm not kidding."

Hugo was amused and detached simultaneously. And he was good with that combination seemingly. I'd heard he ran his own consulting firm. Crisis management, he'd told me. But before Hugo had time to react to what I'd told him, there was another person leaning in, a face right there, just below eye level, looking up.

"Kiyomi," I said. "You know Hugo Sullivan?"

She didn't look over at him. She was focused on me, Kiyomi with her laser intelligence, her immediate and reassuring control. "Stephanie," she said. "She's calling."

"What time is it?"

Didn't matter. "Your dad, Teo," she said. "He's fallen."

Lechon Kawali

"How'd it happen?" I asked Stephanie, who was making him tea when I got home. He was sitting on a chair near the front glass shaking his head.

"Stupid," he said. "So stupid. I was just coming down …"

He gestured at the concrete stairs that descended from the loft. Midway down the stairs had a landing, then a bend to the left as they tracked along the curved south wall of the suite.

"Missed the turn, I think," Stephanie whispered.

"Stupid!" he said again.

"It's okay, it's okay." I put a hand on his shoulder and he physically contorted, his face twisting to a grimace.

"Not okay," Stephanie said. "Emergency I think, Dad."

I called a taxi and took him over to St. Paul's. After midnight on a Friday night. The place was slammed. Drug overdoses and bar fights. As the nurse wheeled my father down the hall to an examination room, there was a man on a gurney in the hallway with a nail sticking clean through his hand. You could see the head of the nail on his palm and the spike emerging between his knuckles.

"*Jesus Christ,*" my father said, wincing.

"Not funny," said the nurse.

They gave my father Tylenol 3s. Then we waited, nearly four hours in the end, during which time I could see the bruise blooming yellow and turquoise across his collarbone and up the side of his neck as he lay there on the gurney. His eyes drifted closed, though I knew he wasn't sleeping. Then after twenty or thirty minutes, I remember his eyes suddenly popped open again, searching for something, finally finding their focus far through the wall, past the blood pressure machine and the monitor, the keyboard, the hanging otoscope, and defibrillator paddles. "Dad?" I said. "You okay?"

"Subic," he said.

"What about Subic, Dad?"

And here his eyes refocused again, finding me. He squinted. He seemed to place me unexpectedly in the scene. He put fingers to his mouth, dry lips, cracked and slightly blue. I poured him some Gatorade from a bottle I'd bought in the lobby on the way in.

"You cold?" I asked him. "I can get a blanket."

"Did I ever tell you about Subic?" he asked me.

"No, Dad, never did."

"Oh boy," he said. "Coulda gotten myself killed. All of us."

"*Killed?* Well, now you have to tell me," I said.

"Harbour all full of wreckage," he said. Then suddenly he was blinking, looking up into my face as if he'd only just realized I was there. "Where's the doctor? Did the doctor come?"

"Not yet," I said. "It's Friday night, really busy."

"My shoulder," he said. "Hurts like a sombitch."

"Subic Bay," I said, to distract him.

Subic Bay was another Simms idea, my father said. Came up over whiskey one night after the power station job and before they had another one. Funny how Simms in his aloha shirt and chomping on his butt of a cigar, all wet from chewing and most of the time not even lit, actually ended up being the one with all the ideas.

"Course Maitland could fix anything mechanical," he said. "I was impressed. But Simms ended up being both smarter and dumber than I thought."

The Subic idea was to buy a minesweeper out of the surplus supply at the U.S. naval base, just seaward from the small city of Olongapo. The Americans were cleaning house. It was like free money, Simms said.

"We buy one. We steam to Manila. I got this French guy who'll set us up with a buyer. We make some green. Easy."

"Who wants one of those now?" Arthur asked. "War's over."

Simms shook his head like Arthur was simple. And there was a silence just then during which only the chirping *kuliglig* could be heard, clouds of them in the low jungle all around. "You ever hear of Vietnam?" Simms said, sucking his teeth. "War's not over, over there."

Maitland was looking off into the darkness around the camp. Arthur watched him and wondered if flying Hellcats off the *Essex* was even a true story. He'd seen Maitland sizing up the land, checking ridgelines as they moved. He'd seen the man cleaning a pistol in his tent, quick, sharp movements like he'd done it hundreds, even thousands of times. What struck Arthur that moment, watching Maitland assess the darkness, birds shrieking in the jungled hillsides around them, was that most guys would make up flying Hellcats to look tough. Arthur thought Maitland might have come up with *Hellcat pilot* as a cover story over something much nastier.

"Well then let's make some green," Arthur said to Simms, aware of himself play-acting, pretending that all this was completely familiar and normal.

———

"How's he doing?"

"Drifted off."

"I'm Dr. Velasco. Hi, Mr. Wolf. Can you wake up for me?"

He blinked a number of times, head back on the pillow, then squinted up.

"Hi, Mr. Wolf. I'm Rosa Velasco. Can I have a look at your shoulder?"

My father gestured vaguely.

"It's all right, Dad," I said. "Dr. Velasco's just going to open your shirt here."

"Chart says he's on blood thinners," Velasco said to me.

"Warfarin," I told her.

"He's bleeding into the tissue here," Dr. Velasco traced her finger along my father's collarbone. "This looks painful, Mr. Wolf. Were you playing football?"

"Mateo?" my father said.

"I'm here, Dad. You want water?"

"Teo?"

I leaned in close to him. "Right here," I said.

"Is the doctor here?"

"Dr. Velasco is right here, Dad. She's just going to look at your shoulder."

"Velasco," he said, his expression drifting.

"That's me," she said.

"Kumusta ka na, Doktor Velasco?" my father said.

She looked down at him, eyebrows high. My father was smiling widely, not really looking at her, past her, to the ceiling tiles.

"Sa Olongapo kinain ko ang lechon," my father said to the doctor.

"Did you now? Lucky you!"

"What?" I said. "Is that Japanese?"

"Filipino," she said. "He's telling me he ate roast pig in Olongapo. My grandfather used to roast the pigs when I was small, Mr. Wolf."

"Masarap iyon."

"Kailan ka ba sa Pilipinas, Mr. Wolf?"

"Nineteen forty-eight. Tokyo too," he said to her. "Ikaw ay masyadong medyo."

"Okay then," the doctor said. "So you're going to want to get him off the thinners for a while."

I nodded.

"Otherwise, just have him rest. It's bruising. We'll take some pictures but it doesn't look like anything's broken. Fall on the stairs?"

"At my apartment," I told her.

"Maybe have him sleep on the main floor tonight."

I phoned Stephanie from the taxi on the way back as he dozed against the window. She said to call, though I could tell I'd woken her. I could see the dawn already over the harbour as we cut through Gastown, a blush of rose. "Crazy night," she said. "You were a smash hit."

"Was I?"

"Magnus told Zaina. Zaina told me. He's very happy."

"That's good I guess. We want him happy."

We were into Cordova, almost home. There were tents lining the hoardings of a construction site, a shirt drying over a guy wire, a man in a dumpster, a woman on a bike. Milling circles in Pigeon Park just down from our place. I felt an enormous sleep coming.

Orinoco

Ten days after his fall in my apartment, my father was back home in Alberta and out buying groceries when he had a stroke.

My sister, Simone, called to let me know. The grocery store was in Beaumont, the town nearest to his farm. He'd been at the checkout and suddenly couldn't speak. He was opening and closing his mouth, producing nothing.

"The cashiers all know him," Simone said. "They got him into an ambulance. The hospital called me."

"Jesus," I said. "How is he?"

"They gave him thrombolytics," she said. "Clot-buster drugs. Some of his speech is back though he's still mixing things up, saying his leg hurts and pointing to his shoulder."

"Christ."

"Question: Emerg in Vancouver after he fell. Did the docs tell you to stop his blood thinners?"

"They did," I said. "Was that wrong?"

"No, he was bleeding," Simone said. "Only the cardiologist in me says it might have been nice to start those up again a few days later."

Ten days was pretty much textbook for stopping Warfarin, my sister told me. At that point there's no more medication in the system and the patient is unprotected. "He's eighty-nine," Simone said. "He was on thinners for a reason."

I had my hand over my face, standing in my tiny office at the back of the restaurant. Through the big glass window into the dining room I could see servers rushing around getting ready for our media open. Delphine and an assistant were loading wine bottles into the Otto. I could smell stock and fumet, brown butter, pork bones searing in oil. Linnie and Bell were hunched at their stations, powering through prep. Kiyomi caught my eye and cocked her head. *All good?* I made a face, *not really*.

"I'm so sorry about this," I said to Simone.

"Not your fault," she said. Then: "Jonah's back."

"From Japan?"

"I guess. He's out on the farm now for a few days."

"Should I come up?"

"It's up to you, Teo," she said. "We'd be glad to see you. But there's not much you can do."

"We just opened," I said. "We're completely slammed."

"I get it. Totally get it."

Stephanie thought I could take the time. Magnus said *sure, go* but in the end I didn't. The media open was on us. I had to be there. We were doing full menu for the first time. Ten apps, ten mains. We got hammered, but the team came through. More than that, really. I remember taking a thirty-second breather toward the end of service and seeing them all. Linnie and Bell working shoulder to shoulder, combining elements, finishing plates, hardly a word passing between them. Gracine and her apprentices rolling over seamlessly to pastries and desserts. And Kiyomi, well. She was everywhere: quiet, fast, precise, artful. One glance up and Kiyomi was the first thing I'd see, humming quietly as she worked, sledgehammer strength, gun-sight focus, rapid yet delicate hands. And I can't deny I didn't see this as well: For a young woman who looked like a skate kid half the time, Kiyomi was really very beautiful.

———

I hardly remember three months after that. We got our reviews. We got our raves. Our reservation book went solid black for three months out. We had high-five moments when new reviews hit the corkboard. Kiyomi said, *Nice, Chef. Nice work, everyone.* Then we all turned back to our flames and grills and wood countertops, our trays of microgreens, flats of iced fish, marbled slabs of brisket, onglet, bavette. I had moments in the midst of this flow where I'd remember my mother with such intensity that I'd glance up through the glass and imagine I might catch a glimpse of her in a banquette, shaking my head at myself and drawing a smile from Kiyomi.

"Having your own private moment there, Chef?"

"Having my own private moment, Sous."

"Frites," she'd call. "Frisée lardon, chicken, confit."

Frites. Frisée. Confit. Oui, Sous.

Three months of blur. And then I suddenly felt it: we were there. Things were snapped into place. We were a *brigade*, small but tight, down to essentials. Six of us on stations, three apprentices, two *plongeurs*. Everyone in command of their zone. Ninety days of packed houses and I could call an order from the pass and know exactly who would answer from what exact spot in that gleaming kitchen. I didn't even have to glance up, though I did on occasion just for the pleasure of it, the satisfaction of things working. *Mise en place.*

And after service, just as it had been in Paris, there were those other crucial grooves. All those servers and cooks in the downtown places, all tumbling out staff entrances and into shining alleys, all sparking smokes and glancing back to see the room lights fading blue, the show over for another day. So up we went out of Gastown in our ones, and twos, and threes, all ending up in the same place to pack in close and let the tension drain away, to tell our stories, make our complaints, to celebrate, to hook up, to deny the coming day. Only in Vancouver, Pigalle wasn't a neighbourhood or a string of cafés. It was a single place, every night: the Marine Club. Once a private club for stevedores, long since claimed by punks and hipsters and food industry types, servers, cooks. There were ship pictures on the walls and a jar of pickled eggs on the bar that nobody ever touched. They had a Hammond B3 organ in the corner and a man named Frank who worked the keys for gin and tonics, noodling his way through his eccentric repertoire of standards.

Kiyomi took me there at first, of course. It was always going to be my younger sous who picked up the zeitgeist after only weeks in the city, bringing me up the long staircase from Homer Street to the door with the porthole where a bartender named Stash would buzz you into that low and dingy room jammed with people, so many of whom Kiyomi knew already to greet, to fist-bump, to high five. Kiyomi and I wandering in with the others from Rue Véron and we got the looks, the inquiring glances, the friendly nods. At the time I revelled in it, the obvious way that our exhausted faces attracted the gaze. I took it as admiration, just as I'd taken all the glances in Frankie's direction in Pigalle to have been the same. We were the spot getting all that press, all so early, and all of us so new. Kiyomi with her Chez Panisse stardust. Me just over from France. I experienced it as a purely positive thing, in those early months, like no new rising star could ever be quietly resented.

"Hey Stash," Kiyomi would say, pulling out a stool. "Set Frank up, would you?"

So Stash would pour off a G&T and holler across the room to the organist: *From Kiyomi!* And Frank would smile wide, then start in on his signature tune, which was the theme from that old TV show *The Jeffersons*: "Movin' On Up."

"Kiyomi!"

Someone calling over. Kiyomi greeting them in return, cool and already connected.

People were spilling by. The cooks from the tourist traps and the hot spots. Kids, most of them, younger even than Kiyomi. But not always. There were three pastry cooks from one of the big hotels uptown who came down together and who Kiyomi called the *Mille Feuilles*. They were even older than me and had a stern quality I associate with making croquembouche and things with delicate foam and architectural layers. But they'd come by the table themselves in due course and talk to Kiyomi, whom they seemed to admire.

"How goes it, girl?"

"Doing good, honey. You?"

"Well I'm not young and *famous* but I'm surviving."

Magnus never saw any of this, of course. He wasn't in the restaurant during service for the most part. And he'd be long at home before the Marine Club hour rolled around. But he would have seen the same adulation from his own angle: He was watching the money come in. We couldn't physically process more covers, rolling over two lunch and two dinner sittings six days a week. Magnus thought the rush would last a few months before returning to normal. But it was six months on rails, then eight, then a year. And it wasn't more than a couple of months into year two before Magnus started talking about opening a second one.

"It's a brand moment," he said, down on his knees, picking yellow baby zucchini out from under the plants he'd grown near the bottom of his enormous garden. No sign of excavation for the new house. "Véron is everywhere. You're everywhere. But you're not only Véron. You're this next thing. You're Magic Wolf, baby, and we're in the season for this dream."

I was holding a metal pail, loading the zucchini he was handing up to me. That was rather poetic for Magnus. *The season for this dream.* Maybe he never said it at all and I only imagined it, or Kiyomi said it. I have to admit it doesn't sound like something Stephanie would say. But we were dreaming. In our ways we all were, dreaming ourselves forward and upward along that snaking path.

Of course, Latin American was where we were going next. I say of course because Magnus knew it before I even made the pitch in his garden that day. My father's footsteps were going to be mine too — Magnus willed it so. Magnus saw the *story* there. And so I pitched it to him with enthusiasm, as if it had been wholly my idea.

Spain was the launch pad, the inflection point. After abruptly leaving Asia, it seems my dad had wandered, more or less nomadic. There was a stopover in what was then Ceylon. There was a Suez transit. There was time in Italy and France, though it always seemed that the first place on this long circumnavigation that he really remembered vividly was Spain: Madrid, Barcelona, but especially the north coast Basque jewel of San Sebastian. He remembered fresh fish cooked simply in olive oil and garlic, charred octopus on skewers, smoky green olives, white anchovies.

He'd returned to Toronto briefly after that, presumably to settle down. But it didn't stick. I had to wonder if Jeanie had played some role in that, but I never asked. The story just took a turn at that point for reasons he never explained. He was in Toronto. And then he was suddenly heading south. And then it was all Latin America after that: Guatemala, Columbia, Peru, Venezuela, snaking his way toward Guayaquil, Ecuador, as if some kind of beacon had been activated.

"You'd just gotten back home," I said at one point, over the phone.

"Back," he said. *Back.* As if he didn't get the word.

"Maybe Toronto just didn't feel like home anymore."

He paused a long time, this new cadence having taken our conversations since the stroke.

"You know what I hate the most?"

"What, Dad?"

"I sound dumb, stumbling for words."

"You don't, come on."

"But I used to be …" he started, then he had to wait for it. "Articulate. I used to be."

Then he laughed, which was a relief to hear. My father was in the end still persuaded by life's essential absurdity.

"Back, but not home," I prompted. This felt important to me.

"Kinda both, kinda neither," he said, then laughed again. "Like Schrödinger's cat."

I thought I knew that feeling now that Stephanie was flying to Toronto herself seemingly every other week. All good news for her these busy days. The book was coming together. The book was making prepublication waves. "*A Year in Provence* … for women." That was the ad copy, in essence. But now her agent was talking to documentary filmmakers, television writers, European publishers. She'd call late at night after long days, exhausted and excited. I missed her terribly. *There, and then away again.*

"Maybe I was just restless," my father said, returning to the question. "I'd been in Spain. I saw bullfights there. But I wanted …"

I thought I knew what he wanted even as he grasped for words. He wanted to get out further toward the edge of things, maximal distance from where gravity naturally took everyone else. He was adventuring. So now he was following Latin lines. Chiapas. Comayagua. He marked passage of the Panama Canal as had my mother with her family only a few years prior. Only my mother had transited by tracing the locks and the water en route to Ecuador. My father crossed it the other way, one side to the other, by bridge, eastward near Paraiso, then down the coast, into the bush.

"Modern Latin," I told Magnus that day, who was now rooting in the loamy soil of his Belmont farm, pulling out yams for my bucket. "The food of adventure and discovery. Bright and light flavours, new takes on old plates. Arroz con pollo, mole, cazuela, feijoada, street corn, fire-grilled white fish with garlic. Let's have a Taco Tuesday. Let's have a raw bar with oysters and tuna and daily ceviche specials laid out on the ice. Let's throw on pintxos for weekends because they're amazing and flexible by season, and people love them, and because for me in some strange way this all starts on the beachfront in San Sebastian, a piece of bread with a smear of quince paste, a slice of P'tit Basque and a fat white anchovy."

Magnus had rocked back on his heels there in the dirt, squatting and staring up. "You got a name?"

I had a great name, I thought. It had a great sound. And it had a great feel, which to me was of foliage and smoky fires, trucks on dirt roads, silent ocelots deep in the green.

"*Orinoco*," I said.

Magnus was nodding, smiling widely. "Love it," he said.

Were we going too fast? Were we being greedy? Did Magnus believe in me too much?

I didn't think about it at the time. And certainly Magnus didn't. He'd phone me to chat about Orinoco, or call me up to Belmont Farm, which is what we'd both started calling his undeveloped acreage up there. We'd sketch more of the idea, talk locations, leases, buildings that might come available. Magnus had designers doing drawings before we had a room. Sweeping arches, flared columns, polished tile floors with waves of mosaic colour like the beach promenade in Copacabana.

Which was Brazil, I pointed out. One country Arthur Wolf hadn't visited. Just saying.

Didn't matter. Didn't matter. It was all going to be very hybrid modern. Ian Fleming meets Oscar Niemeyer with a raw bar at the centre of the room, a big circle of ice and mirrors and piles of seafood. It was all going to be way cooler than Rue Véron, Magnus said, which was only ever intended to be *charming* with all that shabby Belle Époquery, modelled so clearly on the Montparnasse greats: Le Dome, Le Select, Closerie, Le Dauphin.

I'd nod and smile. Suggest a new dish. Then rush back downtown to help Kiyomi and the team with afternoon prep.

"Today's toast?" I'd ask, because she'd evolved the idea in what I thought was a very smart way. We always had the *traditional* available, the plain version from my mother's memory. Then we'd pull together an uptown chef-y version.

"Anchovy butter, Chaumes cream, yellow heirloom."

"Nice. And …"

"Baby cuttlefish grilled in a puff box," Kiyomi would say from right at my elbow, then run on down the specials.

"How about something old school today?" I said. Another of Kiyomi's ideas. For lack of shelves in our apartment, Stephanie had left a fair number of our cookbooks at Rue Véron, displayed now behind the bar. Kiyomi thought this was the coolest thing ever and leafed the pages until this one came to her. Some updated reference to the pantheon, the Michelin firmament. Madame Point. Alain Chapel. Paul Bocuse. Outhier, Pic, Guérard, Vergé.

"Beautiful spring salmon today," Kiyomi said. "We could do the Troisgros one with greens."

"We have sorrel?"

"Arugula."

"Absolutely does *not* work," I said. "Does anyone really think arugula tastes like sorrel?"

"Gee, sorry, Chef," Kiyomi said. "I'll think of something."

"I know you will."

Moving and moving. Everything in motion. Sliding past each other, all elbows and hips and bums. Steam billowing and things rising upward. *Behind, behind.* The fall "best-of" lists were out and Rue Véron made every local one, a couple of the nationals. We had a wall of five stars on TripAdvisor, Yelp. *EnRoute* magazine put us on the cover of their Best New Restaurants issue. But even all that didn't prepare us for what happened after the *New York Times* hit. Nobody even knew they'd visited.

"Travel section," Magnus said on the phone that morning. "It's a thing on Vancouver, but you might guess the writer never left Véron. And pictures."

I found a copy. And there we were, Kiyomi and I side by side. Her Parmesan sablés on tomato jelly with parsley oil. My dish arriving on a straight line from wild nights in long-ago Belleville, a big slice of foie-stuffed rabbit pooled around with that mahogany sauce, Coteaux du Layon and demi, shaved truffle.

I pinned up the article on the kitchen corkboard. Everyone hugged everyone. Everyone smiling. I made a midday family meal of tomato toast and roast chickens in a vinaigrette over greens, had Delphine uncork a whole bunch of bottles from the Otto. I offered a toast to my mother's memory, very short. To my father too.

Kiyomi hugged me again. We all ate and there was a lot of laughter. And in my memory now, it's as if the phone rang the very next moment, just as Ali and Ivan were loading the dishwashers and everyone turned to afternoon tasks with another slammed evening ahead. But maybe it wasn't even that day or week. Maybe it was a month later. But he called. Frankie did. I remember Kiyomi picked up in our little office at the back of the kitchen. She came to the door, squinting, confused. "Tran-keel?" she said.

"Okay," I said, hand out for the phone. "Gimme that."

Of course he'd seen the *Times*. He'd seen his own dish up there, made that one night when the hotel guys brought the case of champagne and everyone had gotten bubbly drunk.

"A tribute," I said, but he wasn't calling for credit.

"You did good, Tranquille," he said. "That bunny looks entirely edible."

"Fucking hell, Frankie," I said, laughing now, as was Frankie himself. It was somehow so absurd. And as I remember that conversation now, I'm struck by how little of that epic collapse at the end of Paris was even on my mind. It was just good to hear his voice. To hear him sounding like his old self — confident, expansive, funny, in charge. No regrettable circumstances. No Gauthier. No drunken misbehaviour. Not even Ines just then. I saw Frankie giving change to a homeless person, plating a dish with fanatical precision, buying a round, telling a story, making a toast. Frankie the mentor, the legendary friend. I thought of a nice-looking macaron girl on a chaise longue, a spaghetti strap off her shoulder and a satellite passing overhead in the inky Parisian sky.

Of course, he did have a reason for calling. This wasn't just congratulations or a chance to rib me about getting famous on plates I'd first learned in Frankie's kitchen. He did both those things. And he asked after Stephanie. He seemed genuinely happy to hear of the Femke book. He told me a bit about being back in Quebec. Trois-Pistoles it was. Back home. The simple life. Fishing and hunting. Cooking at a restaurant attached to a bowling alley. More than poutine, he told me. Trois-Pistoles Five Pin was home to Frankie's own Boudin Noir Meatball Torpedo Sandwich. They called it Le Formidable. "I tell you," Frankie said. "I sell thirty a day. Forty. They're good."

"I'll bet they are," I said.

"Maybe I make one for you?" Frankie said.

"Bring it on, man," I said.

"Okay. I'll come to you."

"For real? What?"

"Well, perhaps," Frankie said, and now the long pause. "Listen, Tranquille … listen, Teo my friend. I have a serious question. Or maybe I say *proposal.*"

"Let me guess," I said. "You're looking for a real kitchen. You're looking for a job."

Long silence. I was joking. But Frankie wasn't.

Stephanie had questions, as I knew she would. "What about your all-woman kitchen?"

"Led by women," I said. "Frankie slides in at sous, working for Kiyomi."

"What'd Magnus say?"

"Magnus is persuaded that we need another person so I can focus on Orinoco. He says it's our *brand moment*."

"What does that even mean?" She was packing a suitcase, off for Toronto again. After that, London for a week. The documentary was happening. The production company was in the U.K. It was easier to go. Have a sit-down, as the film people said.

"I kinda thought Frankie might like working at a bowling alley," Stephanie said. "Like it might appeal to his contrarian side."

"He's getting some notice," I told her. "He's making fifty pounds of boudin noir a day and shipping it all in hero sandwiches."

"So why doesn't he keep doing that?"

I was sitting on the edge of our bed in the loft, watching her pack. I could raise my eyes from watching her there and see the mountains, dusted in snow. There were whitecaps in the inlet. The light was hard.

"Le Dauphin was Frankie's identity," I said. "Maybe he wants some of that back."

Stephanie sat suddenly next to her suitcase, then she slumped to the bed full length, as if out of strength entirely.

"What?" I said.

She handled all this so differently than I did. Her book had sold in England, Germany, France, Italy. Other places. She believed in the project, but felt dwarfed by it on occasion. I didn't have enough sense to see my own situation the same way. Quite the reverse. At the time I just assumed I deserved all the attention and saw no potential for danger at all. So someone stopped me on the street, recognizing me from a review or profile, and I'd happily engage, make small talk, once even catching myself talking longer than the other person had expected or even wanted.

"On the street," I asked Kiyomi. "People ever stop you, say hi?"

She rolled her eyes. Kiyomi had her ferocious work ethic, like no degree of success could be assumed. But she'd also learned the hard way that you didn't let people blow smoke up your ass.

I sensed it coming. "Is this about Chez Panisse?"

Partly. Maybe.

So I pressed a bit and out it came. She'd done well there. She'd had the owners' trust. And she could have gone further but then a relationship with a cook went bad.

"Worse than bad," she said. "I discover he's sleeping with servers barely out of high school."

"And you were sleeping with him first?"

"I'm a fucking adult, Chef," Kiyomi said. "And he wasn't my boss."

"All right," I said. "In that case: What a jerk!"

"Hot, though," she said, thinking back. "Rock climber. I like lean protein. What can I say?"

"So you meeting lots of nice Vancouver boys now, Sous?"

"In all my free time, you mean?"

I might have thought on occasion that Kiyomi slotted in where Ines had once been, the work sister. But that was never right. Kiyomi was no kid. She wasn't up from the coast into the big city. She didn't need looking after.

"Fact is I've always picked them badly," she said to me.

"Who was it before the climber?"

A Wednesday night after service. The dishwashers were running. Ali and Ivan mopping floors. Delphine and the bar manager were sipping wine at the bar. I remember Stephanie was in London around this time, early morning for her. She was probably in a breakfast meeting.

"Married guy," Kiyomi said to me. "Only I didn't know. So that also sucked. But he did not sleep with a server, I'll give him that."

"Sorry about the bad luck," I said. "You eating, by the way?"

"You making me dinner, Chef?"

"I'm a nice guy," I said.

"Sure," she said.

"Oeufs de maman?"

Kiyomi shook her head. "Not loving the name."

I looked over at her.

"Mom's eggs. I don't know."

"You're sick," I said to her. "Never once thought of that."

"Well, you wouldn't. But I'm hungry, so feed me."

Sitting there on a worktable, hands around her knees. Black hair, those dark eyes sparkling with amusement and insight. So I banged a skillet onto a flame and got some water boiling, fixed up a couple of jammy soft-boiled eggs. Then I fried off toast cubes in duck fat and tossed it all together with a couple of gratings of Alba truffle that had arrived that afternoon from our picker in Oregon.

"Thanks to the chefs patrons," I said. "In Paris."

"Uh-huh," she said taking a big mouthful of soft egg and crouton in a spoon. "Okay, this is ridiculous."

"The Pellery Pricks," I said. "One of their mothers made them these eggs like this before school every day. Later, they put them on their first menu. Maybe it should have been oeufs comme Maman les a faits or something. Only oeufs de maman is what the Pricks called them. And you didn't mess around with the Pricks."

"I wouldn't mess around with these eggs either," she said, chewing and talking.

"My last morning in the Le Dauphin kitchen," I told her. "I made the Pricks these very eggs."

"Question," Kiyomi said. "Why *pricks*?"

I gave her the overview. Rolling pins to the back. Paring knifes thrown into walls. Cuffs to the ear. Testicles grabbed on occasion. "That morning, though, I take them up their eggs. And I'm pretty sure by that point already that I'm leaving."

"Cause of getting grabbed by the balls and such," Kiyomi said.

"That plus stuff. It's complicated. Point being, I was going to hand in my resignation. So I make these eggs and serve them. I open my mouth to quit and they offer me exec."

"Nice," Kiyomi said, wiping up last smears of egg yolk with a piece of baguette pinched between her fingers. Then she looked up sharply. She held my gaze.

So I told her. What did she think of taking on my role? Executive Chef, Rue Véron. I'd be shifting focus to Orinoco, but she wouldn't be alone. We were bringing in a sous to work with her. Very talented. Very experienced. But she'd be in charge.

"What?"

"Interested?"

"Course I'm interested."

I extended a fist and we bumped. Then, as seemed only appropriate, we went out drinking. The Marine Club, of course, where we hunched over the bar and Stash set us up with brandies and beers. People flowed in and flowed around us. The regulars. The newcomers. Saw the *Times*, man. Very cool. Fist bump. Shoulder slap. I wanted Kiyomi to myself. And eventually, just sitting there, round after round, eventually I almost did.

"Last call," sang the Mille Feuilles as they glided by toward the door, gazes lingering.

"Kiyomi is getting a promotion," I announced to them.

"Oh, is that what they call it?" Then they were at the portholed door and the cold air was rushing in from the street, up those long stairs.

"Well, I suppose they could go fuck themselves," I said.

"Why do you hate the *mil fwee*?" Kiyomi asked. "They seem to really like me."

"Always watching us," I said.

"Maybe you took it the wrong way," she said. "Maybe you're drunk."

"I'm not sober," I allowed.

"Maybe it's past your bedtime," Kiyomi said, as those last drinks arrived, some particular brand of tequila that she assured me would hurt my head in the morning.

"No bedtime," I said. "Steph's in England. Book stuff."

"Steph the writer. She's cool."

Our shoulders were touching. Frank jump-bopping through his version of "Ain't Nobody Here But Us Chickens." Kiyomi smelled like cinnamon and leaned in close, our voices low. I was seeing us both as if from above, hunched over the cracked lino bar next to the cigarette machine, me out past my bedtime. A kind of Pigalle moment. And Frankie was going to walk in the door any minute and take over. He really was.

"Here's the rub," I said. "This new sous."

"The rub," Kiyomi said. "You're pissed. You're a lightweight."

"I'm a lightweight," I agreed. "This new sous."

"Frankie," Kiyomi said. "François Coté."

"He's a genius," I said. "Frankie Formidable."

"I'll try to measure up."

"You will," I said, and my arm slipped around her shoulder, pulling her close. Whispering into her ear. *Just some things you might want to know.*

She made a face and shook her head. She didn't understand what I was saying, what I was vaguely warning her about, if that was, in fact, what I was doing. I wasn't quite making sense.

"Definitely gotta get you home, Chef," she said to me. Her face close. She hadn't shuffled off my arm so there we were pretty much nose to nose. That smell. Cinnamon, tangerine, sweat from service.

I texted her later. I must have been in bed. She obviously was. She wrote back: *You fucking woke me up, Chef.*

Ines, I texted. Or started to text. I don't know exactly where I was going with that or if I typed it by accident or what. I wouldn't have remembered it at all had Kiyomi then not texted me the next morning at 7 a.m.

Wake up, sunshine. Luv, Ines.

I didn't bother trying to explain to Kiyomi, or myself for that matter. I went to Rue Véron and strapped on my whites. I let her laugh there at her station, banging her way through a small mountain of chanterelles and creminis, tossing the trim in for a veg stock. She was laughing, looking at me. She said, "You're a bad date, man. Feed me dinner then call me the wrong name. Shit." The others looking over, but just grinning. Laughing, all jokes all around. All good, I thought.

"Get some coffee poured into the hangover here!" Kiyomi called through the pass.

Café pour la gueule de bois. Vite!

She wouldn't have heard the same echo I heard, of course. Frankie calling out the same thing on that first morning those years ago. Kiyomi only grinned as the server called back *Yes, Chef* sharply, and rushed out toward the bar area. *Yes, Chef.* As if everybody had already heard the news of the changes. Kiyomi moving up. As if this whole business were already spilling forward, rolling onward relentlessly.

Pickled Eggs

Out of Subic Bay and past Mayagao Point, Arthur powered up the sweeper to ten knots and an enormous vibration started through the vessel, so bad that the decking began to shudder and Simms's coffee mug hopped right off the chart table and smashed to the bridge deck.

"Jesus H," Arthur said. "That'd be barnacles on the prop."

Simms took the wheel and called down to Maitland to kill the engine. Arthur then went back to the stern where he stripped down to his boxers, dropped a ladder over the side, and climbed down into the salty swell. It was cold. But it also didn't take long in the water to confirm what he'd been pretty sure was going on: white barnacle shells crusted all over the prop blades. And he cursed himself colourfully there in the water for not checking this earlier. *Sombitch cocksucker fucking bastard shit.*

Then Arthur climbed up and dried off, then returned to the bridge to deliver the bad news. They were going to have to cut speed so they didn't shake the rivets out. And that meant Manila South Port at 2100 hours if everything else went right.

"Arriving at night, in the dark," Arthur said to Maitland and Simms when they'd gathered for the news.

Simms shrugged. They'd brought Arthur in for his ship-handling savvy. Maitland was just the stoker, Simms himself merely the dealmaker.

"Your Frenchman is going to be on the jetty waiting for us when we're in," Arthur said. "Duffel bag with cash, as discussed. That's all I need to hear."

Again with the face, the hands spread wide. *Easy, Artie. It'll happen. It'll all play.*

But Arthur knew this was going to be trickier business than Simms was making out because he'd already found ampules in the mess garbage, a hypodermic set in a plastic case. In Tokyo they sold as *Hiropon, Zedrin.* So of course Simms was going to turn out to be a meth addict in addition to drinking bakudan.

The things you don't know about people.

"Simms," Arthur said, figuring if he was skipper, he'd better start telling this jackass what to do. "Run on down to the galley and get me a couple of pickled eggs and a mug of joe. Black. Then let's get this tub moving."

Stephanie, who was back from London, put a finger to her lips as I closed the apartment door quietly behind me. I pulled her into a hug. Over her shoulder I could see my father's head lolled back on our couch, faced to the window, the blue light, the mercury glow, the machinery of the port. He liked the port, he told me. He liked that Stephanie and I had settled in a place with a view of the gantry cranes and the water. Those were good things, my father thought. He didn't seem to remember that he'd fallen down the stairs behind him. He never mentioned it.

"You guys were up late," I whispered, pouring myself a glass of wine from the bottle. Stephanie was drinking Rieslings those days. I spun the bottle and saw it was Alsatian.

"He was telling stories," she said. "Philippines. Subic Bay, some boat he bought and sold. Did you know he hung out with a guy who shot meth between his toes?"

"Add that to things I did not know," I told her. "How was Rue Véron?"

"Fantastic. Foie with pears, duck confit. I had duck salad. The place was packed."

I'd hoped he might come try Orinoco, where I'd been spending all my time since opening the month before. I had hoped that might be the reason for the visit, to come see my new thing. Come eat pintxos and ceviche. But apparently not.

"How's he been doing?" I asked Simone, who called me before my father's visit.

"He's coming up on the anniversary," she said. "Mom's death."

"Right," I said. "Ten years. Jesus."

"So he might talk," Simone said.

"About Mom?"

"About life. I don't know. He's started talking about his travels. He's remembering things that happened, people he met along the way. Also, other things about what happened to Mom during the war."

About Mom? This was new. Nobody had ever really talked about Mom's history. And in Anglo–West Vancouver in the 1970s, if you were a Holocaust survivor, you just kept it to yourself.

Simone didn't linger on that point either. The point was she didn't quite know what to make of the things our dad had been telling her and perhaps she even felt awkward hearing them.

"I'm good at explaining the medical stuff," she said to me. "Details about aphasia or CVAs."

"What's a CVA?"

"Cerebrovascular accident. Sorry. My point being I'm out of my depth on personal stories. Weren't you the one always more in tune with that stuff?"

"Maybe," I said. "I don't know. Anyway, thank you, sister."

And so my father came out to Vancouver, not much curious about Orinoco, the project that his own travels had inspired. Interested only in going again to Rue Véron.

"The place from Paris," he said, smiling. "Take me there."

"Orinoco has empanadas," I said. "Arroz con pollos. You remember the Orinoco?"

"Oh yeah," he said. "I had a cheetah near there once."

"An ocelot, I think," I said.

"Yeah, that's right. Little fellow. These farmers had it," he said.

"You rescued it," I reminded him. "The farmers were going to kill it."

"Oh, I don't know what they were going to do, Teo. That was years ago."

Stephanie was standing behind my dad. She put her hands on his shoulders, just rested them there. And he reached up with one of his own, fingers calloused and stiffly bent, arm across his chest to rest his right hand on her left. I was seeing that wild animal in some strange synaptic flash, bound up in wire by the two men. Did my father have a handy ocelot cage in the back of his truck? I'll never know. On a dusty road, he unpacked his roll of bills and snapped free the elastic band. The farmers thought he was nuts, but off he went. *Yanqui loco.*

"Loco in the Orinoco," I said. And he grinned like a kid. But Stephanie shook her head. He wanted to eat at Rue Véron. So Rue Véron was where they were going.

That night on my return from work, while my father was sleeping, Stephanie and I sat near the window at the end of the room, city stretching out. We could hear him snore, little purrs in and out.

"So?" I asked her. "Did Kiyomi treat you right?"

"Kiyomi was great," Stephanie said. "Frankie came out to visit."

"Oh, did he?" I said, sipping the wine, looking across at my sleeping father. "So Kiyomi lets her sous out of the kitchen?"

"Not sure he asked her," Stephanie said. "I guess because it was me."

"Right, of course. His one true love."

Stephanie shook her head. *No.*

"Does he look like he's settling in?"

"I'd say so," Stephanie said. "With the beard now? Looks like white Jesus."

"White Jesus on a rocket bike," I said. "And the tattoos."

"He didn't show us his tattoos," Stephanie said. "What'd we miss?"

"A skull smoking a cigar," I told her, pointing just over my heart. "Right here."

Stephanie stifled a laugh.

I shook my head. Of course, I knew this had to be inspired by Gauthier, that scorching afternoon in Paris, tempers flaring. Only it perplexed me, this whole idea of Frankie being inspired by the man who so devoutly wanted him dead. So I didn't raise it.

"And sober," Stephanie said.

"Twelve stepping," I said. "A changed man. Has he apologized to you yet?"

It hadn't taken long for Frankie to get to this part with me. And while I understand that the process is important for the recovering alcoholic — what did Frankie say: *relieving the mind, loosening the chains of regret* — I'm not sure the same amount of thought went into how the receiving party might feel.

"Frankie, you don't have to do this, honest."

We'd gone to the Marine Club directly from the airport. I thought that would be the proper start, one hour into friendship Phase Two. I'd suggested a drink and he'd grinned mischievously.

And then we got there and up those stairs to the doorbell at the top next to the famous porthole. Frankie was loving everything he saw. He loved the framed pictures of ships and dockyard cranes. He especially loved the jar of pickled eggs on the bar that appeared to have been there since the Second World War.

"Give me one of *those*," he said. At which point admiring heads turned while he ate not one but two, which the bartender, Stash, then insisted were surely on the house.

"And the guy playing the organ!" Frankie said, as the Hammond B3 started in.

"His name?" I said to Frankie. "Is Frank."

"Send that man a drink!" Frankie said to Stash, who then poured off a G&T in what was a practised set of motions, since people in the bar bought Frankie rounds at a rate of about twice an hour.

Hey, congrats on the new place. Someone calling over. I turned and nodded thanks. Frankie took my arm and squeezed it. "Look at you," he said, because he remembered Pigalle too. And he no doubt remembered how he had once been squiring me around, the man of the hour.

"And for you?" I said. "Drinks on me."

Cranberry and soda. And that's where Frankie Phase Two really began: With the juice. With the explanation. With the quick move from the bar to the pool room in the back where Frankie took the chance to do a little further work on his Step Nine: *Be Willing to Make Amends.*

"Seriously, man," I told him. "You owe me nothing."

But Frankie wasn't settling outstanding accounts between us. He was clearing his personal air for what I assume were his own personal reasons. And against that metric, which alcoholics are apparently not expected to explain to anyone, it was crucial to Frankie that I appreciate just how sorry he was — very sorry, wished he could go back and do it again, but couldn't of course, because nobody can — very, very sorry that he'd lied to me about Stephanie. A lie of omission, Frankie said. The excised detail being that when he and Stephanie had arrived together in Paris freshly minted out of the CIA, they'd been engaged.

I guess he might have just been flat messing with me. Certainly, that night with Stephanie — standing next to her at the window, whispering because my father was asleep right there on our sofa, head back, softly snoring — I had no reason to believe that Frankie would lie about it. And had Stephanie really lied herself? She'd say, way back then: *Together but not together.*

Roommates, she'd said. He'd wanted her to stay. But she didn't.

Maybe this was a lie only in the same way that Frankie appeared to think he'd lied to me. In any case, I couldn't resent an omission to which I had myself contributed by never asking anything further. If anything, I loved her more. And that moment, that night, something new bloomed in me. Here's another thing the alcoholic is apparently not coached to consider: These epiphenomena that spin outward after confession, supplication, absolution.

I forgave Frankie. I forgave him entirely for whatever it was he thought he'd done wrong. And a month later, there were Stephanie and I, looking out over the harbour, my father asleep behind us.

"Stephanie," I whispered there in the blue darkness. And I remember putting my hand in your hair. "Marry me. I'm asking. Please. Will you marry me?"

———

We made our way in descending darkness. There was a flashlight in a kitchen drawer I dug out and used to light our way. Outside the blue glass, the city stretched, my father asleep as if on a stage, that high window, those stretching waters, all that winked and stirred and streamed across the surface of the city and the black water beyond. I helped him lie down on the couch bed. I'm not sure he ever really woke up. It seemed he might still be dreaming.

"Dark water," he said. "Teo?"

"I'm here, Dad. Let me help you lie down."

She said yes. She said yes. I wanted to tell him then but it would have to wait until the morning. He'd be so pleased. He loved you like his own daughter, Stephanie. He'd always say how smart you were after you'd spoken on the phone. *You found a smart one there, just like I did back then.*

"Was Mom smart?" I'd ask, playful. "She married you."

"Go on, you. She could have been a doctor. That's where Simone got the idea."

Sleep, Dad. Just lie down here. I'll get another blanket.

Creeping our way upstairs and into the loft. That one small light to make our way.

"He told me about bringing that minesweeper into Manila," you whispered that night. "Said it was pretty scary. He said they might have been killed."

We laid in the silver light after making love. You laid with your head in the crook of my elbow, tracing a finger across my chest. I knew this part of the story, or I thought I did. *Wreckage in the bay*, he'd said. So I saw him there, belly on the deck, bobbing in Manila Bay just off South Port. And I thought I could feel the ghosts of a hundred ships lying in the flickering deep below him, superstructures rising like blades in the water, ready to gut you open, drag you down. The piercing tip of a radio tower. The torn sheet of a funnel. A radar array. Cranes and crow's nests.

Arthur with his own small flickering torch he'd found in the tiller flats. The thing was the size of his thumb, not too helpful. But it was all they had. Arthur on that cold decking, watching those rising spars and spans in the dusty deep. Signalling back to Simms at the wheel, praying the man wasn't meth'd up at that very moment.

Starboard. Starboard. Steady on. Steady. Port now. Port!

We are all praying to make it, I figured. All of us at our various moments. Calling out directions, beaming down the light, bobbing there in darkness just off the black pier, the rumble.

Water St

A changed man. When I said that to Stephanie the night I proposed marriage, I'm not sure I even believed it. I'd known Frankie for five years in Paris. All that Pigalle and Belleville action. All those exuberant plates and nights and *demi en pression*. All that brandy. The cocaine and the racing bikes. Macaron girls and cases of blanc de nuit. I'd never previously and never since met anyone as regular in their commitment to adrenalin and vice as Frankie was. He ran on a very distinct current, Frankie did, all the levers pushed forward at once, then pulled back for the precision and focus of his Le Dauphin service, then all pushed immediately forward again, all the needles into all the red zones and all the red lights flashing their overload warnings at once again.

I have no idea what he was like in Trois-Pistoles when he first returned to North America. I only knew that he'd apparently quit drinking there. And I found myself wondering if there had been some kind of a mishap. Maybe another angry uncle. Something about his eagerness to leave Quebec — just as he had once been very keen to get out of Paris — left me thinking he might have been motivated by a dispute or a threat.

I never asked him about it. Every time it came to mind, I'd have a reason to leave the question aside. There were lots of reasons a person might want to leave a small town. I knew that much myself. Besides, events in Vancouver were already speeding up again. We had enough to think about. And Frankie in Vancouver was himself changing before my eyes, vaulting upward, seeming to put whatever trouble he'd had very far behind him. This much I couldn't have predicted: That the inversion of our Paris relationship — Frankie needing a job and me being the connected local willing to provide it — would itself be so quickly reversed and returned to what seemed much like the Paris original.

Frankie landed in Vancouver and proceeded to conquer every challenge the city famously puts to newcomers. Inside a month he'd found a spectacular rental, a house in Mount Pleasant with a big porch looking down the slope to False Creek. He'd grooved in at Rue Véron so fast that Kiyomi talked about him now like he'd always been there. And he was such a born networker that I swear he knew every person in the Vancouver food scene by name by the end of the second month. Suddenly, being out at night with him was like we'd never left Paris. That would be Frankie with his cranberry and soda and his arm draped around my shoulder, pulling me across the Marine Club to meet cooks he knew. I remember when he introduced me to Jules and Jeremy, the chefs who'd once worked in the very location where Rue Véron was now located.

"Legends, these two," Frankie said. "Just don't ask them for any *secrets*. Major NDA."

"So where are you now?" I asked them.

"The Food Caboose!" Frankie said, like I should know. "Hush-hush place out back of the Sun Yat-Sen Chinese Garden."

Jeremy shrugged and looked at Jules, who smiled at him like they were used to people doing the talking for them. And no need to say much anyway because Frankie was off again talking about the fabulous meal he'd had at the Caboose, establishing that he was now a regular at an underground place I'd only heard whispered about and which people said had a waitlist longer than Rue Véron's.

Jeremy and Jules listened to all this patiently, not much reaction beyond what was polite. I caught one glance. From Jeremy. A quick crack of the eyes, up and away, a flattened smile that suggested there was more to be said, just not at that moment. And then they melted back into the crowd, Jules's hand trailing a finger that Jeremy touched with his own as they navigated their way to the portholed door.

I might have thought more about that, about how little they said, their quiet remove, the quick glance. *Legend*, Frankie said. I believed it. Only I failed to note properly at the time that these particular legends didn't hang out at the Marine Club, or not anymore. I didn't see the obvious, that Frankie had asked them to come, not to meet me, but that I might meet them, and that he might be the one to make the introduction.

What I saw at the time was only how Frankie now stood in that room, how the crowds parted for him as he pushed his way back from the bar to the pool room, his cranberry and soda hoisted aloft. How it had taken such a short time to get things back into that Paris arrangement. Which is roughly what I was thinking that night when we finally found a spot at a table against the wall. And Frankie leaned in to speak over the noise. And here, all at once, Frankie was asking me, six months in, *Did I have any problem with him dating Kiyomi?*

"I'm asking because I also know that you have this thing about two people in the same restaurant."

This thing. What I'd actually told Frankie on arrival was that I didn't want him dating any of our servers. In fact, *we* didn't want that, as in Magic Wolf. Those organized young foodies

Magnus had hired were moving this whole business forward in time. No more dining room date farms. We had policies now. Servers were usually young. And even if they weren't, a guy like Frankie was going to come off as some kind of superstar. I mean Bib Gourmand. Which gave rise to influence, which gave rise to choices made differently than they might have been otherwise. Which gave rise to regrets, people getting hurt. Which gave rise to no, just no.

Frankie didn't argue with me, though I could see the bemusement in his eyes. "Yes, Chef," Frankie said. "Kiyomi told me her little unhappiness from Chez Panisse. These things are very regrettable. No servers."

Six months later he's asking me if it's okay for him to date his boss. And he kind of had me there. Loophole.

I called her up and suggested a drink. And when she came through the portholed door that night, I saw she'd smartly left Frankie behind. So in she came and over to the bar, where I put the question to her directly: Frankie. Dating. Why was he asking me and not Kiyomi herself?

To which she replied, "He asked you? Seriously?"

So that started and within a year they were living together.

"Whoa," Stephanie said. "But that's all good I guess, right?"

"Of course."

"What?" Stephanie said, teasing, but just. "You've always said Kiyomi is *great*."

Yes. Yes of course she was more than great, though Kiyomi was also then pregnant in about three months and the mother of a beautiful baby girl in another nine, leaving us without an executive chef at Rue Véron. Of course, I supported her in all this. Lucy was the girl's name.

Stephanie was back from the second book tour. She'd shipped container loads of the follow-up book, *Beyond Femke*. She was appearing on book television and flying off to speaking engagements in the U.S., Denmark, back to France. We'd been trying against a wall chart of her periods to get pregnant ourselves. I remember the doctor's appointment on Burrard Street just across from the hospital.

"You are ready to *bear*," the doc said to Stephanie, a slim, braceleted hand on her forearm. Benny was his name. Not doctor something, just Benny. So Benny declared Stephanie ready to pop with babies. Then he turned to me and started in on immotile sperm. There were laminated sheets that he brought out with pictures of those little proto-tadpoles swimming away. If a man was fertile — equivalently to, say, Stephanie herself — well, then their sperm swam like dolphins up the fallopian tubes. The immotile sperm on Benny's diagram were like exhausted salmon, gasping in the shallows.

"Dude," I said to Frankie, the first time I met Lucy and he insisted I hold her. "I've known all along this was coming and still I'm in shock."

"Me too!" he said. "But Teo, my man. You and Stephanie. You have to go for it. We could all have children together."

Magic Wolf HR was progressive. We had a dental plan. Women or men could take maternity leave. But Kiyomi and Frankie decided she'd be the one to stay home. I didn't really think any of the others were ready to take her place. Or maybe they were ready and I simply didn't want to upset the Rue Véron rhythms: Linnie, Bell, and Gracine being so grooved-in. So we hired outside: Charlie, a trans guy, a superb cook with fast hands and unfailing palate who had himself survived five years cooking at Brasserie Place Bellecourt in Lyon. Charlie was through Vancouver heading to Whistler to ski and saw the advertisement. We'd received maybe half a dozen reasonable CVs. Then Charlie came in. Frankie and

I asked him a few questions and we didn't even look at each other to compare notes. We sent him into the kitchen to make lunch, to watch him bang off plates from our own menu with what was prepped on hand. Dried duck breast salad with mustard greens and sherry vinaigrette. Our bison tartare plate. Charlie even whipped up meringue, which he drizzled with coffee sauce and topped with peaks of maple minted whipped cream.

"I take it you've been scouting us," Frankie said.

"Like I could afford it," Charlie said.

"You're hired," Frankie said. And again, he didn't even have to look at me. He knew what I'd be thinking having sampled those same plates.

So it was that Charlie slid in at sous. And inside three years of his arrival in Vancouver, Frankie took over exec from Kiyomi and had his own kitchen again. He had regained that and quite a lot more, I had to occasionally reflect. He had a beautiful partner, his adorable daughter, Lucy, toddling around. And I could admire the crowd forming around him at the Marine Club, or stand half-stunned at these big Sunday family gatherings we were having up at Belmont Farm and watch Lucy and Magnus's kids, and those brought by others in the Magic Wolf world, playing tag and hitting shuttlecocks, kicking balls and shooting slingshots into the trees, then all lining up in a disorderly queue snaking back through the grass as cooks from Orinoco laid out Brazilian roast suckling pig and picanha steaks on skewers, platters of ceviche, and jugs of adult and kid versions of sweet sangria.

Standing there with my arm around Stephanie. Standing off to one side, squinting slightly in the rising breeze.

Maybe the wobble at Orinoco should have been my caution flag. I think, in retrospect, that we moved past it almost too quickly for anything like a lesson to sink in. Of course, it's also important to remember that the whole thing was entirely my fault and I knew it. So I was happy moving past this episode as quickly as possible.

The fact was that Orinoco was playing catch-up to Rue Véron by that point, which had surprised Magnus and me both. Rue Véron was purposefully old school. Orinoco was the more modern room and we'd had really strong first-month results. But after Frankie's arrival — and I have to acknowledge, especially after he took over as exec — Rue Véron hit a new and unexpected level. Frankie had his game back, no denying it. He and Charlie were what Frankie and I had been in Paris, though honestly more. The room didn't get bigger, so the crowds appeared the same as before. But now they were using an online booking service and people were reserving dates out as far as four, even five months.

Frankie and Charlie's menu changes were the main part of this whole shift, which took us some distance from Paris back toward Canada and Trois-Pistoles. They were stuffing and deep frying pigs' feet, simmering hocks in maple syrup and Pepsi. Charlie had developed a line of individual pot pies — chicken, wild mushroom, salmon — all wrapped in one of the most delicate pastries I'd ever tasted. We were selling those in a white tablecloth dining room as well as the freezer section of gourmet food stores. I understood how financially successful this was proving to be. Magnus was happy to share the results. What I have to admit now is that I doubted the whole project would last. Frankie's homey nod to rural Quebec reminded me of those long-ago meals in Belleville. But that connection only made me think of the idea as small, perhaps better suited to a home kitchen, surrounded by drunken friends. Magic Wolf was on a different level than that, I felt. And for the first time in my relationship with Frankie, I felt as if I had the more senior perspective, seeing the longer view, the more serious and global reputation we were trying to build.

I simply could not have been more wrong. Maybe I was the more serious chef by that point. The world apparently did not care. The world chose Frankie. And it did so by a status mechanism that exploded Frankie past local and national critics and colleagues and onto the most global food stage imaginable.

The Veuve Clicquot/BMW Best 100 Restaurants in the World had never honoured a Canadian restaurant in its history. This was the place where you found El Bulli, The Fat Duck, The French Laundry, Chez Panisse, Noma, and all the others. In only the second year that they worked together, Frankie and Charlie were chosen by the votes of over a thousand chefs and food writers and critics and placed into that celestial food firmament. And they didn't squeak in either. Rue Véron entered the Veuve at number twenty-five, nestled in there neatly between the legendary Troisgros and Alinea in Chicago.

I'm not sure Magnus knew about the Veuve. Certainly, he didn't know the list had come out when I called him that morning. But he was going to know everything soon enough. Because in an instant, Frankie was everywhere in the press. Executive chefs tend to suck the air out of a room, I knew that. Charlie was done disservice in this, I knew that too. But I said nothing to Magnus at the time because what the hell was there to say? White Jesus was getting the coverage: *Saveur* and *Bon Appetit*, *Eater*, *Food and Travel*, *Gourmet*, *GQ*, then *Esquire*, the *Robb Report*, and everybody in the world who talked about high-end food after that, which was, by that moment in history, a staggeringly large community. Frankie thrived under this adoring scrutiny. He had an unrivalled camera face, we were all learning. He projected deep seriousness, as though possessed of some profound cultural truth. And yet he somehow remained the same *bon vivant* he'd always been. Maybe it was the beard. Or the tattoos. Frankie had become one of the new high priests of a freshly energized food world, admired abroad, revered at home.

Magnus, I know for one, went from not paying much attention to Frankie as sous to absolutely adoring him as exec. "Do you have any idea what this means?" he asked me during that period, as if I hadn't introduced him to the Veuve only a few weeks prior. "Frankie has levelled us up. That's permanent. That's for the duration. And he's taking Rue Véron with him. Magic Wolf too."

At the time I was just as excited about this as Magnus. I did own a share of the company, after all. But maybe I was even more invested than my old childhood friend. I'd come up with Frankie. He was my cohort, or so I saw it. In my private reflections, even then, I was pretty sure I was as good or better a cook than Frankie. But I chose to let the fact of his coronation cast a regal halo over me as well. Frankie heading into the stratosphere promised to draw all of us into orbit. And I was going to go happily along for the ride.

If there was a downside here, it was simply that his success increased the pressure Magnus was already applying to Orinoco. Frankie had levelled us up, fine. Rue Véron was leading the way, great. But Orinoco was fading by comparison. The best minds in Magic Wolf marketing were talking about juicing the brand, getting us into similar and sympathetic play. And to them — to me, let's be honest, I did not fight this effort at all — that meant trying to push Orinoco international, somehow.

That's where the idea for me to start travelling emerged. I was going to hit the Latin road, just like my father had those years before: Quito, Santiago, Lima, Miami, Havana, Puebla, Oaxaca. This was all getting pretty far afield from anything that resembled my father's own travels. But I took it on in that spirit of adventure and discovery that I imagined were central to my father's travelling years, and that we'd grafted into the very core of the Orinoco brand. I didn't even get to Venezuela during this time. Magnus had people look into insurance for me and we began to realize the political instability of the region, so he called it off entirely.

"Sure, I'd like a good empanada recipe from a family living in El Tigre," he told me. "But we can't have you getting kidnapped. I mean, we'd probably pay the ransom. But we'd feel bad."

So I took trips in and out of these other places. We used local tour guides to set us up with local families. We'd always make some kind of community donation. Then I'd go in and sit with the *avos* and *abuelitas* with my Moleskine notebook at the ready. And home I'd come with my recipes and preparation notes for Ecuadorian Aji Costeno, clam ceviche with canguil spicy popcorn, arroz a la cazuela, sea bass with yuzu, and pork and lamb shoulders slathered in huacatay paste and wrapped in banana leaves. Moles, adobos, pipianes. Poblano, apple, and pasilla, and a simple pumpkin seed pipian verde that I brought home with me from a visit to a family in the highlands of Veracruz.

Latin American Casalinga. That was how all this was distilled by marketing. And that's exactly how I was told to put the information out in interviews. Which is how I ended up getting quoted — in the *Flat Fish* blog, not huge at that time, but by far enough readers to get the first rocks of the avalanche to tumble — saying the following most idiotic thing: "Well, as Paul Bocuse himself once said, we learn it all first from our mothers. So I've been travelling, meeting other people's mothers. At Orinoco, we steal from the best."

I have a lot of questions about what the hell was going on with me when I said that. Was I tired from travelling too much, from being pampered in nice hotels? Magnus was flying me business. I had a company Amex Platinum card for expenses. And it might have been those things. But as I look back, what I see quietly dominating the picture is the fact that Orinoco was being asked to play catch-up to Rue Véron in the first place. Quietly and without ever articulating this, never to Stephanie, perhaps not even internally, I saw myself once again being pushed to join Frankie on some higher plane.

Meanwhile, Stephanie and I were coordinating phone calls between time zones. Australian Central to Mountain. Eastern to Greenwich Mean. Pacific to Central European. I could have asked any number of questions about that alone. How does this work? For how long does this work?

But I think I know now what the real question should have been as soon as I read that article. I should have simply asked: How is it that I could not stop talking before working my way all the way down through travelling and meeting grandmothers and learning recipes to where I got to the word *steal*?

Did I perhaps believe on some deep and unspoken level that, for people who had reached the heights we had, theft was no longer really a crime?

Ultimately, Magnus sent me to Japan. That was actually the end result of the situation that started developing almost immediately after the fated interview. It certainly wasn't my pitch for a new restaurant that did it. In fact, when I tabled my idea for restaurant number three, a Japanese izakaya beer hall concept called Oishii, it generated resistance from everyone. I thought it was a perfect move myself. It hit all the right marks in my mind. My father had been in Japan postwar so it continued the storyline of the other two concepts. Plus, now I felt I could draw on some of my own memories. There were all those family meals when I was a kid out in Japantown. And it was my dad who inspired the restaurant name, although he wouldn't have known it at the time. Out eating at Kamei Sushi or somewhere similar, my father ordering in fluent Japanese. Prawn tempura. *Toro.*

And then with the first bite of sashimi I ever remember taking, that word: "Oishii!" my dad said — *delicious* — my mother laughing, looking so pretty. And then the bite itself: the melting cold, the saline note, the entire living sea.

So I pitched that. And I framed out the concept for them as compellingly as I could. Vancouver had sushi already. We'd been eating it here since I was a kid. What we needed was Japanese fare that went down in more of a bar setting. Good beer, loud music, communal seating. Oyakodon, unagi on rice, steaming bowls of gyūdon as my father had once described eating for breakfast at a stall outside the Tsukiji market.

Everyone in the meeting that day waited for Magnus to react first. And he did with a look that I basically recognized. He got the gist of it. Only something was holding him back, which of course meant the marketing people jumped in with all their objections.

"Oishii sounds like squishy," one of them said.

"Oishii means delicious," I explained, which of course I had explained already.

"But that's Japanese," the marketing person said.

"Well, yeah," I said. "This is a Japanese concept."

"But most people don't *speak* Japanese," the marketing person said, like *checkmate.*

There were other objections. But Magnus cut off the conversation after only a few minutes and the room fell silent. Maybe, Magnus said — and here he had his fingers pressed to his temples like he'd just gotten a headache — this just wasn't the time to start a whole new concept based on a whole new cuisine. Maybe we should focus on getting through the next month or so without further damage.

"Maybe we should stabilize the ship," Magnus said.

I didn't like being reminded of my misstep in front of a bunch of kids in golf shirts being paid twice as much as me. But I could take the point. We were, after all, in the middle of learning something very difficult at Magic Wolf. We were learning the strange dynamic that covers both media shitstorms and the two ways in which a Hemingway character once described going bankrupt.

Gradually, then suddenly.

During the gradual part, the whole business of me characterizing our project as *theft* just didn't seem to travel far. We had protestors. There were people standing in the street outside the restaurant with signs. But they came and they went, never quite gelling into anything like a crowd. Online, meanwhile, the Magic Wolf PR people were picking up chatter, which then spread to local papers. But even that seemed to stay essentially contained.

How would you feel if someone rifled through your mom's recipe box and set up a business with the ideas? asked one Orinoco reviewer on Yelp. There were replies and some other posts about this. Our star rating dropped below four. But the reservation book did not seem overly affected.

The blog *Flat Fish*, who'd run the original interview, followed up with an editorial at this point that sharpened the point of criticism a degree: *White people travelling in places they think are exotic, poaching ideas, packaging them …*

And a week later a community newspaper ran a long editorial under the headline: *Colonialist Businesses Generate Racist Profits.*

That one resonated inside Orinoco, where the shift in the conversation to racism generated notable anxiety. I had my exec, Dario, and his sous, Pedrina, into the back office to talk with me about it. And yes, they were both scouted because they'd come from the right places: Belize City and Durango, respectively. I'd been the one to lobby hard for that sort of hiring precisely because I wanted people who'd cooked moles before, who'd eaten empanadas and ceviches. In the case of Dario and Pedrina specifically, I wanted a married couple who'd cooked at Bomba de Sabor, the legendary Oaxacan restaurant in East Los Angeles. And if people like that were willing to move north of the border for Magic Wolf,

I was going to be the person who championed them. It was the right thing to do and they were a huge score for us.

"Did we have permissions?" Dario asked, brow furrowed, stressed. "From those who shared their lives and family foods with us?"

Written and signed, I explained. "We also made monetary donations in every community we visited. Plus, we credited individual women on the menu. Rosa's scallops with hazelnut mole. The alioli de piquillo. Who was that?"

"Brigitte," Pedrina said.

"Quito," I said, remembering. "Brigitte Molina."

"But we're only using their first names," Dario pointed out. "Could be anyone."

"So we change that. We add last names. Maybe an online map with the recipe site of origin."

"Only then maybe a thousand Zagat tourists show up at the Molina house," Pedrina said.

"Okay not that," I said. "What about contributor photos? We send photographers to get beautiful photos of each of the women."

Neither of them were convinced. And I thought I understood why. I'd gone travelling in a way that was out of reach to any of my chefs, my cooks, or my front-of-house people. I'd taken Magnus's money and secured ideas that were local and specific and that a lot of people who worked at Orinoco connected to personally, having eaten the same dishes in childhood. People who worked for me *knew* the women who inspired these dishes. They knew the people whose ideas we were using to sell a culinary experience that none of the *avos* and *abuelitas* could possibly sell in the same way, not Rosalito Perez or Monica Reyes or Mariana Cabrera or any of them, whether they were listed on the menu or not. So it really was an exploit, by very definition: *to make full use of or derive full benefit from.* But I was the one who'd done the exploiting. And in using the ideas, in using the services of the very people I'd hired,

Orinoco could be seen as a kind of *hack*. Trespass in a good light, theft in any other, just as I had myself said.

So we weren't at the end of this thing. If Dario and Pedrina weren't certain, then the entire restaurant — that family of people working there, the entire experience we were trying to bring to people — none of that was certain either. But my slow awakening didn't serve any mitigating function, as it turned out. I was arguably past exerting any control at all even before this one:

Congratulations, Chef Matthew Wolf, whose father made his money skull-fucking Venezuelan poor people while being protected by dictator Pérez Jiménez.

That's when *gradually* tipped over and headed toward *suddenly*. I can still induce an anxiety attack just by thinking of the first moment I read these words. It was in a Facebook post to the Orinoco page run by Magic Wolf Media. I wasn't online much myself, but Stephanie saw it and phoned me, mid-afternoon, which was strange.

"Teo?" she said, in a voice I just knew. Something was not right.

My exec, Dario, opened the computer in his office, then closed the door behind us and showed me the page. "It's not good," he said.

And he was right. I felt skewered through, impaled by something that came from the future and was heading right through me to upend the whole past. Anonymous, of course. And the Magic Wolf Media people deleted it right away. But that only made things worse. We were silencing debate at that point, which couldn't be silenced anyway since the original post had long since been screenshot and reposted to Reddit and 4Chan.

We were in the full flow of things now. We were in the white water.

I could comment on the memes here. But maybe it's enough to say that you should avoid having your name come up repeatedly online right next to the word *skull-fucking* if you don't want to see certain kinds of really gothic, really horrifying images. But those images came, they flourished, and they spread. And I suppose it was a kind of discourse that grew around them, too, that flooded the bulletin boards and the social sites, that spilled out physically into the streets around Orinoco. Five people with protest signs one day. Then twelve. Then a spot on the local evening news claiming the number had risen to thirty.

Stealing Culture = Spreading Racism

Be the Solution: Don't Go In.

Magic Wolf Media was maintaining a presence on just about every platform out there at that time: Twitter, Flickr, Tumblr, Instagram, Foursquare. All the Orinoco stuff started getting tagged up with comments and questions. The whole thing was virulently contagious. In the end it took only a couple of weeks to complete the transition from *gradually* to *suddenly*. And that moment of completion was marked by our first call from BuzzFeed. We didn't give the interview. They ran the article anyway under the headline: *Who's Afraid of the Big Bad Wolf?*

"So listen," I said to the gathered group over a special Orinoco family meal. I'd made the morcilla toast and the empanadas myself. Pedrina and Dario were laying out the rest, a big pot of feijooda, platters of cured meats, smoky chorizo, jamón ibérico.

Everybody was freaked out. I could see it in their faces. And before I could even speak, a voice came from the back. "So who was your father?"

"He's still alive," I said.

"Who was he, though?" The question again, friendly, open, not a challenge exactly.

"He was a traveller," I said. "A nomad."

"He worked for an oil company," someone said.

"He was an engineer," I explained. "He was an electrical engineer."

And I tried for more. I tried for a version of the whole story in just a few minutes. The long journey through Asia. Through Europe. The turn south at Toronto. Then Central America. Then South America. To Ecuador, to Venezuela, to the Orinoco, to San Tomé. A journey on which a marriage and a family were made. My family. And we were of those places, too, even if my parents had started their journeys thousands and thousands of miles away from one another and from where they landed.

I saw empathy in some faces, confusion in others. Anger too. And I reflected on what it meant that these people I'd hired had to walk through a crowd of picketers to get to work that day, to get to this family meal, to get to me standing there at the front of the room trying to explain things.

Feed the Hungry. Eat the Rich.

Magnus called me over for a follow-up meeting. He did this with a terse phone message, leaving the impression that me being fired was not entirely off the table. I didn't call Stephanie. I sat with my head in my hands for a few minutes. I felt useless anger surging. Then I called a cab to head over into West Point Grey.

"You know what grips my shit?" Magnus started, as I walked in the door to his upstairs office. "It's the part where I have to admit that what they're saying is not entirely wrong."

"Well, they're wrong about my dad skull-fucking anyone," I said.

"I don't know," Magnus said. "Oil companies in the sixties weren't exactly UNICEF."

"Jesus, Mag," I said. This from a guy who'd idolized my father, called him sir.

But I'm not sure he even heard me. "And as for those Mexican ladies, no point denying we're making bank off their family recipes. That much is just true."

We were in his office on the top floor of his Trimble Park house, with those wide views of the sparkling glass city. Magnus's three-acre slice of Belmont Avenue — where ordinarily the palaces and chateaus and haciendas sprawled — was still a waving field of spelt and Kamut, tangled green hedges of prize-winning Lakota winter heirloom squash.

"Isn't that what you wanted to do?" I asked. "Make food, make bank?"

He was sifting through papers on his desk as we spoke. "I'm just saying that labelling a sauce to show it comes from Carlita Pizarro from Villavicencio … I mean, that's just more bank for us, not for Pizarro."

There was a knock at his office door just then. He cracked a glance at me. He asked, "You mind if Frankie sits in?"

In came Frankie, who gave me a slap on the shoulder as he moved through the room to the leather sectional couch, where he slid into a comfortable position, legs stretched out across the hardwood, heels of his Adidas kicks resting on a vintage Afghan war carpet.

"So here we are," Magnus said.

"I fucked up," I said. "Is that what you want me to say?"

"Well, you did say *steal*," Magnus continued. "Which I might have phrased differently myself."

"Teo, don't beat yourself up," Frankie said from the couch, looking entirely relaxed himself. "We have an idea."

There can't be many restaurant owners who could even contemplate what was then laid out for me. Of course, there aren't very many restaurant owners who have bought and sold airlines either. But what Magnus and Frankie had apparently devised was a royalty system. We had all their names and contact deets, these *avos* and *abuelitas* faithfully recorded in my Moleskine. We knew the granular detail of our menu unit sales. So we paid Rosalito Perez a micro-slice of profit every time her cachuchas fritas sold.

Same for the bright red pescado adobado with Monica Reyes's name next to it, or the pulpo Gallego Mariana Cabrera showed us, a recipe we could have gotten elsewhere, but not with her unbelievable crispy duck fat potato croquettes.

"Give her credit. But give her a royalty too," Frankie said. "Send them all an annual cheque."

Magnus was nodding, looking over at his superstar. "We're not talking thousands, right? Just something fair."

"Of course," Frankie said. "And the signs. The picketers."

"Right," Magnus took the tag. "Racism is a nasty allegation, Teo."

"I'd like a chance to address that," I said.

"So we skip that one," Magnus said.

"Sorry?" I said.

"It's impossible to respond to that allegation. So you just bleep right over it and move on to income inequality."

I didn't really remember hearing anything about income inequality.

"*Feed the Poor*," Frankie said. "*Eat the Rich*."

"That's what they're saying," Magnus explained. "They don't have as much money as they think we have. And that's upsetting to them."

"Okay," I said.

"So we feed the poor," Frankie said. "We respond directly to the criticism."

"Frankie is suggesting we actually feed the poor," Magnus repeated.

"Let me just see if I got this," I said. "Frankie is suggesting ..."

"Don't be like that," Magnus said. "We're trying to help you here, Teo."

I turned to Frankie.

We design a coupon program, Frankie explained. Every four-top full meal at the Orinoco generates a meal ticket we distribute in the neighbourhood. Those meal tickets would then be redeemable at an Orinoco food truck set up somewhere nearby. Tacos, empanadas, bowls of chili, whatever made sense.

Magnus was clicking his keyboard as we spoke, reading an email on some separate matter, no doubt.

"Do we also eat the rich?" I asked, but I don't think he heard me.

"And we get the message out there," Magnus said, wrapping up. "We communicate. We talk to the picketers. Give them coupons. Generate some positives."

"Well, that just sounds great," I said.

"You should be relieved," Franke said.

"Help me understand why I would be relieved," I said to him with a flare of irritation.

Magnus shook his head. He gestured at Frankie again.

"Because these are things we can deal with," Frankie said. "Some shit you just can't."

I looked over to Magnus for help. But Frankie was on his feet already, tapping his watch and looking at Magnus. *We good man? Gotta fly.*

And Magnus sprang to his feet to wrap an arm around Frankie's shoulder, guiding him toward the door, whispering something, patting his back as he left.

I was nodding, watching it all. Hard not to admire how Frankie had pulled that off in a five-minute meeting, solved Magnus's problem by keeping Rue Véron well out of the way. Sure, Frankie would never have messed up that *Flat Fish* interview the way I had. Still hard not to admire the moves.

Magnus returned from the door to his desk and sat heavily, letting out a whoosh of breath. Then he rocked back and seemed lost in thought. Finally: "That guy's going to be bigger than Jesus, I swear."

"What was he talking about? *Some shit you just can't.*"

"He's a sensitive guy. He reads things in the culture. I respect that."

"Magnus," I said. "What the fuck was he talking about?"

"Ass grabbing, that kind of thing," Magnus said. "People say you're stealing from poor people is one thing. People start saying your kitchens are all *rapey* and you're fucked. That would be Frankie's feelings anyway. So you hear the news about Le Creuset?"

I'd never heard anyone use the word *rapey* before. But then I hadn't heard whatever this news was about Le Creuset either, and that promised to be the happier line to pursue. This doesn't look great on me, I fully realize. But that was the sum of my reasoning. So I dropped it.

And here Magnus brought me up to speed on the news. Yes indeed. François Coté, new Le Creuset Global Brand Ambassador. It was a thing.

"You know the brand values of a flame-orange enameled cast iron cocotte?" Magnus asked me.

I spread my hands. "Durability?"

"Family, loyalty, excellence, and respect," Magnus said, holding up a finger in turn for each of them. "Frankie goes and gets some of that and brings it on home to Rue Véron. You simply cannot buy that shit. Now where were we?"

"I have no idea," I said. "I'm completely lost."

"The Orinoco message," Magnus said. "Tell Dario to promote those coupons to the picketers. And make sure to give them out. Generate some positives."

Then he leaned forward. And I thought: Here it comes. And for a moment, I feared the worst.

"Which is all a *cost*," Magnus said. "Even that token royalty is a cost. Those coupons, that food truck. That's a big cost. And all that cost off Orinoco's bottom line is profit lost to us, to you and me and Magic Wolf."

I listened to those words. I felt them hanging in the air.

"But here," Magnus said, and he leaned back in his chair now, the light of the dropping sun making a burnt orange halo around him. "Here is also where your big idea comes in. Oishii. We're doing it, Teo. I've decided. You're going to Japan. This is good news for you. Think of this as really good news."

Akasaka

My dad's second stroke was a hemorrhagic one, moderately severe. He was at his farm when it happened, alone. He ended up speed-dialing Simone, which was lucky. Her husband, Greg, answered and from the confusion he figured out pretty quickly what was going on.

"Dad," he said. "Dad, listen. I want you to sit tight."

"The name," my father was calling out. "What is the name?"

Greg called Simone, who was just leaving the hospital. She dialed the paramedics and then headed out to the farm and let herself in. Then Simone had to wind her way through a maze of boxes and stacked papers, mouse scat evident on the stairs, the kitchen a complete disaster again, all the way to the top floor calling out, "Dad, Dad! Where are you?"

Simone could see through the window that the ambulance had arrived on the gravel drive below. She heard them come into the front hall. "Dr. Wolf?" the paramedic called. "Dr. Wolf, are you here?"

Simone called them upstairs, which is where she finally found my dad in the master bedroom sitting on the bed he'd shared with my mother all those years.

"Dad, I'm here," Simone said, kneeling in front of him, taking his hands, feeling for his radial artery and visually timing the rise and fall of his chest.

"What's the name?" he asked her.

"What name, Dad? I'm Simone. Simone is my name."

"No!" he called out, feebly tugging on Simone's coat.

"Just take it easy, Dad. The guys here are going to help you."

"The name." And now there were tears in the corners of his eyes. "Remember for me."

Simone looked at our father, nearly crumpled there, his skin translucent and his eyes clouded, his fingernails uncut.

"Lilly," my sister told him. "You mean Lilly, Dad. Lilly is her name."

And my father's face went slack-jawed, his mouth open. He stared over at the men who'd entered the room, as if noticing them for the first time. Then his milky eyes drifted back to Simone where they finally rested.

"Lilly," he said.

And he lay back on the bed and curled into a ball, where he would have stayed had the paramedics not been there to help, to lift him onto the gurney, to wheel him out through all that strewn domestic garbage and chaos, down two flights of stairs and out into the Alberta clear, birds singing, the wind sifting the uncut berm grass. The dogs were long gone by that point. Simone was relieved that, on top of everything, they did not have to deal with our father's unruly outdoor dogs.

"Is he in pain now?" I asked.

"I don't think so," Simone said. "Not from the stroke."

"Talking?"

"Garbled," Simone said. "But listen, Teo …"

I waited. It was four in the afternoon for Simone, seven in the morning for me in Tokyo, standing at the north window of my room in the Capitol Tokyu, high over Akasaka. I could see the Meiji Shrine far below, hear the bells and the chanting there.

"I'm not seeing it likely that a lot of function returns here," she said. "So he's probably not going to be able to say a lot more."

"I'll come home," I said. "I'll call Stephanie and we'll meet there."

"Listen," Simone said.

"I can get a flight for this afternoon, be in Vancouver tomorrow, Edmonton in a couple of days. Stephanie can come in from London."

"Teo, I'm not saying come or don't come. But two days is probably the same as coming in two weeks or whenever you're back."

"Three weeks," I said.

"Same," Simone said. "He might slide a bit. But these things are often very gradual."

Gradually, then suddenly.

"Jonah?" I asked. "Have you called him?"

"We spoke, briefly. He's back in Tokyo."

So there we were, poised. Thousands of miles from where we'd last seen each other, but likely less than a few miles apart that moment. There was quite a lot that might not have happened if I hadn't done what I did next. But that was me, standing there at the glass, looking out over Akasaka, silver morning light. Me with my one final question.

"Do you have a phone number?" I asked Simone. "For Jonah?"

Kiyomi and I were doing a Japanese Culinary Intensive at the Tokyo Sushi Academy down on Shin-Ohashi Dori just outside the old Tsukiji Market location. When I got to that intersection on our first morning and saw the street name, I thought of the gyūdon that my father had described eating right around there. It might have been at a stall outside the building directly across the street. There was something of a temporal kaleidoscope spinning in my head just then, all those spiralling decades connecting then to now.

"What year?" Our *sensei* at the academy was Chef Yugi. His name, he informed the class, meant *heroic second son*.

"Nineteen forty-eight, thereabouts," I told him.

He nodded and raised his eyebrows. "Still pretty hard time in Tokyo then," he said. "Maybe not gyūdon. Maybe more like motsuni don."

Motsuni translated roughly as "making the ends work," which was itself a euphemism for using the nasty bits, guts, offal. Or, in the case of this particular gyūdon substitute, sliced intestines instead of other cuts of beef.

"You scrub the intestines with salt," Yugi told us. "They still make it at Kitsuneya over there in the old market. I'll take you later if you want."

I think he found me and Kiyomi amusing. Most of the others attending were catering types and private cooks trying to add something to the playlist. There were a couple of tattooed Australian guys who cooked contract on private yachts, roving all over the world. Two young women from Argentina who did Japanese-themed weddings. The rest were locals either getting ready for their very first jobs or taking cooking classes for fun. There were no other people brushing up on technique and developing menu ideas in advance of opening an entirely new restaurant. And when that word leaked, it led Chef Yugi upstream to Magic Wolf, which led him to Rue Véron.

"Veuve Clicquot number fifteen," he said, shaking his head in amazement at the ranking we'd by then reached. "François Coté. You know him?"

"My kid's dad," Kiyomi said. And here Yugi's eyes went wide. *What?*

That morning I hung up after talking to Simone, it was the Friday of our first week. We'd been introduced to ichiban and niban dashi, saikyo shiro miso, slicing techniques for fresh and seawater fish. We'd done oyakodon and gyūdon the day before. I went down to the lobby to meet Kiyomi as we'd been doing each day that week. As I came out of the elevator, she said, "You don't look so hot."

So I told her about my dad's stroke. And when I'd finished she put a hand on my arm and squeezed, looking up at me.

"I'm sorry, Teo. I really am. Hug?"

We hugged. I held her and I felt her take in a big breath as if to restore us both, her chest swelling and tightening against mine. Then we had to hoof it to the Tameike-sannō Station to hop the train into Ginza.

Kiyomi being there had suddenly been everyone's idea at once. Frankie floated it. Magnus agreed immediately. I was all for it. It just made perfect sense. Lucy was four, Kiyomi wanted to come back to work. The plan all along had been to research and open Oishii by the year-end, a third fall launch to cap what had been, despite my Orinoco foul-up, the best financial calendar year Magic Wolf had ever had. Since I'd by then moved almost entirely over to concept design, Oishii needed an executive chef, a face for the brand. Kiyomi was half Japanese …

It wasn't complex reasoning. But it was good enough for Magnus. And Kiyomi seemed pretty happy about it. Maybe she was glad to get out of the house. Who knew what it was like living with Frankie by then? He was a confident guy to start with. Then he took over his wife's restaurant and rode it to stardom. Although we didn't necessarily talk about it directly, I sensed Kiyomi was quite ready to get back behind a cooktop herself.

"How would you feel about travelling with Kiyomi? Go get your yōshoku on."

What Magnus didn't know, what nobody at that point knew, was how much time Kiyomi and I had once spent together before Frankie had come to Vancouver. Back in the early days of Rue Véron, we'd been bumping elbows and hips, sliding past each other, *behind, behind.* Twelve hours of that, most days. Team intimacy is a real thing. And since Kiyomi and I were side by side across from the other three *chefs de parti*, we were a kernel within the whole. She had this thing, this ass pat. I never thought much about it. *Nice work, Chef.* And there would be that slap to the butt, like football players do. I will say this, I never patted her ass in return. But we'd change into and out of our whites in the locker room at the back. I saw Kiyomi in bra and panties more often than I did Stephanie, who was travelling more than ever at that point. So Kiyomi and I would be together after work as well, drinking and talking, texting later. Maybe I'd have the odd moment of wondering if it was all entirely right. But those thoughts were easily chased away. Out on the town, sometimes with others, sometimes on our own. We'd go to her apartment, which was at that time over a bagel shop off Main Street. There was nothing happening beyond wine and conversation. But somehow I also never told Stephanie about any of these evenings either. Once, I lied.

"I tried you like five times," Stephanie said. "Including five in the morning, your time."

"I'm so sorry. I took a sleeping pill."

"Since when do you take sleeping pills?"

Which was a hassle because then I had to get a doctor's appointment so I could get a prescription so that I'd have the pills when Stephanie returned. Then I had to answer all the doctor's questions with made-up answers too. *How long have you not been sleeping? Have you been feeling depressed or anxious?* Et cetera, et cetera.

But we hadn't done anything, I'd remind myself. Nothing wrong. Nothing to keep secret. And I'd tell myself that even after I'd fallen asleep on Kiyomi's couch after sitting and sipping wine until one in the morning. I'd tell myself it was all innocent except that I knew what I felt. And I knew that we texted each other at all hours. I knew that she told me things about her family and past lovers, that she'd ask about Stephanie on occasion, always in a particular way.

"What's she think about me?" Kiyomi would ask. "All up in her husband's *stuff*."

I worried about that. Kiyomi warned with that statement that she saw us as being indiscreet. And you're okay with indiscretion until suddenly you're not. Two human and sexual beings, sitting there talking, not reaching out to pull each other into an embrace, not pressing our lips and bodies together, every single gesture of which I would work through later in my mind and which I knew she did herself.

"I think about you." I don't remember the specific night she said this, so common had these become.

"Me too, Sous," I said.

"No," she said, looking at me in a different way.

"What?"

"Isn't this all very fucked up?" Kiyomi said, her expression sliding, as if to foreshadow all that might come, affection, sadness, frustration. Was there even a trace of anger in that poised, early moment?

I leaned forward as if to examine her more closely, as if to inspect what exactly she might be telling me. I was trying to tease, to amuse. But her expression didn't change.

"So what do we do now?" I asked her.

Kiyomi waited before answering. Then she put a hand to my chest and pushed me slowly back. She said: "Nada y pues nada y pues nada."

I nodded like *sure, of course*. But I was watching myself as if I was on a security camera, wondering about the man I was seeing, wondering of what dark range of things he might be capable. And

I desired her more in that moment than I had in any moment prior.

They say *sexual tension.* But it wasn't even tension. I'd call it sexual certainty, the sense that we were two parts of a thing that would snap together tight were only some catch to be released. That much, I felt strongly at the time, was a sympathetic vibration between us, a positive and private thing we shared.

Behind, behind.

Then Frankie had moved to Vancouver to work at Rue Véron. I'd been distracted by opening Orinoco so I didn't watch it happen. But some powerful chemistry apparently surged between them. I saw Kiyomi less and less, everything mellowing out. I remember a text Kyomi wrote me at some point during this time.

I kind of miss you.

And I wrote back. *In bed alone. Come on over.*

Long pause. Then: *Oh Teo. Don't.*

Kiyomi and I arrived in Tokyo during cherry blossom season. We'd go up to Chidorigafuchi Park and walk along the moat under all those pink petals. High blue sky, racing clouds. We took the train to Meguro one Sunday, I remember, walking under the cherry trees that lined the river. We ate okonomiyaki at a place called Osaka Soul, egg pancakes doused in a dark sweet sauce, criss-crossed with Kewpie mayonnaise, dancing with katsuobushi fish flakes. She showed me pictures of Lucy on her phone.

"Looks like Mom," I said.

"People say she looks like Frankie," Kiyomi said. "Same grey eyes, dark hair."

"I can see that too."

"What was he like in Paris?" she said, still looking at the picture.

"Frankie was kind of my hero, honest," I told her. "He got me a job."

"As a guy. Was he nice?"

"Very popular. He knew everyone."

"Girlfriends?"

"I assume so. Though you know kitchen life. We had only so much time."

"He dated Stephanie," Kiyomi said.

"Briefly," I said, looking away. "They were just friends by the time I arrived. Then, of course, you know what happened."

"Right," she said.

"But everyone loved him. That much is true. *Formidable* they called him. You know why?"

She shook her head.

"Because he was ferocious in the kitchen. Fast, exact, powerful. Just like you. Then he'd stay out drinking until two in the morning and never be late in the morning."

"Not anymore," she said.

"All cleaned up now, of course. Good for him."

"All cleaned up," she said, and laughed. "And you. *Tranquille.* That was you, Mr. Cool?"

I told her I kept to myself at first and didn't get too fussed about being teased for my French. So they thought I was chill even though I was completely green and actually pretty much freaked out about everything. "I bluffed, basically."

"I can see it," she said, leaning back as if to frame a picture of me better. "You could pass as cool, Chef."

It was yakitori week that Monday at the Academy. They had the coal-fired grill boxes set up in the kitchen for us when we arrived. Chef Yugi had brought his prized clay pot of tare sauce with him, which was warming next to the grill. Mirin, sugar, soy, Muscat wine, and chicken stock. Chilis as a preservative. Yugi told us that if you worked in a yakitori restaurant for ten years, they might let you take some of the prized sauce away with you when you left. He'd had his own longer than that. Once a week he'd heat it up to sanitize it, otherwise no refrigeration required.

One of the Australian yacht chefs came in late as he was speaking and began to set up his station. Chef Yugi pointed at one of the tattoos on the Aussie's forearm, a large set of black Japanese characters. He said: "That's my aunt's name." Then he just carried on talking about yakitori and tare. We'd be learning how to skewer and grill every part of the chicken, he informed. Breast, thighs, wings, of course. But also the liver, heart, gizzard, the neck meat, the skin, even the cartilage. Everything from the tail to the comb. And he ran his pointer across a map of the chicken doing so, tapping it home as he went.

Tebasaki, mune, momo, reba, hatsu, sunagimo, seseri, kawa, nankotsu.

"Everything from the kanmuri to the bonjiri," he said. And then he laughed and pointed his pointer at me, hunched over my counter area, scribbling notes. "Chef Wolf is learning Japanese in four weeks."

"You're thinking," Kiyomi said at dinner that night.

We were way up in Adachi City, in a restaurant called Sutaminaen Yakiniku. They specialized in offal and of all the places in the city that Chef Yugi thought we absolutely must try, this was the place. "Your dad, he eats motsuni don," he said. "You should try this one. The best horumonyaki in Tokyo. But you'll never get in."

Kiyomi and I looked at each other.

"For my Veuve Clicquot superstars," Yugi said. "I will call."

We needed a train and a taxi to get us close. I had a hand-drawn map in my notebook with Chef Yugi's Japanese-language instructions. I handed these to the taxi driver, glanced at Kiyomi and shrugged.

Ten minutes later we were down a narrow alley, opposite a garage. The windows of the restaurant were entirely steamed over. A woman took our coats outside and put them into a large yellow garbage bag for storage in a shed across the way.

"Smoky," she said, pointing at the restaurant windows and waving a hand over her nose. And inside we saw that the place was, indeed, shrouded in meat smoke. People hunched in around low tables, drinking beer and sake and shōchū, flipping small pieces of meat on the spitting grills.

I was thinking, I was having a moment unlike any other on the trip so far.

"You're seeing Oishii," she said. "Tell me. You like this?"

Something like it, I said. Food for being together. Food for joining. I thought my parents would have enjoyed Sutaminaen. I knew they would.

A series of platters had started to arrive. Beef liver and tongue. Square slices of tripe, bristling with comb. Round rings of intestine and aorta. We were eating with focus, Kiyomi and I, both of us seeing it, the common energy.

"Yakitori and yakiniku," I said. "These are sexy things."

"Smoke in your eyes and tan-suji fat on your face is sexy."

"It kind of is," I said.

Kiyomi laughed. "You put me in a good mood, Chef."

I waved over two more glasses of sake. I was pleasantly buzzed and a perfect balance of hungry and full. "Aren't you always?" I asked her.

She shrugged and sipped. Set her glass down and looked at me. "Formidable and Tranquille," she said. "That's pretty good, actually."

I waited.

"Frankie is always this huge show, telling stories and flaming shit in brandy."

"And I'm the retiring type," I said.

"Not saying that," she said. "But quieter. Maybe subtler."

"Subtle, me?"

"Kinder," she said. "Romantic too."

"I heard that once before," I said. "Not everyone finds it a great quality."

"Beats cynicism and cold ambition," Kiyomi said, "of which dudes tend to have plenty. Sorry, going all fangirl on you here."

"All good," I said, lifting my glass and clinking with her. "Fanboy, fangirl."

"Tell me," Kiyomi said.

"Anything, Sous," I said. "Ask me *anything*."

"Serious," she said. "Tell me more about Frankie in Paris."

Her hair had fallen down over one eye, her chopsticks clicking as she picked up small pieces of thinly sliced beef shoulder. When this last platter had been delivered, the runner from the kitchen had beamed widely at me, pointing at Kiyomi and rubbing his stomach to signal that she was a very good eater indeed.

"We used to hang out in Pigalle after hours. He made a nice toast to me after promoting me to chef tournant. He said ..." I coughed. I hadn't thought of this in a while. "He said I was his best friend."

She looked at me a long time. She was serious. But perhaps also growing a little sad in that moment. I sensed it lurking. Maybe nothing dark. Just somehow darker than before. *You put me in a good mood.* That was fading and whatever worked against her mood had returned.

"Why did he leave Paris?" she asked me.

I thought about that for a second. The truth was that I didn't really know for sure beyond what the *chefs patrons* had told me. "Some kind of misunderstanding," I said.

"About what? You said everyone loved him."

"He was a Bib Gourmand superstar," I said. "Now he's a legit international name. You know what the whole Veuve thing means, right?"

"I sure do," Kiyomi said. "Frankie has told me many times. But I get the feeling I'm not being told something else. What went wrong in Paris?"

I stared at her. She was my friend and I had a wicked crush on her, realizing maybe just that moment this was something I'd have to face and acknowledge. Everyone deserved better from me. Kiyomi, Stephanie, Frankie. So this whole conversation was becoming one I didn't know how to navigate.

Still, she waited, staring back.

I cracked, a little. "There was a personal disagreement," I said. "Not with me."

"No," Kiyomi said. "With a man named Gauthier."

I sat back in my chair, put my hand through my hair. Okay, so she knew about Gauthier. "Yes, that's the guy," I said. "A very difficult and troubled man. Did Frankie tell you?"

"Frankie has been getting texts from this guy Gauthier," she said, then. "No, he didn't tell me. I'm a bad person and I snooped. It started right after he hit the Veuve list the second time. After the big profile in *Eater*."

I winced. I was aware of a group of men at the next table watching us, sensing tension.

"These texts are threats, Teo."

"Gauthier has serious issues," I said. "But I don't think he's actually dangerous."

Why was I even saying that? I'd seen myself how dangerous Gauthier could be. I just couldn't bring myself to believe he'd really do anything about that old grudge, that old misunderstanding. Was Gauthier going to fly to Vancouver? It was a dumb question to ask, even to myself, and at exactly the moment Kiyomi added one more detail, her expression confused, worried.

She said, "Gauthier texted something about an abortion."

It didn't mean anything, really. Or at least, it didn't mean anything more than what I'd known already. Somehow Gauthier remained convinced that Frankie had messed with his niece despite both Frankie and Ines denying they'd ever been remotely involved. I tried to tell Kiyomi a tidied-up version of what had gone down. I left out Gauthier beating a man bloody in the alley out back of Bar America in a rage elicited by the whole fiasco. But I could see that the details weren't landing squarely. Or that's what I thought I was seeing at the time. I thought she was trying and failing to sync my characterization of the *bon vivant* Paris Frankie who liked his ladies to the sober family man that he'd become. Lucy's father.

But I don't think it was that. I think what I was seeing was a crack opening. A crack of real doubt.

"Do you think Frankie cheats on me?" Kiyomi asked. "As in presently?"

I reached across the table and took one of her hands, squeezed. "Kiyomi," I started.

"I should be able to ask you of all people," she said. "And before we were married, Frankie was pretty active. I saw it myself."

"Active?"

"In the scene. Active as in dating, hooking up. Active as in private dinner parties at his place, which happens to be our place now. He doesn't anymore. But he's still Frankie."

"Parties?" I said. "With Rue Véron staff there?"

Kiyomi leaned her head to one side, looking at me. Was I really this dumb?

I absolutely was that dumb, apparently. It had never crossed my mind that Frankie would have socialized with Magic Wolf people after the warning I'd given him. I didn't ask Kiyomi directly if she knew of him sleeping with our own servers. I felt in the moment like I'd heard enough. It felt like a betrayal in principle if not in the specific details. And something like a wave of nausea swept me. Nausea and then anger.

As for cheating on Kiyomi since they'd been together, well I hadn't seen anything directly. And I certainly wasn't going to destabilize the whole Oishii project by speculating. So that's what I told her.

"But you'd tell me if you saw something?"

"I would definitely tell you," I said.

She didn't say much in the taxi back to the hotel. She just sat there, her eyes closed. When we got to the Capitol, I nudged her and she leaned over and put her head on my shoulder. "Carry me," she said, like a kid.

I didn't go to her room for a night cap. I wanted to and was about to suggest it. The moment was off. Or maybe the moment was just my last one of sanity in that whole business, seeing damage and hurt ahead for both of us and acting with the appropriate caution and respect, maybe fear.

I stopped the elevator at her floor. "You okay?" I asked her, holding the door. She stood there as if she might not get off. Then she nodded.

"Thanks, Chef," she said. And as she stepped past me, she smacked my bum with the flat of her hand. Pretty hard.

Jonah had agreed to meet for dinner the following evening, Sunday. He suggested Densetsu in Ginza, which was a very hot noodle house at the time. I wondered if Jonah even knew how difficult it would be to get in.

I texted Kiyomi in the morning to see if she wanted to join us but she didn't answer for a couple of hours. Then when she did, she just wrote: *In spa. Never leaving.*

Then a few minutes later: *Sry abt last night.*

I called her. She said, "I told you I'm in the spa."

Head massage.

"Oh, that does sound nice," I said.

"If someone had given me one last night maybe I wouldn't need it today."

"One thing," I said.

"Yes, Chef."

"Gauthier is not exactly a great character witness," I told her. "Bit of a psycho, in fact."

"Oh, now I feel better," she said. Then, "So, off to see *heroic second brother*?"

"He would technically be the first brother."

"The man shooting pictures of tattoos."

"It's art," I told her. "He's famous over here, you know."

"And did you know that if one of his tattooed people came to the spa at the Capitol Tokyu Hotel, they wouldn't be allowed in?"

"Is that so?"

"That is so," Kiyomi said. "I can see the sign from here. Okay, have fun."

"Will try."

"And don't be late. Tomorrow's a school day."

"Yes, dear," I said. Then I got dressed and headed off to look for the noodle shop that Jonah had recommended.

Meeting up with my brother had surely been optional. The fact was Jonah and I hadn't really spoken in years. We exited childhood the way some siblings do, I suppose. After a decade and a half of fighting, which really meant fifteen years of my older brother trying to dominate me in all ways, I suppose we had our separate reasons to just go our separate ways. Perhaps I suggested meeting up because of our father's condition, imagining he might want civility, if not affection, between his offspring. But I have to allow that perhaps it was my own neediness also. Jonah off in Japan suggested to me a self-reliance that I knew my father had once shown in life. Maybe I even thought Jonah understood something about our shared history that I didn't quite yet. Of course, I was never going to ask him anything directly about it. But maybe seeing him would give me clues.

Densetsu was in a busy alley in Ginza. Ramen wasn't quite yet the phenomenon that it is today, but Densetsu had made some key city lists by that point already. So there was the long lineup out front that I expected when I got there about seven in the evening, probably three dozen people in a queue that snaked back from the entrance between pylons arranged for the purpose. When I pulled up, Jonah was already there, not in line, but leaning instead against the railing of a white metal fire escape coming down the side of a building.

He stuck out his hand to shake. "Bro," he said. "Heard about Dad?"

I told him Simone's latest news and Jonah nodded, wordless, then gestured toward the restaurant that we should go in.

He looked good. Trim, silver-grey suit, white shirt open at the neck, hair cut short. He was working out, I guessed. Thick arms, flat stomach. I was reminded that Jonah was always good-looking, with his symmetrical face, square jawline, and those intense brown eyes that had a flinty trace in them. Even a head taller than him, I felt like a slouch in my rumpled blazer and T-shirt, my chef's paunch.

"Popular," I said, noting the line. But Jonah just indicated that I should follow. Then he stepped to the cloth and pulled it aside, speaking in low Japanese to someone inside, then turning again, beckoning.

Cutting the line at Densetsu. I was looking forward to boasting to Chef Yugi about that one. But there we were, brushing past all those waiting and into one of Tokyo's hottest restaurants. All because of Jonah. And as the guys behind the counter called out their greetings — *Irasshaimase, Jonah!* — I could see it in their eyes, too, those young cooks bent over the steam, looking up now, smiling, eyes on him alone. I flashed on Frankie here. The man on whom the gaze possessively fell.

And he was like Frankie in more than one way, I was going to learn. When I went to order beer, Jonah shook his head. He didn't drink alcohol. Then he quickly cut off whatever else a person might think on learning that detail.

"No reason. No crisis. No AA meetings, okay?" he said. "Getting buzzed: just don't fancy it."

Jonah didn't live in Tokyo, he informed when I asked. He just worked here regularly. His home base was London, where he'd bought an apartment in South Kensington off Brompton Road. That made sense, as Jonah had picked up certain English verbal manners. The uptick in tone toward the end of a sentence. Certain phrases. *Don't fancy it.* When we were seated at the quiet far end of the bar, he extracted the one-sheet menu from the holder in front of us and he said *right, then.*

"This is tori paitan soba," I told him. "These guys are legit."

But he just nodded absently, running his finger down the menu.

"You look great," I told him. "I keep waiting for you to get fat and you just refuse."

Again, no particular uptake. He just raised his eyebrows and made a face like the comment slightly confused him.

We both ordered the paitan soba. And it came quickly, unbelievably good, creamy, chicken-y, with a truffle back flavour and shiny beads of fat glistening on the surface of the broth. Jonah slurped it up without much comment, exactly as a local might. I tried to draw him out. Whether he had a girlfriend or a wife. I could see him trying to answer, trying to engage, but struggling. It seemed almost as if he didn't have much interest in the answers himself. Food was a non-starter. He knew a good bowl of noodles but it appeared to be the last thing he wanted to talk about.

"You were always really fixated by this stuff, weren't you?" he said, shaking his head again, eyebrows flickering up and down, amazed at what I'd become.

"Food?" I said. "Sure. Learned that from Mom."

"Yes, I do remember that. Teo in the kitchen making cookies."

He told me he only ate one meal a day. It was good to be hungry. It focused the mind and sharpened the senses. Plus, people were pigs. People ate way too much.

"Hey, guilty," I said. But I managed to keep him talking about his workout routine for a while. Jonah was apparently part of a group who went running in the woods near the Hikawa Gorge west of the city on weekends carrying logs on their shoulders.

We talked about his work for a bit. But beyond telling me about an upcoming gallery show, he wasn't particularly forthcoming. His personal life, not much more to be had. No wife, no kids. Yes to a girlfriend. She lived in New York and was a lawyer. But no spill of details. I had to finally ask what her name was, which seemed to surprise him, like why was that something I needed to know. *Tabitha*, he said finally.

Jonah kept eating steadily through all this. Now he seemed to be waiting for the next set of questions. And not wanting the conversation to run dry before we even quite finished our noodles, I went to shared childhood memories here. It didn't seem like such a terrible idea given we'd barely seen each other in all the intervening years. I tried remembering some of our boyhood West Van exploits: the rock fights, the injuries and property damage. One story I recounted in detail was the time Jonah climbed onto the roof of the school and took the Canadian flag down off the main pole and ran up his Montreal Canadiens jersey instead. Of course, he got in trouble. The principal took him down to the office. But then the school ended up having to call our father because Jonah refused to submit to the strap, which was standard punishment at the time. My dad came all the way from his office downtown and Jonah ended up getting off without any punishment at all.

Jonah raised his eyebrows at that and cracked the barest of grins. Then he said, "You're very nostalgic, aren't you?"

"Hey, it's a good story," I said.

Jonah had finished his noodles by this point, slid the bowl away from himself an inch or two, crossed his hands on the table in front of him. He had the air of someone who maybe hadn't originally felt this get-together was strictly necessary, but had finally thought of something that needed to be said.

"It's like these restaurants of yours," Jonah said. "What's the famous one? Rue Véron?"

My first one, I told him. We'd made the Veuve list.

"I read about that," he said. "You were quoted somewhere saying it was inspired by Mom and Dad."

Well, it was a Paris-styled French restaurant. Mom and Dad were both in Paris at points after the war. I'd gone there myself later and worked for five years. So yeah, that was kind of the restaurant's story.

"And now this latest one," Jonah said. "What did you say it was going to be called?"

Oishii, I reminded him. "It means *delicious*."

"I speak Japanese, Teo," Jonah said. "I know what oishii means. I guess I'm just wondering why the word would mean anything to you."

"Because Dad said it," I told him. "The very first time we ate toro sashimi."

He glanced over at me, unimpressed. "Of course he said it, Teo. He spoke Japanese because he worked here. That's what he was doing here. Working. You understand that, right?"

"More than that," I said. "It was his big adventure. Japan, the Philippines, around the world to Europe."

"Sorry?" Jonah said. "Did you say *adventure*?"

My turn to shrug. How else did you say it? "He was kind of a nomad at that time," I said. "A wanderer."

And finally, I got a laugh out of him. So loud I saw faces turning in the small restaurant, people checking us out.

We'd been at dinner all of forty minutes. It was still before eight. I was thinking, I could take a taxi and be back at the hotel before eight thirty. Maybe I catch Kiyomi and we grab a drink in the lobby or watch a movie in her room.

But now Jonah had swivelled to me. At last, his attention secured.

"Here's the thing, bro," Jonah said. "I'm gonna have to set you straight on that whole strap story."

So he did that. And it certainly didn't take long. The fact was that the school didn't call my dad because Jonah had demanded it. And he didn't get off without punishment either. They called him because that was our father's arrangement with the school. If Jonah got into any more trouble, Arthur Wolf was to be called so that he might attend the premises and administer the punishment himself.

"That's right," Jonah said. "He came all the way out to West Van from his office downtown. He beat me, Teo, you getting this? He beat me with that strap way harder than the principal ever would or could have done."

"Okay," I said, a bit stunned. "Didn't know that."

"Nostalgia!" Jonah said, with a grin, lifting his water glass to clink my empty beer bottle. "The Happy Wanderer. Is that who you really think he was?"

It sure sounded stupid the way he was saying it. But there was no turning back now. Jonah was animated suddenly and moving on ahead. He sent someone a text and then we were on our way to Shinjuku, up through the flying night. I hardly had anything to say about this; it was just all suddenly happening. And here my brother was transformed into the loquacious tour guide, pointing out landmarks from the taxi. Impossible not to see his point here. I was a nostalgist, an emotional, romantic tourist. So Jonah was going to help me do some happy wandering for a bit. Up into Shinjuku. Down into that tangle of streets north of the station. *Omoide Yokocho.* Translates to "Memory Lane," nice touch. So we found our place that night at a cracked yellow Formica counter and I watched Jonah order drinks and more food although he was never going to touch any of it. Momo skewers. A plate of tempura. Shishito peppers.

"Dig in!" he said. The friend he'd texted earlier had just arrived. She was gesturing to the food herself, as if I were a child.

"It's good!" she said, smiling widely, lots of teeth.

Eva, from Moldova. One of Jonah's models. Also apparently a woman with whom Jonah was having sex, at least judging from the way she stuck her tongue in his mouth and he then guided her onto her stool with a hand slipped deep under her ass from behind. I remember she was nearly six feet tall with enormous eyes and platinum hair. She was dressed in red plastic, best I could make out, a kind of impossible magazine-only type of beauty. Guys stopped and stared. Probably ten of them in the time we were in the bar.

Orange koi. That's what I remember. Brilliant fish shimmering the length of her arms with iridescent scales and bulging faces.

Eva said, "You are baby brother. Jonah says you work with François Coté!"

Her eyes as big as saucers.

Yes. Yes it was really true. I worked with François Coté. And Eva exhaled in wonder just as small glasses of brown liquor poured over ice showed up on the table. She toasted me and knocked hers back. I did the same and felt something moving, something coming in through the air from the alley behind us, in through the open windows there. Two more drinks arrived. Eva hoisted hers and looked at me. I was suddenly ready.

"To the happy wanderer!" I said. And I raised my glass to Jonah. I felt a spark of defiance that had nothing really to do with conviction, and everything to do with the farmy liquor made out of sweet potatoes that was burning through me. "God bless the happy wanderer!"

Jonah with a sideways glance at me. A wink and a grin. The soul of mischief. And he actually started singing the song right there in the bar in Shinjuku. Quietly at first. *Oh I love to go a-wandering, along the mountain path …*

"Come on, Teo," he said. "You know the words."

"*And as I go, I love to sing! My knapsack on my back!*"

The cooks and servers behind the counter were now laughing along with this performance. And who knew Jonah had such a good voice? A rich baritone. And people were stopping in the alley outside the glass, staring in. Jonah was now standing, conducting with chopsticks. And the whole place then joined in. Me too. There was nothing to do but join in. All of Tokyo sang for Jonah with one thunderous voice.

Valderiii! Valderaaa! Valderiii! Valderah-ha-ha-ha-ha-ha valderiii! Valderaaa!

And I sat in the middle of it all, playing along, singing along, my knapsack on my fucking back.

Huge applause and much laughter when it was over. I made a good show of joining in, standing, taking my own bow for having inspired it all. And by the time I was seated again next to him, I could see Jonah had grown a degree more serious. He was thinking something over, deciding whether it should be said, then obviously concluding that it couldn't be avoided.

"I hate to be the bearer of bad news, bro," Jonah said, eyes glistening white, a hand just now reaching out to pat my shoulder in an ironically consoling way. "Happy wanderer is such a nice story. Only it's just not what the old man was doing."

"Just working," I said. "I get it, okay?"

"More than that," Jonah said. "*Better* than that. He was busting out, getting free. He was on the run, Teo."

"From what?" I asked, now quite confused.

"Not from *what*, from *whom*," Jonah said. "His first wife, Teo. A fine young lady from Forest Hill. Name was *Jeanie*."

Wife.

"Dad knew what he wanted," Jonah said. "And young bride Jeanie wasn't part of it, so he *ghosted* her. Then he ran and ran and ran until he met our mom. Only then did he make his escape."

Eva tucked in at my elbow, looking at me from close, pinching my arm like *wake up, you're dreaming.* And here came Jonah with the final words on the topic, leaning in, a bare whisper: "Easy does it, Matthew. Steady on."

I went straight to Kiyomi's floor when I got back to the hotel. Knocked loudly, which was stupid. She'd obviously be asleep. But she came to the door in a long T-shirt, then stood there yawning, looking at me as if making up her mind.

"What the fuck, Teo," she said, but then turned and walked back into the room. I caught the door before it closed. I stepped inside.

She poured a scotch for each of us. *For relaxing times, make it Suntory time.*

"So your dad's a bit more complicated than you thought?" she said, climbing into bed and pulling up the sheets to her chin, propping her scotch glass on the pillow beside her. "Does it really change anything?"

It did, actually. My mother not being first kinda changed things for me. More than that. It changed me, I thought. It was the difference between choosing an adventure and breaking out of prison. It was the difference between telling that story all those years, about myself, about my restaurants, spinning yarns without even knowing the truth, mistaking this crucial thing at the heart of the foundational family lore.

Only, I didn't ever say any of this to Kiyomi. I could have. I could have said, *Of course Frankie cheats on you. I never saw it but I knew it. He cheated on Stephanie. He's cheated on everyone. I've always known.*

Or maybe this would have been better: *I'm not trustworthy either. I've been lying since I met you. Let me share my sweeping, generalized anguish with you. Come with me now into these deeper, larger currents.*

Instead, I just stood there looking down at her. And the room seemed to rotate slowly with these thoughts, allowing me to circle Kiyomi as she lay in that bed, allowing me to see in all directions and across the decades. I saw her looking at me. I saw myself setting the whiskey aside, sliding out of my clothes and under those covers, into the warm crook of her arm. Kiyomi didn't say a word. She stayed very still as I curled against her. Then she rolled away and onto her side, arching her back, pressing herself into me, pulling free her T-shirt. She went little spoon in my arms, skin to skin, my face in her thick black hair. And with her hand she took mine and pulled it around her, around the swell of her belly and downward.

That's how I remember Tokyo ending.

Mario's Mac 'n' Cheezery

"Dad, it's Teo."

His eyes were open but unfocused. His lips were blue. He was getting enough oxygen, the nurse told me. That's just how they sometimes looked.

They. The very old. People sliding down the slope toward the end. Was my father accelerating toward the end? You wouldn't guess it. He slept. He opened his eyes and he saw me. I could see him seeing me. I'd take his dry hand and hold it. I'd tell him how things were going. *I've been in Japan.*

Or I'd sit with my head in my hands in that long-term care facility at the fringe of the city. Brown grass stretching away, dirty snow. I'd pace. Then, every fifteen minutes or so, I'd try again to make contact. Say his name. Say my name. I didn't ask any stupid questions. We were past questions.

Escaping. On the run. Well, then. Let him run.

Kiyomi kept flashing back into my mind. Me in my brainless distress.

"So, you know what the experts say?" she said to me at Narita the next day, standing in line to check our bags, heading home. "It's in about a thousand relationship blogs." And she counted off the best advice on her fingers. "One: end it immediately. Two: be honest about it with everyone involved."

"Be honest."

"Well, yeah," Kiyomi said. "You can't be lying to people."

"So that means you've ended it already?" I asked her.

She stared at me. "I don't know. Have you?"

My heart was racing. I'm going to say 120 beats a minute. I was out of breath standing there. What I thought was: I could follow the experts' advice this very moment and get us our best possible outcome. Kiyomi and I would have shared a weak moment. But we'd move on and let the whole thing sink into the blackness of memory.

What I did immediately instead was say no. Not over. No decision.

"Oh, Teo," she said, stepping toward me, my arms around her, her face on my chest. "This is so fucked up."

Which was how I discovered that Kiyomi, like Stephanie, was not a crier. That was me tearing up there in the airport while people in line behind tried not to stare.

"Shhhh," Kiyomi said. "Okay now."

Then we were on the plane, we were in a taxi heading downtown, we were in each other's arms again. Late nights. Oishii staggering to life. Frankie was in London shooting commercials for No Hungry Child, a global poverty action group. He had his face on London buses. He was doing something in Yemen. Kiyomi didn't seem to know where he was half the time around then. I know Stephanie was in Lyon, then Lisbon. She called me from her hotel there. She said, "I'm so exhausted."

This is so fucked up. I thought it, but never said it. I felt fear and a sickening variety of desire, like you'd walk into traffic to get it, whatever it was.

I texted Kiyomi. *Are you up?*

A minute later: *Chef, we meet the demo guys 7 a.m. Get some sleep.*

I miss you.

Sleep.

What's fucked up is me. I'm so fucked up.

No answer.

You free Sunday for dinner?

Wait. Wait. Go to the window. Check again.

No answer.

After that short visit with my father, I met Simone for dinner at a roadhouse restaurant south of town called Mario's Mac 'n' Cheezery. Crap food, I figured, but Simone picked it so I wasn't going to say anything. It was where she used to meet my dad, she told me. But it was also on the highway, convenient to the airport. And everything about the trip was being squeezed by my own realities back home. I'd look at my phone and there would be two dozen new messages, every single time. I wasn't even answering the ones about the restaurant, only personal ones from Stephanie and Kiyomi.

"How was Japan?" Simone asked, sliding into the booth looking out over the parking lot. She was carrying a black nylon notebook sleeve that she slid onto the bench seat next to her.

I gave her the big picture. Cooking school. Brainstorming the new menu. Japanese izakaya diner beer hall kind of thing. Not sushi. Rice bowls, skewers, and such. But I didn't really want to talk about any of this and of course Simone sensed that. So after nodding and listening, she finally said, "And you saw Jonah, who told you a few things I'm going to guess."

So we got down to business quickly and directly, always Simone's way.

"I knew the name *Jeanie*," I said. "Only, not the marriage part. That bit was new."

"Because he was ashamed of it," Simone said. "But I know he was planning to tell you. He only told Jonah on his last visit."

"How about you?"

"He told me around the same time. But I knew from before. Mom told me years ago, Teo."

I nodded. That hurt a bit. But Simone and my mother had always been close. "So this doesn't bother you? Mom not being his first wife?" I said.

Simone looked at me. "Does it bother you? We're talking fifty, sixty years here, Teo."

Fair enough. We both ordered Mario's Favourite Pizza Macaroni, a brick of mozzarella and pepperoni mac and cheese on a puddle of marinara sauce. Not great. Not even good, really. But I was hungry, so we just ate that together and tried to catch up like normal people. Kids and school. Simone asked about Stephanie and I said she was doing great. Very busy with the second book, which was now being packaged with the first book for a television series involving the BBC, Canal Plus, and a production company out of Los Angeles. They weren't talking about a single season. Stephanie's agent thought the whole thing had real legs. She'd be gone months, though the producers were promising to fly her back every three weeks.

"Sounds like a big deal," Simone said.

"It is a big deal," I said. "Stephanie has become a big deal though she's not sure she loves that."

Simone smiled and nodded. Fame wasn't something she would have ever considered. Every day she just did what doctors do, going on call, doing rounds, seeing patients in clinic. I'm sure people thanked her. Maybe patients wrote her notes after treatment. Simone would have just politely accepted these without comment. She really was, in that respect and others, a great deal like our mother.

"You want to see some pictures?" she asked me.

Simone slid the notebook sleeve onto the table, extracting various envelopes. She'd been out with Greg to sort out the farmhouse after the second stroke, she explained. They'd found boxes. She opened one envelope between us and slid out some black and whites. Arthur on a ship's bridge, shirtless. Shots of the engine room. Subic Bay. Two men on a fo'c'sle standing next to the enormous links of an anchor chain. Leather jacket, aloha shirt.

"Maitland and Simms," I said.

"Kinda shady looking," Simone said.

"Black markets, I heard."

"And worse," Simone said. "Gun running. Methamphetamines."

"He told me some of this in the hospital in Vancouver," I said. "The whole minesweeper thing."

"They were selling to a French guy out of Vietnam," Simone said. "Things got dicey in Manila."

"He told me they could have been killed."

"They were late into harbour, he told me," Simone said. "I guess this French guy thinks he's getting cheated. Some big argument ensues. Honestly, it sounded like the Marx brothers when he told me. The Marx brothers with guns."

"But nobody actually got killed, right?"

"There is some question about that." Simone said as she dropped her finger onto the photograph, onto the aloha shirt with pineapples. "Dad said he never saw either of them again. But this one looked like he might have gotten winged. Did I just say *winged*?"

"You did."

"Dad's word, not mine."

She was leafing through the envelopes again.

"They saw some real shit," I said. "Mom and Dad both."

"They did, indeed," Simone said.

"You know, I always remember this one time," I told her. And I described our mother crying in the car that night we drove past the searchlights over the national exhibition midway. How she buried her face in her hands, but we could hear the sobbing. And I wondered aloud now what terror a child would feel on hearing those sirens, the low drone of the airplanes in the distance, knowing that death would soon fill the sky above their own head before falling to the ground all around them. What terror would the adult then later feel to see and hear such similar things and have those memories activated?

"Well," Simone said, "you'd be talking about PTSD there."

"Do you think she had PTSD?" I asked.

Simone wasn't exactly sure. "I'm a cardiologist," she said. "A little outside my area. But I'd say that some very strong and disturbing memories remained for her."

I winced. That was my impression too, despite how little she'd spoken of the war. "What about Dad?" I asked her.

"Highly doubt PTSD," she said. "But people do have brutal experiences without developing that disorder."

I nodded. "Jonah certainly wouldn't think so," I told her. "Jonah thinks all that travelling for Dad was just about making money and escaping from Jeanie."

Simone looked tired all at once. "Jonah thinks a lot of things," she said.

"Also that my restaurants are flaky nostalgic bullshit," I said.

"And you're going to care about that how much exactly?"

Simone opened another envelope of black and whites and extracted some pictures. My dad in a jeep on a dirt road with a low jungle in the background. My mother working in a bookstore wearing a crisp white shirt.

"This is Guayquil?" I asked.

"Librería Científica," Simone told me. "The bookstore. Mom was actually the manager there."

"And he walked in one day just like in that movie?"

"*Notting Hill*," Simone said, "No."

She pulled out some more envelopes and leafed through them, stopping on one, extracting a shot, sliding it onto the table between us. Finally, a shot of them both. It was taken at a party, people milling in the background with drinks. But there in the foreground stand these two exquisite young people. My dad with his gaze so firmly on the camera, his arm tight around my mother's narrow waist. My mother holding his arm, one hand on his shoulder, her eyes up to his face. And I thought I saw the newness of both those gazes, the utter freshness of what both these young people were considering there after their long respective journeys to that very moment.

"This is them meeting," I said. "Photographer conveniently on hand."

Simone shrugged. "They were invited to the same party. And there was a photographer there, yes."

I was leaned in close, examining the expressions on these two young faces. They put me in mind of young people who might at any given time be working for me in one of our various restaurants. Young, with plans, with ideas, with histories that they carried with them to that moment. Young people who needed my leadership, even my protection.

I sat back. "The nomad and the refugee," I said.

"Indeed," Simone said.

"Why do you suppose she agreed to marry him so quickly?" I asked Simone. "Would he even have had a divorce at that point?"

"Annulment, Mom told me."

"So here comes some annulled marriage guy she hardly knows ..." I say.

"Oh, she knew him," Simone said. "She recognized him in some strange way."

I cracked a glance up at her and smiled. "Pretty romantic for you, sister," I said.

"Is being romantic such a crime?" Simone said. "But this isn't being romantic. This is just acknowledging that people have things called emotions. You don't want to be listening to Jonah on that particular topic, Teo. Or on the topic of your passions for that matter, or your restaurants, or what you love, or what you remember."

I had to sit back. Simone was rarely this candid and unguarded. So I just listened.

"Dad didn't leave Jeanie to go work and make money," Simone said. "He left because of Grandpa Jack."

"Died in his sleep," I said.

"He didn't die in his sleep, Teo," Simone said. "No nice way to put it: Jack killed himself."

Nineteen forty-eight. Just a couple of months after Dad and Jeanie were married. Simone was looking at me steadily now as she moved through it. Dad's brother Michael finding the body. Michael calling Arthur to come over and help. "Dad tried to stay in Toronto. But he couldn't."

I was remembering the stories I'd heard: Jack and Kate fighting, pots thudding into walls, knives being thrown. Jack stopping the runaway carriage and saving the day. Jack with his face bruised and split, lying unconscious in his own driveway.

"So these things would be on the mind of this young fellow," Simone said, her finger dropping to the photo of our parents at that party, so long ago and so far away. Her finger first on my father, then slowly sliding across that shiny surface to rest next to my mother.

"And then there's this young woman *here*."

———

On the plane home a couple hours later, I fell into a deep sleep on ascent. The prairies were dropping behind me. The sky was stormy ahead, darkening, going blue. I slept and dreamt. And these dreams wove together with the things Simone had finally told me, things my mother had told her years before.

I saw my mother, Lilly, weeping under those searchlights, white ribbons of light that scraped the clouds overhead. But I saw that she wept for more than the bombs that had fallen. She wept for what came after, for liberation and even beyond. The clattering tanks in the gravel road outside the house where she'd been hiding. The American soldier who spied her from where he sat on the turret and gave her a wink. The sandwich he took from his knapsack and tossed to her, peanut butter and jelly, wrapped in paper. Ambrosia.

Later, liberation would be other things. It would be renewed hunger. It would be school in a tent, a dead body found in a muddy ditch. Liberation would be the news that she was leaving Germany, that the life she'd lost would never be restored. Liberation would be gnawing loneliness. It would be danger. It would be those jeeps that thundered up the Alst road from Sendenhorst one Sunday afternoon, the American soldiers spilling from them, sprinting toward her and the other women who stood near the main intersection of the town. Liberation would be what those women found who ran into the nearby field and hid in the long grass. It would be Lilly herself who made it into a barn to hide. Liberation would also arrive for those who never had a chance, those women who were caught by the soldiers, who were raped in the gravel, again and again. Liberation would be Lilly in the rafters of that barn, seeing it all from a window high above, escaped but not freed.

I dreamt these things on the flight that day back to Vancouver. Racing home to finish what now had to be finished, to try to make sense of the mistakes I'd made, the slim chances I still had, and of course, all that I sensed coming but couldn't possibly know.

Crab Park

In the morning, from the window of our apartment, Vancouver was steel grey and the clouds shrugged in close to the bruised blue mountains opposite the terminal. The ocean heaved slowly, seeming to hold its own counsel, while the sky cracked to the east, ribbons of yellow fire.

The first I heard of the *Blade & Tine* article was from Stephanie, calling from Spain. We had our regular time for these calls, which would fall into the evening her time and whenever I woke up.

Schedule permitting, we'd try for daily. But it was hit and miss with everything going on, with her, with Oishii. We were at demolition, emptying out the space on West Hastings, seeing what we had. It was coming to life, Oishii was, but it had turned into a reeling beast. First few weeks back from Japan, I wondered often about Kiyomi and her return to Magic Wolf, not *if* she regretted it but precisely in what way and how much.

That morning the streets were slick with the rain that came and went, and Stephanie missed me twice or even three times. I heard the last one but couldn't take the call.

"Is that your phone?" Kiyomi said, jolting awake. Nine in the morning. "Teo, that's your phone."

"Fuck me," I said.

"You slept over," Kiyomi said. "It was a sleepover."

I found my phone and pulled up the recents and there she was, Stephanie. But with the indicator that a message had been left, itself unusual.

"What's with three bottles of wine on a Wednesday night?" Kiyomi said. "What's today?"

"Demo results," I said. "So, roughly, if there's anything to save or if Magnus is out another hundred K."

"Great," Kiyomi said.

"You regret coming back to Magic Wolf," I said to her. "Assuming you're not insane, you have to regret it."

"I should," she said. "Only I don't. What'd Stephanie say?"

I listened to her message in the taxi back to our place, weaving through traffic down Main under the train tracks at Terminal, swinging left into Chinatown, north on Carrall. Getting out in front of our building, I let my gaze drift along the street and down to the square onto which Orinoco fronted. I could see the signs of the picketers still there, though a lot less than in past months. I wondered if Frankie's genius coupons were being handed out that moment for torta cubana. But then I turned to head inside, to clean up and phone Stephanie back.

"What's happening?" she asked me when I reached her. She was walking somewhere, on the way to a meeting.

"Demolition was yesterday."

"How's it look?"

"I don't really know yet," I told her. "Just showering and going to head over."

I could almost see her looking at her watch and running the numbers.

"I went for coffee with Kiyomi this morning," I said, which really made no sense at all. We would have had coffee at the restaurant. And I wouldn't go do that and then return home to shower.

"You sound scattered," Stephanie said. "Can I ask?"

"What?"

"Are you wicked hungover?"

"Jesus, Steph," I said. "I got a few pressures here, okay? No. Not hungover."

Flat lie, but not the worst of them.

"Okay, okay," she said, then got to it. "I guess I just wanted to make sure you saw this thing in *Blade & Tine*."

The food magazine in question was U.K.-based and relatively new. But they had big reach through their website and socials. They had a more science-y, empirical take on the hospitality industry and high-end kitchens in particular. The piece Stephanie had come across had run on *Blade & Tine* Spain. *Veneno con estrella Michelin*. "Michelin-starred Poison," she said, rough translation. It was written by an oral historian and psychologist out of the University of Barcelona based on interviews with dozens of line cooks and apprentices from the highest-end rooms in Europe.

"Discovering that a lot of them are run by fucking bastards?" I said. "Not exactly news."

"It is to a lot of people," she said. "Even for us, it's news that people are coming forward."

I opened my computer while we spoke and pulled up the site. I couldn't read the text in Spanish but as I scanned the list I saw names we knew by reputation. L'Assiette Compagne in Limoges. Augustin in Zug, south of Zurich. Brasserie Saint-Priest, which had opened in a suburb of Lyon to huge press the year we left France. There were others, restaurants in Belgium and Spain.

As for the behaviours detailed, Stephanie translated passages for me, the material was unsettling both for how familiar it was as well as how unfamiliar it was to see in writing. Some place with two stars and a tasting menu that cost the equivalent of my present monthly take-home pay. The chef there — one Ekhert Lehner, named and pictured — hit servers with wooden spoons, threw plates at people's heads, pressured employees for sex, once turned a propane torch on an apprentice and gave him second-degree burns across both hands. And while he was one of only two chefs named, Lehner had lots of company in as-yet anonymous form, stories from kitchens across the continent, all mutually collaborative in the details. Hitting, screaming, butt- and breast-grabbing, advanced states of drunkenness and other impairments.

"Ever hear of Belle Vue?" Stephanie asked.

I heard *Bellevue* and thought of Frankie. But no. This was Belle Vue, a forty-seater on a quiet, flower-lined canal in Strasbourg's Petite France. Chef Alveré Langlois, a towering six foot four and sixty years old, whose prize-winning Great Danes wandered freely in the dining room in defiance of local health codes, had yet earned his third star the year before. But *Blade & Tine* moved past the stars and the dogs pretty quickly to the psychological paradox that gave rise to such refinement emerging out of such archaic brutalism on just the far side of those swinging doors. Past the pass you entered another world, one that Chef Langlois apparently considered necessary in the creation of beauty, a world of spasmodic and senseless abuses, somehow normalized in the production of dishes like the house specialty: Bœuf, spaetzle, pomme de terre crémeuse, citrouille moelleuse, raisins grillés. These words in handwritten fountain pen script across the daily carte, elegant calligraphy by Alveré's wife, Yvette, who ran the front of the house with her own stern hand.

If the Langlois duo distinguished themselves, in addition to their relative size — Yvette barely cleared five feet — was the way in which they not only directed the violence toward those beneath them, but occasionally and explosively toward one another. So it was that the *Blade & Tine* article achieved a kind of horrifying climax with the retelling of one story by an anonymous *commis*. The kitchen, like I remember Le Dauphin for the most part, was silent other than orders coming in and those repeated back by the line and station cooks. At Belle Vue this was fanatically observed, such that if a line cook had to cough or sneeze during service they were instructed to crouch down behind their stations and cover their mouths with small terry cloths provided for that purpose. The chef and his wife, however, when they found themselves in the kitchen at the same time, were quite prone to loud and long disagreements, many of which had nothing to do with the restaurant at all.

"It started with a disagreement about the dogs," the *commis* described. The chef was screaming. His wife, Yvette, picked up a cake knife from the pastry station and brandished it in her husband's direction. Alveré Langlois grabbed the blade with one enormous hand, pulling it from his wife's grip and opening a deep gash on his palm doing so. Already bleeding copiously, he swung his other hand at her, a haymaker that knocked Madame Langlois to the black-and-white tiles, where she lay entirely unconscious.

The *commis* was working for the *garde manger*, he explained. So that's who took charge. The *garde manger* took Madame Langlois's right side. The *commis* took the left. "Et puis nous l'avons jetée dehors."

They laid her in the grass outside the staff entrance to the kitchen. Then they all dove back to their tasks.

"Holy shit," I said. "Never saw anything quite like that."

Stephanie wondered if a rolling pin across the shoulder blades wasn't just as bad. And she was right, of course.

"Nothing from Paris?" I asked her.

"Wait for it," she said. "It'll come."

Which pissed me off somehow, Stephanie's certainty on the point. Hadn't her own book editors asked her to stay a little positive on Paris, stay on the Femke upsides and minimize the war stories? Yet she just knew somehow that it was all pivoting in our direction soon enough. And I held this against her somehow despite all she'd suffered herself to justify the feeling, some reeking dude at Jardin Jardine with his hand between her legs, pressing her up against the metro shelving. And I snapped at her. *Maybe we have to think positively.* Which pinched off our call that day.

Or maybe some part of me was afraid already of all that I'd watched over the years and said nothing about, all that I was even then myself doing.

I texted her five minutes later. *Sry. Bit frazzled.*

She texted back. *I could come home for a break. My agent could ask for me.*

But we didn't decide anything that day. *Luv u. You 2.* And I remember sitting on the edge of our bed that morning with my head in my hands until my phone buzzed again and there was Kiyomi, already over at Oishii and wondering where I was at.

The Oishii space was just around the corner from Rue Véron in the 100 Block of West Hastings. But our third project was turning out very differently than our first. Rue Véron was a modest size and we had modest ambitions for it originally despite what it had become. And when it got to the facility itself, everything we touched there — floors, walls, plumbing — was rock solid courtesy of that very expensive restaurant that had gone bust there the year prior. Oishii was turning out the complete flip side. The space was huge, Magic Wolf's biggest footprint by far. It also had been a restaurant prior, though not high end and closed way back in the '90s. Oishii was also the first of our locations to open in a room we didn't own. Magnus had negotiated a low monthly lease payment in return for getting no money for improvements from the landlords. This was all part of the plan to keep capital outlay low because, also very unlike Rue Véron, Oishii came to life with significant expectations.

Magnus had been very clear on this when he first approved the concept. Rue Véron was the flagship. Orinoco was the popular local spot, though barely break-even now that we were giving away our profits. Oishii was there to make up the slack — cheap to start to run, but a volume play. Lots of people eating lots of food and drinking lots of beer. Oishii was to be our revenue generator, our compensating cash cow.

Conceptually, I was feeling great about it. Kiyomi and I had come back from Japan with a particular kind of volatile chemistry bubbling between us. We'd vowed not to have sex again but would spend our days together 24/7 otherwise, not infrequently crashing in the same bed. I thought all this was showing on the Oishii menu in a very good way as we crunched through development in the Orinoco kitchen after the restaurant closed. We were building something there in the wee hours of the morning, something I thought had a real chance to be popular. Gyūdon, oyakodon, soba noodles with dipping sauce, karaage fried chicken, tonkotsu sandwiches. Small plates packed with umami wow. Barbecued pork belly with white miso and gochujara. Crisp duck confit ramen with shoyu-mirin-dashi. Black cod with grapefruit and charred cabbage. We had a signature dish in these chicken meatballs we adapted from the tsukune Chef Yugi had shown us. Light in texture, bright with sesame and green onion, they came grilled and drizzled with pineapple tare, served on a banana leaf. These were going to sell. They were going to be our tomato toast, I thought. And the first time Kiyomi and I made them together — it was four in the morning, the whole city outside utterly still — we just stood there chewing and staring at each other. It was a real moment, standing there eating that meatball that we'd made together, figured out together, carried home from Japan together. It was a kind of love. I loved Kiyomi right then.

"This meatball," I said. "It's like the baby we brought home from Japan."

"That's a really problematic metaphor, Chef," Kiyomi said. "But I do sort of get it."

"Can I kiss you?" I asked her.

Ever kissed someone when you're both eating the same thing? It can be really intense. And it was that one time for Kiyomi and me, too, all the while knowing how wrong it was, what outward-spreading ripples of damage I was forcing myself to ignore, willing not to exist. It was all sexy Japanese meatballs in the moment, an idea that was going to deliver everything that Magnus had demanded.

Volume. Big crowds and noise, big flavours, big cash flow.

Or it *would* deliver if we could just figure out the room. But here we were hitting snag after snag. Nothing we were planning was expensive. Kiyomi and I had settled on lots of wood: plank floors, long communal tables, smooth cedar benches. The kitchen would be open at the back. Yakitori bar down one side and craft beer bar down the other. Grill boxes along the tables. Light bulbs hanging on wires strung across the room. But from the moment we started the demo, everything we touched crumbled, and those killer lease terms meant Magnus had to pay to replace everything that did. We'd hoped to reuse some of the ranges in the back, some of the hoods, maybe even the bank of refrigerators. But with the space gutted, we could both see immediately that it had been exposed to the elements for far too long: squatters, wildlife, vegetal growth of a bewildering range. The equipment was all beyond cleaning, units caked in grease, mould inside the ovens, animal scat and pigeon guano in the hoods. We had an industrial cleaning outfit in and they took one look and backed away. Wouldn't touch it. So we had to get the demo guys back in, rip out the equipment, and truck it all to the transfer station.

Magnus phoned from Los Angeles: "That would be sixty thousand dollars over budget in the first three weeks. And we have no kitchen. I'm super impressed."

"Is this karma?" Kiyomi said, standing there on our second or third day of discovery.

But we hardly had the time to commiserate because it was plumbing day. Apparently, even after discovering all the kitchen hardware had to go, even after tearing up the floor tiles and putting a foot clean through the subfloor, thereby discovering it was entirely water-rotted, even after all that — at which point I was feeling Kiyomi and I deserved some breaks — we ran a water test and the dining room pooled with water and all the kitchen-area drains backed up.

The plumbers came in and I pretty much could have written out their diagnosis in advance. Nothing could be salvaged. It all had to be replaced. Refrigeration, sinks, drainage, water and gas piping plus related fixtures. The bar area would need new freezers and ice machines, beverage taps, sinks, faucets. Then the bathrooms. Magnus no longer joked about the overruns in our weekly calls. And I knew he was tracking us closely now. His people at Magic Wolf were paying attention. They'd pay every bill and keep us moving toward objectives until the Magnus metric said that it no longer made sense.

Then it would all be over.

But we never quite got to that. We replaced the plumbing and the entire subfloor. Week five we realized the walls would need so much patching we might as well redo all the drywall. Tearing all that off then revealed the termite problem. Week six we discovered the fire damage on the rear wall of the room, where the deep fryers of the old place had at one point apparently exploded into flame. Week seven we found the source of the smell toward the back, which was a below-grade crawlspace full of rats.

I knew several exterminators by name at that point and we were two hundred and fifty thousand over budget by the end of three months. We had a conference call with Magnus that I insisted Kiyomi sit in on. *Hey, we're doing this together.* I didn't read the signs very well. She might have preferred to leave the Magic Wolf business to the Magic Wolf partners. I was trying to be inclusive and ended up putting her on the spot when Magnus went snarky on the call and said something about a forty-thousand-dollar Tokyo honeymoon that was now looking like a minor budget line item compared to everything else.

"Did I seriously fly you business class?" Magnus said. "I'm too nice a guy."

"He's too much a fucking dick," Kiyomi said when we were off the phone. "What's this about a Tokyo honeymoon?"

He didn't mean it that way. That was just Magnus being a fucking dick. She nailed it. But there was a different charge in the air now. Something harder shaping itself there. She was frustrated and I couldn't blame her. We had a restaurant to get open by the fall. Or we did until late summer, when we realized there was no way we'd get it open before the spring.

"Spring works," I said to her. "We can make it work."

"Fucking right we will," Kiyomi said, cross-legged in a big leather chair, holding a glass of wine. I was lying across their living room on a big sofa. Lucy was asleep. But Kiyomi didn't look at me for a long time after agreeing we could do it, weighing her thoughts.

I waited, watching her. I was thinking a lot of things in those moments. I was thinking of her sexually, no point pretending otherwise. I was thinking about that tsukune meatball kiss. But more, I was swept by the sense that I didn't know at all what she might be thinking in the same moment, how she might be feeling about any of the dense pattern of things that we had now shared between us. All I knew was what I could see sitting there, cross-legged, black hair pulled back in a scrunchy. One look at her and I could see that she was beautiful and smart and fragile like the rest of us. But seeing that didn't change what happened next.

The glance up, the gaze held. She said, "Teo?"

"Yeah, Kiyomi," I said. "Tell me."

She said, "Frankie's home tomorrow. Will you stay?"

We walked from Gastown down across the tracks to Crab Park together. I hadn't seen him on my own in a long time. It brought back Paris. But it brought up feelings too. The smell of the sea reminded me that the world had turned over, that we'd tumbled down the side of it to find ourselves in this very different place together. He'd lied to me any number of times, I knew. I wondered more than ever if he'd done anything to deserve all the explosive success he'd seen.

But that was still me there with my old Paris friend, François Coté, global superstar. We were standing shoulder to shoulder in the harbour breeze, across from the towering orange gantry cranes, the Lego bricks of those container terminals — red, blue, white, green.

"How was London?" I asked him.

"London was fine," Frankie said, squinting with the breeze, as if he were trying to remember. "Then I was in Yemen shooting that commercial. Then I went to South Africa."

We stood there silent, gulls screaming in the updrafts off the shore. He wanted to ask me about something. I didn't know how to help him get there, so I let the silence ride.

Finally, "Did I tell you about Omega?"

I looked over at him. "Omega what?"

Omega the watch, he said. Then he showed me the expensive-looking wristwatch he was himself wearing, which I hadn't noticed prior. Speedmaster, he said. He'd received it as a gift from the company. They were talking to his agent about a sponsor deal. This was an enticement.

I laughed, incredulous. I was thinking: How did this happen that Kiyomi and I both end up married to people who are represented by agents?

"Well, I guess that's pretty amazing," I said.

"We'll see," Frankie said. "It's a brand decision."

So Frankie now made brand decisions. This was not something to which I'd been previously exposed, Frankie deliberating really in any way. Frankie had always been the most instinctual and intuitive person I'd ever known, from Pigalle to Belleville all the way to his highest intensity kitchen-robot mode. Now he had experts. He had refined choices to make, like whether repping Le Creuset, No Hungry Child, and Omega at the same time lent to any coherent single message. And he chewed his nails now, too, another something new. I saw it when he raised his wrist to show me the Speedmaster with its whirring dials and tiny round subsidiary faces. Frankie's nails were stumps, his cuticles ragged.

But even then, at that moment, standing there on the grassy berm in Crab Park, I thought I knew what topic Frankie was trying to raise even if he'd told me his Omega news instead. Even if he was levelling up again, even if his body was giving off signs of deeper crisis for all the upward trending, I thought I knew the root thing that must surely be on Frankie's mind, whose wife I'd held in my arms less than twelve hours earlier. He'd suggested the walk. I'd let him lead the way. We were there on the grass, looking out over the waves, the heaving sea.

"You're wondering about Kiyomi," I said. "Wondering how she's been doing."

Which prompted Frankie to turn sharply, to look at me, eyebrows up and head cocked. Curious. All of which told me in an instant that he hadn't been thinking about Kiyomi at all. Frankie was thinking about the future. Frankie was worried. Frankie was thinking about *Blade & Tine.*

St. Paul's

"I've missed you," Stephanie said.

"I'm sorry about on the phone the other day. The whole *Blade & Tine* thing. The restaurant exposés. The idea that Paris is next on the list."

I looked at her lying there, head back, long throat exposed. She'd called her agent and set up the break. Hadn't talked to me about it. I guess she made a judgment call on the phone that day. It was hard to say what Stephanie sensed. She'd have been a good poker player for someone who'd never played a hand in her life. It's not a blank expression that does it. It's the fully crafted thoughts and plans that the person feels no particular need to share. No need, no reveal.

Stephanie never had much reveal.

Now she said, "I guess I just wonder why you'd be worried about a magazine article, if that's what it is. Not like you threw knives or pressured people to fuck you."

Had there been pressure? It didn't feel that way. When I thought of the mess that I'd made with Kiyomi, I thought of her leaned over close to me in the Marine Club smelling like tangerines, or texting me a picture of herself, or asking me to stay over the night before Frankie came home. I tended not to think of me picking her out of a pile of resumés, hiring her, promoting her, owning a share in the company that sent her monthly cheques.

I'd made Stephanie what we called our prom date dinner: rib-eye with Béarnaise sauce, tater tots instead of frites, arugula with peach and parmesan. I'd lifted a Bordeaux from Rue Véron earlier. Château Haut-Brion. Very fancy juice that I would have to cover with Delphine at some point. We carried our second glasses upstairs to bed. We'd been talking about travel, the hassles of airports. I told her I was having a recurring dream that I was lost in Narita, wandering around, no luggage, no passport, then I realize I'm also wearing only my underwear.

"And did you also forget to show up for one of your final exams?"

"Exactly," I said.

"So what are you stressing about, Chef?"

She never called me that, so I rolled over to look at her and see what it might mean. But she hadn't heard herself say anything strange.

"I'm bored of me," I said. "Let's talk about you."

She didn't have dreams like that, she told me. She was just exhausted all the time. She was missing being home, being settled, going for Sunday brunch, walks on the seawall. "I want a dog," she said. Then she rolled her head over to look at me, her ringletted hair spilling over the pillow, shining in the street light that was coming through the high window.

"A dog," I said.

"Not sure I can do what we're doing much longer."

"What're we doing?" I asked her.

"No dog, no kid," she said. "Parallel nomadic lives."

"I never go anywhere," I said.

"You were all over Central and South America for the better part of a year. Now I'm doing it."

"Isn't that what success looks like? Demands on your time all over the world?"

"It gets old," she said.

"You want to settle down?" I said. But Stephanie was being quite serious.

"And at some point," she said to me, "it stops being freedom and becomes just drifting around."

Stephanie sipped her wine, rolled her head back to look out over the city.

"After Spain you're home," I said. "We'll get a dog."

After Spain. It sometimes felt like there was never going to be an after for Stephanie. *Femke* and *Beyond Femke* had been *New York Times* non-fiction bestsellers now for over a year each. The movie that had become the television show had now grown beyond the Pigalle restaurant, beyond Femke De Vries, beyond Stephanie herself. It was time to talk about women in the kitchen more generally. So the show was being built on episodes about women running restaurants in England, France, California, Spain.

"You know what this is going to end up being about, Teo," she'd already said to me.

Of course, we both knew the answer. It was going to be about the path women followed and the one obstacle they almost invariably encountered. Stephanie herself had Jardin Jardine. My mother had her horrors. My sister, too, it turned out, who had a story from med school that sounded a lot like others I'd heard. Of course, she didn't do anything about it because, in her words, it was not in her interests.

I wondered just then if Simone would watch the *Femke* TV show when it finally aired.

"Oishii opens in the spring," I said to Stephanie as we lay in bed that day. "Let me get there. Then I leave Kiyomi to do her thing and I come join you in Spain."

Stephanie was distracted. She said, "If we can't get pregnant then I'd like to adopt."

"A kid and a dog," I said. "I'm in."

"You're joking, I'm not."

"Spain," I said. "Shorter term, I join you in Spain for a month and we walk the Camino."

She looked over at me sharply. We'd never discussed it. All those years prior in Frankie's Belleville apartment, he'd told me of her interest. *At some time in my life, this is very important.* For a second lying there, I wondered if he'd been making that part up. But then she did react, finally. Up on one elbow, looking down at me now.

"What made you think of that?" Stephanie asked me. "You're not even cursed to have once been Catholic."

I try to imagine what you were seeing that night, your husband having just raised something that you'd never raised yourself, that you'd carried inside instead.

"Way back then," I said. "In Paris. Frankie mentioned it."

You dropped back onto the pillow. "I see."

You didn't speak for a long time. And then when you did, it wasn't really a clear answer. You just repeated again that you thought changes were needed. You wanted me to focus on Oishii, get it open, do what I could to make it a success. But you also wanted me to engage seriously with the idea of adoption, even if in the end we didn't do it.

Nothing here to disagree with. I waited for you to get to it. Whatever was the actual thing you now wanted to say.

"I want complete truthfulness between us," you said. "There hasn't been."

My breath caught. I held it. Then, "No, there hasn't been."

I lay there, breathless. Then I got up and went to the bathroom, ran a glass of water, drank some. Returned to bed. "Well, since you raised it."

You said, "Frankie. Frankie and me."

I waited.

"When we went to France we were together. We were actually engaged."

Traffic from the streets below. Taxis and voices. Tires singing on the wet pavement. One siren in the distance. I imagined an ambulance for some reason, reaching now to stroke your hair, to run my fingers through those ringlets, along those golden lines. I saw your throat pulse as you swallowed. I saw that rarest thing, the bead of moisture at the corner of your eye, the seed of a tear that would never fully form, never fall.

It's okay. It's okay.

Fingers in your hair. Palm to your cheek. Up on one elbow now myself, looking down. That lone siren dopplering away. I could have volunteered what untruthfulness I had myself been protecting. I wonder if I had just then, if we might have moved on through it more quickly. But the conversation never returned to me that evening. And perhaps it had not registered to you that I was really capable of concealment, such was my emotional and outward way of engaging with others. What was in seemed so reliably to come out.

So we listened to the siren there in bed, that night. And I saw it so clearly in my mind's eye, the boxy van with the flashing lights, slowing at intersections, making its way uptown toward St. Paul's hospital. I send a thought out in their direction, the paramedics and doctors, the one in distress. To us too. A pulse out to the universe of need. A prayer, I suppose. Why not? A prayer said to the spreading, holy darkness.

Let's just make it through. Dear God just help us make it through.

Oishii

And we did too. Oishii did. Gradually, then suddenly the path ahead of us was revealed.

And we slipped on down it. Over the winter break, we got the floors and walls in, the furnishings. By February the plumbing and lights were done. The kitchen came together. The installs were clean. And in the early spring, we felt good enough about progress to set the opening for April. I chose my dad's birthday, the twenty-third. I asked Kiyomi if she was okay with me marking that date and she agreed but I could see she was thinking of other things.

"Let's just get this thing open," she said. "Can we do that?"

"We can do that," I told her. "We're doing it."

She was standing, admiring the new ranges, running her hands along the brushed aluminum surface. Imagining herself in action. I was standing at the main service station on the other side of the bar.

"And I'm thinking out loud here," Kiyomi said.

"You're the exec," I said to her.

"I'm thinking I just want to take this place and sort of run with it on my own," she said, across the bar at me directly now.

"Well, sure." First beat, I didn't get where this is going. Second beat, I did. "Oh, you mean ..."

She meant on her own as in maybe a little less of me. She meant she really regretted we'd had sex again the night before Frankie came home. She meant that she recognized my feelings for her had deepened and that it somehow disappointed her now. All this hurt, honestly. And I'm not proud admitting it. A lot of other things should have stopped me from getting to the hurt part, but there I was. "Oishii is yours," I told her that morning.

"Gonna be honest, Chef," Kiyomi said then. "Not really enjoying having to tell Frankie lies every time he says he loves me."

That was heavy for Kiyomi. *You're okay with indiscretion until suddenly you're not.*

She sighed. "Okay," she said. "Good talk."

"Well, I'm not sure what to say," I told her. "The truth is great, yeah? But I'm not sure I can handle Frankie knowing it."

"Veuve BMW season is on us," Kiyomi said. "We need the talent happy."

"There's more going on than that," I said.

"If you listened to Frankie, you'd think that was the only thing going on in the world. I've learned you make these lists and then you're in agony for a year worrying you'll lose your spot. Or worse, get dumped altogether."

"I highly doubt Frankie's getting dumped," I said. And I was believing this too now, despite having never been able to get my head around Frankie being picked by Veuve in the first place. However it flattered me as an owner of Magic Wolf, it perplexed me in every other way.

But here Kiyomi was looking at me again, in this new direct and penetrating way she was developing, this *seeing right through you* look that I had previously associated strongly with Stephanie.

"How old will your dad be when we open?" Kiyomi said, finally.

"Coming up on ninety-two," I told her.

"And how long was he married to your mother?"

I had to do the math. "Fifty. Fifty-two years."

Which Kiyomi seemed to think about for a minute before quietly shaking her head, then turning to go into the back without another word.

My father himself was never going to see Oishii. He wasn't travelling anymore. Simone said she'd come down with Greg for the launch if they were invited.

"You're invited," I told her.

"I'll take some pictures and show him," Simone said to me. "Not sure how much he's taking in at this point. But he does react to things on occasion, so you never know."

After all the setbacks, all the unhappy surprises, all the pest control visits, all the extra costs amounting to three times the budget, we were actually ahead of schedule a month out to go time. Kiyomi had run ads and had a flood of resumés. People with high-end experience. People from around the world. No Japanese diner/beer hall concept hired as easily as one connected to Magic Wolf and Rue Véron. Nobody anywhere hired as easily as a restaurant connected, however tangentially, to François Coté.

Kiyomi handled all this. I stayed out of the way. We weren't texting in the evening anymore. Frankie was home. And Kiyomi had been right about the run-up to the Veuve BMW announcement. He was stressing over it. I left them alone. So it was Kiyomi who sifted all those applications, reviewed backgrounds, called references. She picked her own team. Then three weeks out from launch, Magnus and I met and reviewed the hires and he seemed to notice for the first time that the Oishii org chart made no mention of my name.

Magnus said, "Remind me what you do here?"

"I'll host the launch," I said. "Then maybe I'll retire."

"Yeah, right," Magnus said. "A thought."

I waited.

"What about we get you back to Véron?"

"You're not telling me Frankie is leaving."

Magnus actually laughed. "Not a chance. I just handcuffed that guy with a bonus deal. Charlie's bailing to open her own place."

"His own place," I said. "Fantastic."

"Not really," Magnus said. "Kind of leaves us without a sous."

"Gracine?" I suggested. "Bell maybe."

"What about you? Get you back in there. Get you back in the game."

I could see what he was trying to do here. The Orinoco crisis was mostly behind us. Dario and Pedrina had told me there was still the odd protestor in the street outside the restaurant when they came in. But they'd been bringing them coffee and tortas, having a smoke and a chat, restoring goodwill. Now with Oishii apparently out of the ground and built around Kiyomi's crew, Magnus was just trying to find me a role. Frankie and I had already worked together, so you could certainly argue that this all made a certain amount of sense.

Still, I felt angry hearing Magnus make this suggestion. How many times could things possibly break better for Frankie with me playing a pivotal role? Paris goes sideways, I defend him, and he ends up thriving in Trois-Pistoles. Things go south in Trois-Pistoles, he calls me, and I cover him with a nice job offer in Vancouver. He heads west, flukes into some monster accolades that change his life, ends up fraternizing with my staff, impregnating one of my best friends, then taking over the very restaurant I'd originally designed to memorialize my parents. After all that I'm just going to slide back in there and start working for the guy?

"I sense feelings," Magnus said. "Relax. Charlie's given us lots of notice. We'll find someone."

"Do that," I said. "Better yet, let Frankie find himself another sous. In the meantime what about the next project? Let's get me working on that."

Magnus didn't respond directly, but we both knew this wasn't on. Restaurant Four wasn't happening until my Japanese diner/ beer hall concept started paying back the cost overruns. "Speaking of which," Magnus said. "Oishii's gotta hit the notes, right? Fun, loud, high volume."

"We have internalized these messages, yes," I said.

"What about Kiyomi?"

"What about her?"

"Something Frankie said. Something about her being off since Tokyo."

Off. It troubled me to hear Magnus say it, to register that Frankie had noticed. Of course, it all troubled Magnus, too, only for different reasons.

"The Veuve BMW," I said.

"We need that thing," Magnus said.

"Frankie needs it."

"No," Magnus said, looking at me sharply then. "*We* need it. So keep an eye on her."

"She ran Véron before you knew Frankie's name," I said. "Don't be worrying about Kiyomi."

All those years since Paris, since *why do you need a penis to work a decent kitchen in this country?* Since the very fact of Femke, the restaurant, the book, now the show. All that time and distance and travel and pretending we were learning and progressing and there we still were, returning again and again to the same spot, the same moment.

Of course, this was me deluding myself. I see that now. Because at no point in that whole discussion with Magnus did I really seriously entertain the idea that Kiyomi off, Frankie off, anybody off might really be mostly about something I had done. Me in my brainless distress.

I remembered her opening the door at the Capitol Tokyu in her long T-shirt. *What the fuck, Teo?*

I tried to focus on helping Kiyomi. Let's get this thing open. Let's get that kitchen up and running. But the reality of those last couple of weeks is that I was largely a spectator, watching her clear hurdle after hurdle on her own. I showed up every day even though I had no official role. I laid carpet. I stacked bottles at the bar. I hung antler racks on the wood-panelled walls, Japanese monster movie posters. I screwed in light bulbs. But she fought the fires still flaring up daily around us.

Literal fires. We had ourselves a nice gas explosion two weeks out. One of the yakitori guys was trying to light the grill with the butane wand intended for the purpose. The charcoal didn't catch after several tries so he went in search of matches and left the gas valve on the wand open. By the time he'd returned with someone's plastic cigarette lighter, he wasn't sparking up a tendril of fumes, but a gas bubble the size of a Volkswagen Beetle. I saw it flare, a ball of blue and white. I felt the boom of it on my eardrums, saw the glassware bursting on the bar shelving behind him. But that was Kiyomi sprinting from the kitchen before I could even move. That was her helping the guy toward the shower in the staff washroom. She had him in there with all his clothes, cooling off the side of his head where the hair was singed short. He couldn't hear properly for a couple of hours, but he went back to work. I saw her expression. She was responsible. Kiyomi was in charge.

Not the only incident either. Oishii was committed to showing us we were opening a restaurant the hard way. We had a kid knock over metro shelving where we stored fifty-kilogram bags of uruchimai rice. That was Kiyomi manning a broom. A dishwasher got his hand caught in an ice cream machine he'd been cleaning but hadn't unplugged. That was Kiyomi taking him to emerg. That was her wrapping bandages around the hand of a line cook who'd sliced off the top of his finger with a *gyuto* blade.

It went on. We lost power in the neighbourhood the day before the open. Three o'clock in the afternoon. I was out front laying cutlery on the long tables and heard the crack and fizz of a control box failing on a pole in the alley out back. The room plunged to semi-darkness and I heard twenty people groan at once. Most of our deliveries for the next day had just arrived and now the bank of walk-ins moaned briefly themselves and fell silent. Salmon, urchin, tuna. About fifty kilos of chicken and wagyu.

Kiyomi handled it. Dry ice into the walk-ins. She sent a kid running up the block to buy candles at a party supply store. And there we all were, prepping yakitori skewers by candlelight. *Mune, momo, reba, hatsu.*

"Let me help," I said. "I know this."

And she let me in. She said to her crew, "Chef Matthew, people. Elderly but reliable."

I stepped in there, prepping skewers, rolling tsukune meatballs, portioning pork belly. The power came on at noon the next day. I'd been home for exactly four hours' sleep. Kiyomi hadn't left the place — slept on a Therm-a-Rest under a table, she said.

And then she was off down the line. *Behind, behind.* And she touched the small of my back as she passed, sending a shiver through me. A singe of excitement, of nerves. A trace of fear too. Couldn't explain it.

Frankie on the grass looking out over the harbour that day had been thinking about the *Blade & Tine* story, not Kiyomi as I'd first guessed. By the time I caught up to him after talking to Magnus, his mindset had almost entirely reversed. He was thinking a lot about Kiyomi when what he really might have wanted to pay attention to was the new story out that week in *Le Monde*: "Cuisine Toxique."

If *Blade & Tine* had made ripples, *Le Monde* made waves. And yes, Stephanie had been entirely right. Once Michelin-starred restaurants were in the crosshairs, then Paris restaurants generally were never far behind. But in focusing the story on one city, *Le Monde* really set things on a different track for Magic Wolf, for Magnus, for me. Because no discussion of Paris kitchen abuse could be contemplated without mentioning Le Dauphin. It wasn't the only example raised. But it was prominent. The Pricks were named. The rolling pins, the knives, the thrown plates, the testicle grabbing, which got my attention because for all those years I'd assumed that one had happened only to me.

Not so. *Le Monde* had spoken to dozens of people who'd been in the same kitchen. And from apprentices to station cooks, all anonymous, of course, they were telling the same stories. Many were women, who'd by then joined the ranks at Le Dauphin and in other Paris brigades, and who had their own uniform details to share. Breast grabs, ass rubbing, erection grinding, being scared to go back into the walk-in when certain chefs were around.

But what surprised me most about that *Le Monde* article was that somewhere along the line the reporters managed to source someone who knew about the death of Clémente. That was strange, because only Gauthier had been around long enough to remember the incident first-hand, and no way the legionnaire was dishing trash about his *chefs patrons.* But there it was. Anonymized, the exact restaurant name left aside perhaps on the advice of legal counsel. But *somewhere* in Paris, at *one* of these kitchens being unpacked in all that grim detail, there had been such a violent argument between an exec and a station cook that knives had been drawn. And they'd gone at each other, swiping and stabbing the air, the end only coming when the exec slipped and fell on his own filleting knife. He'd managed to do this such that the knife went right through his neck behind the windpipe. Dead on the scene. No criminal charges. Welcome to your inside look at Paris fine dining.

"How is it you never told me about that one?" Stephanie asked me when she called later that day. She'd of course read the piece. Everyone was talking about it. And the incident was immediately being linked to Le Dauphin, which was leading everyone in my world toward Frankie and me.

"Well, it was a decade before my time," I said.

"But you'd heard."

"Yeah, I'd heard from Frankie, from Gauthier. It was Le Dauphin lore."

"Which is really sick, right?"

She was right, even if I'd never thought of it as sick before, that we repeated the story, that we all shuffled back and forth across the very spot where the man had bled out on the tiles.

Behind, behind.

Frankie wasn't directly mentioned in the *Le Monde* piece. But there was one detail. Frankie wouldn't have missed it. And in the end, it's pretty clear nobody else did either. In translation it read roughly: *One cook known for affairs with young servers ended up fleeing France. He's famous now, sources said. Though nobody was willing to say his name.*

I met him at the Marine Club a couple nights later. I remember the place seemed empty to me, or at least much quieter than usual. Frankie wasn't looking great despite the very large, very new Omega wristwatch, a Seamaster Planet Ocean with an orange stripe on the diver's bezel.

"Holy shit," I said. "You got the gig."

He nodded. Frankie Coté was now on London buses as well as billboards in Singapore, Hong Kong, Tokyo, probably Paris too.

But he was far too distracted to discuss all that. I remember him ordering a pack of chips and a pickled egg, mashing up the chips then dropping in the egg, fishing it out all covered in bits of potato chips, popping the whole thing in his mouth. His fingertips were red. His eyes weren't clear. He said he'd smoked a joint and he was eyeing the bar in a way I hadn't seen since his arrival in Vancouver all those years before. Frankie poised. Frankie on edge.

"Do you think I could?" Frankie asked me. "Teo, man. You think?"

"About what Frankie? Hey, what's on your mind?"

"One drink," he said. "You think I could? Or I drink it and every fucking one of the seventeen that would follow."

I didn't know how to answer him. I didn't have that skill myself, none of that self-knowledge. I was on my sixth beer already and the whole evening was sliding. I could feel it moving sideways, like a pre-drunk dizzy spell.

Frankie said, "You'd tell me if you knew for sure about Kiyomi, right my friend?"

He seemed very stoned all of a sudden. I had to doubt it had only been pot. "What about her Frankie?"

"She's having an affair," he said. "I'm sure of it."

It is strange to me now that in my memory this moment sticks to me not by how this made me feel exactly. I felt the tremor, of course, the feeling of things underfoot growing unstable. But what stays with me more is how I felt the room change, as if with these words. A sifting quiet seemed to fall. And I realized that the room was not, in fact, empty as I'd earlier thought. The tables were all full, just as normal. Only no one appeared to be gesturing to us or venturing over.

I felt glances, certainly. But were these wary now? Did they come to us over turned shoulders?

By that point Frankie was already wandering away from me and back toward the pool room. I'd followed at a slight distance, separated somehow from this drama I was witnessing. Frankie approaching groups of people at their tables, extending a hand. Small talk that I couldn't overhear. But nobody rising to greet him. No embraces as I'd seen so many times before, back slaps and shoulder squeezes. All rather dark and sombre just then. And I noticed the Mille Feuilles, too, just then, huddled toward themselves, faces turned inward, one of them on her phone and furiously thumb-typing in whatever words the moment demanded she record, send, share.

Frankie making his rounds. Me with a shoulder to the wall boards under a framed black-and-white picture of the ship plying the mid-Pacific waves, the caption in silvered handwritten script: *S.S. Rakuyo Maru.*

I watched Frankie from my spot on the wall. He seemed at that point hardly aware of my presence. He made his way around the room, table to table, as if he was off on a long sea voyage of his own, just now saying his goodbyes.

Sea to Sky

We made the launch, just. That's what it felt like to me. We barely cleared the hurdles to get Magic Wolf's third restaurant open. We put out the fires and took the wounded to emergency. We fielded the interviews after *Blade & Tine* came out and then the more pressing inquiries that started after *Le Monde*. We carried on in stiff silence after Magic Wolf PR put an end to talking about these things at all.

After a recent article published in Le Monde, *there has been unwarranted speculation about a much-valued member of our team …*

But we came through it. We launched the weekend before April 23, which was my father's ninety-second birthday. Oishii opened. Oishii, which complexly linked to my parent's fraught travels. Oishii, which I associated with all those happy family sushi meals as a kid.

Oishii, which — I was still intent on telling anyone who would listen — meant *delicious*.

We went with a Monday when both Rue Véron and Orinoco were closed. So people from across the Magic Wolf world came.

This was when all the cafés were open as well. Pharmacy, Jaytown Grind, Cue Seven. I never counted but I'm going to say we had seventy-five employees there plus significant others. Plus Simone and Greg. Plus friends and friends of friends. We were packed. I seated Simone and Greg with Magnus, Zaina, and Stephanie over at the yakitori bar where they could really see the action.

It seemed to me that a lot of circles were being completed that night. Magic Wolf had reached a stable high level. And here were all these faces from our entire history to provide perspective. Or at least, that was the effect they were having on me, arriving all at once with all the others. Charlie, Dario, Pedrina, Gracine, Linnie, Bell, Delphine. I was more than a bit emotional. And while all those voices overlapped, I floated in the middle, watching the bar, watching Kiyomi in action behind the pass. She didn't look up though I willed her to. She was prepping a long line of plates. Sashimi, I saw. She was wielding that *yanagiba* like the sword it was, perfect slices, clean slice, fold away, gently stacked. A meticulous, deadly set of motions. And I remember hearing Magnus's voice at the bar just then, talking to Zaina and Stephanie. I couldn't be entirely sure. But it seemed he was telling one of those stories about boyhood mayhem and damage. The tires rolled off the bridge deck maybe. Or was it the bulldozer we'd started up and which crawled itself right into Horseshoe Bay?

Then it was service. And I worked a rustic room of long tables, packed with people, layered over with DJ tracks and laughter. I worked a room that was working on its own. And Kiyomi shimmered at the top of the space, under the hot white light of the pass, in the reflections of the blades and aluminum surfaces, in the voices of her crew, tuned so tightly to her. *Yes, Chef! Yes, Chef!*

Plate after plate came out. Paper-thin slices of salmon sashimi with yuzu dressing. Pillowy kimchi gyoza. Spot prawn tamagoyaki. Udon carbonara with salmon roe. Pork belly with miso. Tsukune chicken meatballs.

"Okay, *those*," Magnus said, after eating one with his fingers. He was drinking a dark beer, glass nearly empty.

"Right?" I said.

"I thought this place was going *down*," Magnus said, draining his glass and raising his hand for another. "My dude had me scared."

Stephanie smiling, shining also. I see it in memory. I see how beautiful she looked that night, a momo skewer between her fingers, first bite between her teeth.

"Teo?" It was Simone, up close. She hugged me close. "Mom would be so proud." And I cried a little into the top of her head, one hand pressed to my face. But even that felt safe in the moment.

Crisp seared duck breast on soba in dashi. Charred cabbage. Wagyu sliders. Chicken cartilage skewers. Perfect mini-bowls of oyakodon to finish before the platters of brightly coloured mochi and kanten sweets. I was ferrying out the sweets on long rectangular plates, sliding these into place in the middle of the common tables. Did they hear me talking about my father and mother here? Was that evident in the dishes that were coming out of that kitchen, the long track away from home and around the world, winding and turning, overlapping and retracing steps toward this room?

I can review the question now with clarity. At the time I could only think about this in a glancing and unfocused way. And perhaps that's why I didn't notice for so long that night that Frankie hadn't been there for the entire meal, only really seeing his absence the very moment he chose to arrive. I heard the high-pitched snarl of that rocket bike pulling up out front. Then in he came and I saw the room's eyes swivel. I felt the place brighten. It makes me wince to think of it now, the timing. But the room's gaze did swivel to Frankie with his white teeth, black hair, grey eyes. He took me back, Frankie did. He'd shaved his beard. White Jesus gone. Paris Frankie was back in full, a helmet tucked under his arm, handsome as danger. And I was no longer angry with him, as I had been talking to Magnus earlier. Magnus who'd himself risen from his bar stool and was crossing the distance to his star chef, arms outstretched. *Brah.* The one-armed shoulder-to-shoulder hug, the back slap, the drink held gingerly at arm's length in the other hand. Because while in my memory he'd only just walked in, only just swivelled the room onto himself in that familiar way, Frankie, it seemed, already had a drink in his hand. A tall, narrow glass of Pilsner with spilling foam. Frankie was drinking again.

I wish I had stopped that moment to look carefully at either Stephanie or Kiyomi. I can't be sure what I would have found, only that there would have been clues, evidence of some critically different reading of which no one else in the room was quite capable. But that was me heading down the more familiar path, an almost involuntary matter. Magic Wolf was magic after all. And I was entirely in the spell. I forgave Frankie again in that moment. I forgave him again for his outrageous good fortune, even the arrogance that might have given rise to indiscretion. I forgave him for things that I honestly had no idea if he'd ever done.

Matthew Wolf ascending a bench, beaming. Matthew Wolf with a glass of his own raised high. Calling out. Calling out to the gathered assembly.

My almost ninety-two-year-old father lay in a hospice with his eyes on the ceiling. I'd visit him the next week to celebrate on the twenty-third. But who's to say what he saw in that pixelated air that night? I'm only sure now that he was seeing something. It was written there.

I spoke in French, for obvious though entirely subconscious reasons.

Attention! Attention! Loup Magique!

Maybe things didn't come to an end either gradually or suddenly. Maybe the seeds of destruction were there all along, both benign and deadly. Thinking back, it seems to me that the calculations only made sense if the situation, as a result of some fundamental feature of Magic Wolf itself, had been a catastrophic failure both in potential and fully realized all along. Or, kinda both, kinda neither, just like Schrödinger's cat.

Certainly to a point, there was a progression that could be dated to a calendar, linear and causal. After *Blade & Tine* in March had come *Le Monde* in April, just as Stephanie had predicted. And with *Le Monde* reaching Paris, they also reached Le Dauphin. And after Le Dauphin was out there, a version of this logic held that Frankie was going to be next.

And he certainly wasn't kept waiting long. May dawned. And on the first day of that month, one week after the Oishii opening, the waves broke on Frankie's shore. I thought I had by then settled everything internally with him, all forgiven. But it turned out there was much more volatile material in me than I knew at the time. *Ressentiment*, the French would say. And when the word "rape" was finally used, it all burst into flame again, every tinder-dry and brittle memory of his meteoric rise and the way I'd helped him every step of the way.

The May 1 article appeared in *Flat Fish*, the same blog that broke the Orinoco story a seeming lifetime prior. They'd by now grown with the times into a sprawling foodie-experience website with a YouTube programming and content generation arm. The source they were relying on for the latest story was unnamed. But Frankie was in full colour.

François Coté was now out there in print and on screens. And the source was as detailed in her allegations as she was devastating. Frankie and the source had dated. And yes, the source allowed, the relationship had been consensual at first. But she'd been only sixteen years old at the time. She'd also been living on her own in

Paris, hundreds of kilometres from the smaller city where she'd been born and raised. The trouble started after the first month of dating. That's when jealousy, violence, and an impulse to control and dominate entered the picture. And that is also when the source said that on at least three different occasions, Frankie did not listen to "no."

Abusif. Tyrannique. Prédateur. Violeur.

Part of what disturbed me about the allegations was that the details seemed to place these incidents during my own time in Paris and in the very same physical locations where I'd been so many times with Frankie myself. That same bar in Pigalle was described where I'd once seen Frankie fight with the waiter from Polidor or stand drunkenly singing over by the jukebox. His apartment in Belleville, same thing. The source seemed to know the layout, the rubber trees, the outdoor dining table, even the Moto Guzzi that Frankie had parked there during those years.

But the allegations themselves were more sickening still. Frankie had submitted the source to humiliating rituals, forcing her to pose naked sitting on that very same motorcycle in front of industry friends, powerful hoteliers, and wine reps. On another occasion when Frankie's friends were over, she'd been locked in a wardrobe at the rear of the house, having displeased a drunken Frankie in some way she couldn't even understand. If she objected to any of this treatment, the source said she'd be disciplined, including using what Frankie referred to as *asphyxia érotique*, wherein the source would have to again strip naked and force her own throat into Frankie's open hand, which he'd squeeze tightly, at one point so tightly that the source passed out and fell, bruising her cheekbone on Frankie's concrete floors.

All these details were specific and ordered. No one made up this sort of thing for well documented reasons. There's shame in public exposure for the minority of women who do speak up about being assaulted. And by a brutal double standard, these same women are made to feel culpable, even responsible for the sexual violence they manage to survive.

I didn't specifically think about any of those studies or statistics, mind you. I just subconsciously accepted that an account of assault that included a description of a Tabriz prayer rug in Frankie's bathroom did not read like fiction, much less fantasy.

If there was one detail that didn't sit quite right, it was that the source knew about Pique 22 and the infamous incident involving tuna salad ordered for a dog. I didn't think Frankie would have told that story anywhere outside the Le Dauphin kitchen because of how he had been humiliated by it. But he certainly did hate Pique 22 as described. And he certainly was capable of irrational anger when gripped by the memory of that particular insult. So who knew what Frankie might have said to someone he was trying to get into bed, or thereafter in anger for one reason or another?

All that I've described here so far happened in rough sequence. Up to that new *Flat Fish* piece, up to May 1, things seemed to be linear, causal, and accelerating. What distinguished the situation as it developed after that day was its startling nonlinearity. Everything went everywhere all at once. *Ressentiment* did that to you. And while it spread like an infection through my community, I see now that this was nowhere more true than it was in my own case. In my head, in my heart, in my conscience. Something had been lying there dormant, but both benign and deadly. On May 1 and in the aftermath, I opened Schrödinger's box and looked inside. Then things crystallized into a single reality that could not be avoided.

"You were in that kitchen with him in Paris. You went to his house. You were his best friend," Magnus said to me. "You didn't see any of this shit?"

We were in his Trimble office again. I was staring out over that view of the glass city, those blue mountains rising beyond.

The fact was I hadn't. There had been abuse at Le Dauphin, for sure. There'd been tyranny and predatory behaviour on the part of superiors. Only, I never saw Frankie do any of this to anyone. And I certainly never saw or heard about anything similar to rape.

Still, in the day it had taken Magnus and I to sit down and talk about the mess, it had already become an exponentially bigger mess because there had been an informal kitchen meeting over at Rue Véron the afternoon before.

"Sorry, meeting?" I asked Magnus when he told me.

Delphine, Linnie, Bell, the apprentices, even the two dishwashers were dragged in. Charlie was also there though I'd learn later that he hadn't wanted to go. Delphine had insisted, even though he was a week away from his last day with Magic Wolf.

"Meeting about what exactly?"

"Great question," Magnus said. "A meeting not contemplated in the fucking HR manual, I can tell you that much. A meeting to fuck things up a great deal further for us and get everyone worked up and hysterical."

"Called by who?"

Delphine, it seemed. Or at least, she was the one to pick up the phone at the end of this meeting and call Magnus at home, something she'd never done previously. Delphine called Magnus at home, in the evening, and informed him that if he didn't suspend Frankie immediately and ban him from all Magic Wolf properties, then the whole kitchen crew was walking out that same day. Walking out or worse.

"Like what kind of worse?" I asked.

"Like talking to the press worse. Like suggesting Frankie was doing that same shit at Véron. That's liability, my friend, if you haven't sniffed that much out already."

I thought I got the picture. And it explained Magnus drilling down on what I had or had not seen in Paris.

"Listen," I started.

"I am most definitely listening," Magnus said to me. "And any good idea would be most gratefully received."

"Since Paris ..." and here my voice tailed off. In that particular meeting, which was on the Monday, May 2, I was entertaining what would be my final reservations that might have mattered. After that, everything went everywhere inside me too.

"Since Paris fucking what?" Magnus said.

He was angry like I'd never seen Magnus be angry. I'm not sure I even knew he had this kind of anger in him. This was *Magic* we were talking about here, unflappable. Magic, who one-strapped a nylon backpack to lawyers' meetings because he didn't care what lawyers thought. Magic, who backed Kiyomi and I when we ran a quarter million dollars over budget on Oishii. Magic, who'd always believed in me, and who needed more than ever to believe me now.

"Since Paris, I think I've heard enough," I told Magnus. "Frankie's done something really bad here. I've heard enough to know."

Magnus paced and breathed. Then he threw himself into his leather desk chair.

"All right then," Magnus said. "HR will suspend his ass first thing this afternoon. We'll talk to the lawyers, but bottom line is no fucking way he's coming back."

"Jesus," I said, stunned to feel everything so suddenly in motion.

But Magnus wasn't hearing me anyway. He was thinking ahead.

"Phone calls," Magnus said. "Has Frankie called you?"

Three times the night before, in fact. Five more calls in the morning.

"Did you answer?" Magnus asked me.

"No," I said. The truth.

Magnus nodded. Good. Better for all of us that Frankie didn't know anything, certainly not that legal was now in the picture. Magnus told me he was also bringing in a crisis management outfit to assist the Magic Wolf PR team. "You remember Hugo Sullivan?"

Sure, sure. Of course I did.

"I'll get him synced with legal and he'll be our quarterback on this," Magnus said. "Don't do shit without consulting Hugo."

"How's Kiyomi?" I asked.

"Don't contact her," Magnus said. "Zero."

I'd texted her two dozen times by that point already. No reply. But all right, no contact then.

I wish I could report that I took a step back at this point to make some kind of a list of pros and cons, arguments for and arguments against, anything in the way of a two-sided analysis of any kind at all. I didn't, other than possibly my call to Ines. But even that isn't quite right. Because I called her thinking I knew for sure she was the source. Who else could it be? I called her to commiserate, to cry on the phone about what she'd been through, to confirm the evil that I was convinced had been uncovered.

I tracked her down through Instagram. She was living in Avignon. Happily married, two wonderful kids. But if any of that surprised me, nothing about that conversation that followed was going to be any less surprising. Ines immediately said she was shocked by the article, which of course she had read.

"*Flat Fish*, what is this?"

Just a name, I said. Point being, they'd gone wide with the story. And while the follow-up press wasn't quite as direct about saying Frankie raped someone, they were repeating the story that his reputation had been critically damaged. That serious allegations had been made. And people understood what that meant.

Ines caught something there in my description of these things. "You don't think this story was from me?" she said. "That I talked to them? Teo?"

I was stunned. "Yes," I told her. "I assumed it was."

"Teo!" she said, shocked with me now.

"Well, didn't he, with you?"

"Didn't he what?"

"You know," I said.

"Of course we slept together, Teo," Ines said.

"Ah, Jesus," I said. "*Oh God.*"

"Why, Teo?" Ines said. "What does God have to do with this?"

"You were fifteen," I said. "Sixteen."

"I was seventeen by the time it happened," she said. "In France this is of age."

"So who is the person in the article?" I asked.

"Well this is not me!" Ines said. Now she sounded mad. "And Frankie would never do those things!"

"I'm sorry, I'm sorry," I said. "You were still too young for him."

"Well, if I remember you were interested in someone else," Ines said, sharply.

"I thought of you like a sister."

"Yes, I remember that quite well," Ines said. "I didn't feel exactly the same. So Frankie, we sleep together. Maybe four times, five times. But he never force me."

And with that, the line ran silent, but for a thin crackle of static that still connected Ines to me.

"Then I discover I have a baby," she said, finally. "So I return to Le Havre for the doctor."

"You had an abortion."

"Yes, Teo," she said. "A woman does sometimes. I was in such a time."

"And you told your uncle, Gauthier," I said.

"I didn't have to tell him," Ines said. "He knew."

I can see now that this was the moment when I probably should have started asking some harder questions. But I didn't. I discounted immediately that Gauthier could be behind all this because I just couldn't see the man ever being that covert. He had a tattoo of a skull smoking a cigar on his chest for fuck's sake. A guy like Gauthier hates you and he takes you out with a pool cue. Plus, Frankie had apparently lied to me about so many other things earlier, I felt justified wondering what else he might be concealing.

Of course, I'd also lied over the same years. I'd concealed things from Stephanie, from Kiyomi, even myself. Add it to the fact that I'd been lying pretty spectacularly to Frankie himself, from Tokyo and onward.

It didn't tip the scales for me. It didn't make me cautious or suspicious. And perhaps this was an impulse born of denial, fear, confusion, guilt. I didn't express reservations because I didn't have any. And I say that knowing that Ines had shared a detail that seems rather more pressing now with hindsight, something entirely new to me: the fact that Gauthier and Frankie had been tight friends when he first arrived in Paris. Gauthier had mentored the young French Canadian. Gauthier had fancied they had something in common: rural upbringings, Francophones from outside the mother country. When Gauthier spoke of Frankie in those early years, he'd say *mon cousin Canadien* in an affectionate and familial way.

Something changed. Ines didn't care to speculate. It had happened long before she even got to Paris. But I knew, even then. Had I been honest with myself, I could have recognized that Frankie had taken something from Gauthier without trying, just as he had taken something from me. It's hard to even admit this now. Frankie hadn't even been trying as he climbed from station to station, to the Bib, to the Veuve BMW, to international fame, climbing up the backs and shoulders and then standing on the heads of people like Gauthier, like me. The man was on buses and billboards and he hadn't broken a sweat.

So maybe Gauthier had had enough. And maybe, in some novelistic world, Gauthier might have enacted his plot for revenge after all those years, made up a story layered with facts that people would recognize, seasoned with shocking details from imagination, combined into an outrageous story of unforgivable offense. Maybe Gauthier did design this whole thing, get some female accomplice he met in Bar America to make the *Flat Fish* call, then release the whole thing into the world when the time was just right.

Maybe. But by the time I had even briefly considered this scenario, which I found utterly implausible based on the Gauthier I'd gotten to know over those many dinners at Le Mouton Noir, it was pretty clear that the truth was less important than the explosive reality of what was happening out there right that moment. Because after *Flat Fish*, the follow-up stories and social media and news coverage were putting the final nails in this thing. To the world as it could be deciphered online and in print, Frankie was dead already. And that much was true even before attention pivoted to Frankie's last job with Magic Wolf, even before attention starting swivelling to Magnus and to me.

Nobody went on the record from Rue Véron. But someone said enough off the record to bring it all shuddering home. He'd dated servers, if not at Rue Véron, then elsewhere. He'd thrown big parties when he first arrived in Vancouver. He'd pissed on his own front lawn in front of people numerous times, it seems. He'd been in arguments. He'd offended people. He'd gotten into a shoving match with a chef from a downtown hotel who said he'd been humiliated as a result. Frankie had made advances, inappropriate comments, and just generally made a lot more people uncomfortable than you might have guessed he had time for.

My phone was ringing every five minutes at that point, Frankie almost every time. I'd mash my finger down on that side button to decline each time because I was furious with him but also deeply confused and I had nothing to say.

Veuve BMW removed us from the rankings and the reservation book tanked almost immediately. Le Creuset, No Hungry Child, Omega. They all called Magic Wolf, with whom the endorsements had been structured. And you knew what that was all about.

I think this part of the implosion took only a couple of days in itself, during which time I listened to a single voicemail from Frankie. I don't know what made me finally listen. I'd been deleting them up until then. Sitting in Victory Square on the steps around the cenotaph, right there in the heart of that zone that had been my Vancouver for so many years. Rue Véron just down there. Orinoco around the way. Oishii a stone's throw to the east. The cafés, the employees who relied on Magnus and me. I was sitting there with my back against the base of the triangular obelisk with its ghostly words etched on its three sides:

Their name liveth for evermore
Is it nothing to you
All ye that pass by

And just that moment, someone did call out, someone I didn't remember. Or maybe we'd never met. Just walking down the sidewalk on Hastings Street and seeing a dude from the neighborhood. *Heya, Chef.* And on they went, off to the east as my phone began to ring again, buzzing in my pocket, then in the palm of my hand.

Decline.

Wait. And then the follow up buzz for the message, which this time I did not immediately delete. I thought of Pigalle that moment instead. I thought of all those greetings I'd heard called out for Frankie over the Paris years. All that recognition directed toward him. And I thought of that and what a pitiful sight I made having finally achieved the same, slumped there against the cold stone.

Phone pressed to my face, hand shaking. Frankie's voice in my ear. He'd heard about the Veuve bailing out. He'd heard about the cancelled endorsements. He was in Mexico somewhere stranded because Magnus had cancelled his credit cards.

What is this? Why don't you answer, man? I can't get through to Magnus. I can't get anyone. I have some affairs, man. Listen to me, Teo, my brother. I sleep with people. But I didn't rape anyone!

Frankie in tears on the phone. Frankie sobbing. Not even to my ear in that moment was any of this the sound of guilt. It was the sound of desperation and fear. It was the sound of the same feeling I was having myself sitting there, the fear of being consumed in the fire and obliterated.

And that wasn't a sound I could afford to be near. No one could. So I listened to the message a second time. Then a third. Then I deleted it and blocked Frankie's number.

"For a clusterfuck," Magnus said to me, notably calmer than our first meeting. "This one is really quite epic."

We closed Rue Véron temporarily in early June, in part to deflect media inquiries. Because of a clause in Frankie's contract relating to sales, that allowed Magic Wolf to release him against a prearranged severance. But Legal then disputed the severance due to alleged negligence on Frankie's part and sent a letter indicating he would not be paid. Magnus had, meanwhile, agreed to pay Rue Véron staff some tie-over funds so that they didn't all leave. But that was only going to last so long under the best circumstances, and then we lost Delphine and the entire kitchen to resignations on a single day. And with Rue Véron now effectively dead, that was the moment media attention turned back to Orinoco.

Pedrina and Dario and their team did not deserve this. We'd been safely out of the news for most of two years due to their efforts. But imagine the poor timing that Magnus had quietly decided a couple of months prior to wind down the food coupon program, close the Orinoco food truck. Once Rue Véron was down, once attentions shifted, people picked up that detail very quickly. And after *Le Monde*, after *Eater*, after the *L.A. Times* and *Food & Wine*, and all the others, what should we have expected them to think? My catastrophic interview ran again. Obviously it did. I had said the exact stupid thing that was being reported. So that went everywhere. *We steal only from the best.* Full text in *BuzzFeed Tasty*. *Eater* picked it up. It was now a big topic that Frankie had given me my first job in Paris and that I'd then hired him five years later, even though I'd never thought once to deny it.

I was sleeping poorly around this time. And I remember that things were tense with Stephanie, who'd said very little through all of what had happened since Oishii opened. She'd been the one to draw my attention to *Blade & Tine*. She'd been the one to predict that it would circle back to Paris, which it did in the article that had run in *Le Monde*.

I don't think she saw it coming, how fast it would all collapse onto Frankie, onto Magic Wolf. I do know that at some point she stopped reading what was being written about him, about us. She did that and a tightness grew in our conversations when I'd raise it, when she'd sense my anger toward Frankie. And I know she was stunned when she heard that I'd blocked Frankie's phone number.

On learning that detail, she looked at me in a way that I'd never seen. I was a stranger to her. And it troubled me to see such wariness in her eyes, as if I'd somehow revealed that I could myself be dangerous.

"You don't think that at any point in the past three weeks, it might have been a good idea to get his side of this story?"

Those words just hung there full of incredulity and judgment and sorrow. And I was angry again hearing them. Angry to think that she was rising to Frankie's defence. Angry to think that I was following Magic Wolf protocol here, laid out by Magnus and Legal and Hugo Sullivan's crisis management experts. But that I had never disagreed. The reverse. I'd started declining Frankie's calls before anyone.

And in Stephanie's eyes now, after those earlier feelings, after the sorrow in particular, something new had crept. Stephanie was wondering if she and I would make it.

On the night that would mark the end of things, if not for us finally as a marriage, then at least for this phase of things between us, I remember that Stephanie and I had actually tried to have a normal evening. We'd eaten dinner together, which I had stayed home to make. Some sausage, potatoes Lyonnaise. We'd had a little wine, maybe even a bit more than we should have. And I remember that when we stumbled up to bed together Stephanie fell into the sheets with a strange sort of laugh, at nothing really. And then she was asleep. And I tried to lie awake next to her. But, with my eyes closed, I had that vertiginous feeling, the sense of the ground onrushing. I lay quite still. I felt a delicious sense of falling down, tumbling down, like a stone speeding to the end of its flight. I saw blood spatter from a head wound. I saw Magnus lying bleeding in the long grass. I fell from a ledge and it was perhaps only with this last image, a shining black surface fast approaching, that I realized I'd slipped into tipsy dreams.

I heard my name being whispered, again and again, as my hands boned out halibut and mopped down the sides of a pot of three-day wine sauce that looked like blood. I heard Jonah singing a dirge-like tune. I saw my father hunched over a dead body, Simone and Stephanie in a restaurant together, leaned in toward one another in a tense conversation that I was sure was about me.

I gave that Oishii toast over and over again. In this dream it was like a puzzle that refused to be solved. *Attention! Attention! Loup Magique!*

I see Frankie and his old Moto Guzzi. I see a winking satellite in the deep blue sky above.

Our third restaurant. Wow. I want to thank Magnus for a lot. Don't get me started. My oldest friend, people. Saw this guy take a rock off his head once. He seems fine though.

Steph. Thank you. Thank you endlessly. Paris is a long time ago. But it began there. We began there. And we've made it this far, right?

Lilly and Arthur both in the spiralling blackness. They are rising up over the world, tracing their arcs of travel across it. I saw that the sky above them flowed with silver, like mercury.

I need to thank two wonderful people who are both here tonight. Two wonderful role models in the kitchen. Kiyomi, please. Take a bow. Come on.

Clapping and calling out. *Oishii, Oishii!*

And then of course, the one, the only …

And here there were big cheers in advance of his name even being mentioned. Everyone smiling and thumping the tables and looking over at him.

Vous connaissez tous cet homme! François to some. Frankie to others. To me, always Formidable.

Wait, wait.

Holding up my hands. Holding them back.

Mais personne ici ne sait mieux que moi, que Frankie est aussi une bonne personne et un grand ami.

A slow, heaving silence had settled.

A true friend. And that's not all! Wait! I want to thank the great people of Veuve Clicquot BMW who just put our little restaurant, Rue Véron, Frankie and his brigade, on their new list at … number SEVEN.

And the roar returned. It filled the room and there was no single voice, just the joint one. A roar like a boat firing up its engines astern to bring it to a stop alongside a pier. A new continent stretching into the dark from the traveller. The eye looked up and could see only lights, and houses, and a starry horizon beyond.

My glass in the air again. I see you, Stephanie, my glass extended, my hand trembling. I see Kiyomi, standing behind the yakitori grill, unsmiling.

But now my phone was ringing again. The phone was ringing next to my head, on my night table. Ringing and ringing as if Frankie had never been blocked.

I jerked awake from my dreams. I would figure out later that it had been two months since Oishii opened, two months to the day since my father's birthday when the call came in. June 23. Summer was on us. And here Magic Wolf reached the end, all the way past the top of the arc and down to the very bottom. This was the moment that movement stopped. This was the dirt.

"Hello?"

Magnus out of breath, as if he had perhaps just run upstairs.

"What the fuck, man. It's two in the morning," I said, switching my phone to the other ear.

Stephanie, groggy beside me. Waking up still in her clothes. "Is that Frankie?" she said.

"Magnus, man," I said. "Talk to me."

Magnus looking for words.

"What's going on?" I was pulling free of the sheets. Standing. Starting to move without knowing where or why.

"Fucking fuck," Magnus said. "It's bad. It's Frankie."

He had been riding his newest bike. That's what Kiyomi told *Eater* in the long interview she gave about the tragedy. Summer was on us now, the beaches filling in Vancouver, the cafés bustling, the seawall an endless parade of walkers and bikes. Kiyomi did the interview on the front porch of their house in Mount Pleasant.

I recognized the furniture. Only, you could see packing boxes through the window and when the camera pulled out in the final shot, there was a moving van in the street.

Ducati 848. In signature red, of course. Kiyomi knew the bike to its details because she'd bought Frankie the bike herself. A gift to her husband. *Husband* was the word she chose. Six months later, a gift that Frankie had taken out the morning after Kiyomi had left their home with Lucy and gone to stay at a hotel downtown. It had been a temporary thing, she thought, staying away. Everyone needed some time. Frankie had contemplated his circumstances and decided that he didn't have even a short while left. He'd taken the Ducati out across the bridge and through West Vancouver, around the corner and onto the Sea-to-Sky Highway which would have taken him to the resort town of Whistler had he ever intended to get that far.

When did he decide? I wondered about that. He might have woken up that morning to the half-empty bed, the kid's closet empty, suitcases gone. He might've decided right then and there, or ten minutes later over a coffee — grind the beans, burp out the double shot — decided right there that it was the very last one, that there was no point and would never be a point for another.

Or it could have been weeks before. It could have been when his phone went silent. Maybe that's what he thought of that morning with the gulls screaming as he wound it up through the RPMs over the crest of the Lions Gate Bridge. He could have caught the shock of cold air shouldering down off those blue mountains, wound westward, uncorked the Ducati at the Eagle Ridge bluff and wound it out up those famous curves. The water below, the sky above.

Of course, it's entirely possible that he didn't think it through beforehand at all. Frankie was a man of impulsive action, after all. Perhaps he only made the decision in the split second before there was no taking it back, in the flow. That would have been a few feet before he reached the gap in the concrete barricades, according to police estimates of his speed. There was a gap at the curve where he left the road. And the rider would have had to aim carefully at that opening to make it cleanly through.

Vehicular suicide, subsection rocket bike. Dude checked out off that highway at 150 feet over the forest below. Estimated speed 180 kilometres per hour, given the distance he flew. That's what the policeman said.

Frankie in flight just that one more time. He was in all the papers. He was burning white-hot on every social platform. Frankie was trending hard. Trending up and falling down. Frankie arcing through the night, Ducati screaming, crashing into the cedar trees. He broke to pieces, my old friend Frankie did. He passed in an instant through those final layers. I can't say I know that he came to rest. I'm not sure you could call it rest. But he didn't move again. That much, we do know for sure.

"Frankie didn't pay much attention to the press," Kiyomi said to *Eater*. "Until they started telling all those awful stories about him. Until his friends stopped returning his calls. After that he cared. He cared about that silence. And he cared about what you wrote, what you printed. Because he knew that both together meant he'd never work again."

There's about a ten-second pause in the video here. I can report that because I've watched it many times.

Then Kiyomi picks up again. "Frankie couldn't live without working. Are you going to include that detail? He couldn't live without the thing that you all took away."

Hugo called. We were in the dwindling days. But the press was very much still around. Hugo said to me, "Listen, we're not going to ask you to do any more of these. I'd just like to do the *New York Times* and that's it. And yes, I'll be right there with you."

I was sitting there in the boardroom at Magic Wolf. Magnus slipped in with one of his lawyers. He shook his head at me, then dropped his forehead to the polished wood in front of him, groaned.

Then he sat up straight again and looked unruffled, as if a mood had passed.

"Véron is done," he told me. "I have an offer on the building, fixtures. The Otto too. I loved that thing."

I hadn't heard. "Who?"

"People who bought Duke's," he said. "Fucking hate that. But it's the right move."

"Are we good?" I said. "Like did we lose a lot?"

"A lot?" Magnus said, like he didn't know what that meant.

"What about Orinoco?"

Magnus looked at me like I was simple. Of course they'd shut that down too. "Sunk cost baby," he said. "Hey, better get that phone."

The console phone in the centre of the table was ringing, all the lights lit up. Green lights. Red lights. So there I was sitting with two reporters from the *New York Times* who asked me, maybe their second or third question, how I felt about Kiyomi Sakaguchi quitting Magic Wolf, leaving Oishii. Who would be her replacement? Could there even be a replacement? And here I looked down the table at Magnus who, even though he shrugged like — *of course, sure, this was clearly coming* — was just as clearly hearing it for the first time.

Kiyomi had given the *Times* her thoughts already, though she seems to have been brief. She had made the one short statement, then declined to say more. Frankie had dated a lot of people before they were married. But he had never dated anyone at Rue Véron other than her. And he had never raped anyone anywhere in the world.

Then she went on to say that her own recent split from Frankie had been a long time coming, but unrelated. She also said that she thought it was unfair that a big organization like Magic Wolf, with all of Magnus Anders's billions behind it, would try to pin this whole thing on her late husband when there had been far worse behaviour from others in the organization. People with whom she had herself closely worked and travelled, who were themselves in positions of power and should have known better.

At which point Hugo leaned in and asked the reporters for a second, muted the mic. Then we all sat there, stunned, staring at each other. Waking up fast.

As my father lay dying, I made my way slowly into Gastown. I got on the elevator and rode it to the top. I was taking accounts. I was trying to reassure myself. We'd managed pretty well, Stephanie and I, hadn't we? We'd built a nice home together. I really liked the flat-iron look of our building. I liked the location. When I got off the elevator and made my way to our front door, then opened it, I took in the high expanse of glass. I always liked that high window. And standing there, I was able to remember vividly the post-purchase satisfaction all those years before. *Look at what we've done. Look at us. The two of us.*

As my father lay dying, Stephanie was in the loft, packing for Spain. I heard her doing that. And I remembered how after Magnus's phone call came in at two in the morning on that tragic night, Stephanie had sat up in bed next to me and we'd cried together. It was very black out that night. We couldn't understand anything. But strangely, after what had been a long hiatus, in the grainy darkness that night, after tears and more tears, we'd wiped our eyes and surrendered to what was then the terrible mystery of Frankie's suicide. Then we made love. Gently, very gently, like we didn't want to make a ripple that extended beyond our own bodies, these two bodies here that we had chosen to join.

When I came in that afternoon, as Stephanie packed upstairs for the trip that we had known was coming, as my father slipped into that most peculiar of dreams that comes before the end of all dreams, I was thinking about that *New York Times* meeting, cut short by Hugo and the lawyer simultaneously. I was thinking about the heated conversation with Magnus that had followed later on the bluff at Belmont Farm. And coming in, there was the sound of drawers opening and closing. There was the sound of my wife calling down.

I went upstairs and sat on the bed and watched her folding shirts and skirts, underwear, bras.

She spoke, finally. She asked how it went.

"It's over," I told her. "Magic Wolf."

She turned around, caught my gaze. But she didn't say anything, just stared for a short time, then went back to packing.

"Rue Véron is dead," I said. "They closed Orinoco yesterday. Oishii was the last one standing after everything, but Kiyomi's just quit. Nobody deserves any of what's happening and real estate is hot right now so Magnus wants to sell the buildings. Oishii could have saved us. It really could if only …"

"Stop," she said.

This time, she did not turn to look at me.

"Just stop," she said. "Don't go through it. Don't torment yourself."

Finishing the packing. Fixing the suitcase clasps now, cinching those belts in a bid to get it all into the overhead compartment and not have to check bags.

"Hard not to," I said.

And then, "I called Kiyomi."

I breathed in deeply. I held my breath.

"Somebody had to," Stephanie said.

I waited.

"I called to say sorry about Frankie," Stephanie said. "I called to give condolences."

I let my breath go slowly, slowly.

"You know, part of me thought that we would have a good talk about him," Stephanie said. "Part of me thought that I'd tell her no way Frankie raped anybody. And I expected that she'd agree with me. And then we'd have some kind of a moment agreeing, two women who chose that particular guy as a lover, who loved that guy during the time that we loved him. Do you understand what I'm saying here, Teo?"

"I don't think so," I said.

Stephanie sighed. "What I'm saying is that those two women I'm talking about ended up talking about you instead."

Stephanie shook her head, standing over that suitcase. "Why the fuck, under all these circumstances, would Kiyomi and I be talking about *you*."

And here you took your hair back and put it into a band. Then you had your phone out because flights were flights and taxis were needed. Spain was coming. Spain had to be done, whatever part of your work the trip would involve this time. But I could also tell that you wanted to be there differently now than you had before. Now it seemed necessary, urgent even.

I started to talk. I started to tell you. Apartment visits. Sleepovers going way back. Late-night texts. Tokyo, of course. Tokyo. Brainless distress. One more time afterward. But I remember so clearly how you were shushing me the whole time I tried to get through this.

There was no need to go over it again. There was no need to explain.

"I left you a note on the kitchen table," you told me.

"Can I kiss you goodbye?" I asked.

You didn't have to. I would understand now if you'd said no then. But you didn't. And so with dry lips, that's what we did then.

The kiss done, you said *goodbye*.

Tiradito

"I have a question," Lilly, my mother, said. "I mean, an important question."

"Ask," Arthur said. "Ask anything."

"Tell me again about your work."

He told her. It was with a different outfit than he had with been on his earlier travels. But the work was much the same. And then he stopped because it was clear she was heading somewhere else with this line of questioning.

"You must travel with this work," she said.

"I must," Arthur said. "But I also want to."

"And how long do you intend to keep trapping around?"

English was her fourth language, Arthur had learned recently. It came after German, after a pretty good grasp of French, after picking up near-fluent Spanish.

"*Traipsing*," he said. "The word is *traipsing*."

"Answer me," she said, though she smiled. He had a stern face but it melted entirely when you looked at him a certain way. She'd noticed that. Cedro, the boy she'd been dating before this one had arrived, had never softened once as they kissed or talked. Cedro was good-looking, but with hard edges. With this Canadian, Arthur, well, he looked stern. His eyes were cool, protected. And then they lit up. Lilly had even registered that Arthur's eyes seemed to light up when they landed on her.

"I intend to *traipse* around a little farther," he said. "Then I intend to find a beautiful young woman to marry. And then I want to have children. And then, I don't know."

"Oh, I see," Lilly said. "Just like that."

They'd been dating three weeks, if you could call it dating. At the party where they met and had their picture taken by the photographer, they'd only danced, hardly talked. But at the end of the evening, Arthur asked her where she lived. Of course, she refused to tell him.

"But how will I see you again?"

Did she want to see him again? Cedro would be furiously jealous. But Cedro was turning into a bigger bore every date they went on, every trip to the beach with his friends. Cedro was a beautiful young man. But sadly, he knew it.

"You can pick me up at work and drive me home tomorrow," she said. "Then you'll know where I live."

Five o'clock sharp. The dingle of the bell at the bookstore. And there he was standing next to the front shelves, dust motes descending. But what Lilly noted most strikingly is that the first thing he did was pick up a book, not even look around the shop for her. She peered from behind a shelf of German fiction. He was leafing through black-and-white plates of Picasso sculptures.

One whole week of that, driving her home from work. Then, on the Saturday he took her to dinner at a little restaurant near the apartment he was renting, where they ate a red snapper prepared *tiradito*, with spicy chiles and onions and lots of lime. They ate other things too. But neither would ever remember that part of the evening. Just the snapper. And then the conversation, which went way past midnight until they heard the owner of the little restaurant, which was, after all, attached to his house, quietly clear his throat as he snuffed out candles at nearby empty tables.

"I will see you for church tomorrow," Arthur told Lilly. "And on Monday, I'll pick you up and take you to work also. Then I'll take you home. Or perhaps for dessert."

And so two more weeks unfolded, very much like the first except he was driving her both directions now, to home, to work, back again. It was his way, Lilly reflected. He quietly suggested what he clearly believed to be already laid out before him, an indelible set of directions on a map in his mind, footsteps plotted out into his future. She'd been pushed out of Germany. She'd been pushed out of beautiful Paris where she would have happily stayed. Pushed out across the ocean to the place where her family had found refuge. She was grateful to be alive. Oh, grateful, ever grateful.

But she was grateful for this, too, this possibility of a new direction.

At the end of three weeks, she finally asked him the question, which was very forward of her, as it suggested a judgment, like she thought *traipsing* around the world was something that had to come to an end at some point. Like maybe *traipsing* was something Arthur had been allowed to choose by the very same vast and unknowable forces that had prevented her own choosing.

"I have a question," she had said.

And then, after other things, after other discursions in the conversation, he returned to that.

Arthur said to Lilly, "I don't think I answered your original question honestly."

She looked at him a moment. "Well then?"

And Arthur said, "My traipsing is over when you marry me. Lilly, will you marry me?"

Now this, Lilly did not expect. And for all her spine and moxy and strength, for all the terror she'd seen, the way it marked her with secret knowledge that made her different from those around her, she could not suppress the tears that surged.

Hands to her face, sobbing.

Arthur had no idea. "I'm sorry," he said. "I'm so sorry. Did I say the wrong thing? Are you already engaged? Have I done something terrible?"

"Stop," she said to him. Then she blew her nose into a hankie that she'd carried all the way from Pforzheim. Münster, Telgte, Albersloh, Pigalle, Genoa, Curaçao, Baranquilla, the Gatun, and Pedro Miguel Locks. My God, would it never stop?

Then she composed herself and Arthur himself sat back an inch, still obviously worried he'd said something impossible, something that would end everything. He looked very afraid, and Lilly saw that plainly. The man with a future who had offered to share it with her. Nobody had ever done that before. Most people she'd known in the past ten years hadn't had much of a future themselves. And most boys, if they were lucky enough to sense that they did have a future, had no clue how to share anything, much less that.

She breathed in. Breathed in deep, held it a second. Arthur appeared to mirror her. He appeared to do exactly the same. Up went his shoulders and out went his chest. They were frozen there opposite one another. One thousand, two thousand.

"I need to know *why*," Lilly said to Arthur. "I've known you three weeks. Why would you ask me to marry you so quickly? Why would you ask me at all?"

Out went his breath. But it was not a deflation. Lilly could see that immediately. It was resolve. It was what you did when you were determined to take another breath, and another, and another one after that.

As my father lay dying, he saw that he was crossing a great canal, but he was going across it on a bridge and not through it along the water as was the more typical transit. I think he saw other things, too, that moment. I think he saw someone approaching, lights under the water and circling overhead into the heavens above. I think he saw the way that north-south and east-west met right at that spot and in that moment, and how it became a sphere in the middle of which he was suspended. But not alone. He saw these things and saw that it was not a crossing at all, but a re-joining, a closing, a coming home. Someone was there. Someone was drawing close.

Because … Arthur said, though not just Arthur, another voice too. Two voices now, criss-crossing and weaving together in the silver current, in the never-ending mercury flow, a sentence that would never be finished.

3

AFTERWARD

Taberna do Bispo

We made it to Zaurautz all the way from San Sebastian. I say we, though I was technically alone. There's something about the solo long walk that puts you into a silent community of other walkers. So there would be people you pass on a bend in the trail as they stop for water, standing in a patch of shade. And you nod. Then you see them again on the rocky downslope into town. Another face you saw that morning. You nod again. *Bon Camino.* Maybe you'll even exchange a word on the terrace in Orio, sipping the best tasting Coca-Cola you've ever had in your life.

"Con hielo y lima?" the bartender asked me in the café.

I could hardly speak with fatigue, but I managed. *Si, si.* Ice, please; lime too.

Then I went outside and there were some of those same Camino faces.

"How are you making out?"

"A little tired."

Laughter all around. Sipping that Coke and staring straight up to the skies overhead. Westward, westward and wondering why.

I couldn't have explained to anyone what exactly I was doing. I read the note from Stephanie on the kitchen table. I sat on the sofa and read it again. It was extremely short. So I read it several times more and tried to imagine what Stephanie had hoped I would do with it: not a statement of her feelings, not a question about mine, not an order or a request.

I folded the letter and put it into an envelope. Then I was forced to make my own plans.

In Zaurutz the white beaches were empty, the terraces too. The economy was bad and the Brits were apparently staying away. I sat at a table and smoked Fortunas and read *Don Quixote*, which I'd decided to carry with me the whole way. I ate a calamari bocadillo and sipped a cheap Rioja. Later I wandered up into Muzika Plaza and found a hotel on my first try. Everywhere there were empty rooms. There was a boy banging a drum in the plaza, standing in the concert gazebo. I watched him for a while, his face a mask of determination.

Zaurutz to Deba, from Deba across the high green hills, along stony paths, feet sore already. Day three, was it? Day four? Making it the entire distance in twenty-four days was impossible on foot. There would be a few trains involved. But getting there somehow was my only objective.

I remember telling Serena from Michigan, climbing around the lighthouse south of Pasajes San Pedro. *Yeah, I'm kind of on a schedule. Meeting someone. Hoping to.*

And she pressed a Spanish-English dictionary into my hands. *Schedule or no schedule, I'm just, like, really worried about you walking all the way across Spain without this.* Then she disappeared up the trail, walking at a speed I couldn't have quite matched jogging. I climbed the hill, past a graveyard, gasping in the heat. I stood in the shade of a towering, gnarled oak, catching my breath, pulled out the dictionary, and looked it up. *Horario*. Schedule. *Peregrino* for pilgrim, which lead me then to *perdido* for lost, which was the best by far so I stopped and put the dictionary away. Standing there at the crossing on that wild shoulder of Basque greenery, high above the heaving, Windex-coloured sea.

I also brought T.S. Eliot. *The Four Quartets*, my mother's copy. I never saw her read it myself. But she must have at least once because there were parts underlined. Eliot, who was messed up on Jews and crystal clear on death. I read those underlined bits.

> *If you came this way,*
> *Taking any route, starting from anywhere,*
> *At any time or at any season,*
> *It would always be the same: you would have to put off*
> *Sense and notion.*

There is a common conversation had out there on the trail by those who are seemingly cast out along it. The conversation is about *why*. Why do this? Why come this way? Ned and Brit from Denmark, testing a relationship maybe a little on the early side. They'd been together a year, Brit told me. She'd wanted to do the Camino all her life.

I said, "I know someone like that."

Ned said, "She make me do this." He thought he'd blown out a knee coming over the rocks from Deba to Markina-Xeimen. We sat in the main square opposite the big church, sipping beer. Ned had a plastic bag of ice cubes over his kneecap. Brit looked at me and rolled her eyes.

"We do this for the freedom," she said to me, as if that much were obvious to anyone. As if there could be no liberty that did not take you down the Basque Hills and across the sands of the Playa de la Arena, up to El Haya, down the blaring Cantabrian motorways, the misty back lanes, through the shaking pines and fragrant eucalyptus, the red dirt, the gossiping donkeys, the halting breeze.

But that is the answer I hear the most often. They tell you they're heading to the festival at Santiago, or they're meeting friends in Finisterre. They tell you they're travelling on the cheap before finishing a last year of school. But most commonly, they talk of freedom, which is a jarring answer if you associate the word with autonomy, self-definition, individual routes through the maze of life. On the north coast, there is only one way to Santiago de Compostela, and you are reminded of your surrender to that path every kilometre or so by a yellow sign or a scallop shell indicating the way forward. This way. Up that hill. Turn left past the churchyard. The markers make rudimentary the human day, collapsing all options, all routes, all avenues to one. Freedom. Really?

After Serena from Michigan, I stopped giving any of my muddled reasons why I might be there.

I cooked six months' worth of old family dinners for my father when he was ailing, I could have said. *I found most of them still in the freezer after he died.*

You see, people would just stare at you if you said something like that. So it was this, instead: *Porque estoy perdido.*

And people seemed to accept that. And I could lose myself in the days. Five or six and I was marooned in the flow. No way out but through this thing. I thought about Charlie as I walked, who I'd gone to see in Vancouver before leaving. He'd shut his place down. Vegan dumplings down Kingsway. Excellent stuff. Busy as hell, getting raves.

Charlie shrugged when I asked about it. He said, "I dunno, after everything I just lost interest in doing all that." We'd met for coffee at Jaytown Grind, which Magnus had sold to a family who'd moved to Vancouver from Karachi. The place was doing well. You sat in Jaytown Grind and wondered how anyone could fail to become rich running a coffee shop. The pastries were insane. We had these apple crostadas dusted in cinnamon. Absolute heaven.

Charlie sat listless in his seat. There was something there, something he wasn't saying. I pressed, stupidly. I didn't really know Charlie that well, only that he'd impressed me from the beginning. That Frankie and I had seen him right away for the talent he was.

He sighed. "I guess I'm kinda surprised how it all went down with you and Frankie. You knew him."

"Well, everyone knew him."

"No, no," Charlie said. "I worked for him. I didn't go to his house for parties or text him at night. Right?"

Sure, fair.

"So it all seems a bit fucked up to me," Charlie said, now looking at me steadily.

"It was a fucked up situation," I said. "Emotions running high."

Charlie's gaze revealed curiosity and a degree of disgust that I was just noticing. "You know what I read?" he asked me. "About this whole shit show?"

I started an answer. But Charlie's question was rhetorical.

"I read this *Vanity Fair* article about the French Legion guys, like that one Frankie worked with, the one who hated him so much?"

"Yeah," I said. "Name was Gauthier. Legionnaire."

"So this *Vanity Fair* piece is writing about what those Legion guys would do to new recruits, make them lean into their hand and choke themselves. It's like a thing in recruit hazing, not even just the Legion. Ever see *Full Metal Jacket*?"

Charlie hadn't touched his apple crostada. And I sensed he wasn't going to either. This get-together hadn't been his idea of a good time, getting the pastries to go with the coffee, having a little chat about how life was going. He'd been waiting instead to see what I wanted from him. Which was something like absolution, I suppose, a nod from a person I respected indicating I had not been alone through these past weeks.

Charlie's gaze let me know pretty clearly that as far as he was concerned, I was alone.

"I didn't know that," I said. "About the choking thing. The Legion."

"No," Charlie said. "Didn't think you did. You know who pointed out that article to me?"

I think I did see this next part coming, even then.

Kiyomi, Charlie said, pulling on his jacket, making to leave. Kiyomi who really probably of all the people involved deserved better, all the people involved who remained living, anyway.

Then he left. And I stupidly said sorry sitting there. Charlie out the door and on the sidewalk already. I said it to the open, busy room, just sitting there with my hands folded uselessly in my lap. "I'm sorry," I said.

Which was nobody's idea of an important result, I'd learn soon enough. I met Magnus later that same day. The topic came up.

"You think I'm not sorry? Only, who fucking cares if I'm sorry?"

He blamed me and I didn't even have the strength to argue. I wanted to jump off that grassy bluff, the most expensive farmland in the Western world. I wanted to dive into the ocean and make my way to sea, to live with the dolphins, invisible under the waves. Stephanie was gone three weeks by the time Magnus and I finally spoke. I was sick to my stomach every minute of every day.

Magnus again: "So be sorry if you want to be sorry. But don't tell me about it. Fuck, man."

Remember the Break the Dull Steak Habit girl?

I could have said it. He wouldn't have remembered and I would have certainly sounded insane. But I could have reminded him. *Do you remember her marked up with Sharpie, sectioned like a side of beef?*

I didn't say a word, just looked out at the ocean, felt Magnus fuming, felt sick.

Before leaving Vancouver for Spain, I flew up to see Simone. I couldn't help thinking maybe she had answers. I remember she listened to everything I said, long-suffering as always. Then she zeroed in unexpectedly.

"With your guy, Magnus Anders," she said.

"My oldest friend."

"Who now has a boatload of money," my sister said.

"Call it a billion."

"Which is seriously amazing on one level," Simone said. "As a kid he was such a twerp."

"Where are we going with this, counsellor?"

I looked across the table at her. One in the morning in her suburban home. She'd long sent Greg and the kids to bed. My sister had set a bottle of Greg's scotch on the dining table next to me and was even sipping a small pour of it herself, not her normal pattern for one in the morning on a weekday. Such was the moment upon us.

"Men like our old neighbourhood friend," Simone said. "Your erstwhile partner. You gotta realize these ones don't have a lot of experience with losing. I meet them fairly regularly. Life's been one long win. So Magnus didn't want to hear that you're *sorry* because Magnus himself does not really say *sorry*."

"Okay," I said.

"But then nobody else wants to hear it either," she added.

"And what's that mean?"

"It means that in these cases being sorry just doesn't make anything better. A whole bunch of people gotta stop grabbing women by the boob and expecting them to hop in bed. Stop doing that and you don't have to be sorry. You get that, right?"

"Yes. Yes, I do."

"And maybe you people should also stop stabbing each other while you're at it. Was that for real?"

I told her that Clémente's death was indeed for real. Simone just shook her head.

"So you thought Frankie did something really awful," she said. "Like terrible."

"Well, he kind of did," I said.

"Just not the thing people said he did," my sister said. "Not the thing you thought. And probably not the thing whoever spoke to *Flat Fish* said he did. And these, Teo … these would be distinctions with a true difference."

"But he slept around," I said. "He was a dick with a lot of people. And I looked up to him. You know, for a lot of years I thought he was …"

"You wanted to be him," Simone said. "For which he did not deserve to die."

Long pause. This was all disturbingly insightful. My head was in my hands.

"Only, you also did not kill him, okay? Worth remembering that too. How long has it been?"

"A year. Roughly this time last year Frankie killed himself and Stephanie split for Spain. I thought she was coming back in a month until I read the note. Did I show you the note?"

"Several times," Simone said. "The fact is I never knew Stephanie that well. I saw her about three times. You guys were always so busy."

There was silence for a stretch. My sister was watching me. Finally, she said, "You're depressed. You're broke."

"Not quite."

"Pretty broke. Plus, your wife is gone a year now and no, the beard absolutely does not look good. You're drifting, Teo. You're lost."

"That much is undeniably true."

Simone poured herself another tiny scotch. She cocked her head, looked at me.

I waited. I waited.

"*Bon Camino*," Simone said. "Go be lost then, Teo. Go be free."

So it was Simone who seemed to know best in the end why people did this kind of thing. And it was the trail itself that would steadily prove her words right to me as I walked. It's the way people talked about the whole adventure, these *peregrinos* themselves. To be free. To feel free, which I suppose is allowing for it all to be an illusion.

I walked with a political science student from Germany, a nurse from Norway. In Bilbao I shared a bottle of wine with a bookie from the U.K. We were in the plaza out front of the Catedral de Santiago de Bilbao, and here it comes again, same story, every time.

The bookie said, "I just like the freedom. Just walking. No hassles, right?"

Maybe the Irish cheesemaker came closer. Yes, I actually did meet one of those. Isibéal was the name on the card she gave me. *Isibéal Campion Creameries.* She was in her seventies, I guess. Had a farm outside of Donegal that she had left in the care of a friend. She had sharp blue eyes and a wide smile. She wore a black bandana wrapped tightly around her head and a long wooden rosary around her neck. She was also wiry and fit and walking quite a bit more spryly than I was by that point. But she stopped to watch me photographing flowers outside a café coming down a seaside road toward Castro Urdiales. She said to me, "That should be a nice shot." And when we got to the point in the conversation where we talk about *why*, she said, "Well, I guess to change my mind about a few things."

Nobody talked about religion, faith, metaphysics. None of that. Nobody said because they slept with a good friend's wife and then their father died and then the friend killed himself when he was accused of rape. Nobody said because they were crushed by guilt that it was spreading around inside them like poison, or that they missed their dead parents, or that despite fucking up everything with their wife and not even hearing from her in a year, she yet remained the last thing worth walking for.

People didn't say this kind of thing because it would suggest the pilgrimage was not really your own doing. It would suggest you were not free. That you did not feel free. That you were somehow forced to do it, forced across each of those eight hundred kilometres, driven across the land with no idea if you'd end up anywhere better than wherever you'd been when you lost control of your own affairs.

I was admitting all that to myself that day coming down into Castro Urdiales one stop west of Bilbao. My Irish friend had gone on ahead. But I saw her later on the waterfront at a restaurant on Paseo Maritimo opposite the marina, all those sailboat masts waving and sparkling in the low evening light. She was there with a Korean theology student and a couple from France who both worked for BMW. They took four months off every year to walk the pilgrim trails that spider webbed across Europe. They'd done a thousand kilometres when I'd met them that day and would cover fifteen hundred more by the time they returned home late summer. The man said he'd lost fifteen kilos by that point. And he showed us all the extra holes he'd had to add to his belt.

I thought: We're all marooned. We can't stop or turn back. So now every single step depends on each of the others. Each footfall, each crunch of broken stone, scuff of dust, kicked pebble skipping ahead. Each step is now both the tiniest of non-events and a phenomenon as large as the universe. Each footstep, in the moment we take them, is all we have.

But then the platters of food began arriving, platters of octopus and smoked ham, anchovies and green olives, and then the *pièce de résistance*: a whole monkfish cooked in oil with slivers of garlic and served with bread. The theology student stopped our hands and we prayed, the only grace I heard said aloud along the entire way. I can't remember what he said although as I raised my head and inhaled that beautiful smell, as I raised the utensils to serve the others, I saw Isibéal was watching me, first my hands and then my face. She saw something there. My guilt maybe. My desperation.

Then we ate and talked about home, just a bit, not overly. Mostly the deprivations of the trail. Our theology student had come with bad shoes, cheap sneakers that were now blown out along the sides. He had enough money for duct tape, which he'd wrapped around what was left of his footwear.

Though when we were finished dinner, I saw Isibéal pull the theology student aside and force money into his hand. This happened off to the side and his face was wide with wonder. I saw the tears bead. I turned away.

Then I slept. I crashed. I went deep past dreams. And I awoke huge-spirited. I woke full of the energy of my plan.

"Get to the Primitivo," the Germans had told us at dinner, speaking of the mountain route from Oviedo over the remote inner hills of Asturias and Galicia and down to the walled city of Lugo. "Hurry through Cantabria if you have to, but take your time in the mountains."

So that's where we all were going, walking our separate speeds, marking our own pains, our own inarticulate determinations. I felt it all bend that direction, the whole trip winding now toward that one part of the route. To the Primitivo. To the Original Way of the medieval pilgrims.

I pulled out Stephanie's letter before departure that day. I read it again, all thirteen words of it. Then I carefully folded it, tucked it into its envelope, then into my pack.

In my mother's *Four Quartets* that night, I tracked the bits that she'd underlined however many years ago she read it last. I turned pages and found these words:

If you came at night like a broken king,
If you came by day not knowing what you came for,
It would be the same, when you leave the rough road
And turn behind the pig sty to the dull façade
And the tombstone.

I crossed Cantabria and the pilgrim ranks winnowed. Days along through the sprawling estuaries of the Tina Menor and Tina Mayor, past the flat expanse of inland water reflecting the sky, past the blue-green hills, past the clouds shooting in to gather at the foot of the Cantabrian mountain range paralleling my path from the Basque Country behind us all the way to the Galician border. Climbing the long slope into Asturias, I got properly lost in a hillside eucalyptus forest short of Unquera. Not metaphorically lost. I couldn't find myself on my own map, which meant I'd followed a narrow track several kilometres past a marked turnoff, swatting bugs in the heat, running gauntlets of thorns, while below me through the fragrant trees I could see the road I was supposed to rejoin dropping farther and farther away.

I stopped. I retraced steps. I tried different trails that all fringed out to nothing in the brush. It took me two and a half hours to get down and across the valley — overheated, scratched, sweating, hating myself — and climb the final steep stone path to Colombres, where I'd hoped to stay.

It was approaching the summit that I got my first real taste of pilgrim's euphoria. Endorphin flows, runner's high. Call it what you like. For me it was the sudden head rush sense of my own movement, like the thrill of liftoff in an airplane, only writ down to human scale and speed. As I climbed that hill, I felt the chain of those thousands of steps connecting, hundreds of thousands now, a chain pulling me onward and upward. I felt the earth roll under my feet as if propelled by my own very motion.

I took a picture at the crest of the hill, my phone held out at arm's length. There was a *capilla de animas* here, a little stone chapel set up for recitation of the angelus. I didn't know the prayer, but I was gripped by a feeling, an exhilarating sense of lessening, the world briefly rendered inconsequential. A summit feeling. And I thought of my parents, of course I did. I thought of those circling paths, winding and converging. Running away and toward. I was going to look at this photo later, much later. I looked a bit mad, standing there, seized by the moment, by memory, out of breath.

I have no pictures of the moment just following. Fifteen minutes later when I discovered that both the hotels in Colombres were closed. That I was going to have to carry on through to El Peral, a series of gas stations and truck stops on the highway to Villaviciosa, where tankers and big rigs howled by, and none of the restaurants were open, and the bartender who handled room keys at the motel ignored me standing there, willing me on and out of his jurisdiction. I stood there ready to crumple with fatigue. Twenty minutes in which I spent wondering if I was going to have to hail a taxi to the next town or sleep under a hedge or what exactly.

Summit feelings don't last. I should have known they wouldn't. Memories carry you only for so far, plans likewise. The world returned. But so, too, did Isibéal just then, whom I'd assumed must have walked on far ahead of me. But there she was making a perfectly timed entrance. In she came to that bar with an air of complete authority about her. Her Spanish turned out to be impeccable.

Two rooms, she said. *One for me, one for him. Yes, we're peregrinos. And we need rooms.*

I thanked her, of course, but she was gone in the morning early. I never saw her in Oviedo either, where I stayed an extra day to try to mend my feet. I drank cider and ate a meal of slow roasted lamb shoulder with stewed red peppers. I walked in the old square. And then I was on the original way, once again submerged in the motion. Up and down. That's the inner and outer topography of walking for weeks on end. Once you're locked into it, once you're truly surrendered to it, thrown out along it, the trek becomes an endless cycle of arrivals and departures. Always entering or leaving some fold in the land, climbing or dropping off a ridgeline, a valley behind or in front, the roll of a hill stretching upward or downward ahead of you. And after a couple hundred kilometres of walking, it seemed to me that I'd been coming forever on some new set of views and possibilities, the real constant of the trail its everchanging sameness. That and the sounds of sheep and cowbells, the hovering cries of birds.

The trail dwindled to a point. It narrowed and turned, like a nautilus shell. It directed me to some inner part of itself. Past Oviedo, past Grado and Tineo, I turned to the heart of the Primitivo. Four long, mountainous days lay ahead, 120 kilometres in total. Tineo to Polla de Allende, then to Grandas de Salime. From there to A Fonsagrada, and finally to O Cádavo and on to the ultimate destination of every westward bound pilgrim I'd encountered in all those days: Santiago de Compostela. And as I left Tineo in the pre-dawn blue, rose light colouring the clouds to the east, I felt myself arriving at the heart of the matter, turning with the inner spiral.

The trail was full of pilgrims that morning. I looked for Isibéal but did not find her. Crossing into the valley, westward toward the Sierra de Obona. Spanish kids and older couples. People greeted one another. They said *bon camino*. Past the glowing green summit over Piedratecha, all of us descended the long, straight forest path through stands of red pines and bright yellow canola. I walked for a time with a schoolteacher from Galway. She did this, she said, for the freedom of it.

Onward and onward. The days compress and stretch simultaneously. In Berducedo, with no other pilgrims around, I asked the old woman running the corner store if she can make me a bocadillo, and she nodded and shrugged and retreated into her own kitchen through a doorway past a shelf of plumbing supplies, returned a few moments later with a sandwich cut roughly from a loaf of dark bread, thick wedges of cheese, folded layers of jamón serrano. In a roadside café just past the Alto de Lavadoira, where the washroom had a wasps' nest in it and a crew of red chickens ran riot out front between the legs of the table, the woman who owned the place had laid out a bowl of hazelnuts for pilgrims, with a small hammer provided for cracking. On the ridgeline near Buspol, wind turbines churned the sky, emitting a steady, low roar and "wielding more arms than the giant Briareus," as Cervantes would have it. And just past those turbines, right where the path led behind a farmhouse and onto the open hillside above the lake, I came across a man and a woman. He was sitting in front of a small grotto with a statue of the Virgin, sitting with his head in his hands, the woman, I suppose his girlfriend or wife, fretting nervously behind him.

"What's wrong?" I ask.

She told me that the gate at the end of the lane was closed and that there was a bull in the paddock beyond. And since there was no other way around, they were considering the fact that they'd have to go back down that long, steep hill we all just climbed, all the way back to La Mesa, where she thought the *refugio* was already full.

I stood sweating and wondering. Then I moved as if on someone else's legs, numb from the waist down, stumping forward through the thick earth. I walked to the end of the lane and I pushed open that gate. I didn't look at the bull standing a dozen yards to my right. I just started walking and kept my legs in motion. It was the product of pure exhaustion. Maybe a trace of inspiration too. Step and repeat. It's what you did. It's what they did. Step and repeat. I followed them through that pasture. My mother and father, but Stephanie too. Step and repeat. There was no terrifying creature there, no magnificent creature with curling horns and rippling flanks. I saw a cow. So I crossed that field and through to the end, while the bull gazed up into darkening clouds and never stopped chewing his cud for even a moment to consider me.

Spiralling and spiralling. The dust is rising, and I can see the spire of the church in the town below and across the water. Something shifts in me again. The larger place where I might be heading.

I caught up with Isibéal finally in Grandas de Salime. There was a little green shuttered restaurant around the corner from the hotel. She was sitting on the terrace and waved me over. They served a menu that ended up being enormous. But we were both hungry. Gallego followed by slabs of Chuletón con pimientos, followed by Tarta de Santiago. We were giddy, gorged by the time we were through and the litre carafe of wine that had been clunked down on the table at the start of service was nearly gone.

She asked about my parents. I don't know what prompted the question. She knew I was from Vancouver, that my wife was involved in television. Somehow, my cheesemaker friend drilled back to my parents. And when I told her Dad was a nomad and Mom was a refugee, she leaned in.

"Nomad how?"

"Wandered all over the world. Who knows why?"

"And refugee?"

Holocaust survivor, I told her. She lived but she'd had what they used to call a bad war.

"And what happened afterwards?" she asked.

Well, that was really the largest question, wasn't it? But I took a stab at it. I told her about the two long paths converging finally in Guayaquil, Ecuador. I suppose I took up more than my share of the conversation doing all this. But she listened so closely, it all felt drawn out of me.

It was night by then. In the distance, perhaps at a community dance or a house party, someone was playing the Galician pipes, a reedy spill of festive notes, rippling the air. We ordered a small glass of brandy each to close these matters. Isibéal seemed to be lost in thought. And so was I until she spoke.

"The prisoner wants to be free, and so he roams," Isibéal said finally. "The refugee wants a home, and so she seeks and seeks."

"Who said that?" I asked her.

"Oh, just me," she said, laughing. "You have a lot of time to think when you're making cheese."

"But how do the nomad and the refugee ever get together?" I pressed. "If he's always roaming and she's always seeking a home?"

Isibéal smiled at that. "Well," she said, holding her rosary beads tightly in thin fingers. "I think it cycles around to the same thing in the end, you know. The nomad wanders until he has no idea at all where he is. Then when he's finally good and lost, he starts looking for a place to rest as well."

And here a finger slipped unconsciously to her bandana, shifting it slightly where it had slipped to reveal her baldness underneath.

"And what about you, Isibéal?" I asked her. "Has the trail changed your mind about anything?"

"Oh yes," she said. But then she only smiled widely again and said nothing. So I took these lessons she had learned to be a private matter between her and her fate. And I didn't ask further about them.

With those things said between us, Isibéal and I wound down the evening by listening to those Galician pipes in the distance and imagining all that lay ahead: what we knew, what we dreaded, and those things for which we could only hope.

And just as we took our leave from one another that final time, she took my hand and shook it quite vigorously in both of hers, looking up at me, that broad beaming smile. She said, "No one who really knows me calls me that, you know. Isibéal."

"Well, what should I call you then?" I asked her.

"I'm going to walk on ahead now and probably not see you again," she said. "But on the off chance, the people who really know me, they call me Lilly."

> *And what the dead had no speech for, when living,*
> *They can tell you, being dead: the communication*
> *Of the dead is tongued with fire beyond the language*
> *of the living.*

Across the roofline of Spain, where the bare hills rolled away in all directions. Through small towns, stone buildings daisy-chained along the ridgeline. I split the sole of my right shoe just before the walled city of Lugo, standing on a dusty track just as a kid driving a small herd of black-and-white cattle came into view.

Vaca! Vaca! he called. And I stood to one side, tucked into the gorse as the animals milled by. That was the one time I cried for Frankie, standing there. Useless tears that dripped off my nose and vanished in the powdery dust.

In Lugo I was going to eat the best roast chicken I'd ever tasted, sitting in a café on the Praza Maior.

And I was going to think: nomad, refugee. We've all been there.

———

After twenty-three days, the destination seems unlikely to live up to the route. Santiago is rain-soaked and clogged with pilgrims. They walk singing down the flagstones next to the cathedral. They gossip in the square. We watch each other. We take pictures. I wait for a glimpse of Lilly but she does not appear.

I'm both empty and full, just as I might have predicted.

It's July 22. I'm staying in the nicest hotel room I've stayed in since the beginning. Top floor looking out across the wet city toward the cathedral. I can't sleep. I open that letter again. I'd been opening it daily all the way across Basque Country, Cantabria, Galicia. Reading your words, then folding the paper carefully and putting them away.

I read your words again that night in Santiago de Compostella, Stephanie. I read them lying again in bed. You were never going to write that much, I would have always known. I was, in the end, the one who was talking all the time. You spoke only when you really had something to say.

Still, I was impressed with the brevity. That note you left on the kitchen table, when I finally had the nerve to open it and read. It said only:

> *You could meet me at the Taberna do Bispo. July 23 would work. Next year.*

If we were going to talk things over, if we had any hope of figuring things out and moving on, then we could do it walking the Camino. But not soon. *Step back. Consider yourself.* I took that to be your communication, Stephanie. So I didn't reach out. I didn't text. I didn't ask through channels how you were doing. And for all I know, you're not here now. For all I know, you've long since come to your senses and changed your mind.

Of course, this idea that you'd walk the Camino in reverse was pure perfection. I saw that right away. No way we were walking it westward the way everyone else does, starting from the French border at Irun as I had just done. You were proposing we start in Santiago, start at that restaurant that might otherwise have been a reward for completion, work your way backward from there and across the country in an easterly direction from the terminus all the way back to the point of origin.

If I was going to join you, I took your message to mean, we weren't going to be pilgrims on this road at all. We weren't going to walk for completion. We were going to walk to be undone instead, to dismantle what we'd become, to return to the beginning. And we could walk the road in that direction to that end, or not bother at all.

Why walk the whole thing in the westward direction first? Why not just fly direct to Santiago to meet you? Well, that would be the natural question. I'm asking it myself, lying here wondering if I can possibly do the whole thing again in the reverse direction. But if you're not here, Stephanie, then at least I will have put in the miles to get to the start point.

I get up from the bed and I can hardly make it to the window. I'm limping. A blister burst climbing the stairs. I hobble over and lean on the ledge, looking out. Across the blackness and through the sheets of rain, they've turned on the cathedral lights now, the whole Gothic structure glowing silver, mercury, gold, blue. The clouds wreathing around it, underlit and vaulting, as if to extend the structure high into the swirling sky. And I know then that I've walked all this way to see this sight. This garish, amazing, crazy sight. Touching the beyond.

I text you. First time in 372 days. I've been counting. July 22, a year later. It's all I have left.

I thumb in the words. I write, *I'm here. See you tomorrow?*

Then I wait. For a minute. Then two minutes. Then I pour a glass of water and watch the tremor in my hand make rings. Five minutes. Six.

Then, there you are. Just this in reply: *Okay then.*

But there are those three dots blinking and glimmering again, another text in progress, a thought developing, suspended, then arriving. You're looking out at the same rain-slick cathedral spire, I realize. We're taking in the very same view.

You write, *Santiago is shining.*

Acknowledgements

Thank you Russell Smith, whose editorial guidance was smart and made the book much better. Thanks to all at Dundurn who believed in the book and contributed to it. Thanks Erin Pinksen. Thanks Laura Boyle. Thanks Jen Hale. Thanks Rajdeep Singh. I'm very lucky that circumstances aligned such that I could work with you all.

Thank you Chef Adam Busby, who told me hair-raising real-life stories about working in Paris kitchens in the '80s and '90s, most of which made their way into the book in modified form.

Thanks also Chef Hiro Tsumoto of the Tokyo Sushi Academy, with whom I spent a happy week learning about Japanese cooking. Understanding dashi has changed our home cuisine, Sensei. Thanks also to Chef Shinichi Yoshida of Tokyo Cook for teaching me about soba in your kitchen at Souga.

Thanks Yuki and Aiko Aida, Haji, and Yukari Sakamoto for the help you each gave me in visiting Tokyo. Getting to know the city, even as a wide-eyed culinary tourist, has been one of the signal rewards of my travelling life.

A final word of thanks in the culinary realm goes to the two real-world legendary restaurants whose menus inspired the cooking of the character Frankie: Au Pied de Cochon in Montreal and La Fontaine de Mars in Paris.

The lives of Arthur Wolf and Lilly Kuppenheim, who meet and marry in this novel, are modelled on the lives of my parents, Richard Taylor of Toronto and Ursula Kuppenheim of Münster, who circled the globe postwar — as a nomad and a refugee respectively — to meet by chance in Guayaquil, Ecuador. That said, as far as I'm aware my father was never involved directly with criminal elements as Arthur Wolf seems to have been in Subic. I miss them both very much and continue to be inspired by their lives and their memories. I'm grateful to the editorial board at *Brick Magazine* — to Allison LaSorda and Madeleine Thien in particular — for their support in publishing part of my mother's story in *Brick* #110 that came originally from an early draft of this book.

Most crucially, thanks to my immediate family, to my wife, Jane, and my son, Brendan. There have been challenges between my last book and the publication of this one. Yet you continued to support and believe in my writing when a non-trivial number of others stopped doing so for their various reasons. Meanwhile, we survived the pandemic together. And you two weathered the additional ordeal of me writing a novel at the dining room table while all the other pandemic madness was going on. I owe you everything.

About the Author

Photo by Kate Whyte Photography

Timothy Taylor is the bestselling author of novels about contemporary people with contemporary problems, almost invariably of their own making. Taylor is also an award-winning magazine journalist who has written about food, travel, sports, visual art, business, physics, and once about a group of Russian mathematicians who believe the Middle Ages were a fiction added to the official account of human history by the Vatican.

Taylor has been a food enthusiast since childhood, when his father paid him a nickel a piece to eat hot pickled peppers. His home cuisine was Latin/North European much like the main character of this book. His family also once lived in Venezuela where he was born and where, at the time, they had a pet ocelot. Taylor taught himself to cook at university using a recipe box given to him by his mother and a copy of Jacques Pépin's *La Technique*.

Most recently, he attended cooking school in Tokyo, which has really upped his rice-bowl game.

A professor at the UBC School of Creative Writing, Taylor lives and eats in Vancouver with his wife, his son, and two Brittanys named Keaton and Murphy.